PURA VIDA

Printed and bound in Great Britain by:
CPI Antony Rowe, Chippenham and Eastbourne

Published by Crossbridge Books
Worcester WR6 6PL
www.crossbridgeeducational.com

ISBN 978 0 9569089 5 7

British Library Cataloguing in Publication Data
A catalogue record for this book is available from the British Library

Cover photo: indee.stocker19/shutterstock.com
Cover design by david@patina.space

 CROSSBRIDGE BOOKS

PURA VIDA

**a story by
Helen Babin**

To my wonderful Mum, Sue

I'd like to thank my patient and supportive publisher and editor Ruth, for the help in creating this book, as well as all my friends and family who have encouraged, supported and prayed for me whilst writing this book.

Amy

The Royal Oak. Cosy conviviality. Familiarity wafting over when walking through the front door.

"Alright darling!" beamed Stephie perched on a barstool, her streaky blond highlights radiant in the bar's down-lighting.

"Hi sweetie," Amy cooed back as they hugged.

"Ay up!" murmured a voice suspended in a cloud of illuminated cigar smoke. At that moment Amy felt a familiar sensation like the stylus sliding into the groove of a record. Brass beer pumps. The wooden panelled bar with its flank of upholstered bar stools. Ornate horse brasses and antique fishing rods mounted on old ceiling beams. Paintings of rural life hung as if to fill every piece of available wall space. Nothing had changed. The hug. The smile. The ritual pint of cider. Reassuringly nothing, Amy noted, but a new cigarette machine. Stephie: reliably casual in a strappy halter-neck vest, jeans and leather sandals. Simple, timeless, comfortable. Amy felt immediately scrawny, overdressed and weirdly cheap, despite her Carnaby street designer slashed skinny jeans and her designer baggy shouldered T-shirt from a simple sounding brand in Harvey Nichols.

"Old Sandie's son moved to London didn't he Ray? Out by Wembley wern it?" said Frank the barman attempting to reassure Amy she wasn't the only local that had tried such a thing. Naturally they chose a table out of earshot. Back in the days when Amy and Stephie had worked bar shifts together in the Oak it had been more the type of watering hole for men straight from work. They would stamp zigzagged mud clods off their rigger boots at the door and dominate the bar with talk of topsoil and tippers, low-loaders and JCBs. Those had been lager-drinking days, working-for-weekend-drinking-money days. Drinking had been a pastime since aged thirteen, when they'd been allowed to catch the bus into town. It had seemed that half the school was in 'The

Crown' on a Saturday lunchtime, drinking pints for a pound to be disguised later by Wrigley's chewing gum and Impulse body spray.

"I can't get used to your hair Amy," Stephie jumped straight in with, barely managing to conceal her disapproval. Amy double gulped her Thatcher's, like her father always had done with his first pint after work, savouring the moment.

"Haven't you seen it like this?" Amy retorted, mentally reminding herself that several 'friends' in London had confirmed her new fringe looked sassy.

"I haven't seen you or your hair for months actually. Like nearly a year." Amy quickly glanced at her best friend - since they were aged four - with a pang of anxiety. *Is Stephie angry with me for not keeping in touch better? Did I ignore an important text message?* Amy's brow furrowed into a faint look of pleading as she became filled with a deep pining for the jollier version of Stephie. She hadn't bargained for Stephie to moan at her, and knew she'd crumble into tears if Stephie became aloof, or worse still patronising. But the two friends embarked on their usual Worcester agenda, Amy ensuring to take keen interest in Stephie's run down - how everyone they both knew was, the job she still hated, and her long-term boyfriend Rupe and his family. Stephie sipped her pint in a contented, whimsical way whilst talking about Rupe - head cocked to one side, sighing gently and twisting her torso from side to side with a soft-eyed smirk. Amy waited, blinking at this unfamiliar version of Stephie, until her friend finally extracted herself from her own daydreams, suddenly aware that Amy wasn't caught adrift with her. "So that's enough about boring Worcester. What's the latest in your love life? Are you still seeing that fit guy?" Stephie grinned eagerly. Amy took a swig of cider, squinting her eyes and pulling her mouth into an exaggerated smile, or grimace. "The footballer guy," Stephie helped her out.

"Oh him. Nah, he was just a bit of fun. Nothing serious."

"There must be enough fit guys in London? No-one on the scene?" Amy looked Stephie hard in the eyes whilst she tried to summarise London life. She was finding it hard to get past the presiding feeling that the tables had turned between small-town, steady-life Stephie and her own fast-paced, big-city aspirations. It was clear, this time, that Stephie had gotten over the envy and self-depreciation that Amy usually unintentionally conjured. *What was different this time?*

Amy grappled, wondering if she looked jaded from her months of late-night revelling.

"There are plenty on the scene, every weekend you can have as many romances as you want. But there's too much going on to waste time on that. I'm usually at gigs, clubs, bars on Fridays, Saturday night DJs, cruising the West End, then pubs all day Sunday, live music, the pubs are just awesome," Amy recounted, glancing wistfully out the window.

"Don't you feel kind of like a fish in a massive shoal, sort of lost in it all?" Amy's breathing halted as her inkling had been confirmed. Stephie was happier, steadier, more grounded and confident in herself than Amy was right at that moment. Stephie couldn't help twinkling a smile from under her shimmery green eye shadow to confirm Amy's observations to be true. Amy sighed in resignation to the fact it was now her turn to need reassurance, rebuking even for her silly antics, and cajoling into vodka-lemonade nights in an embarrassingly shoddy Worcester nightclub.

"For real. London. People get lost there. Go crazy. There are loads of Bible bashers on the streets trying to save your soul. Me, I just party hard and hit the gym." Amy tried to sound brave, hoping the mention of partying would lead the conversation towards Stephie suggesting a night out. Amy was ready to accept her old self to return a little, to catch-up with Stephie - Worcester-style; to accept a level of inevitable boredom and awful DJs for the vital necessity of once again being immersed in the safety of true friendship.

"So, how's your mum?" Stephie continued in a more comfortable tone. Amy curled up the right half of her top lip and shook her head slowly.

"It's an absolute nightmare," Amy said as the story surfaced ready for unfolding. Stephie raised her eyebrows from behind her pint, stifling a critical squint. "She's got a new companion, as she calls him. It's a total mess." Amy emphasised 'total' and 'mess', and added with surprise, "Have you not heard about Giles?"

"No. Your mum is so lovely; she totally deserves a top guy only."

"Yeah well, top guy Giles is not. He's a complete nightmare; already driven Rich to move out; caused loads of trouble for me and

Rich by trying to make us look like total heathens," Amy was listing when Stephie interrupted.

"Well, you guys kind of do that yourself too." Amy blanked it.

"Get this. Guess how old he is?" Amy said pausing before continuing with reinforced nods, "twenty-eight."

"Noooo! She's got a toy-boy."

"He's fifteen years younger than her, and there's more," Amy said quickly, getting more animated "He's got twins."

"Twins? Like babies?"

"Little walking, toddling, baby kids," Amy replied waggling her head.

"How old are they?"

"I don't know. Do you think I go anywhere near them?" Amy retorted.

"You've never liked babies or kids, have you?" laughed Stephie, unsympathetically and inappropriately Amy thought.

"It's not funny." Amy blinked for a couple of seconds. "Giles is laying down the law. No smoking *in the garden*, no friends staying over waking the twins up when we get in late."

"I can kind of see -" Stephie tried to reason but Amy cut her words, almost bellowing.

"No. I can see, quite clearly, what Giles has in mind for my Mum. He's after her home, her money, her support, her mothering to him and his kids. It's a joke. She's the joke, she's being a total idiot and being played for a fool," Amy argued, spitting specks of foam from the corners of her mouth.

"Do you think she really likes him though?" Stephie asked at a lower volume, reining her eyebrows in.

"Like him? That's not the point; he's a single Dad with young kids!" Amy exclaimed loud enough to turn heads at the bar, but they were too embroiled in their own debate. Stephie rolled her bottom lip over her bottom teeth, clamped it with her top teeth and set her face to a firm frown. *Why is my best friend being so callous?* Amy's mind demanded.

"Where's the mum?"

"I don't know. I don't want to know. I don't trust him or anything he says," Amy said at a more conversational volume and drank the dregs of her pint. "Don't worry; I'll come up with a plan to save Mum from making the biggest mistake of her life. I can see what he's like even if she can't," Amy said in a tone getting progressively more positive and added, "lucky I'm back here really."

"You girls finished?" Frank interrupted scooping up their empty glasses with clink. "Ray's put one behind the bar for you both. Same again?"

"Cheers Ray!" the two friends chorused at the cloud of smoke.

"What do you two think about this then?" Frank beckoned Amy and Stephie to join Ray "This crazy doctor argues that *all* drugs should be legalised."

"No drugs should be allowed," Ray added in his plain-speaking-farmer way.

"I think cannabis could be made legal, like in Amsterdam, perhaps we could have a smoking room out the back?" Frank chuckled "You girls are out in the bars and clubs, what do you think?" Amy and Stephie looked at each other with forced patience; they knew the conversation was a way to give old Ray some company.

"Why would anyone want to legalise drugs when people get addicted to them?" Stephie offered.

"Ah but old Ray is addicted to tobacco, that's addictive, does him no good," Frank responded with his well-rehearsed argument.

"My old man smoked the same cigars and lived to eighty-nine. That'll do me," said Ray with conviction.

"And government profits from taxes; the tobacco is grown legally, so why not for other drugs? Then it could be controlled properly, without dodgy dealers ripping people off," Frank continued.

"The question is, whether the quality of drugs would be better legalised or not, and the price," Amy added, to which Stephie cocked an eyebrow at her.

"Why do kids want to take drugs anyway?" exclaimed Ray over his freshly filled pint of mild, "when it makes their heads like pumpkins; good for nothing. I've seen it." Everyone giggled at old Ray getting fired up.

"They always do, Ray. Beer and fags aren't enough for kids these days," Frank sympathised, "but think of the taxpayer's money spent on - what does that paper call it? - the war on drugs, the policing, the prisons, the courts, chasing criminals around. Now, the way I see it, you legalise it all - all that stops. The drugs get produced above board, like other pharmaceuticals and kids get educated on it properly instead of lured by drug dealers."

"A bit of wacky-backy is one thing," Ray said through his contorted facial expression, "but all that dirt people putting up their noses and injecting it in, that can't be made legal. What good would that do?"

"What's our vote then?" Frank asked.

"Absolutely no," Ray said.

"I'm with Ray," Stephie said with an air of hidden indifference.

"Me, I think it should all be legalised," Frank said firmly.

"Ridiculous," Ray commented, to which Frank shrugged and held his hand out for Amy's contribution.

"I think people would still want to buy drugs off a street-dealer, rather than from a shop, as the drugs the government would allow would probably be much weaker or modified somehow to make them safer. I think, in a way, drug dealers do the job of getting stuff people want from A to B better than the government could. So, no I don't think legalise it, but maybe decriminalise it. People will always want drugs. It's their choice," Amy said. Frank raised his eye brows and mockingly rebuked:

"You wouldn't say that if you had a son or daughter turn into a crack-head." Just then the front door opened and in walked an unfamiliar man. Amy and Stephie took their chance to scuttle back to their table with fresh pints. With a butterfly of hope rising within, Amy extracted the old Stephie from under the black eyeliner and caked mascara as memories of their friendship flashed through her mind. Simple time together, shopping, out for drinks or eating with each other's families. Amy fantasized for a few seconds of her summer in Worcestershire.

"Did I tell you that Rupe and I are actually having a holiday this year? Three weeks travelling in France and Spain, and possibly Italy too. We're leaving next Tuesday!" Stephie announced, clapping her hands and widening her eyes like a little girl offered a fancy ice cream. Amy tried unsuccessfully to return the smile, but instead took a long swig of her cider.

"Next Tuesday? You so deserve a holiday. You'll have a great time together; you romantic couple." Amy eventually managed to drag the words out of her mouth, "I reckon you'll be buying a house and having babies soon."

"Practise making babies! How about you? What mad adventures are you going off on now you are a graduate? Well done by the way," Stephie unintentionally mocked, unknowing that her comment was like stabbing an open wound.

"I'm not sure yet, probably get away somewhere; get my head around stuff, after getting rid of Mum's new man friend," Amy said flatly as her mind ran frantically through the prospect of being in Worcester without Stephie.

"You mean you don't have plans? You always have plans. How about that resort in Malta you were practically managing by the end of your placement year?" asked Stephie, frowning with a puzzled expression. Amy just screwed her nose up as the sinking, sad feeling crept up on her again. Stephie had no idea where Amy was at emotionally. How feeble and broken Amy felt inside. How all she was seeing of her friend Amy, was now a facade of that once confident, ambitious, studious person that took the world by its collar and judo wrestled it to the ground. Really, Amy was burnt out, heartbroken and mentally shattered from the partying and personality-bending she did to fit into the world she'd been pursuing. "I thought the resort in Malta offered you a managerial job on graduation?" Stephie persisted, to which Amy blinked blankly at Stephie for a long second, realising how little her best friend knew about her conflicted life.

"The job worked out well in Malta, true, they did offer me the job. But the resort was boring; full of honeymooning lovebirds or screeching kids and moaning parents whose bums we have to kiss all day and night," Amy reminisced seriously, to which Stephie broke into laughter.

"But that's travel and tourism management, what you studied right?" Stephie beamed, openly revelling in Amy's dismay.

"Right, but I won't be going back there, I don't know," Amy faltered, intentionally avoiding the real reason; local-boyfriend burnt-bridge problem. "The beaches were gorgeous of course - the sunsets and the sea. The sea was my life there." Amy daydreamed about the coastal rocks with their shoals of pretty fish where she'd swam and snorkelled for hours before and after her shifts. This was where she'd been happiest, head under water, looking in on some real reality. The resort owners had loved her flair for managing people, especially how she'd gotten the best out of staff. They'd marvelled at the way she'd insisted all staff members, young and old alike, should join staff nights out in the local bars. Her infamous skinny-dipping, teambuilding nights at the secret beach, and her straight-down-the-line tone with the shirkers had won the hearts of the hotel owners. Amy was loved by everyone; she made working fun and always had a friendly smile to sooth the worst of hangovers. But inside, Amy was lonely.

"I'm just nipping to the loo." Stephie left Amy mulling her cider-hazed thoughts. The prospect of a summer at home, doing nothing but work, was weighted with failure and depression. It was almost alien after the hectic, whirlwind of her final study year in London. Not that she'd have admitted it at the time. Blinkered to the abnormality of the capital's pace, she'd galloped around like everyone else. Smitten in love, dreaming of a future travelling and working in exotic places with the beautiful pilot boyfriend she couldn't wait to see all week, until she'd rudely found out he was married. It seemed that only Amy alone hadn't seen the blatant reality. Stephie broke back into Amy's reminiscing, looking even more radiant and bronzed ready for the summer sun.

"I think Rupe's going to propose on the holiday. You know he's paying for it," Stephie grinned so widely she looked like she was grimacing. Amy wanted to throw her head on the table and sob so Stephie would scoop her up and hold her mess of a friend in her bosom and promise not to leave her in this state.

"I'm definitely going to be your bridesmaid, right? And I look best in aquamarine or cerise," Amy stitched herself in tightly and smiled back.

After a drawn-out goodbye involving a quick half, whilst Rupe came to collect Stephie, Amy stood alone in the car park leaning on her VW Polo. She sighed, slowly ballooning her cheeks, and looked up at stars smattered across the bright dark sky - a view she'd not looked at for a while. In the car, she scanned through the radio channels tutting at the lack of stations. Classical - *No*. News - *No*. Status Quo - *God No*. Lenny Kravitz - *that's probably the best we have.*

"I wish that I could fly. Into the sky. So very high," she sang along, starting the engine. "I. Want. To. Get away. I wanna fly. Away,"

Amy sang loudly before pulling on to the dark road and driving back to the family home.

****

Amy peeled and chopped onions trying to think of a subject to broach other than the obvious. Rosie cast her daughter a jerky glance like a meercat, then let her eyes wander to the backdoor thoughtfully as she stabbed hairclips into her fuzzy curls. She was ready for cooking.

"You do the peppers and I'll de-salt the aubergine and courgettes," Rosie said placing two red peppers and one yellow around Amy's chopping board. Amy loved Rosie's Ratatouille. It was soul food. Served hot with crisp green salad and warm bread, it was the taste of home. The kitchen was bright and homely, a pleasant contrast to Amy's student digs and the party-people London house-share. A breeze wafted the scent of lilies in from a vase at the open window where sunshine illuminated Rosie's ruby-red dyed hair. Amy almost smiled to herself. She'd found it again. That feeling of being home - it still being home. Rosie's long angora jumpers with sparkly, pastel-shade neck scarves always gave Amy that snugly, 'with-mum' feeling. The healthy glow of Rosie's natural perma-tan from endless hours in the garden reminded Amy of her roots in the countryside. "So, when is the graduation?" Rosie asked followed by another meerkat-mane shake.

"July, I think. Why do you keep shaking your hair mum?" Amy answered and asked without looking up from her chopping, concentrating on pushing Giles away from her thoughts and intentionally enjoying time with her mum.

"Oh. It's just this last haircut makes it feel different," Rosie assured her, "he really lopped some off."

"It looks nice. Love the colour." Rosie smiled at Amy in that loving-mum way and said:

"I've got some of that apple strudel that you loved so much last time you were back."

"Thanks mum," Amy winced trying to recall any memory of the last time she was back, or apple strudel. Rosie always wore floral, loose blouses, often with splodges of colour like a country-cottage garden in full summer bloom. And usually with leggings that reminded Amy of her mum's yoga days. They'd even do yoga on the lawn, much

9

to Stephie and other school friends' amusement at joining in. Rosie had always been the subtly glamorous mum, without her nails painted, instead opting for silver or gold leather sandals or a colourful headscarf. Rosie wasn't overweight, a little tubby around the middle that she concealed with black leggings and long-sleeved vests under all garments. But she was the quietly confident type, and if her new boyfriend wanted an older woman like Rosie, he'd have to take her as she was. Amy hadn't taken the time to really mull over the reason behind what exactly it was about her Mum's new boyfriend Giles that made her think he wasn't long-term relationship material. But if she had taken the time to dissect her feelings and hunches, it would have boiled down to the whole approach to their relationship. Giles and Rosie had a kind of 'matey-ness' that made Amy's instincts sneer with disgust. She had to accept that perhaps it was something they did in front of the twins, to play it down. But Amy couldn't help comparing Giles to Rosie's last boyfriend who she'd been sad to see the back of. He had visibly adored Rosie, lavishing her with affection, patting her bottom, gazing into her eyes over cheese and wine. But it had been the wine that had brought it all to an end - and his snoring. He'd been great fun, always friendly with Amy and Rich. Giles was none of this. Sure, he complimented Rosie's cooking and clothing. He took her out and closed the car door for her. They had long lingering hugs on the drive.

"So, you know your brother Rich has moved in with his girlfriend so that he's closer to town and work?" Rosie said, scooping up and dumping the onions into a saucepan of hot oil. Amy stopped chopping and remained silent. She forced herself to retain the words screaming in her mind. Rosie stirred the sizzling onions for a few long seconds. Then, prompting herself with a deep breath she announced to the saucepan: "We've decided that Giles is going to move in."

"What?" Amy shouted, wrinkling her face like a sneering fox, knife clattering on the chopping board, "Are you completely mental? You're not letting him move in here. I won't let you. You've only known him for a couple weeks."

"No. We've been dating for longer than that. More like two or three months I think you'll find," Rosie turned and patiently corrected Amy. She'd mentally rehearsed this scenario and had a practised response.

"What about Rich? He's moved out to get away from him," Amy protested, her temples straining.

"Well. That's up to him. It's nothing to do with me if they can't see eye to eye." Rosie had now adopted her firm-but-fair Motherly tone.

"Mum!" Amy took a deep breath and sighed it out loudly. A pile of bills fluttered. "It's not just Rich he's been out of order with. He's been having a go at me too. He hates me. He hates Rich. Can't you see? He even threatened me. I didn't want to tell you but he's a nasty piece of work Mum." Rosie's jaw slackened as she drew breath into her chest. "I just don't want you to get hurt and caught up with someone again, and then you can't get rid of them, like the last one," Amy reminded her with a calmer tone and a surety that her point would hit home. But Rosie tossed it aside with ease.

"This is different. I'm entitled to have male company. You and Rich have girlfriends and boyfriends -" Rosie defended, to which Amy closed her eyes against the dejection that word 'boyfriend' invoked. Rosie finished chopping the peppers and scraped them into the pan, "whom I make welcome," she continued. "We're all adults now, Amy." Amy frowned in confusion. *What has that got to do with Giles moving in?* "And you're in university and off living your lives. I want to live my life a bit and have a male companion. And I think it'll be good to have someone around to help with the garden and the barn that needs repairing," she explained convincingly, stirring the braising vegetables.

"But Rich and I are always happy to help with all that," Amy blurted, "you don't need to shack up with a boy -" But Rosie cut her off with a sarcastic guff.

"Of course! You and Rich are just going to start popping back to do stuff." Amy was waggling her jaw and staring at the back of her Mum who double tapped the wooden spoon on the side of the pan, as always, put a lid on it, and turned to face Amy square. "My door will always be open to you and Rich, you know that," Rosie said with a slight upward tilt to her face, her eyes wrinkled in a hopeful plea. Amy squinted her left eye trying to listen, but her mind was numb. "And, I hope that we will always be friends," she added with a final mane shake. Amy's jaw froze, mouth half agape. The backdoor chipped into the discussion with its own UPVC voice. It was Giles.

"You in?" he called, followed by a pitter-patter of small soft-shoed feet. Whatever thoughts were in Amy's head evaporated as a poignant smell-memory replaced them, - the smell of barn dust. Rosie started to walk towards the back door, stopping to gently touch one of Amy's tightly crossed arms and craned down to catch Amy's eye.

"Please Amy," Rosie said softly to her daughter's angled jaw, before letting go and carrying on to greet her soon-to-be housemates. After grabbing her smoking paraphernalia, Amy marched down the hallway, catching a glimpse of blond pigtails in each of Rosie's arms, and exited by the front door. Giles stood in the driveway loading himself up with duvets, bags, and huge cuddly bears from the open boot of his shiny, grey, estate car.

"Evening Amy. Something smells good," Giles said with a nod towards the kitchen.

"What the hell do you think you're playing at?" Amy said in a low voice as she continued across the driveway towards him. Giles stood still; arms outstretched around the bedding as if hung on a cross. Amy was licking at the rivets of dried skin on her bottom lip, staring at him.

"Rosie told you about our plans?" he started to ask until Amy cut him.

"Plans?" she frowned with clenched teeth, "I know your plans alright. My Mum doesn't need you and your kids freeloading off her."

"Clearly she has enough kids freeloading off her already," Giles hit back. Without hesitation he threw his load to the ground and took a step towards Amy. "I happen to care about your Mum. I earn a decent wage. I can look after myself and my girls perfectly well. Your Mum loves having the girls around, which is more than I can say for you, or Rich for that matter." Amy felt a burst of anger and injustice.

"How dare you come in here telling me about my own Mum who you've only known for a month or two? You don't even know her at all. Trying to tell her she doesn't like her own daughter!" Amy shouted, her heart pumping fast and head craning forward.

"Please don't shout in front of my children," Giles replied gesturing to his girls who were sat wide eyed on the backdoor step each holding a homemade ice-lolly.

"How dare you come here?" Amy continued but was interrupted by Rosie.

"That's enough thank you Amy," Rosie said firmly, appearing behind Amy. "I think you better just go and cool off."

"You know what? I can't do this Rosie. I can't bring my girls here to watch this. This is just not working out," Giles said sighing and shaking his head. Amy squinted at him, fighting back foul language. "We can't be here anymore if she's here," Giles announced. Amy's face was contorted with the incredulousness of what he was saying.

"Good. I certainly don't need to be treated like this," Amy answered in a lower tone. But what came next floored Amy.

"No, not good, Amy," Rosie was saying. "Giles is right. He can't bring the girls here to this. This isn't fair Amy. You're being out of line." One of the girls had started sobbing in a stifled way that both Rosie and Giles knew would crescendo. They both hurried over to comfort a girl each. Amy nobly raised her head towards the fields and started to march down the driveway to escape the scene. The pit of her stomach had a dreadful sinking feeling. A small soft-toy pug dog appeared in her lower vision and she saw her right boot make a fast connection with it like a footballer when chipping in a close-range goal. The pug was flung through the air and landed on the holly hedge, followed by a little girl's screech.

Amy perched on the top of piled pine planks stacked against the back of the decrepit barn. Her blood still pumped with adrenaline making her hands tremble as she crumbled weed on to the contents of a cigarette in a rizla paper. Once she'd rolled the spliff she lit it and took a deep drag, filling her chest with the pungent, sweet, herby smoke. 'Tansy' Rosie would always say when she caught a whiff, referring to a common, yellow, flowering weed of a similar fragrance. Occasionally, Rosie would even join Amy and Rich to have a puff on a starry night. Amy scowled at the thought of Giles ruining all of this. The herbs crackled as hot smoke drew through them and hit, with a satisfying ache, deep within her lungs. On exhalation, the driveway scene seemed to float up and away on the smoke. It didn't matter. Amy leant back on the barn wall. The girls would be happily bickering in front of the television, whilst Rosie and Giles would be pouring glasses of chardonnay to have before the ratatouille. The wild meadow beyond the fence shimmered. She suddenly felt very real. Everything felt real. The wooden planks, the barn, the trees with their singing blackbirds, the brightness of the fields, the rustling sound of an invisible breeze in the tall poplar treetops.

Amy felt totally alone in all the grass and trees and flowers. She knew then how she'd been mistaken to think it was still home. That home, the old one, was just a memory now. Everything had changed, except the views. Those memories all seemed irrelevant to the present. Just like choosing to study for a degree based on prospectus words: 'fast-paced global industry', 'broadening your horizons' and 'social impacts'.

An almost harrowing worry started to dominate her mind: withdrawal symptoms. *How will I cope without my life? No parties, no clubbing, no bars of student mates or work colleagues,* she thought gravely at the bleak prospect, as if she'd fade away completely. Rosie's voice echoed in her mind - '*I just want us to be friends.*' Amy found something very unsavoury about that phrase. *Yes, it was the phrase you'd use to dump a school boyfriend. But a Mother to her twenty-two-year-old daughter, what does that phrase mean? We've always got on, until Giles.* 'We're all adults now,' Rosie's voice echoed again. *Mum obviously wants to be more like a friend than a mother.* A tear slowly emerged and stuck in the corner of her eye, as if from a deep well of brine buried somewhere in her face. A vibrating impulse surged from within – it was clear and strong and urgent.

"A summer in Worcester is off," Amy said aloud to herself.

Three Ticos

Three *ticos*, as Costa Rican men call themselves, strolled among tourists on Castillo beach - a daily routine they'd kept since school days together. Warm sand on bare feet melted the day's stresses away as they bantered cheerfully in their colloquial Costa Rican Spanish.

"You are playing this weekend?" Zan flashed a glance at Manuel.

"Not possible! It's the end of the *zafra*. I can't say no to my father for harvesting sugar cane," answered Manuel shaking his head in anticipation.

Zan had his t-shirt off and tucked into his belt, exposing a robust upper body to the waning afternoon heat. He always wore baggy, denim board-shorts, reaching well below the knee; an imported fashion from their Northern neighbours, as were his baseball cap and chunky sneakers with oversized-tongues. He knew all the local 'surf dudes' by name, despite not surfing nor having dread-locks. In fact, he kept his hair cropped short, which accentuated his smouldering, wide-set eyes and boyish tufty chin beard. Zan always acted laddish but his muscular build gave him a man-like machismo. His confidence verged on cocky.

Manuel was always somewhat the odd-one-out, for the beach stroll would commence after he'd finish his day-shift at the local bar, La luna llena (The full moon), so he was always wearing black trousers and a white shirt. Manuel removed his shoes and socks, rolled up the bottoms of his trousers so not soil them with sand-dust and unbuttoned the top button of his shirt before they set off.

"It's an important match this weekend! You work the bar at night and the land by day! No surprise you are too slim," Zan cried, his frown igniting his eyes into a fierce glare. Zan had notably emotive eye expressions ranging from his typical serious-verging-on-stern stare, to a wildly offended, maddened glare. Even one of his rare teeth-bearing grins transformed his eyes with intense caprice.

"You have one job, then go home to rest. Me, I don't have privileges like that," Manuel replied coolly, a little apologetically.

Bandu chuckled at his friends through mouthfuls of spicy empanadas.

"I'm talking about *priorities*, not *privileges* man. We beat those dogs; we are regional champions," Zan threw his hands to the sky as if to pray. "Regional champions! Don't you know this importance?"

Zan pulled at Bandu's arm to prevent him stepping on a snoozing sunbather who'd clearly had too many lunchtime beers. Bandu was an altogether more approachable character, his sun-bleached auburn dreadlocks bouncing at his shoulders. He chose to wear less blatantly branded beachwear. In fact, he chose to wear less clothing all together, rarely covering his top half but for a string of seashells around his neck for good luck, despite his rather chubby tummy. He usually wore whatever shorts or flip-flops were to hand at his home, the latter only necessary when going to a bar or journey out of town. Bandu would always raise a smile for anyone he knew and had an infectious twinkle in his eyes. Even in his early twenties, he still had the look of a typical, tropical beach boy.

"I know. I know. You know my priority is always the team. But *my* priority is nothing. My father makes *his* priority *my* priority," Manuel patiently explained. Conversely to Bandu and Zan, Manuel had a heavier weighting of Spanish heritage giving him a more European complexion and stature; slim, paler-skinned and straight-haired. His quiet temperament gave him a sultry, submissive aura.

"I'll come to speak to your father tonight," Zan said firmly, a finger and thumb expounding his idea to the setting sky.

Bandu laughed out loud almost choking. Manuel shook his head smiling.

"What? I know your father. We talk," Zan responded seriously, his eyes pleading for respect of his status.

"You will be working Zafra too," Bandu said through his laughter. Manuel nodded at Zan.

"It's not justice on our team!" Zan protested like a football manager at a losing side line.

"It's not justice on me," Manuel argued, "I want to play. You have freedom to choose. You can walk away when you finish your work, no responsibilities."

"I have responsibilities," Zan glared. "If the pool doesn't filter, anytime night or day who is called? Something needs repairing? Again it is I. Client loses their keys? Me."

"OK, but only responsible to your boss," Manuel interrupted. "A United States, who cares? You can make excuses if you don't want to work."

Zan fell quiet. Bandu swallowed his mouthful, softened his smile and glanced at Zan.

"I'll play for two in defence." Bandu tried to sound reassuring, but both his friends knew he worked hard enough playing just for himself.

Surfers and little fishing boats silhouetted against the setting sun in the pink-peach Pacific sky. They had reached the end of the beach, the local hangout spot. Calling and nodding greetings the three amigos stole a piece of wall space from a group of younger ticos, who shuffled along without resistance nor greeting. Zan tore a piece of crumpled bread paper and cupped it in his palm, thumbed into it dried marijuana, and then twisted it into a cone. They glanced intermittently at the sunset, as if reading its colours, each savouring a sweetness hanging in the humidity. The sweetness was partly the taste of profits brought by swelling summer tourists. It was in such moments of heavily coloured sunlight that Zan's macho facial expression appeared worldly-wise. But the truth was, he'd never ventured further than his home province of Guanacaste. His worldliness had come to him with the swathes of foreign tourists and land prospectors visiting to surf and party, make deals, and become employers. Zan purposely hung out at local bars, often La Luna Llena, to observe foreigners' body language and sense of humour. Manuel would fill him in on what the conversations held after everyone left. Zan was the type of local that tourists rarely stopped to ask directions. Bandu was occasionally approached and always embraced the chance to promote his handmade pottery, whereas Manuel was a most regular target of questioning tourists, both inside of work time and outside. He just had that reliable, trustworthy demeanour. Yet he never failed to shrink with shyness when face-to-face with girls in bikinis. His family were devout Catholics. Even not-so-tall North American men, known locally as gringos, made him feel hopelessly intimidated.

Zan was never intimidated. He often became overwhelmingly

protective over ticas, the local way of saying Costa Rican girls, when they hung out with gringos, especially the girls of his own village. Zan would sit and stare with a maddened glare. But all the ticos, including Zan, abided by their mantra: *Pura Vida*. These two simple words meant more than what they sounded like - pure, natural, laid-back, tropical blessings. It meant the 'law of the land', and when Zan joined gringos, gringas, ticos and ticas at La Luna Llena's roadside bar, Manuel's greeting of *Pura Vida* to his lifelong friend Zan meant 'be cool, we are together like brothers'. Privately, Zan pined with nostalgic pangs of sadness for the life of his childhood memories. A time when Castillo was still a sleepy fishing village with a sand track in place of the paved 'main-strip' that now brought in streams of SUVs and hire cars. He was just old enough to remember the beach being a place for the fishermen's nets and people on ponies, and when the sleepy beachfront restaurants thronged with a wedding celebration, or more frequently, a festive celebration in honour of a holy saint. Sometimes Zan's wide-eyed daydreams of these days, whilst sat awaiting Bandu and Manuel, gave the impression he was high or crazy. His aloof, detached idling could give the impression he was a transient from elsewhere. But he was born and bred in Castillo, at least on his Mother's side.

"I saw your brother today. Has he finished studying?" Bandu asked Zan.

Zan lifted his head, set his eyes to the horizon and blew out smoke. He envisaged the scene at home - his visiting brother absorbing their mother's praise and adoration.

"Is he a big lawyer yet?" Bandu persisted.

"Don't know, Bandu. Carlito is just back for a week or two," Zan finally answered without breaking his gaze.

"Will he relocate to San Jose?" Bandu continued.

Zan took a drag on the cone-shaped spliff, turned to Bandu, shrugged and passed it to him. Bandu and his smouldering auburn dreadlocks set their own contemplation at the sky, drawing carefully on the spliff, softly blinking, and exhaling gently with ease. He'd always fancied himself as the brother who went away to study in higher education and go on to get a good professional job, a career even. But being the youngest, it had fallen to him to stay with the family pottery business until further notice.

"I bid you a good evening my friends," Manuel said eventually, after his share in the smoking, slap-shaking Bandu's and then Zan's hands.

"I got to go too. Take my shift at the shop. I know my sister will be getting ill-tempered by now," Bandu chuckled, "I said I would return at lunch time."

"Take it easy my friends," Zan replied, acknowledging a pang of jealousy, for both his friends worked in family businesses - being taught their father's trades. This was something Zan could never really shake down whether he was less or more fortunate for missing out. Alone but for a few lingering local boys doing cartwheels at the sea's edge, Zan's breathing naturally aligned with the waves. He thought of his father. It was seven years since his father's tragic death and still he was referred to as his father's son. Local folk, particularly when drunk, would often remark how his eyes were his father's, and he wondered if they simply meant his eyes resembled his father's, as they did, or if it held a deeper implication. Either way, Zan felt he was the walking shadow of his father's memory. A paradoxical shadow both respected and disdained. His eyes searched the curdling pink-orange horizon, squinting unnecessarily, as if looking for an approaching armada. It looked so far away. Unreachable. Like his father. He tried to picture what life would have been like with him still around. If they'd have been richer, connected. How he might have been different. How his mother would have been different. Blinking away his daydream he realised the sun was gone, as were the last of the local kids, and darkness had deftly engulfed him. Casting a glance to the road, Zan started figuring on who would be passing by to hitch a lift from.

Castillo

Castillo. A little cove on the Pacific coast, its ocean pounding white sands. Hot, sunny and swarming with tourists. For over an hour she'd marvelled the view in every direction - the horseshoe-shaped stretch of pale golden shore abutted by dense, green forest reaching up into the craggy hills. *Sun, sea, sand* .... Amy's thoughts trailed off with a warm glow.

A returning feeling of joy and peace. An almost forgotten feeling. She could hardly turn her thoughts back to what she'd flown away from. The turmoil behind her in the UK seemed to float away, diminishing with every slow, deep breath. Giles, the twins, Rosie, Uni parties, the ex-job, the ex-boyfriend - all fuzzy, distant, unnecessary thoughts of aggravation. Even London, where she'd call home a little more than a week ago, with its partying, bars and clubs seemed stressful in comparison. *I don't need any of that. I'm going to be the new healthy, happy, trouble-free Amy.*

Languishing in the baking sun she watched frolicking bathers shouldering into waves, bobbing heads and feet floating beyond the break, a semi-crouching surfer catching a wave before casually plunging backwards behind the rolling water. Further out, the sea's surface was a sheet of sapphire blue glistening blissfully under a radiant sun. Amy listened to the mellow, surf-muffled murmurings. She felt the hot, dry sand trickling between her toes, and her loose hair tickled her naked shoulders. It all felt exquisite. Tip-toeing across the burning sand to the frothing water's edge. She flung herself into the next wave. Dipping, kicking, floating. *I'm so lucky to be here* Amy's thoughts whispered *my luck has changed.*

****

Amy awoke to a shrill cockerel cry at close range. She opened her eyes to pale sunlight streaming through thin cotton curtains. The high-pitched rasping of cicadas rang in her ears.

Amy lay on a single bed under a thin cotton cover printed entirely in comic-strip of unfamiliar superheroes. She listened to the noises of a family preparing for their day: the bathroom door clunking open and closed, clanging cooking pans, a heavy-footed toddler on a solid concrete floor. Rummaging through her suitcase on the bare floor she sensed a presence or maybe a noise. She looked at the closed bedroom door, listening. A couple of seconds later there was a movement. A glinting brown eye withdrew, leaving an empty keyhole, and disappeared with a giggle. Amy shoved a folded paper napkin into the keyhole.

In the kitchen, Alba, the mother of the house, was busily frying chunks of pale-yellow plantain in a large,oil-encrusted frying pan whilst extracting various jars and tubs from the huge vintage American refrigerator. Her three children perched on wooden chairs eating breakfast at a small kitchen table. Amy smiled, hopelessly charmed by Alba's exotic sounding words and cooking smells. She found the words completely unrecognisable, not even telling where each started or ended. After receiving a blinking, blank face from Amy for a second time, Alba simply pulled out a chair and hand-gestured for Amy to sit. The two brothers scampered off giggling, and the little girl continued to eat, partially successfully, milk-soaked cereal with a dessert spoon. Amy sat watching and waiting. Through the colourful fly-deterring fringe of plastic ribbons across the backdoor she could see jerky-headed chickens strolling past, lime-green bushes and smooth brown earth. Grunting and squealing of pigs and the brash interjection from the loud cockerel filtered in.

"Grace-ie," Amy said to Alba when accepting her plate of sliced fruits and toast, followed by an uproar of boys' laughter from the next room. Alba scolded them with a torrent of words.

"Gracias," Alba corrected Amy, who was quietly reminding herself that she was a paying guest in the house and promising not to let the two pesky little boys alter her mood. *I am here to recover, set my life back on track, get a job at an eco-resort saving turtles and learn Spanish.*

After the giggling boys had escorted her to the top of the dusty track and flagged down the language school mini-bus, Amy found herself ushered into 'El Mono Descarado' language school. *Cheeky Monkey* Amy translated the name in her now 'worth-its-weight-in-gold' Spanish-English dictionary. *Descarado* Amy kept whispering to herself sat at a little desk waiting for class to start. She was falling in love with the intonation of the Spanish language, how most every word ended in an 'o' or an 'a', a rhyming language. In a whisper Amy could roll the 'r' sound, she could hear the sound it should be in her head. The induction was held in the classroom constructed like a large tree house nestled in the sturdy branches of a mango tree. Below was an open courtyard lush with cactus, yuccas and orchids.

"Me llamo est Amy. Yo estoy Ingles. Yo tengo veintidos años," Amy read the alien phrase from the white board and sighed with pleasant satisfaction. She suddenly felt as if she'd spent most her life in the equivalent of a grotty little fish tank and had now been plunged into a huge aquarium with shoals of pretty fish and brightly coloured reef plants.

Everything seemed so tantalising: the smells of the empanadas frying at break-time, the tall glasses of freshly-blended smoothies, smiling young women in beach dresses and flip-flops, barefooted guys in surf shorts and tousled blond beach hair. A wave of aspiration washed over Amy and she felt a returning lust for bettering her life.

Adventure

Pouring suntan oil into the palm of her hand instantly induced a string of memories. The first whiff reminded Amy of beach holidays, but this was quickly overpowered by revulsion - the taste-memory of Coconut rum and cheap cola.

"So, what do you teach?" Amy asked, smoothing oil across Louise's broad shoulders.

"I teach in a public middle school: sixth, seventh and eighth graders just inside of Detroit. I'm a Michigander," Louise stated with a hint of pride.

"Oh right. So middle school is like high school then?" Amy asked wondering how this friendly, docile woman she'd struck one of those 'immediately-friends' relationships with could manage dominion over high-school children.

"Yeah, kind'a. Junior high school, which is eleven to fourteens and then they go on to high school after that. I think its kind'a different in England?" Amy tried to remember the age she'd started high school.

"I think so. Did you always plan to be a teacher?" Amy asked, if only for the pleasure of hearing the accent flowing, all rounded and smooth.

"Not really *always,* but I love my job, I'm very fond of the kids, well mostly, an' I figured that I just wanna make a difference. But, it's tough in there. No kidding, teaching is so tough these days," Louise said gazing out over the waves.

"You mean the kids play-up a lot?"

Louise glanced at her before contorting her face ready to accentuate the pitfalls in her chosen field of work.

"The daily problems we face include - victimisations, delinquency, assaults on students and teachers. You know what happened in 1999 in Columbine?" she asked Amy who nodded vaguely, recalling the name. "Happenings like that make people real fearful. The state of Michigan is a 'shall-issue-state'. With a permit you can carry a weapon, and keepin' those weapons out'a schools is real difficult. We have metal detectors fitted at the entrance," she explained as Amy's bottom jaw slackened with her every word. Amy blinked at Louise. "But'cha know the kids still get them in. Would you believe that a child of *six years, shot,* and *killed* a child, the same age, at an elementary in a township a couple of years back? *Six,*" she said, her face wrinkling with incomprehension. Amy pushed her lips towards the centre of her face starting to mouth the word 'what?' "I've worked in a lot'a different schools around Detroit. The townships are real tough. But you know, most'a those kids are just reachin' out. They don't have family support, so as their teacher I can make a real difference to their future. Well I'm hopin' so, anyhow," Louise concluded beaming widely before swigging water from a bottle.

"Wow. Sounds a tough job," Amy understated, "I don't think I could work with kids, with or without guns."

"I'm here to learn the language so I can teach them kids some Espanol. How about you?"

"Me. I'm here to learn Spanish for a job. I've got to get good enough to work," Amy explained hesitantly.

"You mean back in England? Or where you got'a talk Spanish?"

"Oh no, here," Amy replied clearing here throat, "there's a new eco-resort opening, and, I've got a - well hopefully - I've got a job helping to manage the place when its open."

Louise coughed, choking for a moment on her water.

"No way! You got'a job here? Like you're gonna be living here, working at an *Eco resort.* Oh my gosh. That is, *so*, awesome girl." Smiling with surprise, Amy felt herself blush and glanced around at those sat near them. Nobody was paying them attention.

"Come on! Tell me how this came to be," Louise enthused.

"Ok. I can't really believe it myself," Amy replied much quieter than Louise, conscious of her conservativeness. "So, it started in London, a few weeks ago, where I have been studying and working. I was out after work with a friend, mentioned how bored I was in this hotel job and how I really want to get work somewhere with sun and sea, and just like that, a colleague of my friend linked me with this guy setting up an eco-resort in Costa Rica." Amy thought back to that day and smiled at its incredulous consequences. The conversation was hazed by large glasses of chardonnay and the buzz of belonging to a social network: after-work-drinks, ladies in snug-fitting office wear, men suited and booted. Michael, Amy had been told, had sold up, left London and followed his dreams of building an eco-resort in some beautiful beach location.

"Tell me more. How did this happen?" Louise grinned.

"This colleague of my friend said: "You've got experience in front of house, managerial support, and beach resorts, whatever. You've got a degree in tourism! Michael's place will be all eco-tourism, scuba, saving turtles stuff like that," she gave me his number on a card and said: "Give him a buzz, tell him you know me. If I was your age, without kids, a mortgage and a husband, I would not be giving you this.""

"So that was it? You just called, and what, he offered you a job?" Louise probed.

"No. I forgot about it for a while. Then, remembered it. And yeah, phoned him up. He said to come on over, do a course in basic Spanish, and then, hopefully, if it all goes to plan, I'll get to live in at the resort, helping with the guests and organising stuff - saving turtles."

"That is *sooooo* cool. You'll be part of the resort right from the start. You may live here, like, forever! That is way cool. I'm gonna come visit, right?" Louise chortled. Amy's smile had expanded with Louise's enthusiasm as her own words metamorphosed into her new, evolving reality - living on the doorstep to paradise. Beach every day, sunshine on bare skin, flip-flop feet freedom, salsa music in cool cocktail bars celebrating another day in paradise. A restless, heartbroken, stressed-out English girl transforming into a laid-back beach-babe.

"Señoritas!" a voice sang out. Louise and Amy looked up to an old, sun-bronzed man in a sun-bleached T-shirt and over-sized shorts. His droopy, salt and pepper moustache almost concealed his smile.

"Is he selling fresh coconuts? I love those," Louise said.

"What would you do with a coconut, eat it?" Amy asked.

"No, drink it dummy. Have you not seen them? Big green, fresh coconuts with the top chopped off and a big straw to suck up the coconut juice."

"How are you, lovely beauties?" the man asked in Spanish, elegantly tipping his straw hat. In one outstretched arm he carried a branch of driftwood wrapped with around thirty leather bracelets and colourful braided bands. Resting against his leg was a board wrapped in a sarong, with necklaces and earrings made of gems and seashells pinned upon it.

"Did you call these 'friendship bands' at school?" Amy asked Louise.

"We did make these, yeah." Louise casually discussed which stones best suited her eyes and hair with the old, patient man, making it immediately apparent to Amy that Louise's skills in speaking Spanish were already conversationally comfortable.

"Wow, so that's why you're in the intermediate class," Amy marvelled.

"Let's buy each other a friendship band," Louise suggested.
They picked out a little braided bracelet for each other and a necklace each for themselves, fastening them around one another's neck and wrists, as the old man assisted with delight.

"Friendship band," Louise said to him "Amistad."

"Yes?" said the old man beguilement spreading across his face. "Friendship bracelet, I like that. You have a symbol of your friendship together, so you can never forget." Amy and Louise giggled together, thanking the friendly, quirky man.

"May God bless you both," he bid farewell in English. Amy wished she'd gotten a bold gemstone pendant like Louise's, but both Louise and the convincing old man had insisted the string of tiny, pale pink shells best suited her instead.

"Does your tica Mom cook nice meals?" Louise asked Amy whilst bobbing in the sea.

"Yeah, proper home cooking. I think the meat is home-grown too," Amy replied tipping her head back to dip all of her hair in the warm water.

"Cool! How old is your tica Mom?"

"Twenty-seven, I asked her at the weekend. Young to have three kids," Amy replied. Alba had written the number of her and the children's ages for Amy.

"Wow. Twenty-seven and three kids. That's how it is here I guess."

"What like having bigger families?"

"I mean women. Women here like to marry and have kids. Their job is being a housewife and mother. The fathers work. It's still traditional in that sense."

"My Mum did that too, and worked part-time," Amy replied.

"Sure. But your Mom, and mine too, had machines to do the laundry and the dishes. I bet'cha your house-mom does it all by hand, huh?" Louise asked and stretched out floating on her back.

"You're right, she does. How come you didn't want to live with a local family?"

"Take a break from kids. Do my thing. I know if I'd been in a family, I'd be hanging with the kids all the time. Teaching 'em stuff, playin', you know." Amy nodded aware that she didn't really know. Alba's kids seemed to just ridicule her.

"I wonder if she hates it? Being just a housewife. Meeting girls like us who travel from afar to study here, free and independent, whilst she's scrubbing our clothes," Amy pondered.

"I think she's probably real happy to have a husband, and children, and a decent home, and you're an extra source of income for them. Life is pretty laid-back here." Amy raised her eyebrows in doubtful wonder at the blue sky above. "Costa Rica has a high literacy rate, something like 95%, and that's one of the highest rates in Central and South America," Louise lectured as she sat upright and fanned her arms for buoyancy. "Yet there are still strong traditions of what is called 'machismo'."

"Machismo?" Amy repeated.

"Yeah. A system where women are regarded as the weaker sex and are limited in their roles in life"

"Machismo. I kind of like the sound of that word - machismo," Amy added pointlessly.

"You dork!" Louise laughed sloshing water into Amy's face. "Last one to the beach towels buys the drinks," Louise hollered. Amy took pursuit and would have won had it not been for Louise yanking her back by her bikini bra causing them both to dive together into a giggling sand-plastered heap.

****

Under a smoky-blue sky scored with devilish-red streaks of sunset, the two friends climbed out of a clammy little four-by-four. It was Saturday evening and they'd just reached Santa Maria beach town, approximately one hundred kilometres south of Castillo.

"Let's take a swim before sundown," Amy suggested.

Amy and Louise had left tourist hotspot, Castillo, behind for miles of dusty roads and farmland, their hair flying wildly out the car windows. It was a bank holiday weekend, in honour of one of the many saints, and the teachers had earnestly assured students the school closure on Monday had already been scheduled into their individual learning programmes.

"It looks kind of rocky Amy. I hate getting my ankles bashed," Louise fretted, gripping on to Amy's arm. Holding one another's hands as they picked their feet through the shadowy water, before plunging into coolness, dipping and diving, sighing and smiling, the sea instantly dissolved the day's sweat.

"Is it a boat?" Amy squinted at a peculiar sight on the horizon.

"Or perhaps the flash of a light house?" Louise replied.

They watched the silent, intermittent flashes for over a minute before Amy exclaimed: "It's a storm!" The lightning flashes inched around the distant skies like a tumbling ball of clouds. "I've never watched a storm from afar before," Amy marvelled. "It's truly mesmerising. Like a giant electric bulb. Imagine the voltage in that."

Watching the storm, as if it were a film on a vast sky screen, Amy imagined it was an ancient Greek god touring land and sea in his cloudy chariot under the cover of a dark starless night. "I think it got closer to us." she stated after a few minutes. Louise squinted at the sky counting the seconds between flash and rumble.

"You're right. That one is closer," Louise replied after a four-second interval. A portentous breeze skimmed the water's surface, followed a few seconds later by hammering bullets of rain. Suddenly their heads were drenched as if under a humongous shower - one of those Italian shower heads. They could do nothing but spit out the saturating water as it gushed down their faces, into eyes, ears and mouth. A loud ripping sound, like a strip of gaffa tape fiercely torn off a cardboard box, added to their bewilderment. Louise screamed, lurching and clinging to Amy. "My leg!" she shrieked at Amy, who was trying to keep her head above the whipping waves, "Something touched my leg." Amy squinted into the darkness, rain splashing the seawater into her eyes and suddenly felt a spinning disorientating.

"It's a boat," Amy gasped as she felt a taut rope scrape against her leg. Amy pushed her foot against the anchor rope, grabbing it with one hand to gain some stability. Louise was still grappled to Amy's shoulder. "We've drifted. We need to swim for the beach," Amy shouted at Louise.

"Which way? I can't see anything," Louise screamed back, verging on hysteria. All around was darkness and splashing water as if thousands of fish were jumping up out of it. Amy looked up the rope of the boat and considered how they'd climb aboard. Shimmying up the rope over three meters looked arduous, if not impossible. Suddenly the sky directly above illuminated with bright white light. Amy caught a glimpse of Louise's face; a snapshot of a huge grimace. But in those protracted seconds of light, she saw, silhouetted beyond Louise, trees, land, a building with lights.

"Oh my God! We've got to get out," Amy shrieked yanking Louise's arm and starting to stab swim strokes. Fear had hit her stomach, but now she knew which direction to go. Above them, loud bangs and rumbles filled the sky like an angry orchestra of percussion instruments. "Swim!" shouted Amy "this way."

Louise pulled herself free of Amy's arm and started swimming for her life. Another flash of bright white lit the scene, this time for more than a second. And then, at the very same moment, they both saw the thin, white trails of waves touching sand only a few meters ahead. Yet the beach felt so far away. A fearsomely loud cracking-sound directly above made them simultaneously duck and scream. A burst of adrenaline made their legs and arms automatically pump and kick faster and harder blindly forwards. Neither could feel their bodies. Both were fixed on the imaginary sensation of a colossal amount of electricity discharging into them.

Their swimming efforts suddenly became easier as waves lifted them forwards, then dragged them back. Scrambling on shifting sand. Heaving forward, hands digging in, dragging backwards, sand swilling, draining. Lungs burning. Crawling, stumbling to their weak knees. The sky lit again. Louise cried out. Grasping one another's arms, they ran for the trees, as if pursued by a battalion boat.

****

Only after they'd finished their pan-fried fish supper and drained their bottles of beers, did the adrenaline start to drop away. Amy succumbed to her day-long craving to smoke and wandered out into the dark shrubby exterior. She peered beach-ward searching the crawls of wave whites for two rolling corpses, in case they'd not survived after all. Amy's mind had started mulling over something stronger than a beer. On her return, she found Louise elaborating their ordeal to a small audience of backpackers.

"I wanna toast this special occasion," Louise announced sentimentally, "I've planned this trip for a long time. Four years actually, and I wanna thank you for being here to share the moment with me." Everyone chinked their glasses of Cuba Libre - the national rum cocktail of cola and fresh lime juice over plenty of crushed ice, and sucked the sweet, anaesthetising drink through straws. In the pleasant haze of the rustic, 'out-of-town' bar, refreshed from stormy sea breezes, Amy took a wide-angle view of the scene: making new friends, taking an excursion, the sea-swimming adventure. It all gave her a sense of it being a wholesome turn of events. Right then, she sensed a heart-warming hope for a healthy new direction in her life.

Then they met Rick, a tall man in his early thirties from somewhere in the United States Amy hadn't heard of. Amy stifled a smirk at Louise girlishly twisting her hair and taking in Rick's manly, chiselled jawbone, complete with George Michael stubble. With a quick shrug and laugh, they agreed to Rick's request to join their onward trip. The next day they set out promptly after breakfast, and by late lunchtime Louise, Amy and Rick were winding up Monte Verde's steep hairpin bends in the labouring little Daihatsu. Elene, the pretty mountaintop town was little more than a few dozen log cabins, and a handful of quaint gift shops huddled on the steep slope. They checked into the hostel and went to the only restaurant they could find, a charmingly rustic pizza restaurant built entirely from wood.

"The air feels so fresh up here. With a woody, tree-like taste," Louise stated.

"That'll be your wood-fired pizza you can taste," Rick joked.

"Very funny, Rick," Louise smiled sarcastically, slowing her chewing pace.

"I'm only kiddin,'" he smiled warmly at her, "You're right. The air does have a scent of the vegetation here, and that'll be down to the fact that in a tropical montane cloud forest, like we have right here, moisture is collected by the mosses and ferns in the trees from the cloud that actually sits on the forest. Thus, the abundance of species."

"Wow. You know about trees, huh?" Louise responded. Amy saw Louise's eyes glisten at Rick's words as she munched into her chicken and sweetcorn pizza.

"A little, yeah," Rick confirmed leaning back, sipping his beer.

"Why does the cloud hang on the mountain?" Louise leaned forward and rested her chin on her hand. Amy watched, sipping her cola, thinking about the taste of 'Cuba Libre'.

"Well. It's got to do with the elevation, typically between one point five thousand and three thousand meters, and the tropical temperatures around the equator."

"I'm just nipping out for a smoke," Amy interrupted and hurried off outside.

"How could you pollute this pure air?" Louise's voice called behind her. Blowing cigarette smoke into the fresh, quiet atmosphere, Amy pondered the clouds hung all around and whether having picked up Rick had been a good idea. *It might have been more fun without him.*

Single-filing along narrow paths through bushy jungle, the trio were rounding off their day with a forest tour led by a guide calling out species' names in well-practiced English.

"What did he say that bird call was?" Louise said quietly behind Amy. Behind Louise was Rick and then at the rear of the group four tourists chatting too loud to hear the guide.

"Three-something bellbird, and bare-necked umbrella bird, how funny's that?" Amy whispered. Louise relayed the same to Rick, who was craning to listen, his eyes scouring the trees. In a clearing where the guide imparted information to the keen, Amy's mind and eyes wandered into the forest around them. Filing along like ants she'd not been able to notice that every inch of the forest was brimming with living lushness. The stony footpath appeared felted with mosses. The crowd of huge, solid tree trunks looked decorated with twisting vines, sprouting ferns, mosses, lichen, and flowers, all shiny like polished accessories. Looking up, the towering trees' canopies faded into cool mists. It smelt of decomposing wood and spring showers.

"Hear!" the guide snapped excitedly, "That bird call is the resplendent quetzal, which is actually the name of the bird."

This is real life thought Amy *Growing, dying, producing oxygen, nature.*

An hour later, Louise and Amy were strapped in harnesses, watching each other's bottoms climb vertical metal-rung ladders attached to some of those giant trees.

"This is gonna be so awesome. Amy don't-cha forget to take my photo for my class. They won't believe I did this," Louise shouted up to Amy's shoes.

"Okay," Amy shouted back without looking down. They'd had tuition from canopy tour guides and were, in theory, prepared for the 'tree-top tour'. Snaking along narrow, tree-suspended bridges, their safety straps clipped on the thick wire ropes above, dragged behind each owner like little dog leads. At each new tree or bridge they obediently detached and reattached their personal carabineer clip, aware that this was the life-saving element, should one fall. Already, one woman had spooked at the first zip wire and dropped out of the tour, along with her surely disappointed husband. Before launching off down a wire, a thick, leather, 'hawker' style glove was issued to act as a break by dragging it on to the wire. The guides briefly informed the tourists of the height and length of each zip wire before reminding them that the hand of man had never changed the dense, virgin rainforest since earth began.

It was a stupefying exhilaration, flying suspended from a wire at over a hundred meters above a forest canopy. With the pulley whirring loudly along the wire right behind the head, all that could be done was to brace towards the only direction of travel and breathe. Glancing down was both terrifying and awesome. On approaching the landing platform at the end of each zip-wire, an awaiting guide would start yanking excitedly at the system of pulleys designed to slow down the tourist whizzing along the inclined wire. Amy managed to take in, by her third zip wire, the vast swathe of green all around - so rugged and human-less.

"We're lucky our guides are not bad looking," Amy joked to Louise who'd gone quiet.

"I'm pleased you're enjoying it," Louise said diplomatically, frowning towards where the ground lay hidden below. Amy saw that Louise was trembling uncontrollably, her face pale and eyes welling. The platform they shared was over twenty meters high; Amy's legs were feeling quite weak too.

"I'll get your shot on the next one," Amy said.

"Please Amy. I gotta do this," Louise pleaded as tears started to stream down her face.

"This is the longest zip-wire of seven hundred and seventy meters long," the canopy tour guide said, oblivious to Louise's state. He pronounced his v as a b and his r as a w, something Amy would normally have had an internal chuckle at, but her humour had been left at ground level. The other tourists shuffled towards the launch-off platform, as Amy felt adrenaline surging through legs and arms. She traced the zip wire with her eyes, squinting to see the destination landing platform, where the awaiting catcher was a mere dot nestled in the distant green trees. Louise clung to the tree sobbing. "Do not stop. No use the glove to slow. Only at the end. It is very difficult to help you if you stop on this wire. You understand me?" warned the guide. "Do not stop. It is very bad, you no stop on this cable." The guide glanced at Louise and hastily hooked on the next tourist.

"It's the last zip wire," Amy said hearing her own voice wavering. She fumbled in her pocket whilst clinging to the rail, then lit a cigarette, took a short drag and a long look at Louise hugging the tree like a clinging baby koala bear to its mum.

"No smoking," a lady said to Amy, shaking her head "forest fire." Amy exhaled smoke towards the lady's face and frowned.

"It's a cloud forest, damp and wet," Amy said. The guide peered back with an anxious expression.

"I can't do it," Louise sobbed, "I'm going down."

"You can do it. I still haven't got the picture. You can't let your class down," Amy coaxed quietly, trying to ignore her own fear of the stupendous zip wire. Amy had cajoled, motivated and praised Louise through all eight zip wires, claiming falsely, that each photo she'd taken hadn't worked so to create a motivation for Louise. After twenty minutes, Amy and Louise were alone but for the guide, who was discussing on his walkie-talkie whether to take Louise down.

"We can go down the ladder, it is not easy, and we are so high. If you want to do this, we must wait for help, another guide must assist us. It will take one or maybe two hours, for guide to come," the guide explained seriously before continuing talking on his walkie-talkie.

"No," said Amy "we can't wait here for two hours." Louise was sobbing quietly like a child sobbing itself to sleep. "Louise. Why did you force yourself to do this if you're so scared?" Amy asked raising her voice, "I'm scared too you know."

"I'll tell you later." Louise turned her head to face Amy, her cheeks red and wet from sobbing and imprinted with the bark pattern. Amy gawped at her friend for a few seconds.

"Come here," Amy instructed, peeling Louise's hand from the tree and pulling her into a hug. Louise didn't resist but nervously transferred her clinging and sobbing on to Amy. The guide watched silently, waiting, glancing at the sky. "It's okay. You're going to be okay," Amy whispered into a face-full of Louise's sweaty hair and embraced her tightly until the sobbing started to subside. "Look at me," Amy said pulling Louise's face in front of hers with her hands. "You've waited a long time to do this. You're going to clip yourself on to that zip wire and just do it. It will be fine and over in less than a minute," Amy said. Louise closed her eyes and whimpered. "You must have been scared before," Amy said. Louise opened her eyes and investigated Amy's. "This is like a roller-coaster scary. Fun scary. It will all be over in a flash. We're going to drink lots of rum tonight, and eat pizza, maybe chicken?" Louise nodded, wiping her eyes. "Do this and I'll be so proud of you," Amy said. She hauled Louise back on to her feet until she was upright again. The guide shouted something down his walkie-talkie.

Louise shuffled towards the platform edge, keeping her eyes fixed on the guide, who clipped her swiftly on to the cable. With a brief nod and no double-checking whether Louise was ready or not, he firmly pushed her off. Metal on metal squealed as Louise wailed loudly until becoming a dot on the wire. Amy and the guide looked at each other briefly in the way two people alone do. Amy tried not to look at the valley or towards the ground. She lit another cigarette, blew the smoke up into the air feeling a tiny bit braver and offered it to him. He sheepishly accepted it and smoked it gently.

"Do you like your work as a guide?" she asked awkwardly, to which he smiled shyly.

"I love the forest of course, but it's not easy, very tiring, dangerous also, of course." Amy wrinkled her nose at him. "Dangerous," he repeated nodding and wincing, as if at a sad memory. Amy winced back, blinking, and watched him carefully stub out the cigarette. His walkie-talkie spoke. "Are you ready?" he asked.

As Amy plunged forward, and the zipping noise instantly sped up, she started to scream uncontrollably before her voice froze stiff, along with every muscle in her body. She squeezed her eyes closed, but it made the terror of dangling in mid-air on a mere wire worse still. She peeked through one eye at the miles of thick forest, like a helicopter shot on a TV programme, and forced herself to take some stunted gasps of breath. Then she tried to extract the intense exhilaration from her fear. She felt she was high above the world, flying through it, defying death. She sighed out heavily, expanding and contracting her ribcage more than she knew possible, peering around at the vast green world below. The magnitude of nature, its captivating vastness. This small movement caused a very slight swivel, which in turn made her squeeze her eyes closed again and then the screaming started again. All she could think of was falling, free falling until bouncing into one of the soft green sponges. *No not bouncing. It wouldn't be soft*, she told herself, *I'd probably be skewered on a branch and it would take days, even weeks, for a search party to track down my eagle-torn corpse.*

"Retardar! Despacio! Despacio!" someone was shouting. Amy opened an eye and saw the awaiting guide below her frantically waving his arms, tugging on cables. She was coming in fast, and clearly, he wanted her to slow down. She tugged down the glove, but it had no effect. He called again and again. As he abandoned the cables and readied himself, like a defending rugby player for a tackle, she saw his contorted face approaching. She squeezed her eyes shut again. He timed his leap well, wrapping his legs around hers like a crazy monkey and letting his bottom, luckily covered by padded trousers, drag hard along the platform. They both swung steeply upwards before being dumped abruptly on the platform. He unclipped and dragged her away from the landing strip and leaned her against the tree trunk. She could hear her heartbeat pounding and a rush of relief surged through her body as she glanced over at Louise who was giggling wide-eyed into her hand.

"The last time my legs felt like this," Amy said breathlessly, "was after eating too much vodka jelly".

****

The next day brought a stifling afternoon, especially in contrast to the cool cloud forest. Amy awoke from a backseat doze as the trio arrived at the sea-level town of La Fortuna.

"Hey Amy, Louise and I have decided..." Rick began speaking into the rear-view mirror, and Amy half expected him to say 'to get married' or 'to have a baby.' "...that it would be totally awesome if we treated ourselves to an evening at the hot-spring spa resort." A couple of hours later they were wearing fluffy white dressing gowns strolling around rock pools of crystal-clear water. Little wooden bridges and cobbled pathways linked the various pools, some with dams and gushing waterfalls, others were small and screened off by neatly trimmed hedges. Everywhere was landscaped with lush palms and lilies.

"There are eighteen pools, all ranging in different temperatures from eighty-three to one hundred and three Fahrenheit," Rick read from a sign.

"I like the look of that one," Louise suggested.

"Oh yeah, baby!" cried Rick, to which they all laughed.

"Cheers!" the three friends chorused, raising their flamboyantly dressed cocktails. They sat on submerged bar stools at the cocktail bar in the middle of the largest pool.

"To new friends," Rick beamed.

"To new friends," Louise and Amy chorused back. They 'oohed' and 'ahhhed' their way around the thermal pools. Some were so hot they felt their blood could boil, others cooler and refreshing with weirs to bathe under. As daylight faded fast, soft lamp-light glowed from within foliage and behind mini waterfalls, backlighting ferns and banana leaves. Rick opted for the boiling experience again, leaving the two girls together in a small pool hidden by palms.

"I wouldn't be surprised to see Bambi or a unicorn appear," Amy mused.

"I gotta thank you for today Amy. I never would have achieved the canopy tour without your encouragement," Louise said shaking her head and sighing.

"You didn't seem scared to begin with." Louise looked at Amy's face for a few seconds, as if reliving the canopy experience.

"I didn't tell you the reason," Louise squeaked in a high-pitched voice, bobbing her head as if to a sudden burst of an imaginary rhythm. Amy watched her and waited.

"That this trip means so much to me," Louise stammered before bursting into tears. Amy, biting her bottom lip with her teeth, put her arm around Louise's shoulders. It felt awkward both in bikinis and feeling so hot. But Amy watched her cry into her hands until with big sighs Louise composed herself. "My boyfriend and I...," Louise paused, "my boyfriend, Rob and I had planned this trip four years ago, but we never made it. The canopy tour, volcanoes, caving was his kind of thing. I'd rather lie on a beach every day." Louise laughed out loud. Amy listened. "We made a deal, that if I did all of the zip wires, then for the rest of the holiday he'd lay on the beach with me as much as I wanted. So, I kinda had to do it to keep the promise," she explained, her voice stabilising. Amy nodded slowly, waiting to hear more of Rob.

"So, Rob, he's?" Amy eventually prompted. Louise turned her red eyes to Amy, sadly smiling.

"He, he was killed in a car accident," she said with effort, "I, I don't usually get upset like this. I've moved on, a lot, but..." Amy blinked for a couple of seconds before smiling sympathetically.

"But doing the canopy tour and this trip is bound to bring it all back. And you did it. I'm sure he'd be so proud you, doing the canopy tour for him," Amy reassured, suddenly overwhelmed by pride for her friend. Louise sobbed again, this time through a smile. "So, when we get back to the beach, you've kept your promise." Louise laid her head back on the stone edging and sighed up into the night air. Amy felt a strange reassurance in her own 'single' life.

"Look!" exclaimed Rick from behind the hedging, "You can see the hot magma flow coming out Vulcan Arenal." As true as he had said, there in the dark sky a red diagonal glow hung where you'd expect to spot a white moon. At Rick's suggestion they sank into a hot pool with a magma view.

"This is so romantic. I don't wanna get out," Louise said drowsily. Amy caught a glimpse of Rick suppressing a smile at Louise and on impulse, swam to the steps.

"I'm going to get water," Amy said, "let me know if it erupts."

Sat at the bar, Amy gazed out across the illuminated pool sipping a Jack Daniels. A tourist couple sat to her left, evidently in love, and a pair of wealthy looking ticos, dressed completely in white, to her right. As the strong liquor eased her mind she thought: *I bet she hasn't been with a guy since her boyfriend was killed. Rick seems nice. I've got to let them get together. It's so romantic here; I bet that's why he wanted to come here. Love is lovely* Amy smiled to herself glancing at the kissing couple nearby. As Amy ordered the same again, she made a mental promise to do all she could to get Rick and Louise together. She wasn't sure if it was the hot springs or her new friendship that made her feel so invigorated and refreshed. But what she did know was that focusing on other people, as opposed to one's self, made her feel gratifying and gallant. For a moment she even decided to accept that her Mum could be in love with Giles and if they lived happily ever after, well then, Amy would be forced to be happy. *Whatever,* Amy thought to herself slipping into a blissful giddiness. As Amy approached the magma-view hot-pool she could see Louise and Rick's teeth glowing white as they giggled together. The sight brought such a happy feeling to Amy it almost confused her. It was a profound sensation that she was part of something beautiful, special, sacred. She felt part of love blossoming.

"You know, lovely ladies, I got'a hop on out as my skin is starting to shrivel, and there ain't nothing nice about a shrivelled guy. Meet me at the bar when you're ready, I'm treating you both to dinner tonight," Rick announced as he climbed out, bowed and strode off into the foliage.

"Looks like a wedding party," Louise said back at the pool bar looking up at the veranda of the resort building where people in tuxedos and beautiful evening dresses were starting their relaxed evening. Amy nodded.

"Rick seems nice," Amy said, to which Louise nodded into her Pina colada, "and he seems to like you." Louise narrowed her eyes and glanced sideways at Amy smiling.

"You deserve a nice guy," Amy cajoled. Louise smiled like a wise grandma to a child.

"And you? Got a nice guy in your life?" Louise asked. Amy's mind blanked for a moment.

"No. No nice guys at the moment. I don't tend to go for the nice ones anyway." Amy nudged Louise's elbow and nodded up towards the veranda. They both waved at Rick, who was looking dashing in a James Bond way, wearing pale linen trousers and shirt, with his damp hair combed back. He held up his wine glass and then raised a bottle out of an ice cooler.

"Playing it smooth," Louise said through her grin.

"Enjoy it, I say. You deserve to," Amy said.

"*We* deserve it," Louise exclaimed squeezing Amy's arm giggling, to which Amy raised her eyebrows still looking at Rick.

The whole evening had a magical ambiance, from the gourmet dining to the groovy laid-back vibe of the jazz band. The three laughed and ate ice cream and drank wine until late.

"This is so great, huh?" Rick beamed, his tan making his bright, blue eyes twinkle, "tropical paradise with two beautiful ladies. I couldn't be happier."

"This is the happiest I've been in a long time," Louise agreed.

"This is the happiest I've been, ever," Amy added.

"For real?" Rick asked with a hint of surprise.

"I think so," Amy nodded with a creeping sense of self-consciousness, "I've had some great times - music festivals, night clubs, Ibiza, amazing nights out in some of the best bars of London, but tonight is something different. I feel so relaxed from the hot-springs, and the forest, and you guys…"

"Ahhhhh, come here," Louise cooed, pulling the three together for a group hug.

A cold beer in a quiet bar

Louise and Amy sat under a parasol at Café Coco Loco's stretch of beach on a searing hot afternoon. The heat just seemed hotter since their adventure weekend away in the cool mountains.

"So, you got another five weeks of school?" Louise asked pensively.

"Reckon I'll be ready for that job by then?" Amy responded with a doubtful smile.

"Sure you will, no doubt," Louise reassured in that way Amy loved.

"How about you?" Amy asked, feeling the faintest wisp of trepidation at looking into the near future of imminent change.

"I got another three weeks of classes, so I should be able to teach some basic Spanish to my students, and then a few extra days at the back of that. Maybe for another adventure?"

"I'm up for that, definitely," Amy answered immediately.

"Then I'll come visiting your eco-resort. Maybe you can get me a discount?"

"Of course!" Amy replied, re-conjuring that imaginary new version of herself that only seemed to materialise itself fully in Louise's company - an established eco-resort deputy manager, bronzed and fluent in Spanish, calm, responsible, perhaps a little taller. As Louise drifted into a peaceful nap, Amy's thought wandered to Mary-Ellen from New Orleans. It had been on the same stretch of beach Amy had spent a brief hour making a reluctant acquaintance with Mary-Ellen. They were in the same class and Amy was making efforts to avoid her and their conversations that made Amy cringe to privately recall.

"Mamma made it crystal clear to me that I ought not forget who I be. No point in pretending I'm not wealthy in comparison to the folk round here," Mary Ellen had said whilst Amy had tried not to listen.

"Here, a have a swig of this." Amy had offered Mary-Ellen a small, hipflask-sized bottle of brandy.

"It's a bit early in the day for liquor!" exclaimed Mary-Ellen, squinting into the sunlight, her blond hair reflective white.

"Chill out, we're on holiday," Amy insisted, to which Mary-Ellen took the bottle and a little swig.

"You got'a watch y'back here hon," she continued, passing the bottle back.

"I'm not so sure you need to judge the local people in that way. I've not been ripped off yet. My local family is lovely, actually. It's a tourist area, people sell to the tourists. I've just moved from London; you should see how they rip tourists off there," Amy answered as they'd spread out their beach towels.

"Oh sure hon. Not everyone is bad to the bone. But we'za targets don'tcha know? Don'tcha delude yourself and be a victim," she lectured. It had been the same day that Amy had dropped into the eco-resort, at Louise and Rick's insistence, to learn that Michael was away in San Jose, dealing with some legal matter, and the construction works of the resort were some way off completion. As much as Mary-Ellen really got under Amy's skin, she did still feel a pang of guilt for knowingly leaving her dozing in the hot, bright sun that day.

"Hey girls," Rick chirped from behind them.

"Hi Rick," they chimed back.

"How about you Rick, what are your plans?" Louise asked.

"You know, I'm just seeing what happens here. I'm loving the surf right now. I don't need to be back in the Rockies for another few weeks. But I fancy hiking up the highest mountain in Costa Rica – Cerro Chirripo – it's a tropical forest with these giant oaks I'd love to see," Rick said wistfully.

"Wow, sounds awesome," Louise echoed his tone. From behind her sunglasses, Amy caught a glimpse of Louise's gooey expression. "Who's up for a juice? I'm melting already," Louise announced.

"I'm in," Rick didn't hesitate. Amy paused a moment.

"You guys go ahead; I've got to get some homework done."

"Come on Amy," Rick coerced, "It's just a juice. Help you concentrate."

"No really. If you guys want to come and visit me in my eco-resort job, I must get learning. Seriously, I'm not super-fast at my homework like the teacher here."

"I've offered to help." Louise shrugged off the compliment.

"Bring it with you, we'll do it together," Rick instructed.

"I'm going to catch the next bus straight home and plough through it," Amy stated conscientiously.

"Good on you, I say. She's motivated, Rick. You go girl," Louise praised.

"Ok, but tomorrow no refusing," Rick said to Amy, "This is our meeting point, right? End of the day. We meet right here."

"Right here Amy," Louise parroted.

"Cool. Right. Catch you tomorrow." Amy bid farewell, heavy with sacrificial loyalty to the grace of matchmaking.

The next day, instead of meeting at Café Coco Loco's beach strip, Amy sought out the most hidden spot on the beach, up near the estuary. Her plan was to wait for the heat to die down, whilst attempting her homework, then go for a pre-sunset jog and sit-up session, by which time Louise and Rick would have met up without her again, and hopefully, without the threesome friendship getting in their way, will have had time to merge their travel plans together. This was how Amy's trail of imagination was taking her, justifying her intentional avoidance of Louise, who she'd rather be sat sinking a juice or beer with and picking her brains on the mysterious concept of verb conjugation. This was when Amy heard a familiar voice.

"Friendship bracelet." It was the old bangle seller. Amy held up her wrist showing the pink shell necklace doubled for a bracelet, grinning.

"You're a student," he said in Spanish, to which she nodded. "Excuse me, please. My name is Alvero," he introduced himself, eyes twinkling from behind his little round spectacles.

"My name is Amy," she replied, pleased with her Spanish pronunciation.

"The language of Spanish is beautiful, yes?" he continued.

"Difficult," Amy replied using a word she used often in class.

"Can I join you? Perhaps I can be of some help," he politely offered.

After two solid hours of conjugation, Amy felt she had gained more understanding of Spanish structure than from the entire week's classes. All that Alvero would accept for her gratitude was a coffee. They agreed to meet same place and time the next day.

****

"So how was the juice?" Amy beamed at Louise, entering the school snack bar.

"Hey Amy. Not as good as here," she grinned after hesitating.

"I meant how was the juice *with Rick*?"

"It was good. He doesn't know if he's gonna split or not. Seems like he's forest mad. I keep thinking about the Rockies - crystal-clear lakes, roaring fires in log cabins," Louise mused.

"I can't believe he works in the Rockies. Me, I prefer warmth and beaches. I think he's hanging out here for a reason. I mean, why would he change his plans and divert to Castillo? I reckon he's got a thing for you," Amy smirked, bouncing her eyebrows.

"Get out of here!" Louise exclaimed with a huge smile, "you think that for real?"

"Yeah I do Louise. I can tell, the way he makes such an effort and is so polite."

"I don't know, maybe I could leave the teaching behind for the Rockies, and surf holidays," she replied coyly and, to Amy's satisfaction, blushed a little. Barstools scraped on the tiled floor as students filed out of the little café area. "Are you going to show later today then?" Louise questioned as she stood to leave for her afternoon class.

"Yeah. Sorry got caught up with stuff yesterday," Amy replied, wanting ask how things were going with Rick. Louise pulled a doubtful, possibly suspicious expression at Amy, like she did with a student giving a less than acceptable excuse. But later, Amy was sat near the lethargic estuary waiting for Alvero. It was an overcast afternoon; surfers fought heavily with the sighing waves. Alvero patiently spent another afternoon reinforcing Amy's lesson, tirelessly explaining grammar and conjugations. He moved on to drilling numbers and days of the week and had drawn little circles with the two clock hands, neatly annotating each clock face in capital letters. They

43

role-played dialogue until her mind was exhausted and her head dizzy with vocabulary and grammatical rules. She'd just bid farewell to Alvero and was lay back on the sand to stretch her legs that she'd crossed for too long, when a voice snapped her full attention.

"Hey Amy. You showed up." Looking up in surprise, she saw Louise tramping across the sand towards her and instantly perceived her friend's disconcerted mood. "But in the wrong place. What you doing here?" she demanded.

"I thought I'd missed you. Sorry about not showing up again. I needed to make headway with homework, and -" Amy started to explain. Louise stood with hands on hips frowning down at Amy.

"Really?" Louise said unconvinced.

"So, did you and Rick go for a smoothie or anything?" Amy asked a little confounded by Louise's introverted mood.

"Rick didn't show again either," Louise said wincing and looked out into the bay at a boat.

"What! When? Today?" Amy asked as if accused of an injustice. Louise huffed and shook her head slowly. "What do you mean again?" Louise shook her head whilst still looking out at the boat slowly traversing the bay. Amy scrambled to her feet with a twang of overexerted stomach muscles under a rib.

"You both didn't show," Louise said firmly, now facing Amy, "again."

"It was his idea to meet there, what's he playing at?" Amy said in a raised voice.

"Oh, what do'ya know! Here he comes now," Louise said looking beyond Amy in mock surprise.

"Hey girls. Looks like rain, huh? Sorry I didn't make it yesterday or today, I got stranded on this surf beach up the coast," he said grinning. There was a rumble from land direction.

"For two days?" Amy frowned.

"Yeah, the surf was good, so the others wanted to sleep on the beach."

"Ok, you've been stuck on a surf beach?" Louise asked directly to Rick's sunglasses.

"Let's go and have a beer," Amy suggested, "or a cocktail. Sit the storm out."

"You guys go ahead, I'm going to hang out at my house," Louise said tiredly.

"No!" Amy protested forcefully, "Come on. It's the weekend." But Amy was shouting through a yawn, fighting against her own sudden tiredness. It always happened when the sky was thunderously heavy and the air smothered with humidity. Louise raised her eyebrows at Amy. "This weather makes me want to lie down," Amy admitted. Rick gazed at Amy.

"Me too. That's why I'm gonna go take a nap," Louise announced with irritation.

"It's just this heavy weather; as soon as it breaks you'll feel normal again. Come on guys, let's go get a beer or two; hang out," Amy begged before her next jaw-wrenching yawn. Once in the bar, the sky darkened at an alarming rate, like nightfall in fast-forward. Soon after, dense rain fell fast. People huddled under shop canopies gazing out at the washing road, entranced by the bubbling water. Lazing tourists blinked at the hazy empty beach that, only moments before, was full of bathers. It felt incongruous to order cocktails, but Amy did, ensuring they were strong. "You see. When it rains, you just perk back up again," Amy smiled, distributing their second round of cocktails.

"Hey, it was my turn to buy drinks," Rick protested.

"Too slow," Amy smiled back.

"I didn't buy any yet either," Louise joined in.

"You don't buy anything. After waiting on the beach three times," Rick replied.

"It was fine," Louise shrugged, head cocked to one side, smoothing stray hair behind an ear.

"Tomorrow I'll be there, you too, right Amy?"

"Sure. But it's not so easy for me living out of town and guessing the bus times, you know?" Amy replied.

"That's no excuse. I'll hire a car and come pick you up," Rick laughed.

"I'm just nipping out for a smoke," Amy said, blanking Rick's comment. The sight of soggy sand on the empty, rain-swept beach normalised paradise. She thought of her eco-resort job and wondered what it would entail, if indeed Michael sorted his issues out anytime soon, and his wife accepted her into the family business. She took a drag on her cigarette, watching a couple of drenched fishermen wade ashore from an anchored boat, their t-shirts and shorts clinging to their bodies. She imagined herself joining these workers of the bay, etching a living for herself too. *My tourist days will be short-lived* she told herself, *speaking Spanish is priority*. She glanced, eyes only, at her two friends. Rick was becoming animated and the empanadas Amy had ordered were being served. *If only I could just slip away,* she thought glancing up the beach. But then she saw Rick was beckoning her attention, so she re-joined them.

"I spend most of my days flying in a helicopter over the forest, mapping, monitoring the rivers, lakes, snow on the Rockies out in Western Canada," Rick was explaining to Louise, as Amy quietly slipped on to her seat. Louise was blinking softly into Rick's eyes. The smell of spicy empanadas and fresh pineapple and mango from the cocktails wafted around them.

"Wow. I bet it's so beautiful, what a job!" Louise enthused, "Aren't the Rocky Mountains huge?"

"Ok. The Rockies are part of a huge stretch of mountain range that reaches right down the West side of Canada, the US and all of the way to the tip of Chile in South America," he explained, biting a huge mouthful of an empanada. Amy gazed out at the beach.

"I should know this, but I didn't major in geography," Louise blushed, "So, do you have to stay in the mountains on your own?"

"I do have periods of time where I'm stationed out there; I do a lot of trekking, but then I also work at the visitor centres in the towns, it varies really."

Amy took in the setting, her company, the warm rain, how free her feet felt in sandals, how comfortable she was in shorts and a vest over her bikini, how relaxing it was to wear her hair lose down her back, it all felt right. So right. Amy noticed that Louise, unusually, hadn't eaten any empanadas.

"I'd love to see the Rockies, it must be so fresh up there," Louise said dreamily.

"Oh yeah it's fresh alright. And bright too. It's so beautiful, I can't tell you. There are glaciers, waterfalls, still lakes so turquoise blue you can see white clouds reflected in them. Mountain life is like being away from all the craziness of the world." Rick glanced at Amy who shook her head in fake wonder.

"Don't you get scared out there alone in the mountains?" Louise asked.

"Not scared. Lonely, some. A few rangers I know take their wife or girlfriend for a few weeks to stay with them, to share the evenings, or even accompany them on their hikes. My friend's wife is in love with the mountains. She's an artist - paints all day."

"You know, you should go to the Rockies next school break," Amy said more dramatically than intended. Louise's eyes widened. "What do you reckon Rick? Do you have your own cabin?" Amy asked.

"Sure. Of course. You are both welcome to visit anytime," he nodded standing, and headed to the bar. Salsa music abruptly blurted from the speakers, as if announcing the end of the rainfall.

"Rocky Mountains. Reckon you could manage it?" Amy asked, grinning widely.

"I wish," Louise said holding up her glass, thoughtfully looking into Amy's eyes as if wanting to say something. Amy chinked her cocktail glass with Louise's. A few cocktails later, the trio were dancing and chatting with some equally tipsy tourists, to the quiet amusement of the bar staff. Amy went to the toilet and whilst washing her hands took a good, but slightly blurry, look at herself in the bamboo-framed mirror. *What do I look like?* She wondered *Kind? Responsible? The type of girl who can manage an important job at a turtle-saving eco-resort?* The sun-kissed face in the mirror didn't respond other than heavy-eyelid blinking. When stepping back into the bar she was immediately greeted by the sight of Louise and Rick dancing together, an attempted salsa but in more of a ballroom hold. Amy stopped quickly, hesitated, and then beckoned the girl collecting glasses to the veranda where she explained, as best she could, to tell her dancing friends that she went home – to her family. She re-emphasised until sure the girl could repeat the message to relay. Then, in a liquor-infused elation, Amy trotted down the veranda on the beach, cut between shops and made her escape up the road, slopping her sandals through puddles.

The next day Amy was ambling along the dusty Castillo backstreet in her favourite daydream, the one she'd become a scuba-dive instructor at the eco-resort, when she heard a familiar voice call her name.

"Hi Rick. What you doing here?" Amy replied, her mind racing with questions.

"Do you want to get some lunch?"

"Why don't you get lunch here at the school? I'm hoping Louise will be here too, she's got morning class this week."

"I wanted to speak to you, about something I've been thinking about," he replied. Amy narrowed her eyes for a moment and then a glimmer of hope emerged. *He's going to confide in me about his feelings for Louise.* "I want to share something with you, come on. I know you have afternoon class." With raised eyebrows, she let Rick take her arm and guide her back towards the beachfront. In a quiet bar, a little way along the beachfront from Coco Loco, Amy sat with Rick, waiting for him to tell her what was on his mind. He ordered for both from a menu he seemed familiar with. "How're you finding Castillo then? Can you see yourself working, living here?" Rick casually enquired, to which Amy frowned and rested her elbows on the table. The waiter brought cold bottles of beers to the table and opened them before Amy could answer. Rick held his beer up and Amy clinked her bottle with his, forcing a smile.

"What do you want to share with me?" Amy asked after a gulp of fizzy lager, noting how nice it was to be in a quiet bar having a cold beer at lunchtime. Rick replied with a long rambling description of his idea to take a weekend trip up to another volcano, elaborating mostly about the forests, studying trees and his chances at getting a job in Costa Rica. Amy had almost drunk her whole beer whilst he spoke at her. "Look Rick," Amy finally broke into his talking.

"Sorry, I was chatting at you. I just don't know if I'm ready to head back north yet," he smiled warmly at her, gazing into her eyes. For a moment Amy found herself attracted to his cropped hair and golden face stubble. The way he spoke so openly; his gentlemanly tone of voice unbefitting his heavyset shoulders and arms.

"I want to ask you something," Amy began. The waiter brought plates of salad to their table followed by another waiter carrying a big, rusty-orange lobster sliced up on a bed of slaw and lime wedges. Rick grinned at Amy, clearly waiting for her reaction.

"Looks awesome, huh?" he said hardly able to conceal his excitement.

"Wow. I don't normally go for lobster." Amy watched Rick digging his fork into the juicy white lobster meat, thanking the waiters and ordering two more beers. She had a sudden feeling of being with a total stranger. She thought of the school snack bar and Louise eating empanadas. She had a strong feeling that was where she should be.

"Here, try some," Rick said to Amy, holding a forkful of lobster towards her, "it's got an awesome chilli dressing with a squeeze of lime." Amy hesitated but then took the offering.

"Wow, that is gorgeous," Amy said with surprise. The beer, the delectable meal and Rick's chirpy company faltered Amy's intended inquisition until the lobster's shell was emptied. Amy sat back and sipped her second beer.

"Did you enjoy?" Rick asked.

"I loved it, yes."

"Can I ask you something?" he asked quickly, and continued before Amy replied, "You work out right? I mean, you are seriously toned."

"I like to run, get the toxins out."

"I saw you running on the beach the other evening," Rick grinned, "It was you right? Wearing tiny shorts?"

"Oh, those shorts," laughed Amy sitting upright, "I don't know why, they seemed to have shrunk into pants. I think I've put weight on here actually."

"Ok. I'm gonna join you for a run, if that's ok? I need to get in shape." Amy felt herself blush a little under Rick's smile and shifted in her seat.

"I wanted to ask you," Amy proceeded. He nodded a little and hung his head to one side.

"Louise," Amy said, "She's a great girl, isn't she?"

"Sure."

"And, you're a, great guy, and, you two, together?" Rick tilted his head back and laughed loudly, his eyes closed. Amy's smile merged into a frown as she watched Rick hooting. She had a strange feeling she was losing something, or never had something she thought she did have.

"Louise and I?" Rick laughed out loud returning his face towards Amy. Amy glanced around and squirmed in her seat a little.

"You two make a great couple. You have fun together. Aren't you looking for?" Rick reached around the table and held one of Amy's hands. He stopped himself laughing and looked at Amy sincerely.

"You're a sweet girl, Amy." Amy blinked at him, sighing with exasperation. "Don't you see?" Rick said, "Falling in love isn't just about having fun together." He pulled his face closer to Amy. She could smell his woody aftershave mingled with lobster and lime. She noticed how his short, blond chin-stubble looked sharp and imagined its coarseness against her own chin. For a few seconds she longed to be kissed and fall in love. His hand on hers felt strong and manly. He caressed her palm with his thumb making a tingle travel right up her arm and into her neck. "It's about attraction," he said. Amy thought of Louise, pulled her hand free and stood up.

"I've got to go to class," Amy said apologetically, "I think you've misunderstood." Rick frowned at the lobster shaking his head.

"It's ok to be happy Amy. What's with the tough-girl act?"

"Tough-girl? What do you mean? You said I was sweet a minute ago," Amy said louder than intended, the lager flushing her face.

"You act like you're the lone-ranger, don't need no-one, drinking, smoking, tough-girl in town," Rick criticised at Amy's flabbergasted face. "Some London bad boy broke your heart?" Rick flippantly continued.

"What?" Amy sighed unable to find words, "This wasn't about me."

"Am I right?" Rick reverted to his kind, warm way, "We all have broken hearts Amy. You don't get to warm by a fire without flames. Just 'cus you got your fingers burnt once don't mean a thing." Amy just gawped at him in confusion. A flood of feelings swarmed over her, predominantly that she'd been foiled. She started to walk away but didn't get far before his hands were on both her arms. Turning and looking up at Rick's cool expression she felt overcome by anger mixed with that urge to be kissed, whisked off her feet. "Amy," he said with closed eyes, "give me a chance. I'm... I'm a good lover." Something clicked in Amy's thoughts.

"I've got to go," she stammered, wriggling free from his hands and making her escape. Once out on the warm streets, Amy's mind went into a self-rebuking monologue. *What was all that about? All this effort and sacrifice for Louise to be with that jerk. I'm so stupid. I could have been hanging out with her, having a great time, instead of trying to set them up. 'I'm a great lover?' Who the hell says that?*

Afternoon class dragged by despite Amy being forty minutes late, something she was sent to the school reception desk to be cautioned about. Amy just scowled at the school manager's rebuking. But she hardly cared. She couldn't concentrate in the class for being so irked at Rick. But she gradually realised that her thoughts kept returning to his biceps stretching his t-shirt, his firm chest, his lilting accent purring endlessly about trees and forests. She suddenly realised, with a kindling feeling, that he'd asked Amy to join him visiting Costa Rican forests so he could look for work here; to be with her. *Why?* She felt genuinely baffled.

"Amy. Your turn please," the teacher interrupted her thoughts, pointing at the whiteboard phrase.

"Uno libro rojo en la mesa grande," Amy read out. The teacher gesticulated for Amy to continue to give her own example sentence.

"Una cervaza fria en la bar tranquilo," Amy said, meaning a cold beer in a quiet bar.

"El bar tranquilo," the teacher corrected and swiftly moved on with the class.

After the lesson, Amy sat in the school snack bar prodding her coco-mango smoothie with her straw, trying in vain to ignore Mary Ellen's attempts to converse with her.

"What is it with you?" Louise's voice hurtled across the bar. Amy's foot slipped off the footrest of the bar stool as she looked around with a start. Louise's face was flushed and scowling, her eyes puckered from crying.

"Louise, what's up?" Amy asked alarmed.

"Do you think I'm stupid?" Louise demanded. Amy immediately knew Louise had seen her with Rick at lunchtime.

"But -"

"Hatching your excuses for later?" Louise said forcing back fresh tears. For a moment Louise looked so beautiful to Amy, her glistening eyes, the vulnerability of her raw emotions on display, the hurt she housed for Amy. "You're such a liar Amy. Why don't you both just come out with it?" Louise said with a raised voice so that the whole of the snack bar was silenced and watching the drama unfold.

"But don't you see what I'm trying to do?" Amy answered.

"Oh yeah. I see what you're trying to do," Louise retorted, her eyes glaring wildly "I'm not stupid."

"Louise!" Amy pleaded, jumping off her stool, her face burning with blushing.

"I'm through with both of you. I thought you were a friend!" Louise shouted throwing the friendship bracelet at Amy's feet. She stomped out of the school, leaving the students watching Amy. Amy's feet felt rooted to the floor.

"She's wrong," Amy shook her head "I haven't -". The students started chatting between themselves again.

"Hon, let's go get a shake, or a beer," Mary Ellen suggested in a comforting way.

"I've got to find her, and make her see," Amy muttered, rushing after Louise. She followed Louise down the dusty track until reaching Castillo's main street. But Louise had ducked down an alleyway and disappeared from view. Amy peered down the street as if seeking a lost dog. Electric lights were switching on by the second as the sun sank away. She searched at Louise's hostel, on the beach, by Coco Loco and in the bars, as she watched the silent glory of the beach sunset - gold turning orange, turning red then pink, compounding her dismay. She had a strange, growing sense that she was in a film as the leading actress - the drama of the situation; the paradise setting; the warm sunglow casting murky shadows around the streets. The people more hurried than usual, ending their days, returning to homes and their other lives. *Why do I always screw things up? What do I need in my life to stop being so stupid?* Amy asked herself with welling tears.

"A coffee?" a voice rang out of a nearby café. It was Alvero. Amy instinctively smiled at him. He looked different without his old hat on, sat reading a newspaper through his spectacles. He looked a little like Mahatma Gandhi. He stood and pulled out the chair opposite him, gesturing for her to join him. Amy solemnly joined him, and Alvero returned to quietly and continually sipping his coffee, watching the feet of passing people on the street. He placed his empty coffee cup on to the table and lent back in his chair.

"How was your day Amy?" he asked over his glasses at her, to which she shrugged.

"No good day," she answered after drawing a long breath.

"Why no good?"

"My friend - green necklace. She no happy. She thinks me bad," Amy explained. He continued peering at her and nodded once for her to continue. "It complicated." Amy waved her hands, shaking her head, avoiding eye contact.

"It is regarding the man from Canada?" Alvero asked or stated. Amy looked him in his eyes. "My necklaces are very popular," he answered smiling coyly.

"Two platas tipicas," a waiter interrupted, putting plates piled with rice, beans, chicken and salad before them as if it were their order. Alvero glanced nervously at Amy and breathed in the aroma before a shout from the bar prompted the waiter to whisk away the plates again.

"The man from Canada," Amy persisted after the disturbance ended. "My friend - to like - have heart for this man - but," she tried to explain.

"But his heart is for you instead." Alvero completed her sentence, leaning forwards and widening his eyes.

"How? But - I want, help my friend, the two together, but now -" Amy whined.

"It was a mistake to attempt to -" Alvero used his hands as if he were kneading play-dough, "connect friends in this manner. Love is a blessing from God. Natural and pure."

"How you know the Canada man has heart for me?" Amy asked frowning.

"I see him," Alvero pointed two fingers at both of the lenses in his glasses, "every day I am at the beach. To you, the beach is a lot of people. To me, the beach, there are newly arriving tourists, local people, tourists who have been here for one week, some one-month, surfers, and more. It is my professional duty not to approach the same people every day and cause annoyance," Amy listened, "therefore," he paused, poising a pointing finger as a lecturer might do, "I had noticed yourself regularly meeting with your two friends. The jade necklace girl always arrives first and sits next to the café Coco Loco," Alvero explained with eyes and helping hands. "Then you *or* Mr. Canada arrives. But you may not know that Mr. Canada started to sit *in* Coco Loco, behind the screen so to observe the meeting place. When *you* arrive, he joins afterwards. The days you *don't* arrive, he leaves the café by the road and does not join jade necklace girl." Amy frowned with disbelief, partly at Alvero's account and partly at doubting her Spanish comprehension.

"Bizarre?" Alvero shrugged. "I can only analysis this behaviour is because Mr. Canada only wants to see *you*, but you are not always reliable."

"Oh no," Amy moaned leaning her forehead into her hands, "Why am I so stupid?"

"No," Alvero pulled her hands down and found his eye contact, "don't cry." Amy looked at the old man craning to comfort her and saw a lonely, sad person clinging to hope. Up close she noticed how dry his lips were, how gaunt his face was.

"Senor, Senorita. Can I get you anything else?" the waiter asked, clearing their table.

"Yes. Two platas tipicas, a beer, and another coffee or a beer or?" Amy asked Alvero, who was shifting in his seat verging on protesting. "I pay, today," Amy added, nodding a little at him.

"Another coffee, please," Alvero told the waiter after a pause and sat upright twisting the edges of his moustache.

An hour and half later Amy and her taxi driver were lying on the roof of the taxi, looking skyward. The driver's zealous deliberations over the Spanish word *'estrellas'* had found them in a scrubby field to settle the matter.

"Look.... you see... estrellas," the taxi driver had repeatedly said in English, pointing out of his open car window.

"Australia! No. I think not," Amy had repeatedly insisted. And so he had swerved off the road and down a hidden track.

"No, estrellas!" he had said, climbing up the bonnet of his car and beckoning her to follow. *Surely he doesn't think that Australia is out in space* Amy wrangled with herself, considering a pronunciation misinterpretation from his missing front teeth. The vast sky above, when viewed horizontally, transformed before Amy's eyes. It was like a great black canvas smattered with bright pin-pricks, as if flicked up there by a loaded paint brush. Incomprehensively vast, the masses of stars stretched to the sky edges. Suddenly, all above seemed more illuminated than dark. The millions upon millions of stars inconceivably filled the sky. A shooting star streaked across the sky for a fraction of a second. Facing space was staggeringly wondrous, awe inspiring, heart stirring.

"Ahhhaa? Si? Estrellas," the taxi driver boasted, transfixed by nature's largest screen. The sky revealed more by the second, for the deeper one stared the more clusters of stars appeared to the eyes. In any one small pocket, stars of differing intensities and size shone out. "You wanna clave?" the driver asked in English holding up a key. A key turned out to implicate a snifter of cocaine off the key. Before Amy had caught up with the connotation, he'd swiftly snorted his loaded key and was reloading for her. The audience of shining stars, the driver's audacious, gappy smile, the spontaneity of the moment amongst the tall grasses, the riskiness of being alone, letting go of caring, the emotions of the day all summed up to Amy's compulsive response. She swiftly sniffed up the offering.

"I can touch them!" Amy giggled in English minutes later, arm outstretched to the sky.

"Si!" the taxi driver agreed, grasping for sky, giggling as childishly as she was. Soaring intensely, warming within, hearts opening.

"The stars are falling on us!" Amy squeaked through her rollercoaster smile at her lurching sky, hands covering her face.

"No, it okay," the taxi driver insisted peeling her hands from her face. Her eyes slowly focused on his spinning face with the stars safely high above him and burst out laughing with such gusto her legs curled up like perfect Pilates postures. And so it went on. For minutes or hours, Amy didn't know. Keys, star gazing, fits of laughing Pilates. "Si? Estrellas," the taxi driver concluded for the twenty-something time, pointing and waving his finger across the sky scape.

"Stars," Amy said, almost to herself.

"Stas," he repeated "Si? Estrellas."

"Estrellas?" Amy asked the stars above, and then curled up so hard from laughing she rolled over on to her side and would have tumbled right off the roof if the driver hadn't have caught her by her arm. He insisted they climbed down to the ground. Sniffing one more key each he urged her they should continue their way.

When Amy woke late the next morning, sweaty and still, she couldn't recall arriving home or climbing fully clothed on to her bed.

Sleeping dragon

A flock of white, plastic chairs gathered on the pavement outside La luna llena, where half-a-dozen men sat having late-hour drinks by the light of a dim street lamp.

He was staring into the darkness of the alleyway as she stepped into his daydream. Their lines of vision converged as if in slow motion and their gazes locked, naturally, involuntarily. He saw a lean, skulking foreign girl, with an unlit cigarette in her lips. Not the usual tourist-type, introverted from local life by holiday indulgence, nor the scrutinising 'wrapped-up-in-business' land-buying-prospector type. No. This intriguing girl appeared to him as a pensive, purposeful, mysterious female, who moved a little slower than the usual gringas. What her purpose was in his hometown, alone, at the late hour questioned him squarely. Her slender yet muscular arms arrested him first. Then her modestly intellectual air captivated him completely. To him she oozed confidence at a high level, from a distant, exotic land where women equaled, even rivaled men with word and understanding. *She's one of them.* The poise, elegance and understated power of the girl sauntering past him grabbed his lungs and stopped them breathing. *She isn't butch, like some of the surfer tourist girls,* he calculated *but she can probably surf, at least swim well.* He could visualise her pale skin cutting through the water as she paddled a surf-board. Instinctively, the hand that held his lighter outstretched towards her without taking his eyes from hers.

"Do you want a light?" he asked in softly spoken Spanish. His chin and jaw were defined by the overhead street-lamp and, despite being shadowed, gave his piercing eyes a keen, almost maddened expression.

"Thank you," she said naturally as if fluent in his language, accepting the flame to the cigarette.

"My name is Zan. Would you like a beer, Senorita?" he asked.

"I want taxi," she stated in her best Spanish.

"Manuel. Two beers please," Zan called out to the bartender without faltering, and offered Amy his chair.

"Errrr. I want – err – go - Santa Rosa," Amy said.

"Santa Rosa!" Zan asked with surprise, "I live there too." Amy frowned at him, for Santa Rosa was a tiny hamlet outside of Castillo. She was one of only two students homed with families there. She dragged on her cigarette, watching him indifferently, and blew the smoke from the corner of her mouth. Her gaze wandered beyond him for signs of taxis.

"I know your family. Marcel, Alba -" Zan started to list. Amy's eyes rolled back to Zan. The men had fallen silent behind him.

"The children - Alonso, Jose and the little girl. I'll take you to the house, no problem."

"Yes?"

"What is your name?" he asked without blinking.

"My name is Amy," she replied in Spanish, recalling her first ever Spanish lesson. Without averting his gaze, Zan offered her the bottle of beer that Manuel had flicked the lid off and pressed into his awaiting hand. She accepted the beer and chair. And they commenced their struggle through small talk, his eyes fixed firmly upon her as if she were a sparrow that may fly away any moment.

"Is possible for taxi?" she asked again after a while. Zan smiled, nodding to Manuel for two more beers. And so, it went on until the only sign of life on the dark, carless road was a dog snapping at moths under a streetlamp. Amy wobbled off balance when standing to bid goodnight to Manuel.

"Walk?" Zan asked, making two fingers step like feet, "Beach or street?"

"Beach," she replied, hoping it would sober her up by the time they reached the taxis. Zan strolled with ease, gaining the desired sobering effect from the beach, whilst he noticed a primordial skittish excitement stir in the pale girl starting to lollop on the cool shifting sand.

"Sit for some minutes," Zan said after catching Amy's hand as she stumbled. She flopped back on the sand, her hair spreading like a pillow, and closed her eyes. Zan gazed at the dark sea. The waves always sounded different at night to him; heavier or tired somehow. Amy feigned sleeping, snoring in and out to the rhythm of the waves.

"Sleeping dragon," Amy said in English.

"Dragon?" Zan replied. Amy roared a little, then snored again and pointed towards the waves. After a long pause, Zan finally caught on.

"Dragon dormido," he said.

"Si, sleeping dragon," Amy smiled up at his bemused face "dragon dormido."

"Do you want to smoke Marijuana?" he asked. Amy chuckled smugly.

"Yes," she answered, sitting up with some spare stomach muscles. They puffed and passed the joint until it started to burn finger flesh and Zan flicked it towards the waves.

"Pura vida!" he said grinning.

"Pura vida!" Amy copied, wondering what it really meant. Zan blinked out at the white runs of waves in the darkness, wondering who might be around to give them a lift since the taxis had finished for the night, or if she might manage to walk the distance. He dug his hand into the cool sand, picking out bottle tops and coconut shells and hurtled them at the waves, until from the corner of his vision, he noticed she was no longer lay by his side but skipping off into the darkness along the beach. What he shouted out to her had too many words that she didn't understand.

'Estuario muy peligroso,' Zan kept repeating as he got closer to her. As Amy jauntily threw off her top, he stopped and nervously watched Amy gambling over to the water's edge, his eyes straining in the darkness. He shouted to her again.

"Peligroso no problem," she responded with excitement blazing in her wide pupils. She knew they had reached the estuary at the end of the beach, and as for pelicans, she wasn't scared of them, remembering how she'd made a good friend of a pelican whilst learning to fish on a family holiday in Greece. Its huge sack beak, like a wicket keeper's glove, lining up and catching the tasty treats Amy threw it. A different continent, a different estuary, and a totally different type of pelican. It was some days later that Amy learned 'peligroso' means dangerous in Spanish. The low, chasing waves with their dragging undercurrent soon upgraded her dizziness into a disorientating spin. Within seconds she couldn't tell which direction sea or beach, or river was, and Zan laboured waist-deep in the murky waters to haul her back to shore. Back on sand, Zan watched her panting heavily, dressed in only her knickers, laughing with exhilaration or shock or madness. He, also panting heavily but not laughing, wondered how they'd make the four kilometers home.

La vida Costarricense

If Amy had taken the time to scrutinize why Zan was instantly and completely irresistible, why the magnetism and feel of familiarity, mental warning bells would have been loudly ringing. He called for her one afternoon soon after the estuary rescuing episode. Alba and her children had hung in the doorway listening to their efforts to communicate, before exchanging expressive glances confirming that their English lodger was completely unconventional. With tentatively uttered words and a shy smile, he politely asked her for a date. She knew so from simply hearing the words 'con migo', meaning with me, in his sentence, punctuated by a question-mark from a quick bounce of his eyebrows. Amy could hardly stammer a response. She felt she could be back wearing a high-school uniform. She failed to refuse such a polite, formal request, especially following the hours of piggybacking home from the estuary.

After closing the door to him and resting alone in her bedroom, she saw it clearly. He had torn a hole in a beautiful picture, beckoning her to dive right through it to find what exotic mysteries lay beneath the canvas. The *real* people of the wondrous place named Costa Rica felt more alluring through Zan. The more she greeted locals with 'pura vida', bought single cigarettes from the corner stores, drank late-night beers in the local bars and chatted to women returning from working the fields, the more she thirsted for the Costa-Rican way of life. Saturday football matches on dusty village-square pitches, smoking weed through a conch sea-shell to celebrate the village victory, hitching rides on the back of motorbikes and pick-up trucks after missing the last bus home, bread-paper rolled joints on the beach at sunset.

"My house!" Zan had exuberantly welcomed Amy to the wooden bungalow one day. It was down a driveway crossed with a large loop of barbed wire. Amy immediately could see that Alba's home was upmarket in comparison. "I live with my mother and sister," he explained. Amy cast her eyes around the dim kitchen, at old wooden chairs, the stone sink, and a huge blackened frying pan caked in what looked like years of fried oil. But no mother or sister.

"A toilet?" Amy asked, to which Zan didn't hesitate in pointing to a curtain just beyond the kitchen. Inside the shower curtain was a small cubicle with a shower tray base. "This a shower?" she asked a little confused.

"No, it's a toilet, it's ok," he insisted. So, Amy took a pee down the plughole. "My Father." He pointed proudly to a framed black and white photo on the wall. The man had a piercing, determined, almost startled expression, and was evidently Zan's father. Zan took a shower in the toilet cubicle and Amy sat in the big armchair with the father's eyes upon her. *What is that glare, so intense, as if accused? Severity? Eagerness? A zest for survival? A demand for justice and truth?* she pondered, staring back at the haunting photo. She was unsure of her welcome in his home. In the backyard, smoking a cigarette, she pondered the little wooden outhouse, guessing that was where she should have relieved herself, and smiled at the rural feel all around her. It reminded her of the local farm back home - dirty metal feed dishes scattered around the yard, with roving geese and shaggy-haired dogs sleeping in stony potholes. Ten minutes later Zan emerged from his pit of a bedroom miraculously dressed in bright, cleanly-washed football kit. "Que rica," Zan would repeat with a passion any actor aspires to authenticate, gazing into Amy's eyes as if searching for tiny distant islands he believed to be housed there.

"Drica," she would attempt to copy, falling hopelessly flat on the rolling 'r' sound.

"Muy linda, muy bonita," he would continue, singing the extruded 'i' sounds. Amy relished looking up these words in her dictionary. All three meant beauty in Zan's context. Even *rica* meaning rich, as in Costa Rica's rich coast, Amy translated as a sort of beauty. Perhaps rich like devil's food cake she concluded hopefully, rather than financially. Zan sang this same string of compliments every time they were together, to which Amy unfailingly chuckled, like a cooed baby, at its hilarity. But Zan's stormy brown eyes seemed painfully sincere, in a slow-blinking, pleading sort of way.

****

"Bueno, you like Zan?" Bandu asked with a grin over the pool table, "He's a good man and I would be happy to see him with a girlfriend at last." Amy conversed better with Bandu as he always faced her when speaking and he listened carefully to her every halting sentence. In the busy evening bar, where noisy tourists sloshed back beer preparing for the wet T-shirt competition, Zan left the toil of understanding Amy to Bandu. Besides, Zan wasn't one to lose at pool. Practically the whole football squad were in the bar, rivalling the number of tourists.

"I see Zan. He remembers me a salsa, singer?" Amy struggled to remember the CD cover from back in her salsa lesson days and then exclaimed "Candido Fabre!"

"Candido Fabre!" Bandu laughed heartily "Yes, you're right." After the bars would come the beach, where Zan would reclaim Amy to stroll hand in hand, stealing her kisses next to their sleeping dragon. Castillo nights always climaxed to a blurry end:

Smoking and keys.

Soaring and speeding.

Heavy-chested breathing.

Head-blood pumping.

Skin pores radiating cold heat for senseless time.

Warped-out vision.

Internal power surging.

Superman rocketing up into the sky by the force of his fist.

Zip-wiring over the canopy.

"Pura vida!" someone always perfectly summarised in a husky utterance.

****

"You've met your equivalent," Bandu said, sidling up to Zan swaggering along the shore, his eyes scanning the crowd.

"Did you see her?" Zan asked, keeping his eyes averted.

"No. But there are many students," Bandu answered and changed his tone to a sincere one. "Amigo, this English girl, she's fun, but she's not good for a girlfriend."

"Why, what you heard?" Zan asked gruffly.

"Nothing man. She's a party girl. They party different in Europe, you know that, remember that German girl, and the two Spanish girls Juan thought he was in love with?"

"Amy is English not Spanish," Zan pointed out and stopped abruptly. "What are you telling me? Not to touch this girl, Amy?" Zan's fierce eyes squinted in the sun's glare.

"No man! That's your business. Just be careful that she doesn't break your heart." Zan's face stretched horizontally, baring most of his teeth.

"No girl can break Zan's heart," he said pounding his chest like a gorilla. The two friends chuckled and carried on walking.

"So, how you going to land this fish?" Bandu asked.

"She loves the life of Costarricense. She wants the authentic experience. And that's what I'll give her. I'm just being cool. Taking her out to bars, football, and of course I'll take her to the Rodeo. She'll love it. I bet they don't have Rodeo in England," Zan enthused.

"Good luck man. But don't come to me limping like a dog with a stone in his foot when problems arise, ok?"

"Hey, don't be so quick to foretell the future. Watch her experience the life of Costa Rica with Zan. She will want to stay. God has his plan. We don't know it," Zan accentuated with his hands. Bandu halted abruptly.

"She has her own plans. Didn't you hear her say that she will be working at the new eco-resort? She's coming to live already," Bandu exclaimed.

"Well?" Zan shrugged, eyes twinkling his luck, "that's what I am talking about."

"Alejandro!" a woman's sharp voice pierced the beach, pricking the pair's attention.

"Ah, my mother," Zan said squinting up towards the road.

"Alejandro. Come here," Zan's mother snapped across the sunbathers. Zan quickly strode over to her, shrugging his shoulders at her, looking left and right. "What have you been doing? Out in the bars again last night. The night before, the night before that," she ranted before he reached her, "huh? Where's the money for the groceries, the gas, the petrol and everything? What is going on with you?"

"I got the house money, calm down. Why are you so furious?" he asked her firmly.

"Are you getting mad? Why this crazy behaviour?" she asked in a lower tone. Zan stepped closer to her and looked down to her. He took some bank notes from his pocket and counted them slowly.

"Take," he said solemnly, "No need to shout at me on the beach again, understand?" She took the money.

"We need the rest this week, ok?" she said quietly, "Carlos must continue his studies."

"Carlos. Carlos. He should work too, not just study," Zan whispered though clenched teeth and spat on the sand.

"When he completes and works, watch," she replied proudly, "Watch, then." Zan cast a glance out at sea and turned back to his mother with eyes half closed.

"I know that Mother," Zan said with restraint.

"How are you getting home?" she enquired in a new air, "I'll cook pork tonight."

"Come, get a ride with Bandu, he's leaving now. Let's go," Zan urged, taking his mother's shopping bag from the ground by her feet.

Rodeo

"Rodeo! Carnival!" Zan sang "Fiesta del Torros, you have the best guide in town for the best rodeo in Guanacaste, and because Guanacaste has the best cowboys, naturally this, I guarantee you, guarantee this is the best rodeo in the whole of Costa Rica." Amy felt a warm smugness as she clambered out of the car, having got Zan's gist. A loud brass band started up as if to substantiate Zan's claim. "This is the Cimarrona," Zan gestured at the four-piece band and then towards thick, grey smoke emanating mouth-watering wafts of sizzling meats and corncobs, "and this is barbecue traditional." But Amy's eyes were fixed upon something elsewhere. Zan held his breath whilst following her gaze to what, or who, had captured her attention immediately on arrival, and then sighed with a smile. "Marimba. The music of marimba," he announced, proudly leading her by the arm to the mellow, jolly sound. For a full half an hour she was absorbed in the whirring, supple wrists of the father and son duo hammering the little ball-headed mallets on wooden keys that resonated so perfectly on the large glockenspiel contraption. "Like the voice of the trees singing," Zan said squinting his eyes and gently shaking his head. The father, with three little mallets in each hand, swiftly led the songs from the upper deck, whilst his son harmonised on the deck below, his little hands flitting left and right, reverberating notes as does a drummer on a snare. A few people clapped as the musicians ended an epic song and mopped their brows. Zan introduced Amy to the musicians with a pride bestowed on family members.

"Hello, I ham berry please to meet you," the father said in English shaking her hand.

"Is this marimba traditional to Guanacaste? Or to all over Costa Rica?" Amy started her accumulating questions.

"Ok. Marimba is popular especially in Guatemala, Nicaragua and Mexico," the father explained, reverting back to Spanish.

"You have a beautiful marimba." Zan complimented the musician's instrument, which was an intriguing assembly, its long resonators strapped beneath the keys made of long pear-shaped dried gourds set within an ornately painted wooden frame.

"Yes. This is a traditional outfit, similar to the original African balafon," the father went on to explain.

"Marimba is African?" Amy frowned perplexed.

"Originally, yes. The balafon came from Africa with the *esclavos,*" he said.

"Es clave?" she said pointing at the wooden keys with a huge grin. If there was one word, she was confident in, it was 'key'. Between the late-night key snifters and protracted debates with Alba when losing her house keys numerous times, she had ample conversational practise in the words for key.

"A long time before, yes, now marimba is famous in Guanacasta." Amy nodded smiling, but then frowned again at the same sticking point. Zan had started stretching his neck as if he needed to click it.

"How? Africa," she waved a hand up to the sky and far away "and after here?"

"With esclavos," he repeated.

"Esclavos," she echoed pointing to the keys again, doubt sneaking up on her. Zan had turned to wave at someone and smoke a cigarette, leaving Amy to thrash it out alone. Soon a small group of people had joined in the charades game for Amy and it wasn't until a man started to bind up his friend's wrists, to much raucous laughter, and pretend to whip his back, that Amy realised her misinterpretation. Zan watched on at a distance, his eyes flickering intensely around the scene of laughter and amusement. "Oh, slaves," she said gratefully, finally understanding. "Claves y esclaves. Very the same," she tried to excuse herself.

"Let's go. The *Sabaneros* are starting now." Zan stepped in and swept her away.

"Slaves here? In Costa Rica? Before?" Amy attempted to question Zan who seemed not to hear her. His eyes were glancing all around, skimming the chattering, smiling crowd, his perma-smile reflecting the festive mood. His upward nod greeting in recognition of those he knew, and firm hand clasping of friends passing by. Amy followed her swaggering companion, vaguely recalling maps and pictures from school history lessons. She'd always preferred geography but had a distinct memory of a world map with arrows across oceans making a triangle, and ships with deck plans of body outlines. It had seemed appalling to teach such details of history, Amy had tried to ignore it as much as possible. *At least I understood eventually – easy mistake – I'll have to overcome many more to become fluent. To live here. To work here. To be Zan's girlfriend.* And only the latter struck her as remotely tangible.

"You like sabaneros?" Zan asked Amy twice before she realised it was a question.

"Sabeneros?" Amy shrugged her ignorance. Zan cocked his head and looked at her as if she was complex and mysterious. His upper lip twitching his nose as he wondered '*another word she does not know? Or could she have never heard of cowboys before? She is English after all. Do they have them in Europe? I don't think so, no.*' As they weaved through the gathering crowds the *Cimarronas* broke into semi-recognisable jingles and Amy felt a pang of excitement. They claimed a prime spot to watch the action, perched on top of the high fencing right next to the bull holding pen. In the ring, cowboys pranced their tough little horses on tight reins through the arena. Zan took a bottle of beer from a conveniently large pocket in his calf-length shorts, carefully prised the top off with a molar tooth and passed it to Amy, who secretly swooned.

"Sabeneros," he said, casually nodding into the arena as he opened his beer. Amy staved off her self-disappointment at not being able to guess the word, not having her dictionary, and not understanding Zan's body language better.

"Sabeneros," Amy parroted back to him and smiled as if it were a greeting. *Maybe it means 'show' or horses – no horse is cabeo she thought, sipping her beer.* Amy distracted herself by observing the bull below - confined, snorting, goaded with sharp-prong prods to its huge rump. It smelt of hot animal fur. Zan had struck up a conversation with the people next to him. The bull kicked out and flinched its head; hoof and horn clattered against wood. Denim and leather-clad cowboys straddled the fencing, coiling and tying ropes in concentration. Zan leaned over to Amy.

"Cow - boy," he said with a thick Latino accent.

"Cowboys," she said with a smile creeping across her face. Another goal scored.

"Sabeneros. Cow boys," Zan said to the arena. The masculine bravado of the cowboys, the odour of bulls and leather, even Zan's whistling at the cowboys, all felt fun and an easy-fit. Life in the UK suddenly seemed too tame, modern, affected. Even the eco-resort and the language school were tainted of the world she'd left behind. With Zan she felt part of a real, raw, more vibrantly-alive world. Her thoughts were suddenly interrupted by speakers draped up high on posts above them as an announcement blared out. Zan put his arm protectively around her waist. A few men jumped over the fence and jogged across the arena holding rags and flags. A chap-wearing bull-rider clambered to the top of the holding pen and carefully lowered his splayed legs astride the broad back of the bull. It didn't react. He carefully and slowly took hold of the rope looped around the bull's neck and wrapped it around and around his right hand. The bull grunted, shuffling side to side. On the other side of the gate grouped half a dozen men meticulously exchanging shouts to those in and around the bullpen.

A curt yank of a rope flung open the gate and the crowd erupted with cheering and whistling. The bull galloped out into the ring, its rider clinging on to the rope one handed, in the other flailed his cowboy hat above his head. *'Rondero,'* the crowd chanted at every circular twist the leaping, kicking bull made. The rider was thrown in a matter of seconds, triggering a swarm of men to dash at the bull frantically waving their rags and hats. The bull-rider scrambled to his feet, bee-lined to the nearest fence, and was hauled over the top by willing arms. Amy became as enthralled as a little child at the circus. Zan lit and passed her cigarettes and beers he'd signal for from young lads circulating in the crowd.

"You like?"

"The best," she answered with a stirring sincerity. It was then she became cognizant of a truth she'd overlooked - that her series of blunders and disasters in life were not stemming from her own failings, but rather her incompatibility to her previous environments, the most recent being London. Costa Rica, she decided, suited her better. *I've found my place,* Amy breathed with a sense of realisation and relief. The beasty-motion of the stocky bulls transfixed her. The flexing of surprisingly supple backs. Legs kicking forward and back like rampant rocking horses. Their speed and agility. Their ability to halt suddenly and freeze. Their responsiveness to goading. The bulls fascinated her. But Zan drew her attention to the cowboys. Galloping the perimeter of the arena on their horses, whirling lassoes above their heads, they demonstrated 'real cowboy work'. Seamlessly and steadily their horses ran like those trained to carry trapeze artists in a circus.

"Look at these sabaneros," Zan admired, "they are the best in Guanacasta, maybe the best in Costa Rica, maybe all the Americas!" A mounted cowboy galloping clockwise lassoed a bull's monstrous handlebar horns. Seconds later another cowboy galloping anticlockwise did the same. The tension on the ropes instantly tempered the bull's pace as they drew him steadily back out of the ring. Such impressive technical horse-work filled the ring after every bull ridden. Cowboys' horses prancing on the spot, sideways, backwards, their feet raising high, their chins tucked down on their necks. The cowboys were, undoubtedly, the stoic heroes, whereas the bull riders, claiming their seconds' worth of fame, were brave but without elegance, often exiting the ring by diving through lower fencing boards yanked up by the crowd.

"Watch this! Without rope, just the horse, and its feet," Zan pointed excitedly, his hands imitating the brave little horse's feet stamping up and down as it faced off a bull, ushering it into the exit pen. Twenty or more bull-riders escaped the ring unharmed. Then one didn't. It had happened, as in bull riding, within a handful of seconds. A big mottled bull had thrown his rider in the first seconds with a snap of his rear-end. The young guy had hit the ground hard, level with the bull's right shoulder. Unhesitatingly, the bull tilted his rocking-horse motion toward the rider, who lay motionless, face down in the dust. As the bull's front feet hammered on to the rider's back the crowd closest went frantic, hammering the panels on the fences loudly, whooping and jeering, leaning and waving arms at the bull. Mounted cowboys were on their way at top speed, their galloping horses now appearing too small for their pillions. On its next forward rock, the bull accurately lowered his head with a twist and swiftly jabbed a horn into the side of the rider. The crowd murmured in anticipation for him to be tossed upwards. But he didn't toss, just a precise, short stab. Before the bull's next forward stamp, the motionless rider was dragged away by two brave men crawling as fast as they could on hands and knees, like children. Grasping an ankle of the injured man each they dragged him facedown through a waiting gap made in the fencing. The bull continued to stamp in circles where the rider had lain until a lasso snared its horns and its neck jerked back under the control of the cowboys.

"He is very young; only eighteen." Zan repeated the announcement to Amy. Then the brass band started up again and the next bull was prepared. They watched, over the top of the crowd, the injured bull-rider's limp body being lifted onto the back of a pickup that hastily set off down the bumpy road and into the night. Once the bullpen became empty and the Sabaneros' lasso show slowed to a trot, the crowd wandered off to other distractions. The evening air felt alive, like an electric storm was brewing.

"Can you dance?" Zan asked Amy once inside a village hall filled with people and extremely loud salsa music.

"Yes. I like dance," she answered gleefully. She'd half expected him, for all his machismo, to be too self-aware to dance. This was the moment she was to grasp the true measure of a 'tico'. Face to face, stomach-to-stomach they commenced la fiesta. After a shaky start of Amy treading on his toes and clashing her knees against his, she sobered up to the fact that Zan wasn't laughing at these blips.

"Can you hear the clave?" Zan asked, his eyes pricked, a finger from each hand tapping a beat as if two sticks.

"Which?" Amy strained her ears.

"Ok. Listen. Bum-bum pat, bum-bum pat, bum-bum pat," he highlighted a rhythm. Eyes fixed on his, she extracted this rhythm from the multiple layers of percussion, piano and cowbell sounds and tried to wriggle her hips and shuffle her feet in time.

"No. The tumbao. Listen," he almost scorned. "Here too," he said twisting her shoulders a little. *Right, he wants me to move to one of twenty rhythms feet, hips and shoulders simultaneously whilst following him. They didn't teach this in the bloody salsa classes.* She managed, with effort, to follow his lead, albeit a subdued effort and without spins. Zan's eyes cast around the hall, as if to glean the rhythm from around. It felt alien to Amy. Not the seductive, romantic dance she'd always envisaged, but a meditative movement. But she closed her eyes and worked hard at feeling the rhythm. Her legs and feet moved quicker, her thighs pumped harder, soon her breath rasped. He nodded his apparent approval. Then their song came on - *Mariposa Traicionera*, a popular rock acoustic song by a band called *Mana*. A smooching song, as Rosie would call it. Amy pleaded Zan for the slow dance, and reluctantly he swayed with her as the singer sang his melancholic, deep aching love lyrics.

"Mi mariposa de amor. Ya no regreso contigo," Zan sang, his face sad and pained, looking deep into her eyes. She smiled back, melting, swimming, disintegrating in his arms as he sang to her. "You Marisposa?" Zan asked later as they swigged beer from bottles by the bar.

"Me? Mariposa?" Amy smiled without replying and hooked her thumbs together and flapped her fingers into a butterfly. She knew mariposa meant butterfly. Zan pulled her into his arms tightly, squeezing her and muttered into her sweaty hair. In the hot dancing crowd of bare-arms and swishing long, dark hair of ticas, Amy felt giddy and elated. Head-spinning drunk, Amy found the ladies toilet. Young ticas congregated around the sinks, damping down their long hair and re-combing it. The pitch-black toilet cubicle stank of urine. The floor was sopping wet. Amy rolled her white linen trousers up to each knee and went in. She took a pee in the general direct of the toilet and paddled out again, almost overcome by the stench. The ticas ignored Amy as she lit a cigarette and leant against the wall. The spinning settled to a dizzy-fuzziness and Amy stepped back into the humid throng, where thankfully Zan awaited her. The night felt like it would never end. After the salsa came music for the youngsters - Nirvana, Guns'n'Roses, Metallica. For Amy, the songs were straight from her teenage years; discos with smoke machines. Where she'd lacked at salsa moves, she redeemed herself at moshing to thrash-metal classics.   More beers, smoking, keys. Outside sat on hay bales in shadows cast by the huge floodlights. The night spun dizzily on until the hard, bumpy sensation of wheels upon the road.

Monday's newspaper headlines honored the young tico who died from the punctured lung as a brave and talented bull-rider.

Black Jesus

It was mid-afternoon, midweek. The sun was a blazing heat high above Castillo. Listless from her arduous beach run and hundred sit-ups after morning class, there was only one place to really cool down - the Internet café. Packed full of plastic tables with whirring computer stations, strip lighting and droning air-conditioning, it felt an incongruous space for instant relief. But she settled at the allocated station, between two tourists, and logged into her email account.

'Dear Amy,

Sorry I've been unreachable for a couple of weeks. I've been dealing with licenses and permits in San Jose. I hope that your studies are going well and you are enjoying Guanacaste.

Interviewing starts next week. Could you pop in sometime this week for a heads up on the Assistant manager / Front office managerial role? I'd also like to pick your brain on marketing experience you have too, if you wouldn't mind.

Please give me a ring on the resort main number, leave the name of your hotel if necessary and I'll get back to you. Look forward to finally meeting soon

Best regards

Michael'

Interviewing? Amy scowled at the screen. *'Heads-up,'* and *'pick your brain,'* spiked out at her as echoes from that world she'd left behind; that world of drudgery, responsibility, competitiveness, egotism and professionalism. London, where she'd ejected herself from. Amy took a deep breath, straightened her back and opened a new email from Rosie; it had been at least two weeks since Amy had sent a brief 'I'm ok,' email to her mum.

'Hi Sweetheart - How's Costa Rica? Must have a lovely tan by now. How's the Spanish going? What's the job like? Any news on when you'll start? Can't wait to hear all about it – please call soon – everyone asking about you and send their love. Lots of Love Mum xx' ps Shame we missed your graduation ceremony

Amy frowned at the thought of her Mum bragging about her exotic job. *Probably happy she's got rid of me,* Amy thought with self-sympathy, wishing she'd not emailed so much detail about her new life over five-thousand miles of Atlantic Ocean away. With more optimism she opened an email from Stephie:

'Hola amiga!!

How's la playa? (see we've learnt some Spanish too) Bet you're killing it on the dance floor after all those salsa classes we used to go to with your Mum? I'm remembering some of those cha cha cha moves. You were always better than me though. The guys here are caliente!! Not like those pervy old men at salsa class

We're having a great time – arrived in Barcelona last week and now just stuck here – love it. Party every night – just like you I bet?? How's the job going? I'm so jealous – we're definitely coming to visit the resort and complain about lizards in the shower or something – haha.

Bet you're glad you're not at home right now. I totally see your point now. Your mum has lost it. Getting married – what is she thinking?'

"Getting married?" Amy uttered, a bottle of water poised an inch from her lips. Her eyes skimmed ahead over the next words 'shotgun…getting his feet under the table…' She slumped back in the chair for a second and then leaned back to read it again. Somewhere amongst her feelings of shock, outrage and anger Amy also felt a strange jealousy. *It should be me getting married next, not Mum.* The content of her stomach felt as if it was starting to burn. Amy rose, asked for a telephone booth and punched in the family home phone number. Her hand trembled and she swallowed. The dialling tone sounded distant. Rosie's voice sounded.

"Mum?" Amy said.

"Amy! Hello love. Thank goodness you've called," Rosie said

hastily and then shouted away from the phone "It's Amy."

"Mum. Listen."

"How are you? I've been wondering what you're up to."

"Mum listen. Mum. Mum," Amy repeated raising her voice each time.

"Sorry, I'm just excited to hear from you."

"What the hell's going on?" Amy said steadying her voice. There was silence the other end. "You're not doing something stupid are you?"

"I wanted to tell you something. I, I don't know if you, well I hope you will be happy about it," Rosie started to explain.

"Happy? Have you seen the light on Giles?"

"Amy. Please. Giles has proposed to me." Rosie paused "And, and I'm thrilled." Amy's breathing became short pants as she tried to speak, her face stretched with a sarcastic smile. She paced back a little until the telephone cable pulled taught and then hugged her arm over the top of the telephone box.

"Are you joking me?" Amy stammered.

"Amy, please."

"NO seriously," Amy shouted, indifferent to everyone around her, "ARE YOU JOKING?"

"Amy. I know this is hard for you," Rosie said diplomatically.

"HARD? It's not hard for me. I'm in Costa bloody Rica. It's YOU." Over twenty pairs of eyes glanced at Amy.

"But if you could just see how happy I am. Don't you want me to be happy?"

"Mum. He's using you, can't you *see* that?"

"He's got a job; he's got a flat. He doesn't need me," Rosie argued back.

"He wants you to be a mother to his kids."

"The girls have got a mother already, actually," Rosie answered as if rehearsed.

"Yeah? Well not at the weekends they don't."

"She has the girls in the week, and he has them at the weekend," Rosie explained.

"Does he own his flat, then?"

"Yes, they do."

"THEY! THEY?" Amy shouted and peered into the received.

"Please. Tranquillo," the Internet shop assistant said to Amy touching her arm. Amy nodded.

"He's not even divorced, is he?" she whispered growling.

"Amy. He's gone through a painful divorce."

"Yeah? And you want some of the same, do you?" Amy spouted. There was silence at the other end.

"We want to get married this summer," Rosie said through restrained tears.

"How could you do this to me Mum? You don't care about me or Rich any more. You don't want to listen to what we think of your - new bit of fun."

"Now Amy, come on, Giles is a good bloke -" Rosie defended.

"A good bloke," Amy scoffed, "Why did he get divorced from the kid's mum?"

"She's young; she's training to be a doctor now. They got pregnant without knowing each other very well - and it didn't work out between them. But they're both committed to bringing up the girls. Giles is a fantastic father and been through so -" Rosie said eagerly before Amy cut her.

"Mum! Look. Just do what you want. But don't expect me to be happy about any of this. I don't want to see Giles. I don't want anything to do with the wedding. I think you're crazy," Amy said loud enough to turn a few heads from screens again. Rosie was silent. "I got to go; I've got to stuff to do. Bye Mum," Amy said briskly.

"Take care of yourself Amy," Rosie pleaded tearfully.

"*You* take care of yourself Mum," Amy said slamming the phone down, resting her forehead against the receiver.

****

Whiffs of scorched grass, pigsties and fruity compost heaps hung in the warm evening air.

"Have you seen crocodiles before?" Zan asked as they strolled slowly towards the fields behind Alba's house where the huge Tamarind trees gave shade to the cattle. Amy repeated the Spanish word 'cocodrillos,' making a long snapping mouth with her arms. Zan laughed. "Tomorrow, we will visit my friend, he will arrange a car for us," Zan explained as he started to roll a joint. Their weekend away involved the usual elements of time spent together - bars, pool, too much to drink and smoke, keys on a beach, gallo-pinto – the typical fried rice and beans breakfast. Peering at crocodiles off a high river bridge along with other tourists was the only variation to their usual habits. Amy harboured a growing sense of nagging disappointment at the lack of romance or affection between them. They had barely kissed, let alone been intimate. But Amy sensed there was a deep tradition in his culture, perhaps no sex before marriage? After all, it felt quaint and innocent, like teenage courtship all over again.

"I want to take you somewhere special," Zan announced over a café breakfast. Inside the simple wooden-framed cathedral, the somewhere special, lingered the radiance of a wedding celebration. Amy tingled as they walked up to the altar, hand in hand, her chin raised and eyes fixed ahead upon him - the black Jesus, gazing down stoically, suffering in wood. She'd never seen Jesus depicted with a dark complexion before. The life-sized statue nailed to a cross had an appeal of glory and victory, despite the woeful posture. Jesus was naked but for a gold cloth wrapped around his waist. His stomach had a six-pack and the golden crown hung over his thick black hair reflected the sunlight pouring through a high window.

"God, bless us that one day we will be married," Zan whispered when reaching the altar. He then crossed his chest. Amy glanced at him, feeling cheeky and childlike, and copied the sign of the cross. Seeing the cut flowers piled all over the golden alter and smelling the pungent incense stirred a strangely familiar feeling within Amy. It reminded her of a happy ending scene from a Disney fairy-tale film. *Could this be my way out? Out of everything dragging me down. Escaping the cold and stress for good?* Amy wondered at Jesus. The dreamy fantasy whipped up in her mind - marrying into this place, living forever by the beach. Never caring again. Being led and looked after. Zan turned Amy to him by her hand, leant forward and kissed her lips, as if practicing for the day. *He does love you,* all the little cherub faces called out silently as Zan took her photo with Jesus.

Amy floated through the following week in a dreamlike-state. Thinking of Zan - the fantasy, the beaches and dancing. She was steadily falling in love with Costa Rica. Alvero got her through her lessons with his stoic mentoring. He was practically doing her homework for her, whilst Amy internally mithered over the days when

Zan was nowhere to be found in Castillo. It seemed weeks ago that Louisa had left Castillo. Amy had seen, from the beach, the little coach loaded with North American student-tourists depart. Her wraparound sunglasses had caught and contained most of her tears until her eyes felt waterlogged. Rick, Alvero had told her, had organised a party with three other North Americans to hike the highest mountain in Costa Rica – Cerro Chirripo.

A new style of life

"Hey y'all! Have yourself a good weekend?" Mary Ellen greeted. Her face glowed red and shiny with after-sun lotion and her sun-bleached eyebrows were bright blond. Amy sat slumped, her head lain on the desk. *Who the hell ties their hair with ribbons?* Her mind scowled as Mary Ellen seated herself next to her. It was a Monday afternoon class and the first Amy had attended in over a week. "Well I took an interstate bus o'cross into Nic-ar-ag-u-ar. I tell you, I've never been so scared in all my life. It was so awful," Mary Ellen stated. Amy blinked at her. "I had folk's elbows in my head, we all sweating, people staring all the while. I swear to God I knew I'd be robbed."

"So, did you get robbed?" Amy asked hopefully.

"No Mam. God was watchin' o Mary Ellen the whole time. Thank the Lord. I can't tell you how relieved I was to get back here again. It was just plain awful."

"The bus was pretty awful then?" Amy confirmed nonchalantly.

"The bus? I'm a talking 'bout Nic-ar-ag-u-ar. That place is *so poor!* Oh, it was real bad. I hated it. I just felt so harassed. I stayed in one hotel the whole time and waited for the bus back here. I would not recommend it *at all*."

"You *hated* it because people are *poor*?" Amy frowned.

"Well, I paid to visit Granada, on the understanding it's a beautiful colonial town, historic interests and shopping and restaurants. But I was too darn scared to walk around."

"I can't believe what you're saying! You're foreign, and really blond. Of course people stared at you!" Amy said raising her voice as much as possible with her head on the desk. She dragged herself upright.

"Well I feel sympathetic and all that. I donated some money to kids," Mary Ellen justified "I don't like being in a poor place surrounded by poor people. Honey, you sure wouldn't like it neither. It's scary!"

"No, *you're* scary," Amy blurted just as the teacher walked in.

Classes dragged on like fluey winter days in high school had. But conversely to fever flushes in icy cold air, she had chill sweats in tropical heat. Even afterwards at the beach, watching the relentlessly motivated surfers had become exhausting. Days passed by this way and Zan wasn't to be seen. Even his cronies at the estuary-end of the beach hadn't seen him. Amy had found herself alone with the monologues of her mind - *You're a wreck-head,* a paranoid voice accused her. *I can get wrecked if I want to. I'm single, footloose and fancy-free* another, stubborn voice cogently reasoned. *You're Zan's girl in Castillo. Hardly footloose and fancy-free* Paranoia gibed. Stubborn paused, conceding. *I guess I'm the type of girl who needs a man around me,* Stubborn countered. *Maybe Zan and I are not so ridiculous. I could live here, run a business with Zan, and live together in the sun forever. Mum and Rich would visit us. We'd visit England and Zan would be a salsa dance teacher. You and Zan are a pair of wreck-heads!* Paranoia exclaimed, *you don't even understand each other!*

****

It was the sixth and last scheduled week at school. Amy sat on a chair outside the school's office, trying to shake a detention feeling. *Maybe Zan does end up in hospital after all with liver problems, or is it kidneys?* she pondered in a surging cold sweat, with a grinding lower back-ache. She'd been out that weekend, tagging along with students or locals in the bars and later the beach.

"I am Milda, your teacher this week. We are one to one," said the tica who emerged from the office and guided Amy to a small room. "What do you like? What are your interests?" Milda probed, clearly having been briefed on Amy's refusal to drill grammar and admission to not keeping up in class.

"I like music," Amy answered.

"Good. Do you like Costa Rican music?" Milda enquired with glee, "Do you have a favourite song?"

"Mi Mariposa de amore," Amy sang, prompting a beautiful, open smile from Milda.

"Ah. Yes. Mana. It is a lovely song, but sad. I like it very much too," she chatted as if they were friends in a café.

"What is meaning? The song, why sad?" Amy asked.

"Ok. We can write the words and you can translate them. It's a good exercise for you I think," she concluded triumphantly. It painstakingly transpired that the lyrics are of a heartbroken man wishing good riddance to a woman who flits from man to man, like a butterfly upon flowers. With each verse the singer extenuates the pain and jealousy caused by her easiness with men. "It's a beautiful song, no?" Milda summed. But Amy was staring hard, remembering the way Zan sang it to her. *It's our romantic song, romantic!* "You are disappointed?" Milda observed.

"Yes. I am disappointed," Amy conjugated, "because I think, before, the song is romantic, but it is sad. The woman, the butterfly, the man not love." Milda waited, watching tears rolling down Amy's cheeks. "This song. My boyfriend. I have a tico boyfriend. Here in Castillo," Amy garbled, "He, my boyfriend for five weeks, now. He always sings this song. He says to me I am like a butterfly, and before I say yes, because I think butterfly in song is beautiful and love, not bad butterfly," Amy spilled out, "I am not a butterfly." Milda listened with heart and eyes, refraining from correcting Amy's grammatical mistakes as she had so far, then drew a deep breath and rearranged her feet.

"Ok. I will explain. The men here are traditionally *very* jealous. They will be *very* suspicious of their women. A woman's infidelity is a thing man cannot tolerate. Of course, the same is not true for the infidelity of a man," Milda explained then nodded.

"Ticos are very jealous," Amy confirmed

"Exactly," Milda continued more cautiously. "Now, modern women value their rights. Many women say 'no' to men who want to control them. I am studying and paying for my own studies by working here in the school. I choose not to have children yet, so I can have education and become a professor in the University. When *I* want to get married, *I* will choose a respectful man." Amy watched and listened intently, embarrassment creeping over her. She glanced through the window into the corridor and wondered why she was so lost once again; how she got herself into situations; hot tearful situations that made her want to run away each time - Malta, London, Worcester, now here; just a succession of places with people that she wanted to run away from.

"Here, men can be *very* jealous. Do you understand me?" Milda affirmed. Amy nodded, her gaze clasped with Milda's. "I have heard it many times, that when a man suspects his wife's infidelity, that wife *disappears*," Milda whispered, waggling her fingers into two twinkling star shapes. Her eyebrows rose up her brow, revealing a hint of sadness in her eyes.

"Disappears?" Amy repeated, to which Milda nodded slowly.

"Lost. Gone." Milda replied.

"To Go? The woman, is, to go?" Amy's concentration waned from so much Spanish conversation.

"They say the man will take his wife up into the hills, and he will kill her," Milda signed cutting her throat with her finger, "the family does not know anything. The wife has gone." Amy's eyes widened. "You should be *very* careful. You are very attractive and friendly. Here, it is not like in Europe, I think?" Amy frowned at Milda, absorbing her words. "And there is something else you should know. Castillo sees everything. The trees can see and talk. If one person sees you talking to a man on the beach, perhaps a student, your boyfriend will *hear* this, and he will hear that you were *kissing* him. Men are *very proud*. A girlfriend or wife who is like a butterfly is a *big* disrespect."

****

Amy gazed out over the sighing waves at the mauve-tinged horizon, aching for sun-down. Alvero had been really getting on her nerves. The way he dived straight into her exercise book; the way his moustache became animated as he greedily thumbed the pages to see what tasty morsels of Spanish grammar was on the menu to thrash into her. *I'm the one trying to learn this, not you,* she thought watching his enthusiasm, *besides, school's given up on me. We're just translating songs and news now.* Her head felt thick as if stuffed with cheese. *He'd be better off selling his jewellery today. Why do I always attract obsessive people who want to help me?* she thought, unconsciously flashing him a fed up glance in answer to his unheard question. Alvero fell silent and blinked at the pages open upon his lap. Raising his head, he let his eyes join the direction of Amy's gaze.

"When will you have an examination in Spanish language?"

"Examination?" Amy almost scowled. Beneath his moustache and glasses his face looked thin. He had a resemblance to Albert Einstein, a hint of madness and determination in his shiny brown eyes.

"Yes. You study Spanish for examination, no?" he continued.

"No," she answered flippantly.

"Tell me, please, why are you studying Spanish?"

"Tell me, please, why you, in Costa Rica, to sell, that?" she pointed at his wares. He stared at her, his thoughts almost visibly churning in his head.

"Do you pray, Amy?" he finally asked with his head cocked to one side. She winced. "Pray. Talk to God," he elaborated pressing his palms together.

"No," Amy replied flatly, "No religious." Alvero blinked once.

"Not religion, God. Who do think made all of this?" he asked gesturing at the sea, the sand and sky with his upturned palm.

"I don't know. You don't know. Everybody doesn't know," she blurted out and jolted her neck with pride at conjugating the verb 'to know'.

"Yes. Who or what made this entire world, the tiny seeds that grow into trees, the fish and birds and insects and animals and people, the water and rocks and stars and sun? All that mysterious existence is what we name God. The creator," Alvero concluded. She fleetingly thought of David Attenborough rocking in his firm planted stance on some rugged landscape explaining evolution, and asked:

"You think God is nature?"

"The creator of everything," he replied patiently, "You do not pray to the creator?" Amy's mind was blank at such an idea and replied honestly.

"No."

"Jesus came to Earth to teach us to pray," Alvero said in English.

"You speak really good English," Amy smiled.

"Ancient tribes have prayed to gods for thousands of years. More than *eighty percent* of the people in this world are religious, or believe in God, spirit," he said in a thick, but eloquently clear Argentinian-tainted English. "Are you an atheist?" he asked, to which she initially wanted to say yes, but begrudged being in a global minority. Alvero's fluency in English humbled Amy.

"I don't know," she answered, looking to the horizon for an answer to that. Primary school came to mind, dressing up as Mary for the nativity play in the freezing walls of the dim church, or donating tins of beans for anonymous lonely people.

"Do you believe in the devil then?" he probed further, a glint of enthrallment in his eyes.

"El diablo?" she'd learnt that word from a cocktail list. "No. I think, maybe, some people are the same as the devil."

"The devil is *a master* of disguise. He is hidden. Evaporated into the air we breathe. He is everywhere, like God. *Waiting* for you to weaken and fall into his arms."

"What?" Amy scrunched her face.

"To believe in God, is to fear the devil," he continued.

"*Fear* the devil? I'm not sure I ever have."

"You never feel exposed, threatened? Weak, susceptible?" he eloquently posed.

"Sometimes," she shrugged, starting to nod. Her mind felt clearer, like something finally making sense.

"Your Father, the creator, watches over you. Everything you do, he sees you. And the devil is always there too, waiting for a chance with you." Amy heard him but said nothing. And they both gazed at the horizon for slow minutes. She wondered how he afforded to eat and somewhere to sleep from his jewellery earnings. "Me, I cannot live without praying. When I am alone – I pray. When I don't know which direction to go – I pray. When I am sad and lonely – I pray. The creator always listens. The creator always answers. I think the voice is Jesus; He came to the Earth as a man after all." Amy looked at the face exposing his soul and saw a lonely and sad man. "Prayer is very powerful - very powerful. When you pray, speak to God. Ask for help, in a humble way – He will give to you what you really need. I don't mean everything you want –money, riches – no. You must be humble to God in prayer," he insisted with deep felt concern.

"Why are you here, Alvero?" she asked spontaneously. He drew in a long breath, fixed his gaze firmly on the horizon and extracted his story from his memories, like he'd known one day she would ask this question.

"I was one of many victims who *had* to suffer in the name of revolution. The fight for democracy in *La Guerra Sucia* – the dirty war of Argentina," he proudly stated. "I graduated from university in Buenos Aires in 1973. I studied literature and politics. I was hungry for writing, my ambition to be a journalist. And, I became a very good journalist. My most involved work was with the Workers Revolutionary Party and its military branch, the ERP - the People's Revolutionary Army. I followed them, reported on them and I supported them," he gloated with a glint of stubbornness in his eyes. "Once, I housed some ERP guerrilla fighters in my home during a planned attack on the army base at Domingo Viejobueno," he reminisced, proudly embroiled in his memories, "but the dictatorship defeated the ERP and many people were killed." He broke his gaze and lowered his head.

"You have no family? A wife?" she asked him. He sighed heavily, returning his gaze to the horizon.

"I married my girlfriend, Teresa. We had met at the same university, in 1976. Our first son was born the year after. And then our daughter was born in 1978. I continued to report on the killings that the dictatorship was carrying out. Teresa was very scared. She had fear. In 1980 the brother of Teresa and his wife -" Alvero inhaled to continue, but his breath suddenly swallowed his words. His eyes were snagged upon the horizon, "and, and the children of Teresa's brother, they all *disappeared*." Amy held her breath. "Everyone knew that Teresa's brother was a political activist, but the parents of Teresa blamed me for my political journalism. Teresa was very scared, and she wanted me to stop reporting because her husband would be dead next. She and our children could be next to disappear," he explained solemnly, faintly frowning. His moustache was twitching the way it did when munching a *platas tipcales*. "She left me in 1981," he said numbly, "our son was four years old and our daughter was only three."

"Where did Teresa go? And your children?" Amy asked quietly.

"I think, to Paris. But the parents of Teresa would not say. After, I also needed to leave Argentina. Many, many of my friends and colleagues were killed or just disappeared. So, I left. I travel Central and South America."

"Where are Teresa and your children now? Do you know anything?" questioned Amy. Alvero shrugged in an understated way.

"I heard that Teresa returned to Buenas Aires and the children, now older of course, they stayed in Europe."

"Have you contacted them?" Amy probed. But Alvero just waggled his head and sighed. "But your children are far away, somewhere. Your children are thinking where is my Father? Who is my Father?"

"I have God," he stated with a comforted smile, "and Teresa was right, peace is the only way. Not fighting. But back then, we needed to fight. It is sad. She blamed me for her brother and his family dying. I denied this for a long time. Then I believed it and felt guilty. Then I really started to pray and listen to God. I realised what happened just happened. The past is finished now. My children -" he faltered and paused, "my children probably have their own children. Teresa and I can never be the same. Nothing can change now. I have my faith in God, who provides everything for me." They sat in silence for several minutes.

"But I don't understand, Jesus, how does he talk to you, when praying?" she asked.

"OK. Pray to the Father. God. He is our Father. Speak to him like He is your Father. He loves you. He wants to hear you and guide you."

"How does God love you?" she asked.

"Look!" he exclaimed, smiling as if it were so obvious, waving a hand around, "Look! See the beauty all around us. When you eat sweet fruits, God your Father gave that, *for us*. When you eat fish from the sea, God put the fish there, *for us*. When the sun shines and the rain falls, and you drink water, God, gave us everything. No man on earth made these things." Amy thought for a moment.

"When you pray, you say questions? Or ask help?"

"Yes. Anything. He *sees* your heart so you cannot deceive him. I *could* -" Alvero raised his finger as if to scold but cocked his head, "I *could* be a *very bad* man. Bitter, sad, angry, addicted." He straightened his back. "Jesus is a good shepherd. You know the man who cares for the sheep? *We* are his sheep. He knows everyone of us individually," he pretended to count with his finger, "if one sheep is lost, he looks for the sheep to bring it back."

"But why do we 'sheep' need a shepherd, when we can just live naturally?"

"Good question. Because the wolf will kill; the wolf is the

devil," he jabbed his finger at her. Amy smiled, verging on being inspired. "Is your father, your human father, a good man?" Alvero asked.

"He's dead," she answered matter-of-factly and suddenly missed her own father. She didn't know him anymore. She hadn't been able to recall her father's face in her mind for many years. They both gazed over the sea in silence, the rhythm of the waves soothing, and Amy had a distant notion of becoming like a lost sheep since her father had died.

"You should look for your daughter and son," she said.

"For why?" he replied.

"Because, me, I don't have a father. He's gone. But you live." Alvero closed his eyelids down quickly and firmly.

"Ok. I should. But you also, you should pray to God," he said in a faltering voice and turned to look at her. His eyes were damp and shining like two brown pebbles in a stream. She nodded. "Pray for my forgiveness," he pleaded, "do you promise?"

"Ok I promise. I will pray."

"Thank you," he repeated, sighing and nodding to the sea.

"Coffee?"

"Yes coffee," he replied with a smile.

After coffee and sharing a plate of *bocas,* - the local tapas, they bid each other farewell.

"See you tomorrow, on the beach," Alvero said to her when they parted.

"Tomorrow," she answered. But that was the last time they would see each other.

****

Friday morning had arrived before Amy was ready. Her six-week's stay with the family was over. Alba unceremoniously bid Amy goodbye. The children watched the departure as if waiting for one last scandal. Amy knew she must have been one of Alba's worst guests - drunkenly waking the children late at night, the endless lost door keys, and dirty white linen trousers to be scrubbed clean.

Sat on her suitcase at the familiar bus stop, knowing she'd

missed the morning bus to Castillo, she resolved to wait for one of the taxies that may occasionally pass by. *It will give me time to work out where to stay in Castillo,* she thought, ruling out anywhere she'd stayed with Zan. After almost an hour, a 4x4 pickup rumbled along the road and made a sudden swerve towards her, skidding to a dusty halt. Amy could make out two local-looking men, their teeth gleaming white against bronzed skin in the dimness of the cab. Approaching the window, she saw they had matching sun-drenched dreadlocks, decorated with little white shells and gemstone pendants around their bare-chested necks.

"Amy, how you doin'?" chirped a friendly voice in English through the clearing dust cloud.

"Bandu! You!" Amy beamed back.

"Pura vida. Where you going?" he climbed out.

"One of the Haciendas."

"Hacienda Gloria," Bandu announced decidedly. He promptly swung her suitcase on to the back of the truck and ushered her into the back seat. "Now, we will go to surf beach. You know the secret beach Amy?"

"Oh no thanks! I need to -" she started to decline.

"Amy! You know me. Bandu! I friend of Zan. You know. I am understanding, you girl for Zan." Bandu said with eyes widened with mild offence. The secret beach, a twenty-minute drive north of Castillo, lay hidden behind sand dunes, disguised by high grasses. They arrived when the road simply turned into two narrow, sandy tyre tracks engulfed by grasses, where they abandoned the truck. Barefooted, they squelched through mud and parted tall grasses like jungle explorers, until emerging on to a small sweep of rough beach. The cove was secluded and empty of people, and the waves came in from two directions, crossing on to the sands. They threw pebbles and watched the waves for a while. Bandu's friend ate something pink from a plastic tub. "Oats with red fruits," he said, offering her the spoon and tub of pink mousse. It tasted smooth and milky, like the soaked oats drink Alba made and kept in her fridge. After a while they returned to the truck. The waves were not good. Bandu dropped his friend back in Castillo and helped Amy check into Hacienda Gloria.

"Come, see my family shop," Bandu had said, "and we take a smoke." It seemed a safer option than being at a loose end in Castillo on a Friday night.

"Where is Zan?" Amy asked in English when next to Bandu in his cab.

"I don't know, working maybe?"

"I have tried to call him, many times. His mother says he's in hospital."

"Hospital? For what?" he answered.

"Hurting back, his mother tells me."

"Hurting back? I don't know. We can go look for him later if you want," Bandu said, pulling off the road to a shack-shop with a canvas roof, "but first come to see my shop." Amy nodded, unsure if she wanted to see Zan.

"All of my potteries are individual, no the same. All by my family hand. And by the wood to make fire," Bandu explained.

"Your family owns the shop?" Amy asked, taking in the rough plank shelves lined with pots, vases, plates and bowls.

"Yes. Me, and two my brothers live here. My sister up the road." The painted, glazed pottery glinted in bold colours of ochre reds, deep blues, burnt oranges, and gold, intricately decorated with patterns of squares and crosses, zigzags and circles. Some elaborated with symbolic faces and animal shapes, others plain with a single trim. "So, the *'clay'*, I think is the name in English, is from the mountains in this region," Bandu continued, "sand, called Iguana sand, is mixed with barro, from the earth. We look to the moon, for see when is good for take the barro. This is told to me by my parents, and is told to parents by the grandparents, and before grand-grandparents."

"Wow. So, it has been handed down from generation to generation for a long time?" Amy confirmed.

"Yes. Say again, generation -" Amy repeated the phrase generation to generation, "For long time. For more than eight hundred years. It is very old and typical to the Chorotega people." Bandu slipped into his sales pitch and went on to explain which patterns and symbols were passed down from his Chorotegen ancestors, and which designs were of his own invention. He showed Amy his potter's wheel, how he polished the dried clay piece with smooth stones, the range of powdered rock colours used to paint the pottery, and the black, ancient-looking wood-burning kiln used to finally fire the piece. "The fire burns very hot. *Very* hot! Six or seven hundred hot. This fire, we take wood from special trees. The Quebracho tree. The pottery very strong and good. Only the tree how my family told me is used in here." The artisan pottery tour came to an end in Bandu's little bedroom. *Perhaps not the normal routine* Amy pondered. The room was just off the workshop, its doorway screened with a sarong and most of the room taken up with a mattress upon the floor. A couple of old surfboards were propped in the corner. Bandu rolled himself on to his bed and lay back comfortably.

"We have shower with warm water," Bandu said with raised eyebrows. *Don't think about trying to get me in your nice warm shower,* Amy thought. But the phrase echoed in her mind with a blissful imaginary feeling of a nice warm shower. The hot springs had been the last warm shower she'd had, she quickly drop-kicked that thought away. He lifted his knees and nodded to the space on his mattress.

"I'll sit here, that's ok," she said quickly, sitting on the woven grass mat on the floor. A mild panic rose within her. *What am I doing? What would Zan think?*

"I make you café. Café of Costa Rica is rich, no?" Bandu said, rolling over to a small stereo and pressing the play button on the tape deck. Bob Marley's voice meekly entered the space, "but first we smoke." As Bandu rolled a joint, he spoke of his trip to North America. "I love my life in Castillo. It is my home, my love. But much changes. Now lot of touristas, lot of Estats Unidos, buy todo, todo. Make new hotels," he chatted, lighting and dragging on the joint, "I want to travel, Europe, America, to study, to work. But I must work here. The shop is my family. I work for my father. One day. I will, again." *I'm travelling, studying, I've been working. No family business ties. Yet I am envious of his life, the beach, the sun, the fiestas, his pride in his culture,* Amy realised. "So, tell me Amy," Bandu said carefully as he sat up and passed back the joint, "how long are you adicta?" Amy paused, blinked in confusion.

"Me! Adicta?" she asked, dragging on the joint, "what do you mean?" Bandu's coy little smile curled at the corners of his face.

"Amy. You are adicta, no? Cocaina?" Bandu persisted. She passed the joint back to him, swallowing smoke, and then blew a trail up through the corner of her mouth.

"No, I'm not an addict. Why do you ask that?" Bandu's grin reappeared and he cocked his head to one side.

"When you arrive, first, to Castillo, Zan tell me about a crazy, beautiful, English girl," Bandu started to reveal, "he tell me, you and Zan – together - is the best time - so many the same things together." He passed the remainder of the joint back. His eyes squinting and his smile dulled. She watched him carefully now. "I know Zan a long time - forever I know Zan!" Bandu smiled, "I know Zan is adicto, todo, todo, todo - all of time he is adicto. You Amy, are the same as Zan." She dragged hard on the joint, which almost burnt her lips and fingers, before looking at Bandu.

"Me? No, I'm not like Zan. Not all the time," she said with weak conviction.

"Ok. Every week? One time or two time? Every week, no?" he persisted. The phrase *self-medication* popped into Amy's mind.

"Every week? I don't know. I don't count," she said disinterestedly and just stared at him. She suddenly wished to sprawl out on his comfy looking mattress, stretch out her limbs and snuggle in for a snooze. "Addiction is when someone can't stop, when they feel like they can't live without it. I'm not like that. I go running on the beach. I eat healthy food. I work hard. I study. I'm not someone hopelessly addicted to a drug," she justified "I just like to party."

"Yes. That is why you visit Las Americas, Costa Rica. No? Castillo. They say a gringo in Castillo is for two things: one – money, two - Party. You, number two," he said breaking into a chuckle.

"And three - to study and chill out. But I am one. To work. This is paradise for me here. The sea, the sun -" she started to defend her argument until Bandu cut her.

"Paradise! I believe you. This is paradise of party here! That is for why you are here Amy. Of course!" he continued. Bob and the wailers stopped.

"I didn't come here for the party," her words flowed directly from within her, but then she looked with a pained expression to the floor. The sand scattered across the cracked painted concrete stole any defence she had.

"But the party always happen for you," he said gently.

"I didn't know how this trip, how the party scene was in Castillo," she muttered defiantly. Bandu smirked.

"Adicto always find a road to what he wants," he said with self-assurance.

"I'm not an addict," she said quietly, but there was a long pause as Bandu seemed to drift asleep.

"No? How long Amy? How long you party like crazy person?" he continued. She leant back against the bond of her arms wrapped around her knees and looked up. Amongst the cobwebs, her mind rewound over the past few years.

"I came here to get away from the craziness. The partying. My life. My friends. I wanted to get my head sorted. Get a job here. I came for a new lifestyle," Amy said watching the moths dancing around the naked light bulb.

"What is life style?" Bandu asked.

"A style of life."

"A style of life," Bandu repeated, "I like that. I want new style of life also." She stretched her memory to before university, before she'd really lost it - college years, pub-crawls with friends, dancing and drinking all night in packed nightclubs, house parties and summer barbeques, drinking endless cider, sharing whatever marijuana anyone had. College days that now seemed so innocent. So safe. So much more fun. *What happened?* Amy's mind whispered. *Uni* a voice replied. Bandu had peacefully slipped asleep. Amy contemplated him and his persistent words. *Adicta. Adicta.* Bob Marley clicked back on as the little cassette player automatically switched to the other side, a slow, smooth keyboard riff over a sombre, stoned drum-beat, Bob's voice singing - *You're running and you're running and you're running away. You're running and you're running and you're running away. You're running and you're running and you're running away. You're running and you're running but you can't run away from yourself. Can't run away from yourself. Can't run away from yourself.* Amy stood up and walked out of the room, thoughts of coffee and a warm shower and finding Zan trailing behind her as she stepped, to her mild surprise and relief, into sunshine. *The hours pass so slowly in Costa Rica,* Amy mentally dictated to an imaginary diary, *the days are stretched by a fortuitous sun, who reluctantly succumbs to dusk, the one who tempers him into gold and reds and oranges, plunging him into the cool sea.* She fancied herself as a light-footed fox sauntering with a taut belly from a day lacking in eating. After almost two hours walking, and five declined lift offers, she reached hacienda Gloria. That evening she ate alone on the balcony, then went to bed early with a building anxiety she'd be better off out of Castillo with its lure of bars and Zan.

Accused

Parched tongue, eyes aching heavily in their sockets. Rasped throat. Amy forced a feeble sip of warm water. Stomach residue instantly curdling. Grimace. Pained face. One eye open. Dusty flip-flops curved like bananas. Unrecognisable objects. Legs and feet streaked with black grime. Skirt twisted around her middle - the one she'd hitched up getting on that high-up horse.

"What the hell?" Amy breathed, rolling to her feet. Sitting, doubled over, eyes barely open, Amy's mind scrambled for a bearing. Hacienda Gloria, its white painted frontage with bright cerise flowers trailing along its wall. She thought, and hoped, the dim confinements of the room belonged to Hacienda Gloria. She was on the inside of a cabina Amy concluded. It wasn't someone's house at least. Dim bathroom. One eye squinting at the slither of mirror above the sink. Blindness? Left eyelashes glued together. She tugged to prise them apart with her fingers. Eyes slowly rolling, blinking, blurred. Pain, where? Breathe, sweat, focus on reflected face. Sore, crispy blister on nose tip. Point of pain located, raw throbbing.

"No! The hire car." Clammy walls exuded previous guests' sweat and breath. Zan's presence hung in the stifled air. *Damaged. Must be. Where the hell is the car? Where is Zan?* Creeping bent over double. Dizzy, nauseous, short pants for breaths. Feet dragged on stiff legs. Body lowered, like an ailing hospital patient, back on to bed. Bruised bones ached. An elbow, a shin, a hip. *I'm seriously ill. I don't care if I die right now.* Under heavy eyelids the shenanigans of the previous hours emerged. Upturned chair. Screaming voice echoing. Zan enraged. Her shoulders grazing against the wall's rough finish. English voices shouting through the door. The camera. Reaching to the floor, where everything lay scattered. Vice-like pressure on forehead. Sip of warm water. Chemical belch. Fumbling, flicking. Pictures revealing who and where. Snippets of the facts in images: Amy, an absent mind on strings of legs and arms, long hair wild, dusty bare feet, slim and bony. Amy, on a horse. *Oh God what happened in that wood?* Amy and Rasta, Zan's friend they'd picked up, sat on the car bonnet, the car half-ditched. Smoking. Rasta holding her up. Front bumper hanging off. Lots of faces. In a bar. Zan and Amy so very drunk. Amy's eyes shut, mouth smiling wide. *Oh yes, in Santa Rosa. That little dirty toilet. With Zan? With someone?* Car again, crumpled bonnet, headlights smashed, passenger wing creased.

"What the hell happened?" Amy whispered. After an unknown length of time, Amy awoke to banging on doors. Men shouting. It continued for minutes until Amy wondered if it were her door that was being banged. She awoke properly that afternoon, weak and nauseous. She showered, dressed and luckily found a few coins. Biscuits, bread, bananas - anything the little shop opposite had would do. But the sight, when opening her door and stepping out, halted her abruptly. On the reception porch Zan sat waiting. He was sipping a bottle of beer and overseeing a teenaged girl strip a coconut with a machete. Her body language appeared resistant to Zan's unsolicited advice, or perhaps his presence altogether. Amy wished he wasn't there.

"Let's go to your room," he said quietly to Amy, when noticing her. He sat on the wooden chair in the centre of the room. Amy sat on the bed waiting. Zan continued sipping his beer.

"Where's the car?" she asked after a while.

"The car?" he asked with raised eyebrows and then shook his head slightly. Amy remembered signing the car hire papers with the emergency credit card Rosie had given her. "Playa Blanca," he answered as if it were obvious. He cocked his head to one side and stared at her for a few seconds, before rolling it back upright. "I have made arrangements for the car to be returned to Playa Blanca. Today. Later. I have spoken to my friends also," he informed.

"Why me no drive?" Amy blurted. Zan's face broke into his wild-eyed grin.

"You remember the car, Amy?" he asked and waited.

"No." She shook her head with a frown, "I cannot remember."

"Ahhh. Amy. The car is -" Zan punched a clenched fist into his palm, "Blah. The car is no good." He shook his head with disbelief. "And the wall also. You wanted to drive the car when you were very drunk." Amy sat blinking, absorbing his words. "And two men, you nearly broke them too," he added.

"Two men, broke?"

"Don't worry. The men jumped." He flailed his arms like a goalkeeper saving a goal. Amy sighed then frowned, imagining the scene outside the village bar, herself very drunk, ramming the car into a wall, nearly injuring, if not killing, a few local drunks. "You have money? You need money for the man who took the car," he said.

Amy spent the rest of the afternoon in the bank withdrawing more funds from her account. Zan had things to do. He'd strolled off into Castillo without a kiss or even a smile for Amy, saying that he'd return at six. She felt she'd weep but knew she'd probably not have enough fluid inside her to. She held her ticket, that was dispensed like at Sainsbury's deli-counter, and waited with the rest of those wishing to use the bank. It took hours of sitting, waiting, whilst her head felt like it had a large kitchen knife lodged in it. Her thoughts were oscillating between blank pain and trying to piece together what had happened. She remembered driving a hire car, then the heat out on a dusty ranch, being on a horse - her memory was just too torn and her head throbbing so much to really try to recollect.

At six, dressed and ready, she sat silently staring at the wall of her room, trying not to think. *What if I have injured someone? Maybe that's why Zan walked away.* She tried to imagine the sun setting over the sea. It seemed a year ago that she sat on the beach letting a beautiful sunset melt before her eyes with her heart brimming full of the joy of the sight of it.

"What time's the bus leaving in the morning?" a loud USA accent suddenly bellowed in the next room.

"Early man, six am, no partyin' tonight, we gotta catch that bus. Then at Li-beria we change," another loud USA accent answered.

"They must have heard it all," Amy said to herself, "it must have been their English voices trying to help."

****

La luna llena bar was quiet and almost empty as Zan and Amy entered.

"Pura vida." Manuel greeted them unenthusiastically. They took a couple of beers up the steps and into the interior seating area.

They'd never ventured inside before, always sitting at the bar open to the street. Zan sat so to face the street outside, opposite Amy.

"What did you do with Bandu?" Zan asked as soon as they were seated. Amy stared at him blankly for half a second and felt weary at the effort she was going to need to extract the correct words and string them into a coherent sentence. She told him, as best she could, the truth about the few hours she'd spent with Bandu. Zan's face was expressionless. Before he had said anything, a man arrived. Zan told Amy to pay for towing the hire car back to the depot. She handed over the huge wad of cash. The man gave Zan a plastic bag and gave Amy the bill for the car damage. Zan and the man spoke for a few minutes, rummaging in the plastic bag as if something had been misplaced, and then the man left. Zan gave Amy the plastic bag with her walking shoes and hoody inside. They sat in silence. Amy downed the last third of her beer, mentally converting the car damage bill into US dollars and then sterling. It was between £1500 and £2000.

"Buenas," Zan said seriously to someone stood behind her.

"Buenas," a soft voice responded. She turned to see Bandu, stifling a smile. He took a seat at the table.

"What happened a few days ago?" Zan asked Bandu. Amy's heart sank slightly. Bandu answered pretty much what she had said.

"You touched Bandu?" Zan addressed her in a hushed voice.

"No, never," she replied, imitating his tone of sincerity, her heart racing a little. He asked the same to Bandu who calmly answered the same.

"Zan. I don't lie to you. Nothing has happened between us. Nothing. I respect you. And I apologise for causing this concern," Bandu said directly to his friend. He held out his hand. Zan took it returning Bandu's eye contact, and they shook hands. Amy felt like she'd been part of some deal. Bandu left and Zan ordered more beers, still not speaking. Amy wanted to leave but felt sure Zan would accuse her of following Bandu if she did. As the night wore on, she became numb. Numb-drunk, until she was skulking in the dark shadows of the street, with the shady companions she now felt most familiar with. Zan and his cronies, with their keys and cigarettes and ghoulish smiles saying *Pura vida* through white, clenched teeth.

****

The golden green leaves hung motionlessly on the grand Guanacaste trees that stood sturdy and splayed. It was fresh and bright. It was Rodeo day. The arena atmosphere was buzzing with spectators, the music galloping happily into the hazy afternoon's warmth. Amy was sleek and sexy, her tanned legs glowing beneath her skirt as she sauntered into the crowd, flanked by her companions. Zan was holding her hand. Rasta was with them. The floodlights clicked on and suddenly it was night-time. She turned to Zan, but to her horror it was her London ex-boyfriend instead. He was wearing a cowboy hat. She tried and failed to question the companions. They seemed not to notice Zan was in fact a totally different person. Confusion bloomed. He spoke like Zan, he asked her to dance with him. Everyone had gathered around to watch them dance. *"What are you doing here? You cheated on me, and lied to me, and now you're here pretending to be tico,"* Amy shouted angrily as they danced. He smiled an insipid smile. Worried that the real Zan would see her, she scanned the crowd as she was swung around in the salsa embrace. Then, somewhere over the crowded dancehall came a loud tapping sound. Tump, tump, tump. An announcement would be made over a microphone. Tump, tump, tump it tapped again. Her ex was grinning at her in a sickly, satisfied way, wearing his pilot's uniform. Tump, tump, tump, again, this time louder.

"Amy!" a voice shouted. She knew it was Zan. *He's seen me dancing.* "Amy!" the voice shouted again. Amy woke up with a start, panting. She knew it was Zan. He was at the door. She froze still, quietening her breathing. The silence pounded out of her eardrums and into the dim room. She willed him to go. The knocking had stopped but she lay waiting, listening, like a scared cat stuck up a tree, wanting to come down but refusing to budge. After nearly half an hour had passed, she dragged herself upright feeling dizzy and nauseous. Eventually, she stood, but was unsteady and weak-kneed. She staggered out into the daylight and paused. Nobody was there. She needed to get to the little grocery shop across the road to get water and maybe bread, something for her stomach to digest. *'When was the last time I ate? I'm not even hungry - just need water'.* She made it to the porch, sweat already trickling down her back. Relief gushed when she didn't see Zan, or anyone. And over the road she staggered. Luckily no vehicles were driving, as she didn't even check.

"Hey Amy. How's ya doin?" a familiar North American drawl called out. *'Oh no, not Mary Ellen,'* she thought and closed her eyes momentarily.

"Alright?" Amy mumbled as they came face to face over the shop threshold.

"Good thanks," Mary Ellen replied and then paused, as if to locate some suitable words for addressing the wreck before her eyes. Amy was considerably doubled over as she shuffled into the shop. "You finished school now, ain't that right?" she bambled on. Amy nodded."Okaaaay. So where you staying right now?" she went on.

"Just in there." Amy pointed at Hacienda Gloria over the road. She grabbed the nearest bottle of water within reach as Mary Ellen chatted to the back of her head. She didn't hear what Mary Ellen said, just the accent.

"See ya round Amy," Mary Ellen said and left, perhaps taking the hint that she wasn't being heard. Amy paid and quickly left. As she entered the driveway to Hacienda Gloria, two men – ticos - appeared from around the wall. They started to speak rapidly at Amy, frowning and articulating their anger. One was wearing a baseball cap and scruffy clothing, and the other had a sharp little moustache. Both were enraged.

"I don't understand you," Amy kept repeating.

"The car. Santa Rosa, eh? Remember?" the moustached man was saying very clearly. But the rest of what he said Amy couldn't decipher. *'Big trouble. The people are sad for the trouble,'* Amy's head interpreted part of the sentences.

"Three hundred dollars, ehh?" the cap man repeated. He looked angry.

"You crazy girl, understand?" the moustache was shouting at her, pointing at his temple. "Let's go. Let's go to Santa Rosa. Now. You can see. Let's go," moustache man said, taking hold of Amy's upper arm. She protested, but the cap man took her other arm and she was being marched towards a pickup. Amy felt her own feathery weight, unable to resist.

"Somebody," the moustached man glared at her, as though to spit in her face, "took a lot of cocaina. *My* cocaina. Understand?" *'What? But?'* Amy thought, hearing her flip-flops slapping the soles of her feet, clapping the absurdity of it all.

"Thief!" Cap man exclaimed, glancing a sideways accusation.

97

"What?" Amy protested, "Me? Thief? No! Me no thief, nothing!"

"Lots of cocaina. Last night?" moustache man whispered at her face almost calmly, "I want my cocaina or my money." Moustache man was opening the passenger door of the pickup. *I'm being bundled* Amy's thoughts merely stated to herself.

"What's goin' on Amy?" a calm voice said. It was Mary Ellen. They halted and turned to her. "What's your problem gentleman?" Mary Ellen addressed the men in well-pronounced Spanish, looking keenly from one to the other. She had her hands on her hips and a sort of 'am I goin'a have to whoop some ass?' look on her face.

"She owes me three-hundred dollars," moustache man spat. After some time negotiating, Mary Ellen persuaded the men to leave, giving them eighty dollars from her purse. "We'll be back for the rest," moustache man promised Amy, pausing to stare her in the eyes.

"It's a stupid misunderstanding. I don't owe them any money. I haven't thieved anything. Something happened last night," Amy attempted to explain, relief draining through her arms and legs at the sight of the pickup rumbling away.

"Are you sure you're alright, hon? They're asking for a hell of a lot more money than what I gave them. I think they'll be back," Mary Ellen said looking deeply into Amy's eyes. Amy suddenly wanted her friendship. Her caring, honey-coated words. *I need someone like her. Someone safe. To love me.*

"I'm ok," Amy replied, breaking her bizarre thoughts. *She'd never cope with me.* "I just gotta go lie down. I'll be fine. But, look - I'll pay you back tomorrow. Thanks, thanks so much. You rescued me. And, I'll pay you back tomorrow. Ok?" Amy turned and walked away, feeling Mary Ellen's concerned eyes watching her. *Thank God for Mary Ellen* Amy sighed, twanging with shock.

Fight or flight

Stagnant hot air. Twisted T-shirt, stretched tight. Sweat-stuck bra and knickers. Not enough air. Panting in and out. Pause. In and out. Pause. Head hanging over side of bed. Panting in and out. Pause. Poised to vomit.

"God help me", Amy whispered. In and out. Pause. "Help me," she tearlessly cried.

"Just go Amy," a voice said. Amy frowned, wondering where the voice came from. *Must have been in my head.* She broke the heaviness of eyelids and opened her eyes. The crack in the curtains shone daylight. A benign light before the wrath of full sun. Eyes closed. A steady sweep, sweeping of long bristles on a tiled floor became audible. Panting in and out. Pause. In and out. Pause. *I've got to go.* In. Pause. Out. Pause. In. Pause. Out. Pause. Sinking dread. Eyes open. Feet on floor. Adrenaline kicking in.

Amy got herself upright, stuffing clothes into her suitcase. She raked her hands through her clothes to find the little travel clock, a present, intended to wake her on time for work, from her Grandma. It read a twenty past six, if it was right. Tip-toeing along the walkway towards the porch, her suitcase trundling behind her, the sweep, sweeping noise became louder. She stopped. She knew it was coming from the porch. She glanced around. Nobody was about. Stood still. She hadn't withdrawn cash to pay the Hacienda. They only took cash. She had only a twenty colón note left. Sweep, sweep, sweep the brush continued. Amy stood rigid at the corner before the porch, holding her bottom lip between her thumb and forefinger, looking out of the gate to the road and listening to the sweeping. Then a shrill ringing broke into the peaceful sounds. Amy jumped with a start. After the second ring it stopped and was replaced by the sound of a woman's voice indoors. The sweeping had stopped too.

Without hesitation, Amy quickly dragged her suitcase across

the porch. Without turning, she bumped it down the steps and continued straight out on to the road. Looking left, she saw it. The bus accelerated towards her. As it approached, she saw written on a placard in the front window LIBERIA. *Thank God the buses are always late.* She stepped out into the road and waved the bus down. As the driver loaded her suitcase into the belly of the tica bus, panic rose within. With one foot on the step and the other on the dusty road, she paused. *What about Zan?* For a long few seconds she longed for him to run up and stop her, to apologise, hold her in his arms and kiss her, and for her heart to melt and she'd stay. By the end of those fleeting seconds she realised that, even if he did appear and stop her, all the rest of that scenario would not ensue.

"You ok, senorita?" the driver asked, now in his seat. She blinked at him, and then clambered aboard. She gave the driver her twenty colóns with breath held. He put it in his jeans pocket and chatted to someone through the driver's open window. As Amy sat down, the the bus pulled away and started to swing around the winding roads. She felt a gush of relief – a reluctant relief. A relief like she'd escaped fatality. Passing Bandu's silent, dark pottery shop, she peered inside and heard the echoes of Bob Marley's *running away* song. Then trees and fields blurred as she refocused her eyes upon her own reflection - her shadowy eye sockets and long face.

Nicaragua

Liberia's broad, concrete-roofed bus station was cool and bustling with morning commuters. Amy sat on her suitcase sipping a can of orange-flavoured drink and watched the scores of buses arriving and departing. They seemed to go everywhere; PLAYA FLAMINGO, PLAYA DES COCO, NICOYA, SANTA CRUZ, LA FORTUNA, MONTE VERDE were some she recognised. She wondered where she'd go. A SAN JOSE destined bus entered the station and people jostled forwards. Amy winced momentarily, causing the scab on the tip of her nose to painfully crack again. The capital city of San Jose would mean one thing - next stop London. She quickly glanced down at her tanned feet in their dusty flip-flops. *I am running away from trouble but not Costa Rica. I'm not ready for that yet. Forget San Jose for now.* A surge of nausea wafted over her as she broke into another sweat. But she felt a rising optimism after finding a cash machine in the bus station that allowed her to get a wad of money out of it. A bus rumbled into the stand right in front of her, prompting those waiting nearest to rise to their feet and waddle penguin-fashion towards it. The driver slotted a new destination card into the front window. It read: PENAS BLANCAS NICARAGUA. She stared at it for a few seconds and then decided it was the most appealing.

****

Two and a half hours later she dragged her suitcase through the Costa Rican - Nicaraguan border. Amy blinked at the passport controller and his apparent lack of ability to speak his own language, until he released her into the loud crowd of heckling men waving large wads of cash. Changing her cash into a new currency hadn't crossed her mind.

     "I don't understand," she said for the fourth time to the man who'd swept upon her the swiftest. He was young and friendly in manner. "I have been in Costa Rica for seven weeks. The people, I can speak with," she shrugged her shoulders, "And now, I don't understand. Nothing. The people speak very different."

"Yes. Different accent," he replied slowly with soft, warm eyes that smiled, "where are you going?"

"Managua."

"Managua?" he repeated but with a buttery-tongued accent "Why?" She just shrugged, contemplating admitting that it was the only Nicaraguan city name she could remember, and she hadn't even seen a map of his country. "No, no. Please. Managua is too big and too dangerous. You are alone. And a very beautiful girl," he said with a look of distaste. "Please. Go to San Juan Del Sur. It is better for you. By the beach. People friendlier." Amy studied his face momentarily and asked:

"Managua no good?"

"Please," he pleaded "Managua, no."

"Where beach?" Amy replied, accompanied by a bout of anxiety at the word beach. *Beach, trouble, temptation.*

"You. United states of America? Germany?" he asked with a little chin nod.

"English," she replied.

"How is the Queen? And her dogs? And Prince Charles?" he flashed his eyes widely, pronouncing Prince Charles as Preece Childs.

"Prince Charles," Amy chuckled as her tension broke, "Good, I think."

"Prince Childs," he repeated and they both laughed which made her pick up courage. *I can find a refuge, relax and stay out of trouble.* After a lengthy lesson on currency exchange rates and roughly what could be bought at what price, he made sure, twice, that she was happy with the exchange. Not that she had any idea whether what he said was true or not, but he shook her hand and made a note of the two amounts on a tear of paper. Then he gave her a huge wad of córdobas in exchange for her colóns, making her unable to help feeling she'd had a pretty good deal. "Come to meet my mother - it is only eight kilometres that way. I live with my mother because I don't have a wife. I am twenty-eight and no wife and no children. My mother is very nice - she will give you a nice room to sleep in - with air-conditioning," he offered.

"Thank you very much. But I go," she replied smiling and realising how she'd not stopped giggling since speaking with him.

"Do you have a camera?" he asked without hesitation, to which Amy nodded. "Can you take a photo of me, please?" Amy carried out his request and he seemed very happy with seeing himself on the screen. He scribbled his name and address on another tear of paper. "Please send me the photograph," he asked with a smile unbefitting of a person asking a favour. Then, beckoning her to stand next to him, he took her camera, outstretched his arm, and took their picture together. "Look. The bus to San Juan. That one," he said suddenly, "Let's go," and then jogged her case over to the bus and flung it into its open belly. "Your camera," he said as he handed it back, "Goodbye, Amy."

"Goodbye, Ivan," she said pronouncing his name as a true Brit, smiled and hesitated. *He looks so cuddly and safe. His Mum, in a little pretty house with air-conditioning, would probably dote on me.*

"This and this one." Ivan pointed at the bank notes she was still clutching, in explanation of what to pay the awaiting driver. She took a seat on the bus going to the beach town she'd already forgotten the name of. "Don't forget to send the photo," he grinned up at her bus window just as the bus pulled away and he gave her two thumbs up. Amy waved back at the man who'd spun her off in her new direction and hoped he'd advised her well. Looking at the last photo on her digital camera, of her and Ivan grinning like little children, she saw it was one of those photos people took with locals on their adventures. A strange excitement aimed at a camera. She promised herself to send a print to Ivan's address.

****

San Juan del Sur looked far larger than Castillo, with many seaside shops along the long, curvy beach that looped the teardrop of calm, blue sea. Only when strolling along the vast flat sands - for the tide was well out - did she realise that she'd booked into a real backstreet hacienda. The part of town she'd taken a small, modest room had sleepy-feel streets of wooden bungalows with bamboo fencing and gaily painted stucco shops, where elders sat in the early afternoon shade watching and acknowledging passers-by. The hacienda's gently spoken owner had sat upon her street-facing porch amongst her potted flowers with an old toothless man. Together, in sombre respect, they greeted everyone, including an old, one-legged man hobbling on well-used wooden crutches, his empty trouser leg folded and pinned up. The great beachfront, overseeing bobbing fishing boats beyond the wave break, spoke nothing of those hot, dusty streets. Instead there were large stilted wooden buildings with shaggy thatched roofs she'd not seen the like of before. She approached one of these cavernous and exotic buildings, climbed the steps, and gingerly peered into the dark interior. A woman in shorts and a vest sheepishly greeted her.

"Is there food, here, tonight?" Amy enquired. The woman spoke over her shoulder at a man napping on a bench. He awoke, straightened out his shirt and approached Amy with a slightly dazed smile.

"Good evening senorita. Would you like fish, chicken or pork?" he almost whispered in a clear, tourist-friendly way.

"Fish please."

"Good. With rice and beans, plantain and salad?" he continued, making a note on a little piece of paper, unnecessarily.

"Yes please, and a beer also please," Amy added. Whilst the woman went to cook the order the man sat back on the bench nearby and politely made conversation. He was intrigued to learn that it was not only her first day in San Juan del Sur, but in Nicaragua.

"What are your first impressions of Nicaragua?" he asked chirpily.

"The people are kind and friendly."

"Many tourists visit Costa Rica, not so many Nicaragua."

"There are many people from United States in Costa Rica, for holiday, surfing, learning Spanish language," Amy said.

"Yes, Costa Rica has plenty of United States people. Many of the bars, restaurants, homes, businesses are owned by them."

"It is the same in Nicaragua?" Amy asked. The man paused for a moment.

"You know about the revolution - the wars of Nicaragua?" he questioned her.

"No, nothing," she said, to which he huffed a polite disbelief at his ignorant customer.

"You heard of the Sandinistas, and the Somozas, yes?" he puzzled her. Amy laughed at herself and shook her head.

"Tell me," she said starting to enjoy his simple, affable manners.

"Ok. The revolution in brief," he started and drew a deep breath. "Since independence in the 1820s, from the Spanish, we had two political parties - the Conservadores from Granada, and the Liberales from León." The woman appeared from the kitchen, laid cutlery for one on Amy's table and opened a bottle of cold beer.

"Thank you," Amy smiled, "and another beer, for him please."

"She doesn't know about the revolution," he said when the woman glanced at him. Emotionlessly, she nodded and went back to the kitchen. "In the early 1900s the United States got involved with Nicaragua. Many countries from Europe were already involved - with coffee, sugar. Well, United States sent soldiers to help the conservatives rebel against the President Zelaya." He dived into his account talking rapidly and precisely. Amy frowned in concentration, feebly sipping the beer.

"I'm sorry, I don't understand everything, I don't speak Spanish very good."

"Ok. Military of United States *controlled* Nicaragua," he embellished, shuffling to the edge of the bench and using his hands to support his explanations. Amy nodded, her full attention on her impassioned host. "Many people dead - United States wanted *control* for making canal - you know canal?" Amy frowned. "You know the canal of Panama?" he enthused.

"Panama canal, yes," Amy replied with relief.

"Well – before - this canal was planned for Nicaragua." He jabbed his fingers and took the bottle of beer the woman offered him. "It was for that reason United States took control of Nicaragua, with the Conservadores." The woman's voice called from within the kitchen and the man excused himself. After fifteen minutes of staring at the sea, the woman appeared and set a plate of food before Amy, whose stomach instantly growled. A whole fish, scored and grilled brown sat aside rice, salad and plantain piled neatly like a feast. The man appeared soon after. "So, 1927, Augusto Cesar *Sandino*," he quickly continued, "a simple working man - a liberal, he decided to rebel." The succulent white fish melted in Amy's mouth. The delicate, lightly spiced and salty flavours made her feel joy for being alive, as did the sweet, caramelized, fried plantain chips. "Sandino created the rebellion. Not with military but just workers." Amy put her knife and fork down, sipped her beer and tried to listen. He urged her to eat.

"Sandino start war?"

"Sandino started the revolution," he almost shouted, "He is our hero." He sipped half a mouthful of beer, just to wet his tongue. He was just getting started now. Amy munched on. "After, Sandino was assassinated, murdered, dead," he continued in a lower pitch, "then a new leader, Somoza. Many people dead. Somoza was with United States. Many children, women, dead." Amy stopped eating to listen. "Eat, please," he urged again. "So, the revolution continued." Amy flipped over the fish skeleton, having eaten one side of the juicy fish. "Sandinistas, of course named from Augusto Cesar Sandino the original revolutionist, created trouble for Somoza," he explained.

"Sandinistas are people, or military?" Amy queried.

"Sandinistas became a political party," he explained, "fighting for liberation."

"Another war," Amy said gently.

"Another war, this time with help from Russia, Cuba, revolutionists in Chile." Amy shook her head sympathetically. "We had to fight," he accentuated. "My father went to fight, and he died in this war for liberation."

"That is much war and fighting."

"We people need stability," he stated, his emotions running high, "we need positivity. We need belief, faith and security." Amy paused from chewing for a few seconds, *I need all those things.*

"Sandinistas, triumph?" Amy asked through her next mouthful.

"Did the Sandinistas win?" he repeated her question for her, "Yes. Did Nicaraguans win? No, Nicaraguans lost." He took a sip of his beer. "The Sandinistas took control of Nicaragua. But the United States put *pressure* with La contras," he said with a contorted face of pain, "Nicaragua had a Sandinista president but still not peace."

"La contras," Amy uttered.

"The war of the contras completely destroyed our farming, our industry - people were in so much poverty. So much violence continued. The fear of war," he mouthed each word with disgust. Amy placed the knife and fork together on the plate and drained the dregs of her warm beer, sensing he wasn't going to finish on a happy ending after all that struggling. "Now we will watch. Corruption is always in politics. But peace is more important," he concluded. Amy thought of the men she'd seen with missing limbs - how fresh the wars still were - as they sat in silence looking at the sky dimming into a streaky sunset. Feeling after-eating fatigue, she declined a second beer, paid, and bid the couple goodnight. "You are very welcome. God bless you," said the man as Amy thanked him for his company. He sank back on to his bench and laid his head back into his folded hands.

The man's impassioned account of Nicaraguan history rang in her mind for the rest of the evening, and she thought of Mary Ellen. *She'd been right about the poverty,* thought Amy, yet she was glad to be there. The wounded nature of Nicaragua's story seemed befitting to Amy's mood.

Two mountains island

It was a protracted dawn, eased in by the hollow thudding of water lapping against the boat. San Jorge ferry port was the only man-made feature visible for miles around. It was little more than a strip of concrete. There was no land in sight beyond the flat expanse of lake that could be easily mistaken for an open sea. An unfamiliar sour, sweet scent hung in the humid air. It reminded Amy of Monte Verde, but the topography and air couldn't have been more different. She'd taken an early dawn bus from San Juan del Sur to a town called Rivas, then a taxi to the port. The bus had detoured through the town of San Juan del Sur to pick up from different locations, giving Amy a tour of the town she was leaving so soon after arriving. There Amy had almost gotten off in favour of the bright, blue cove cradling backpacker bars, hostels, nightlife and potential befriending. If it hadn't been for the peculiar insistence of the lemonade-doling hacienda owner, she wouldn't have left. *Strange to practically turn away a paying customer,* Amy frowned at the murky waters. *Surely, she couldn't have heard about me from hacienda Gloria?* Amy squinted at the lake's horizon and got a sense that the steady turn of the planet was rolling her around to meet it. The wide, barge-like boat, known locally as a lancha was named Estrella del Sur (Southern Star), and Amy watched men loading on sacks of fruits and vegetables, cheeping crates of chicks, and huge unidentifiable plastic-wrapped items.

"I can take that for you?" a voice said in English behind her. She turned and became momentarily mesmerised by the young man she saw. More precisely by his eyes that were an extraordinarily captivating turquoise colour. So strikingly large were his eyes, every fleck was vivid under the stark, bright daylight. In his almost iridescent Caribbean-sea irises, bright traces of hazel illuminated his eyes further, accentuated by his dark brown lashes and a dusty-peach, tanned skin.

"Oh, thank you," she blurted after a long three seconds. She watched him take hold of her case by its handle and drag it along the boarding plank into the frenzy of people piling up luggage in the centre of the deck then followed him on deck. She spotted a space on one of the few deck benches and, seizing her chance, squeezed in between an old woman and a boy in front of the captain's cabin. Most people filed down-stairs, but Amy had no intention of missing the trip. The hypnotic-eyed guy and his companion sat at the edge of the luggage pile. She raised her hand in a gesture of thanks to him, wondering how he coped with the attention his eyes would surely attract him. Unfolding the small tourist leaflet of Ometepe, Amy set about gaining some information about where she was heading. All she'd been told was its apparent beauty and magical prestige. She learnt that Lake Nicaragua was known locally as Lago Cocibola, and the strip of land that joined the two round islands was called an isthmus. Ometepe was really two islands with a volcano at the centre of each. On a map, Ometepe, with its adjoining isthmus, looked rather like the cogs and chain arrangement of a bicycle. As the engine started up, the last passengers bounced across the plank. One man heftily pushed a large off-road motorbike that was jostled into a safe position amongst the sprawling area of luggage. The lancha chugged off from the port. As Amy caught a glimpse of the green, alluring eyes glancing over at her, feeling her own eyes were positively dull in comparison, she felt a tongue lick her leg.

"He's beautiful. Very big," Amy said extending a hand to pat the dog lying under the legs of the boy next to her.

"Careful. He may bite. Don't touch," the boy quickly warned, wrapping the chain a couple more times around his wrist. The Alsatian-sized mongrel placidly sniffed the palm of Amy's hand, his large pointed ears cocked forward. Amy noticed the boy was in fact closer to her age.

"My name is Amy," she told him with a smile.

"I am Allan - this is my cousin Warner," he introduced the lad next to him, and patting the dog's head added "and this is el Monstruo." Allan wore a black T-shirt with a skull image, cut denim jeans, and plenty of wooden and metal beads around his neck and wrists. El Monstruo seemed to be part of the image. The word *grunge* popped into Amy's mind with mild amusement. Warner was dressed like most of the locals his age - plain T-shirt and shorts.

"Do you live at Ometepe Island?" Amy asked.

"Warner lives in Alta Gracia with our Uncle, the Curo," Allan replied quietly.

"Allan is coming back to Ometepe. His home. To live with me and our Uncle," Warner smiled, patting Allan's shoulder. "For a better life at Ometepe. You will see how beautiful and peaceful it is." Allan almost smiled but his wizened eyes stayed mindful.

"You are brothers?"

"No cousins," they chorused together.

"But Warner is like a brother to me," Allan said with a serious note. After watching the lake pass for a while, Amy took out her walkman, inserted her indie home-compilation tape into it, pressed play and offered it to Allan. One thing she'd learnt in Costa Rica was that her mix-tapes were always a hit. He took it sheepishly, carefully placing the dangly earpieces into his earholes.

"Pass me one," Warner said impatiently when he saw the huge grin open on his cousin's staunch face. Soon Warner's eyes were also twinkling with wonder.

"Which group is this?" Allan asked loudly, to which she listened to an earphone.

"This is the Stone Roses." After listening to Primal Scream, Oasis, Pearl Jam, Nirvana and U2, Allan pointed up ahead.

"Look! Volcano Maderas." The clouds had cleared to reveal a most majestic sight - a mini mountain, rising from the mist of the lake. White wisps clung around its head as if puffed right up out of the old redundant volcano.

"And there, mostly hidden in cloud, is the larger Volcano Concepcion." Warner pointed over to the left at an undistinguishable strip of greenery between shoreline and thick white cloud. Amy silently pondered Maderas emerging before her eyes, casting her mind back to school geology lessons with coloured diagrams of magma chambers beneath the earth along the seams of tectonic plates. In a fantastical million year time-lapse, she imagined a steep cone pushing up out of the lake basin, then erupting and blowing its top off back into the lake. Suddenly, Vulcan Concepcion seemed eerily closer, in front but now also looming over them. A grey-green, solid mass glimpsed from behind the obscuring fluffy, white cloud patches. A steep slope line could be made out to its right side and its girth seemed to go on for further than imaginable. It felt an ominous presence. A giant edifice rooted down in the depths of the earth, where rock boiled and swilled around - red and orange. It protruded up into the clouds like an incisor in the mouth of the Americas, its nerve pulsing with the hot blood of the earth. *If I need inspiration to believe in the creator then here it is,* thought Amy, with a quiet echo of Alvero's words on the wonder of the world's creation. Soon they arrived in Moyogalpa, the destination port that lay on the west coast of the larger island. It was buzzing with expectant people and the boat deck became a throng of luggage reclaiming. Allan offered Amy a lift to Alta Gracia, which Amy's little tourist leaflet map showed to be on the other side of Concepcion island.

"Alta Gracia is the second largest village of Ometepe and very beautiful. Moyogalpa is the largest town, with lots of hotels, but not as beautiful," Warner told her as they jostled along with the crowd towards the gangplank.

"We can help look for a hotel. It is easier with a car," Allan added.

"Ok. Thank you." She reluctantly accepted with a sneaking feeling that her travel plans were yet again being made for her. Since arriving in Nicaragua, strangers were making travel decisions on her behalf. Firstly, at the border crossing, Peñas Blancas, with Ivan insisting on San Juan del Sur, then lemonade-hacienda woman urging her to go to Ometepe Island, and now Allan was intervening directly as to where she should stay on Ometepe.

"Are you heading to Maderas?" a voice said in English behind her. Amy knew it was the guy with the alluring eyes.

"Alta Gracia, I think," Amy replied.

"We're getting a bus to Monkey Island, heading to a backpacker's place at a farm we've been recommended. A lot of travellers stay there because it's very cheap and simple, with beautiful views over the lake," he informed Amy who was detecting his faintly US accent.

"Sounds lovely," she replied hesitantly, trying not to stare at his eyes.

"Come to see the volcanoes and hieroglyphs? Or on a spiritual retreat?" he asked, hanging his face down to one side - almost smiling.

"Not sure to be honest. Just heard it's beautiful here," she over-nodded.

"You like beauty," he stated, which made Amy pause in wonder.

"Beauty. Peace. Nature. Time out from the crazy world," she offered.

"Escaping. Ah-ha," he said accentuating the Ah-ha with a slow definite nod that made Amy's neck prickle.

"But I'm going to get a lift and check out the other side of this island."

"Vulcan Concepcion," he interjected glancing at Allan and then el Monstruo, "Sounds like you got your own agenda." He gave a dismissive shrug and wandered off into the crowd.

"Thanks anyway," she called after him feeling a little fuddled. After a lot of waiting around, the cousins and Amy set off in a pick-up truck, el Monstruo perched precariously on the flat back eagerly sniffing the air. The jovial driver excessively honked the horn and waved at pedestrians for twenty minutes until the pickup truck rolled and lurched off the sandy track and into a paved town. They rolled to a halt in front of a rather grand looking building facing the tree-shaded town square of Alta Gracia. Amy followed her two companions through the beautifully engraved wooden front door and inhaled the cool air from within. It was a reception room with a high ceiling, stone floor slabs and dark stained ornate wooden furniture. Browns and gold dominated the entire room but for the painted crucifixes and saintly figures hung on all four walls. Sitting on one of the two pews facing into the centre of the room, whilst the cousins disappeared into the depths of the building, Amy concluded the Curo was clearly someone religious and wished she wasn't wearing such short shorts. After staring at the faces of startled cherubs for over ten minutes, Amy popped open her suitcase and dragged out a pair of jeans. *There must be a toilet or little room behind one of these doors,* Amy thought as she carefully tried opening all five doors leading off the room. Each was locked. She looked up at the carved Jesus, who was nearly naked and nailed to a cross - His thorn-crowned head stoically hung down as he endured dying.

"Why is Christian religion all about sadness and suffering? I don't get the church's obsession with the symbol of his death," she muttered as she hastily dropped her shorts around her ankles. As she pulled her jeans up over her string knickers and exposed buttocks, she turned to see a solemn-faced man at the internal doorway. Without a hint of facial expression, he entered the reception room, with Allan and Warner following behind him. Amy blushed profusely. Warner gave her a cold glass of cloudy, unrecognisable juice and the man beckoned her to follow him through a door. Gingerly, she proceeded into the little room where he had already seated himself behind a huge wooden desk. He stood, bowed his head slightly and gestured for her to sit on the large, empty chair across his desk. Amy wondered for a second if she'd walked into someone else's job interview.

"My name is Antony, I have been the Curo of Alta Gracia for eleven years," he introduced himself formally with no hint of a smile. His wispy, grey beard and hair appeared too old for his face.

"My name is Amy. I'm from England," she replied in a surprisingly timid voice.

"Ometepe is a special island," he went on, "ancient people believed it is a sacred land and many tribes travelled to worship God here. The name Ometepe comes from one of the indigenous languages. 'Ome', meaning two, and 'tepe', meaning mountain." Amy nodded. "Are your people Catholic?" the priest asked raising an eyebrow.

"Err. Yes. Catholic," Amy replied doubtfully. "And the other, protestant?" Amy added, not intending to question. The priest blinked once at her.

"Would you like to see the church?"

"Yes, please," she answered spontaneously.

****

The church was a huge building facing on to the square a few yards from the Curo's house. Despite its peeling paint, it had an aspect of modest significance, with tall palms gently swaying at the front entrance as if watching over people going about their daily business. A few women sat under the shade of mango trees selling fruits and vegetables or cooking food over little wooden fires. Locals strolled or cycled quietly along the square, some led donkey carts. The priest unlocked the front door with a comically large, long key and they stepped inside the huge belly of the church. Tall, slender columns lined the aisle leading to the graciously curved stage and altar. Simple pews lined either side of the spacious aisle flanked with various glass-fronted cabinets housing life-sized statues of Jesus and other biblical figures. The wooden ceiling was painted white and the floor tiled. The priest paused to make the sign of cross over his forehead, breastbone and shoulders. Amy hesitated, and then copied him.

"This is the old section of the church. These columns were built in 1618," he said.

"One, six, one, eight?" Amy asked him, with a frown of disbelief.

"Yes. It is very old, no?" he answered. After he'd pointed out the principle architectural elements, the priest led her out into the grounds. They walked across the dusty, bare earth where young palms and banana plants were planted at intervals, until they reached an open-sided shelter with a roof supported by wooden stilts and covered with palm leaves. It looked like a nativity scene until, seeing sat beneath the shelter, large pimply stone figures, some of human form with large animal or bird-shaped heads.

"That one is a jaguar and this one an eagle," said the priest. "Indigenous tribes from the North came here to find paradise, following a vision that their prophet had of a place with two hills that is paradise."

"How old, these are?" Amy enquired.

"They were made a very long time ago - hundreds of years before Christ." They wandered through the graveyard until they returned to the huge front door and the key once again locked it up. Amy thanked him for his time. "The people of Ometepe call our island *the island of peace.*" With this he closed his tour and left her with his two awaiting nephews.

"Would you prefer to stay in the town or at the beach?" Allan asked Amy.

"The beach," Amy answered instinctively. The lake had captivated her. A small group of children had gathered around the pickup, cheekily shouting at Warner as he pretended to chase them off. Amy's case, el Monstruo, Warner, and six children were loaded on to the back. Amy squeezed into the cab between Warner and Allan, and two little girls were passed on to her lap. Alta Gracia's paved streets soon gave way to a dirt track cutting through dense jungle. Peering into lush, green forest, Amy felt an excitement reignite. *Coming here was the right decision. I'll escape all the troubles, finally.* Within quarter of an hour, Warner turned off the track and down a steep slope. He pulled up in the yard of a large wooden building, its chimney trickling with smoke, and everybody disembarked. The children, followed by Warner clutching a football, scampered off through the rambling forest that spilt right on to sandy beach. It soon became apparent to Amy that the hotel was the most luxurious she'd seen during her whole trip, with the exception of La Fortuna's hot spring resort. The room she was shown had a soft mattress wrapped in clean white linen, a bathroom ensuite with tiled shower and new toilet. Even the little window had pretty lace curtains. The dining area opened out to the beach and was broad with a low ceiling and bamboo furniture designed for relaxation. Allan and Amy sat in comfy wicker chairs sipping beers and nibbling fried plantain chips whilst a vivacious football match was played before them. Warner was the referee, jesting and fooling around with the sprinting, tumbling barefooted children. It felt incredibly salubrious to Amy. The lakeside, the spontaneity of the moment, the children's revelry, and the beautiful hotel - even Allan's awkwardness kindled a refreshingly innocuous vibe. A woman appeared from the kitchen with a tray of little cups, a large jug of water and sliced oranges. The children ran to her and guzzled the refreshments around the table.

"Do you want to continue and look for another hotel to stay in?" Allan asked.

"No. No it's ok, here," Amy answered, then quickly added "it is more expensive for me, normally I choose less expensive, but for one night, is ok for me."

"Santo Domingo beach is the most beautiful of all Ometepe island," Allan stated. Amy had no intention of looking elsewhere that day, her lower back still had a dull ache deep inside and the bruises on her right calf muscle were causing her to limp. Warner joined them, wiping sweat from his brow.

"Come to see us in Alta Gracia," Allan suggested, "or leave a message here." Amy agreed and thanked them both profusely.

"Ally, ally, ally!" shouted Warner, summoning the departure of the pickup.

"We have to go and eat with the priest," Allan said, "see you soon Amy."

An hour later, settled on a wooden sun lounger, she watched the bright egg-yolk sun setting over the lake. A spectacular array of warm blood-orange red and gold cast across the sky, staining fluffy white clouds the shade of pink grapefruit. The dark water was calm and endless. In either direction along the shore, nothing but sand met the dry, wispy grasses and trees. As the sun burned away unrelentingly, crawling down towards the dark lake, the glory of the wide-screen spectacle mesmerised Amy, utterly, as it had that first time in Castillo. The sun, ironically permitting, just once a day, eyes to safely ponder its beauty whilst it beat a steady retreat from ensuing, inevitable darkness. *Just reminding you how much you love and need me,* the sun kissed a shimmery goodnight on the watery horizon. Amy was left sat in the darkness.

Feeling extraordinarily fresh after a hot shower, Amy went and sat alone in the empty, candle-lit dining area waiting for the special meal the waiter had recommended. She hoped it wouldn't take too long to arrive as sleep was closing in on her. But it wasn't long before a deep bowl of broth and a plate of bread were placed before her by the silent waiter. Amy's tummy rumbled at the sight. She scooped a spoonful of the sweet coconut milk soup and tasted fragrant spices, garlic and fresh green herbs. The large chunks of fish she scraped off the bone and chewed with closed eyes, carefully sucking all the flesh from the jaggy fish spine with satisfying slurps, and with the bread soaked up every bit of broth. *This is healing me, and healing is just what I need,* Amy thought as she retired to her little room, tired and a little dazzled. She knew then that she'd stay more than one night.

Home above the stars

The glowing sun slipped behind the lake, illuminating the whole sky orange. Scuffs of dark clouds motionlessly approached from the North. Amy shuddered a shiver and felt a heavy fatigue despite spending the whole of her first day at the hotel in a sweaty slumber under a blanket in bed. *I must have a bug,* she thought, resignedly plodding back to bed.

The next afternoon, after a nauseous night and a morning of fitful sleep, Amy asked the kitchen-worker for some bread and wandered down the beach. Plonking herself on to a wooden sun lounger, she sat bent-backed, chewing bites of bread and gazing across the empty water. She felt, for the first time in Central America, totally alone. Blinking at the horizon she wondered what she had gained from her whole trip. Thoughts of Zan, Rick, Louise, Alvero, Rosie and Giles trailed through her mind like a rumbling train.

"I'm lost," she stated, as if in revelation. A sudden, depressing, weakening feeling came over her. She lay back, flat on the lounger, her neck bent at an acute angle so to face lake-wards. *When did I become like this?* she wondered mournfully. *Uni,* a voice in her mind responded. Then, she slipped through the door in her memory named Student life - the clubs, the bars, the house parties always spilling into the next day. Young strangers unified by an educational enrolment, crammed into student lettings, werewolves and witches swigging vodka and lemonade. The student DJ – well, that student with turn-tables and vinyl - essential for any decent student party, proudly airing his most cherished tracks; the prearranged drug dealer bringing his chemical mini-market - coke, pills, ket, sometimes acid if he's a bit retro. He'd often be a final year or ex-student, else a local, dodgy but down-with-the-kids kind of guy.

Most weekends they'd partied hard. Nights out on the town.

Girls dressing up together, all night dancing, spying out nice guys. Not that any dates from a night out arose for Amy. Nor with her student chums. They were a pack. Hugging each other's highs. Hanging out in the toilets sniffing up coke, often with a stranger or two they'd befriended in their euphoria. Laughing and joking, drinking and smoking. Quenching thirsts with spirit mixers. That was Uni. Relentless partying. In those two years of Uni, Amy had sniffed, swallowed and smoked drugs at a weekly, then daily rate. She'd hardly returned to Worcester, the boring beer-drinking city. Stephie and Rupe had cautiously visited a couple of times - bearing witness to the extent of debauchery student life had blossomed into. Rosie had called and asked, "Are you cooking for yourself? How's the course going? Have you got enough money left for the bills this term?" *Was that happiness? Were they even friends? Were we all so close? I've been living with those friends for two years. All the parties and gigs, and pool in the pub, and nights in watching films.*

Then there was the weekend job. Or, in Amy's case - the continuation of the partying - but replacing lectures for real work as a young professional weekend partier. There seemed endless possibilities of gigs, bars, clubs, parties and acquaintances after shifts. Sleeping on the last tube home. Another handbag stolen. Fun-loving, entertainment-packed life in the capital. Monday hangovers from hell. Midweek, afternoon pints in Covent Garden under the summer sun. After-work drinks on eleven pm shift finishes. Sunday's early morning hours cruising in a car full of 'friends' between clubs and late bars. Lazy afternoons smoking in the backyard. There were drugs for partying, drugs for relaxing and then alcohol for all occasions – happy or sad, but especially stressed. And stress was an obligatory gift from London itself. Copious wine and rich beers sloshed down by the worker bees of the giant hive. Sweet alcohol - a poison sucked up like fruit flies on over-ripe pineapples, dizzily stealing hours of life, smothering fatigue and responsibility. Malta had been at least a rest from London. But the partying with the hotel staff and the local romance disaster - it all seemed a lost and confused time now. *Was that really fun? Was I so happy? If I wasn't into partying, who is still my real friend there? What was I even doing? Why? Why?* Amy's mind screamed, her breathing quickened, mouth tightened, blinking blankly at the still, dark waters. The sun slipped silently into the inky lake and all around her dusk darkened. She tramped back to the refuge of her room, skipping dinner despite a growling belly.

For the next few uncounted days, Amy did little else than the same triangular pathway between the darkened hotel room, the wooden sun lounger on the beach, and the hotel's dining area. The latter was omitted when she was gripped with nausea or vomiting. But in between the sickness, she had bouts of sharp hunger that she fed with the fish broth, bread and fresh fruits.

One day, whilst watching a boat traverse the lake, a strange notion came to her - she'd become stranded on a desert island. Why else would she sit for hours each passing day peering out across the lake? Simply surviving, conserving energy, awaiting a rescue. *Zan? Why did I ever get involved with someone like him?* She frowned thinking of the drunken times, the rough, brash ends to nights out. *Now I'm on a paradise island, all slender and tanned. And I loathe myself more than ever.* Hunched forward, head hanging - pulling an acute ache through her neck and back - she burst into loud sobs, tears rolling down her cheeks. *I came here to sort my head out. All I've done is make things worse. I've missed the interview for the eco-resort job, I've got men trying to bundle me, I've racked up debts on Mum's emergency credit card, I've nearly run out of cash.*

Amy had started to note how the dusk differed every day, but for the ritual blue-tailed magpies hopping along the shoreline. At least twice, the glorious golden, pink-curdling display of her first sunset on Playa Domingo had played out again. But there had been more dusks that rolled into darkening grey skies torn with a streak or two of golden sunlight. Pink residues, from beyond the horizon, cast out on to clouds mirrored across the lake surface. Amy would watch the inky grey-blue clouds slowly roll over from landward towards the waning sun, as if to follow their sun god retreating from the dark. One evening, Amy had felt stranded on the lounger. Elbow and knee joints aching, hips and ribs pressed hard against the wood. The nausea had returned. She shut her eyes and just breathed, exhausted from her racing mind. When consciousness returned to her, roused by a mosquito nibbling her ankle, she was cloaked in darkness. Clouds had parted above, opening a bluey night sky blathered in tiny crystal stars. She'd felt as though she was the size of an ant, lost on the huge planet - a million miles from home - a home that was out there, beyond the stars, a tranquil place of peace.

She'd imagined it a place where her Dad was. Where he'd greet her with his warm smile and embrace her so tightly, she'd feel he'd crush her bones. He'd tell her everything was ok. She'd be safe and he'd take her home.

"Dad, can you hear me?" she'd cried. "Help me. I need you. I'm lost Dad."

At least six sunsets had passed by before she met another person other than the humble couple running the hotel who only approached her once she was seated in the dining area. It was a typically hot, still afternoon. Amy was digging her toes into the cooling sand and listlessly dragging ruts, daydreaming at the dried grasses that chirped with cicadas being stalked by tiny birds flitting in and out as fast as bats.

"I'm a guide for Ometepe Island. Have you climbed either volcano yet?" a voice had sliced into her solitude. Amy turned and blinked at a young man.

"Volcano?" she asked, repeating the word she'd best understood. He smiled at her with even teeth that, from behind his soft brown skin, appeared to glow bright white. He struck Amy as being as natural and innately part of the surroundings as were the busy birds. Something about his soft, large eyes made Amy feel comfortable to gaze into them as he described hiking the volcanoes and trips to lagoons and waterfalls. "How old are you?" Amy asked, changing the subject.

"Twenty-two," he smiled shyly as Amy raised her eyebrows and watched his face to detect hints of lying.

"My name is Amy," she smiled back.

"Diego." Despite his boyish looks, slight build and casual clothes, Amy found herself captivated by his majestic zeal. It was as if a charm of innocence exuded from his smile. Amy realised, just then, how much better she was feeling.

"Ok. I am very interested, perhaps Maderas? But, when?" she said spontaneously.

"Tomorrow I will work, but the day after tomorrow I can come, early," Diego replied triumphantly, adding "and don't forget, if you have a group the charge is divided, so cheaper for you."

That evening, as Amy watched the simmering sunset, she fantasised about Diego sitting beside her, together gazing at the big, glowing, egg-yolk sun slipping into the lake, and she realised how truly lonely she always was. Not just on that beach, but everywhere. Being a student for so long, being part of a pack, and that being over, it had left her floating. But being on Santo Domingo beach for those days and nights, almost alone, in the stillness, the peace, the relaxation, the solitude, the nature - it all felt so real, so normal, so beautiful. The memories that had re-ran through her mind over the days now seemed bizarre. Those memories seemed as if they were of someone else, perhaps a sister or friend she once had. They had become past tense. And whatever happened next would be new, a future detached from those memories, those mistakes. Amy fell asleep that night imagining hiking the volcanoes, being back in the cool forests like when in Monte Verde - cloud forests, buzzing with earth and leaves, and birds and insects. Amy looked forward to topping up her soul on that feeling of pure, oxygenated life.

Soles to the sky

The pickup rumbled up the steep, rugged track delivering Amy to *La finca Magdalena*. La finca means farm in Spanish, yet the brimming bushes and neatly pruned fruit trees inside white, picket fencing failed Amy's expectations of a farm. Where were the roaring tractors, livestock roaming fields and farmyard smells? Instead of muddy earth the yard was pleasantly carpeted with grass.

"The main crop here is coffee; grown in the shade," the driver informed with a nod over towards the trees, as he hauled her case off the pickup. "We also grow plantains, rice, beans and many vegetables." Amy gawped up at the huge, old, timber-framed farmhouse. It had three stories - a ground level obscured by trees, a middle story edged with a deep veranda under the wide eaves of the massive tiled roof, and a smaller upper level within the apex roof space. Amy wondered if she'd be expected to work on the farm, but on reaching the top of the external steps she was greeted with the sight of the long veranda, clearly arranged for guests. Sitting quietly amongst the stretch of tables and benches, a couple of distinctively non-locals wearing walking boots were pouring over maps.

"The kitchen is here," the driver indicated, "washing facilities at the other end." Amy would have nodded but was halted by the view. La finca, nestled upon the base of Volcano Maderas' tumbling slope, was significantly higher than the land below. Its long stretch of veranda faced out over the sprawling lakeshore. Amy breathed in the view of fields and woodland cascading towards the lake - a mass of leaves and grasses, huge ferns, flowering hibiscus bushes and fruiting trees. Looming to the far left, on the other island, was Volcano Concepcion, its perfectly symmetrical cone rose skyward, ominous and dark, almost a silhouette. Momentarily, Amy became transfixed by its enormity and struck by its unfathomable magnitude of power - a silent vessel of destruction. Half-way up, the trees and vegetation thinned out leaving the top bare, rocky and striped with lava-flow carvings. Below, the village of Balgue was completely obscured by trees so that the landscape was without buildings, roads or other signs of human settlement.

"It's like the garden of Eden," Amy whispered to herself. A rush of relief washed over her as she realised she'd reached somewhere she had been searching for. Here was a place to be restored - a stoic, humble, working place designed to nurture a weary soul. She was shown around the available accommodation that ranged from hammocks on the veranda, camp beds in shared dormitories to private rooms. She opted for a small dormitory with two other women. Rustic and smelling of dust, the bare, wooden room was dim from the low eaves overhanging the little window. But despite the spartan décor, the building's solid beams and naked rafters exuded a humble fortitude.

Later that afternoon, after wallowing in the nostalgia of simple, rural life, Amy wandered back down the farm track to the little village of Balgue, urged on by a longing for the lakeshore. She found a huddle of wooden shack-like homes with their murmurings of families in back yards. A couple of passers-by carrying machetes and hoes habitually greeted her. A flock of hens behind a building squabbled over grain, but not a single vehicle. Amy came to a small stretch of beach and walked barefooted into the shallow water. A large tree overhung the lake creating a cavernous, shady boundary before the sprawling woodland. Its gnarled roots snaked over and into the sand. *It feels good to be well again,* Amy smiled, *and a stranger again.*

On her way back to the farm track she wandered into the little shop and browsed its stock of essentials - sacks of rice, sugar, flours, grains and plastic tubs and bowls. The shopkeeper seemed a confident, busy type of woman and stood at her counter tearing large sheets of brown paper with which she deftly wrapped up scoops of dried beans.

"Are you going to the fiesta tonight?" she asked.

"Fiesta?" smiled Amy.

"The crowning of the queen," the shopkeeper grinned, "a little girl is chosen as the queen of Ometepe."

"A queen girl?" Amy replied.

"It is a procession to honour the Saint of Alta Gracia, San Diego. This is a tradition of nearly four hundred years."

"Four hundred years!" Amy exclaimed, approaching the

friendly lady, "I went to a bull riding fiesta in Guanacaste Costa Rica."

"Guanacaste is cowboy country," she smiled, "here, Ometepians have many fiestas that are very old traditions. Have you heard of the Baile de los zompopos?" It was established, after working at it with her dictionary, that the shopkeeper was saying 'the dance of the leaf-cutter ants'. "But the celebration, where we dance like ants holding branches, is much older. Very long time before - from the indigenous people - the Nahoas, the Chorotegas - many tribes that came to Ometepe. The dance is a celebration of the island's victory over a voracious tribe of ants." The shopkeeper scolded a toddler, who'd wandered in from her private quarters in the depths of her shop, and Amy experienced that same vague, dreamy jealously she'd had when first moving into Alba's house. A yearning envy of living in such purposeful simplicity, rooted securely in traditions and ancestral knowledge. Amy felt, again, like a lonely seed caught up in a modern wind being blown around. The only traditions that sprung to mind were harvest suppers and Morris dancing. She envisaged the ancient tribes of Britain roaming the world pillaging, colonising and taking slaves, setting pathways for poverty and corruption, and raised her eyebrows to her own thoughts.

"Maderas. I want to go," Amy stated, indicating walking uphill with two fingers, "It is easy?" The shopkeeper stopped cutting and wrapping papers and fixed Amy in the eyes.

"You can get lost or stuck up there," she warned. "Understand. This island is sacred land. Our ancestors were careful to respect the gods of the volcanoes. And we too should respect the volcanoes and the power of the nature. It is big, and powerful, and we are like the zompopos." The two women smiled at each other, but the shop keeper's eyes held their stern expression. Amy bought some bread and bananas, bid farewell, and started the ascent back to the farm, daydreaming a life for herself in Balgue - honest, simple, and attuned to nature.

"Welcome to La finca," whispered a voice in English as Amy entered her little dormitory. The room was pungent with scents of lavender and Neroli essential oil. A young woman, with a flushed face and damp, combed-back hair, sat crossed-legged, inhaling and exhaling deeply. Only a faint sweeping sound and creaking floorboards from within the great belly of the farmhouse broke the stillness, whilst outside the indefatigable rooster pierced the hushed hillside with his crowing. The pallid light of dusk cast shadows over the wooden floorboards that were overlaid with roll mats.

"My name is Luka, you are Amy I think," the woman said with a smile. Amy nodded and watched Luka light a few candles at the edges of the floor space, before returning to sit on the matting. Then another young woman quietly entered the room, nodded at Amy and sat opposite Luka with the same straight-backed pose and started to breathe deeply. "This is Yana from Bulgaria, who has the other bed over there," Luka said. "Join with us for yoga". And so, with Luka leading the positions, Amy joined in making each pose. "This shape should be like triangle," Luka explained, running her finger down Yana's bended profile. "This is one of my favourite stretches - we need a wall," Luka said, placing her hand on Yana's back and bending her forward to demonstrate. "We are a right-angle - hands pushing on to a wall - feet pushing onto floor and to pull out from here," Luka explained, pulling an imaginary cord from Yana's coccyx. Then it was Amy's turn - back lengthening as she pushed her hands into the wall, stomach shrinking up as the backs of her legs pulled taught. Concentrated - steady breathing - tension in the right angle. "Look, her shoulders are perfect. The strength is pushing here into the wall," Luka coached, placing her hand upon Amy's locked shoulder blades, "and then pulling in the opposing direction." She ran her finger down Amy's spine and stopped at her coccyx, making the skin on Amy's back contract and her scalp tingle. Breathing deeply through the strain, tasting the warm candle wax and dust, Amy quivered in the stretch. "You have very beautiful shoulders," Luka said running one finger over the fleshy bulge of Amy's shoulder, "and the neck is soft and relaxed," she elaborated, gently squeezing Amy's neck.

Feeling a degree suppler, and mildly fatigued, Amy took an invigoratingly cold shower, dressed in long sleeves, and headed for the veranda.

"I've been here for nearly eight weeks now," Luka said as she joined Amy at the balcony "and this is why I can't leave."

"Such a beautiful view," Amy smiled, as they both looked out over the warm, orange-glowing setting sky, beyond the lake.

"At La Magdalena we can step off the rotating planet and really see nature's beauty - people living in harmony - far away from all the nonsense of the city."

"I can see the attraction here. It really does feel like I've left all my problems behind," Amy replied, filling her lungs deeply with the atmospheric dusk air riddled with exotic bird calls. A day drawing to its interlude soothed by rhythmic cicadas and the aroma of melting citronella candles.

"Everyone always speaks of their problems here," Luka started to philosophise, "I mean us travellers. We come from a land of problems, apparently. But we are the rich ones. How do you explain that?"

"I guess money doesn't solve problems," Amy responded.

"It is our loss of connection with the universe - our spiritual connection. The universe provides everything we need, but we turn from it. We are distracted or greedy or selfish, not thinking of other ones. This waste of energy creates the conflicts and restrictions upon our lives. If we lived in harmony with the nature, our self and each other, we would not realise any of these problems that we perceive to be real," Luka avidly preached. Amy nodded; guessing Luka's subtle accent was German or Scandinavian.

"So how do you live in harmony with nature then? Walk everywhere? Forage for wild food, sleep under the stars?" Amy asked with intrigue, and then was momentarily taken aback when Luka laughed out loud in response.

"You can do all of that, if that feeds you. But it is finding and knowing what *feeds* your soul. We are all different. And we feed from different things. Meditation is my soul food, but for someone else it could be fishing or dancing or singing or teaching or working of the land with his or her hands. We need a connection to environment around you, and for that environment to be natural," Luka explained as Amy nodded in polite interest. "What feeds your soul Amy?"

"Good question." Amy smiled back at her interesting new room-share, wondering what verbs she could conjure up in response to this.

'Cock-arico-oooooooooh,' a rooster cried, penetrating Amy's soon-forgotten dream.

"Senorita. Senorita." A voice filtered into Amy's hearing, followed by a squeeze of her arm. Amy opened her eyes to the dark and her stomach growled deeply. One of the kitchen women was stood over her, beckoning her towards the door. She dressed quickly and quietly as

Luka and Yana breathed in rhythmic slumber.

"Buenas Dias!" a voice greeted Amy on the veranda.

"Diego!" Amy rubbed sleep from her eyes and smiled.

"Forgive me for not returning," he said with twinkling eyes. The kitchen woman who'd woken Amy stood and watched with mild amusement.

"No! I am very sorry for no volcano with you," Amy blushed, her mind searching for words of excuses for his kind almond eyes.

"Please understand - I couldn't come at the weekend. The weather was no good to climb Maderas. When I arrived at Santo Domingo, they told me they had sent you here."

"It was very nice at Santo Domingo but too expensive to stay much longer," Amy explained.

"Well, today is good - the sun will be shining and not too much cloud," Diego beamed. "You feel better now?"

"Yes. Better now. Before, I don't know - illness."

"We climb Maderas today?" he asked finally.

"Ok. We go," Amy smiled, with a spark of adventurous excitement.

"Will you eat breakfast?" the kitchen woman asked, as she'd been waiting. Amy looked at Diego for permission.

"It's best to eat a good breakfast before we go - to have lots of energy," he replied.

"Ok. Yes. I eat typical Nicaraguan plate please, and juice - and the same for Diego also?" Amy asked the cook, to which Diego tried to decline.

"But to have a good breakfast - to have lots of energy," Amy said with a smile.

Within half an hour they'd set off uphill through the back of the farmyard, after each eating a plate of eggs, gallo pinto with toast, and fresh orange juice. The air smelt of rain on rocks. The sky was clouding over.

"Don't worry, I know this volcano," Diego said, his voice tinged with pride. "It is only dangerous if a storm comes. I don't think today will have bad weather. And if we are surprised and a storm surrounds us, I know where is safe and where not to attempt to pass. The people at the farm know exactly the route I use, so we cannot get lost." he reassured. Tramping their way up the gentle slope, Amy watched the farmland trees and shrubs merge into a rambling scrubland dotted with ferns. Up ahead was a mound of forest rising into the sky, and Amy imagined they were little insects crawling on the feet of a giant.

"That tree, the taller, that is the 'little grape' tree. It's called Ometepensis and is only found right here," Diego explained pointing at spangling, jaunty branches, "and the bird you can hear is the yellow nape parrot."

"So where is the coffee?" Amy asked, to which he smiled broadly.

"All here," he exclaimed. "Look!! These are coffee plants." In the undergrowth, bushes with leaves resembling laurel, about a meter in height, were dotted all around. From their branches hung olive-sized berries, deep green or turning red.

"Coffee grows as berries," Amy whispered, fondling some of the firm fruits. Up ahead, screeches and squawks echoed through the trees signalling daybreak. Diego beckoned her into the undergrowth, peering like a jungle explorer.

"Banana rojo!" he exclaimed, bounding into a small clearing where a leafy tree stood. It was about seven feet tall, with luscious leaves a couple feet wide, each growing upwards and out in elegant curves. Amy found its trunk felt spongy instead of woody to touch and remembered someone telling her once that bananas grew on plants, not trees. She thought back to the banana plantation she'd seen from the window of the pickup on the way to Santo Domingo; how the plants had looked like palm trees with tufts of fronds at the top and blue plastic bags around their fruits. On this lone, wild banana plant, grew tight bunches of tiny reddish-brown bananas, in a circular fashion. They were suspended just above head height, like hands, palm-up, with chunky little fingers. But most intriguing to Amy was the stem on which these bunches were hung, or more precisely, the flower and strange pod weighing down the end of it. Seemingly rather disproportionate in size, this pod looked like a large, elongated acorn protruding out of large, vivid flower petals curled back like a pair of big, red lips. Diego snapped off a little line of fruits from the bunch and passed Amy a couple of mini bananas still wearing little tufts of fibres at their tips. Despite the reddish-brown skin, the fruit inside was pale yellow and had a mellow sweetness and firm, meaty texture, unlike any banana Amy had ever tasted before.

As they trudged further up Maderas' slope, the forest became denser and its canopy shielded from the sun. The air felt refreshingly cooler, and the leaf-diffused light was soft upon the eyes. Amy's skin prickled and tingled as if engulfed by a vibrating energy. The plethora of trees muffled birdcalls and distorted their whereabouts. In the total anonymity amongst the towering trees, she felt, suddenly, she was on an auspicious, privileged trip. It took over three hours to reach the forested summit. The loose stones made progress slow and they frequently stopped to swig water and wipe sweat from their brows. The humidity steadily rose as the concealed sun climbed higher by the hour.

"How is the lake, here, in the top of the volcano?" Amy asked, intrigued by the murky green crater lagoon. It was a lot larger than she had imagined.

"When Maderas erupted, the top exploded." Diego flung his arms up in depiction as he proceeded to descend into the steep-sided crater, "and after the crater is here, so the mud forms and the water collects in there."

"When it erupted?" she asked, following Diego down the steep crater's edge, trying to imagine the magnitude of such a blast that would take the top off a mountain as if it were a soft-boiled egg ready for toast soldiers.

"Many thousands of years before," Diego shrugged, "the lake has always been here." They crouched at the water's edge, gazing into the stagnant pool.

"You want to swim?" he asked with a grin, to which Amy scrunched up her nose. "The bottom is mud, and underneath, I don't know - volcano belly," he said dreamily, gazing in a longing sort of way as if he believed there to be a secret door into an underworld at the bottom of the lake.

"Wow, very big!" Amy exclaimed pointing at some absurdly large tadpoles, over two centimetres wide, their eyes clearly visible. "Why, how do the frogs live here?" she asked, imagining ascending frogs.

"People say that the frogs were transported by storms, so the winds blow them up to the top of Maderas," he explained.

"Maybe they climb like us?" she replied starting them off laughing again.

"Come. I know a very beautiful spot we can sit," Diego said leading her up into the forest to a huge boulder that stretched out flat, the size of a king-sized bed. Sat side by side in the luxury of tree shade, they sipped bottles of tepid water and gazed out over the lagoon that now had a mysterious curtain of mist obscuring its furthest edge. There was something moving amongst the reeds in the edges of the mist. After a while a brown duck with a pink beak emerged and plopped into the water, followed hastily by her brood of ten little, fluffy ducklings.

"They say there are fairies and spirits up here," Diego said as they watched the little duck family floating on their private mountain top pond. Feeling a tickling sensation upon her forearm, Amy turned to see Diego's face up close, peering at the arm he was stroking gently with one finger.

"You're so hairy," he said without a hint of disgust or intended insult, to which Amy smiled without finding any words to answer him. "I've never seen hairs like that. They just stretched out!" Amy watched his amusement at her forearm hair and noticed his lack of arm hair, or even leg hair. She felt transformed back to a child. The tickly, tingling sensation travelled up her arm, across her shoulders, continuing up her neck and spread over her scalp. Their eyes met and grinned at one another, engaging in their private conversations. A strong memory of gaiety and innocence washed over Amy, as she'd felt as a teenager - when she was young and free-minded, attracting friendship and fun. The surging feeling was of love. A true love. The love of life. As a child.

Amy looked out over the lagoon. The ducks were gone, and the mist had cleared. The water shone under the radiant sun, gleaming like polished jade. Diego allowed his eyes to study her - her hairline, her nose, her earlobes, the shape of her lips, and then, her upper lip hairs. She studied him back, trying to detect any facial hairs, wondering his real age. He looked young to Amy yet not immature as his eyes held a candid responsibility. Amy suddenly felt the urge to be hugged. To be loved and cared for. To be kissed on the cheeks and neck in that playful, tickling way a loving parent smothers their child.

"You are very beautiful," Diego said sincerely. Amy just waited. "Don't you have a husband?" he asked, to which Amy shook her head giggling. "A boyfriend?" Again, she shook her head. "No children?" he asked.

"No children. Nothing," Amy replied, feeling indifferent at this status.

"You need husband and children," he stated kindly.

"Maybe. One day. After," she replied, not really believing in such a day.

"After? You study?" he asked. Amy nodded vaguely and looked back to the lagoon.

"And you? Do you have a wife and children?" Amy asked, trying to ignore the fact that he looked too young for either.

"I would like a wife and children one day too. I need a lovely girl. Like you. I will be a very good husband. I respect women. My grandmother is a very wise lady, very kind-hearted. She always teaches me how to be kind to women," he answered sincerely. Amy watched his fingers fiddling, busily stripping a tough blade of grass. "You are so lovely, so beautiful," he said again.

"No. I am not lovely. Me, I'm not good," she blurted out, concerned for his blunder. She peered hard at the lagoon, running her tongue along her teeth and making her jaw stick out at angles, wondering if he'd find that beautiful or not. But he was gazing at the lagoon as well. Then Amy became aware that the mist was moving, forming from above or off the water's surface she couldn't tell. It gave the lake an air of mystery and deception. She just watched and breathed.

"Do you have parents?" he asked after over a minute's silence.

"Yes, my mother. My father is dead," she replied without averting her gaze.

"Your mother is alone?" he asked.

"She has boyfriend - a man. Me, I don't like the man much," she gestured a sort of collision of fingertips on opposing hands.

"Argue?" Diego suggested the word.

"Yes. He - very different - my father different," she explained with a doleful face.

"This man. Is he kind to your Mother?" he continued.

"I don't know," she replied casually, "I think yes."

"My mother, God bless her, is a very strong woman. She even travelled to fight in support of the Sandinistas and political movements for women's rights. But sometimes I wish my mother had a new husband," he said wistfully. Amy cast him a quick glance.

"Why a new husband?" she asked.

"Because after my father died, I have always helped my mother to look after my three younger brothers. I want to go to the city, study to be a doctor or a scientist. I don't want to work in the fields all my life, like my father before the war. I want to work and study, but I must help my mother and my brothers," he said resignedly. A day-dreamed image struck Amy - Rosie's overflowing happiness in love, her newly found freedom in finally having raised her own children. Amy realised that her mum was starting a new chapter in her life, the one after struggling as a single parent, mourning her husband's death.

"Maybe your mother also have next husband, one day," she suggested, but Diego shook his head slowly.

"My mother is too old for more children now, and my father didn't have much land or money, so another man is not very interested in my mother for a new wife. If she had a hacienda and land, perhaps she could remarry," he replied, "but even then, she is still married to the photograph of my father. He is a hero of the war." As Amy looked at Diego, who was peering up to the canopy, Zan popped into her mind. *He must be in the same situation as Diego. Trapped, supporting the family home, his mother and younger sister.* She thought back to the times when Zan's mother seemed to be arguing with him, how Amy had perceived it was about money.

"Did you come to Nicaragua in an airplane?" Diego asked pointing earnestly skyward, to which Amy nodded. "Tell me Amy. What is it like flying so high up in the sky?" Amy looked up at the blue through a space in the canopy and imagined returning to England.

"I am scared, a little. The airplane moves very fast. The people sit very close, together," she started to describe, then thought of the cramped local buses. "Well, one chair for one person - the land, is very, very long and down."

"Oh no!" Diego exclaimed, shaking his head, "that is not natural."

"The houses are very, very tiny." Amy put a finger and thumb to a few millimetres apart, grinning at his revulsion.

"I think I will die on an airplane," Diego said.

"But the airplane take me here," she added.

"Why are you here?" Diego asked sincerely.

"I don't know." She started to avert her gaze from him but

stopped. "Before, in England, I study in university, live in London, work in a hotel and study. London is crazy, I have problems. Life is crazy. I think, I go to a beautiful country. Look at nature, the sea, the volcanoes, the beautiful, the people. And, I learn, speaking Spanish, I live and work, next to the beach." Diego's face was one of awe as he savoured the fantasy of studying and working.

"Why was London so crazy? You are very beautiful, and you are intelligent. I don't understand," Diego asked absorbed by her story. She drew a deep breath and then slowly funnelled it out of a corner of her mouth.

"Diego. Before, I am very stupid. I no see," she started to try to explain.

"No. You have been in a lot of education. You can work in good job and earn a lot of money to fly on an airplane. You are not stupid Amy," Diego corrected her with insisting eyebrows. She was momentarily dumbfounded by this stranger who seemed to better know her life than she did. She looked out to the patch of blue sky imagining herself up there in an airplane, perhaps passing her dad floating by on a cloud smoking his Embassy number 1.

"OK. I explain you well. I make problem for me. I no can find good man. No boyfriend, for only one night, after, a different man," Amy told him, pausing to downturn the corners of her mouth, "I am not happy."

"Oh. I understand. You were a prostitute," Diego concluded.

"No!" Amy quickly corrected him.

"I don't understand," Diego exclaimed, swivelling his hips so his whole body faced Amy, "Why you intelligent girl from England cannot find a good man?"

"My head. Sometimes no function," Amy replied, losing her will to concentrate on speaking Spanish. Diego stared at her intently, his head cocked to one side, his eyes flicking over her face, reading, extracting.

"No function? You were having drugs?" he surmised. Instantly Amy dropped her gaze back to the lagoon and slouched her shoulders.

"Drugs, alcohol," she admitted to the patiently blinking Diego.

"I have a lot of friends who have moved to Managua and other cities to study or work. They get addicted very easily - drink too much alcohol, drugs like cocaine and smoking marijuana. Then their lives

133

become so complicated. They have difficulties with relationships, with their family and girlfriends," he said looking a little perplexed.

"Yes, like that."

"And that it why you are sad - because you have boyfriends who are addicted also - you cannot find love when you are addicted Amy," he said without a hint of pride at his astute detective work. Amy turned and stared at him.

"But now I stop. No more alcohol. No more drugs for me," she heard herself say. He broke into a smile.

"By the grace of God," Diego preached. "My grandmother tells me that a good woman for a wife is a woman that respects herself. Then she will respect her husband." Amy smiled back, wishing she had a grandmother like his, and then remembered with a jolt that she had two. *They're probably both thinking of me right now. Without even a postcard yet.*

"I know a very good view. You can see right over Ometepe," Diego said standing and outstretching his hand to help pull her up. They set off into the forest and walked in silence for a while. "Here. We must climb up into this tree," Diego said finally, crouched below a large horizontally-growing branch, signing for Amy to stand on his shoulders. After they'd scrambled up a couple of meters and wedged their feet securely in a twist of the trunk, Diego pulled aside a leafy branch tip to reveal the bright sunlight and blue sky.

"We're so up!" Amy gasped when seeing the aerial view stretched out below. The whole of the island, accept of course the rear of Maderas, lay before them like a map, showing vegetation and hills.

"Can you see Santo Domingo, and then Concepcion after?" Diego twinkled proudly. "No tourists know this tree. The view is very high, no?"

"Like in an airplane," Amy whispered which made Diego's eyes glisten. As she looked at the stunningly clear view, she felt a deluge of adoration for her life. Fortune and privilege felt heavy upon her chest, almost too heavy to breathe. Her perceived dilemmas suddenly seemed so insignificant. *I'm so lucky,* Amy realised as tears welled in her eyes.

They descended in near silence, comforted by coolness and green hues. Amy imagined the great tangle of tree roots intertwined beneath the earth, wondering if the gentle giants ever shared hidden affection with one another, stretching their roots to touch and embrace. Perhaps others jostled for space, or jealous friends wrenched at their foes' roots. She could almost hear the colossal volume of water circulating through their woody tracts and up to their leaves. The creak of a tree trunk, a crack of a branch, and the rustle of leaves aloft - all felt so mystical.

"There are ancient spirits in here, who whisper their prayers to the volcano gods. These spirits still seek sacrifices to please the gods," Diego whispered without hint of jest, "that's what people say."

"But Maderas is dead, no?" Amy replied.

"But the spirits still need sacrifices." Diego smiled in way that Amy couldn't decipher as serious or not. As they slipped and slid their way down the steep, rocky pathways mostly crouching so their bottoms pressed against their heels, Amy tried to imagine ancient tribal spirits remaining loyal to their volcano gods around them. Then Diego detoured into dense jungle and swung back into view on his bonus tour-guide feature - an authentic Tarzan woody vine. By the time they bounded down the easing slope, they were singing, at the top of their voices, the *rojo banana* song.

****

Amy picked her bare feet between the hard, but slimy-smooth lumps protruding from the sand of the shallow water, whilst casually mulling over the potential size of the lake's freshwater sharks. It was the morning after climbing Maderas with Diego and her limbs were aching. Still brimming with joy from the precious moments shared with Diego - the aerial view, magical misty lagoon, the Tarzan vine, the red-banana song, all of it, she was at Balgue's small strip of beach, nestled between mangrove trees that dipped their roots into the lake and buried them beneath the sand. Feeling a presence, she turned to discover a gaggle of shy-looking children aged between about six and twelve. They giggled as they watched what Amy would do next.

"Here. It is good for to swim?" she politely asked, pointing towards the water she was ankle deep in. This only made the older boys giggle even more. "This," she pointed into the water, "from trees?" The eldest, or the tallest anyway, stepped forward and peered at the water.

"Yes. Roots from the trees," he confirmed and then explained, as far as she could gather, that a little further out into the lake, the roots ceased to be a problem.

"You can to swim with me?" she asked, feeling like a child herself. At the eldest boy's command, the children stripped off to their underpants, or rolled up trousers, and enthusiastically ran into the water with a great amount of splashing and shouting. Amy watched, a little flummoxed, as the roots didn't seem to impair the kids' entry into the lake one bit. Amy followed on, careful to tread around the knotty protrusions amongst the sand. As she started to bend and waver into strange postures, the eldest boy took hold of her hand to steady her, until eventually, with the water up to her knees, she lurched forward into a breaststroke. The water was instantly and intensely invigorating. Her hair billowed around her like blanket weed. Some of the boys had already started a game - throwing and catching a small branch - whilst others dipped and dived like little ducks.

Amy drifted a few meters away from them and enjoyed bathing simultaneously in water and sunshine, whilst gazing at the woodland along the lakeshore. The lack of tourists, the absence of any signs of modern life, the simplicity, being a human minority in nature majority made her feel humbled, alive, awakened. Glancing over at the boys she thought how the eldest had referred to her as mujera, meaning woman. *Of course, I am a woman to them,* she thought with a touch of regret. The clouds appeared to be so high and randomly stretched across the sky, as if chasing each other to faraway lands. A bird shrieked in the mangrove, followed by a flapping and squawking of one chasing another out of his territory. Then silence fell, and the sound of her own breathing became the predominant sound. Amy drifted into a semi-dozing state. Her father again casually drifted into her thoughts.

"I'm sorry Dad for being such a bad daughter. I know you would hate what I've been doing. I hate what I've been doing. I've been a mess, a shameful mess," she said up to the looming Maderas. "I'm sorry to you Zan, for breaking your heart, for the trouble I've caused in your home and village and humiliating you. Everyone told you that I'd take off and leave you and they were right." She gazed up at Maderas' hulk, sat huge and squat like a giant woman's back, feeling so small and timid and ashamed of herself. With the sun blazing down upon her head and the children's squeals in the background, the world around her suddenly seemed to draw in close. It felt as if trees, water and earth were all as much a part of her as her own breath and heartbeat. As if anything she did or thought or said would be known, felt, judged or witnessed. She lay in the water as if suspended in a hammock with her toes peeking out in front of her. *This is believing. This feeling that I'm being watched, listened to. Saying sorry and pleading for help. Maybe I am doing it,* she thought. Alvero popped into her mind with a strange longing sentiment. *What did he ask me to pray for?*

"God," she whispered up at Maderas, "My friend Alvero. He's a good kind man. He helped me a lot. Please help him to find his children one day; to find peace with himself. Oh yes! Please forgive him for whatever he did." Those last words echoed in her mind, as she blinked slowly, breathing heavily. "To find peace within myself and be forgiven for all the bad things I've done," she added with an emotion she didn't recognise - a sort of hope or desire but with more determination. "God. Thank you for keeping me safe, for all the beauty around me, the food I eat every day. For the people who have helped me, for this moment here. Please forgive me and free me from my bad wa…"

Suddenly her shoulders were abruptly jerked back, and her entire head dunked under the water for a couple of seconds. As soon as she felt the pressure release from her shoulders, she reversed the sinking motion upwards with a peddling of her arms, broke the surface again, gasping a breath of air. She turned to see the children laughing aloud.

"Did you think it was a shark?" a giggling boy asked as the eldest boy scolded him from a few meters away. Amy waved with a mild smile, spitting out water. After coughing a little she started to giggle to herself. And, to the children's delight and surprise, she ducked under the water and stealthily swam over to the nearest legs she could find making a grab at them. Soon after, a handstand competition was initiated. Amy joined in by copying the children swim down and cling to the roots with their hands, whilst sticking their feet above the surface, soles to the sky. The raucous laughter from the children told Amy that even her best underwater handstands were hopelessly far from vertical. After the game had gone on for quite some time, as Amy was determined to reach a vertical hold, a yelling from the shore interrupted them. Immediately, the children swam towards the man at the shore. Amy followed, and as she did, it dawned on her that she'd lured the children into the lake without so much as questioning any of their abilities to swim, nor even thinking to check with parents. *In fact,* she thought *I don't even know how many kids came in the water with me.*

"Thank you," she shouted as the children scampered off up the beach to find their clothes, to which the man waved back in a friendly manner.

Waterfall fall out

"Good evening ladies," a man said in English. Amy turned and looked into those alluring green eyes from the boat. "We meet again," he said to Amy, "I'm Yarron."

"Hi. I'm Amy," she replied, willing herself not to gawp at his eyes.

"And this is Gabriel." Yarron introduced a local looking boy stood next to him.

"Good evening," Gabriel said in English, setting down his display board against a bench on La finca's veranda. Gabriel exuded a soft, warm energy that swept over Amy and Luka like a gentle breeze, as he gave both an eye-twinkling, friendly handshake. He had quite a collection of handmade jewellery on his board - all unique he insisted. Polished gem-stone pendants, rings, brooches, necklaces, bracelets and even cord belts. All had his bold, simple, striking style. Amy instantly liked Gabriel. His lack of desire for words attracted her, as did watching the dimples in his chubby cheeks that gave him a childlike innocence.

"Who has heard of San Ramon waterfall?" Yarron asked sipping his beer.

"Perhaps a good connection with natural environment?" Luka smiled to Amy.

"Hiking, forests, fresh volcanic water to cleanse the body and mind," Yarron said.

"Sounds amazing. Has anyone climbed Maderas?" Amy enthused, "I went up with a guide, a local boy. It was amazing, and I really want to climb Concepcion too, if anyone wants to form a group, I could contact the same guide and -" but Yarron cut her words.

"You don't need a guide to climb the volcano," he disapproved, "they say that because they want your money, and perhaps for some unfit people - then maybe ok - it is good. You don't need that. Of course, the local boys are going to ask you to climb with them." Amy squinted at him for a few seconds. Yarron shrugged as if speaking a common knowledge.

"But a few people have said the same thing to me - it is best to take a guide just in case," Amy tried to challenge. Gabriel was fiddling with a stubborn bracelet, oblivious to English language.

"Look, if you want to *get it on* with a local guide, that's up to you," Yarron answered smirking with raised palms.

"I'm not trying to *get it on* with any guides, or locals, or anyone, actually. If I was, I wouldn't invite you guys along too would I?" Amy defended with a rising irritation. Luka smiled wanly at Amy.

"I'll take you, us all, up Maderas," Yarron promised into his beer bottle.

"I've got no problem paying a local guide. They should profit from us being here. It's their home, and we are visiting. They have local knowledge," Amy continued, cocking her head like a ruffled parrot.

"Oh please," Yarron exclaimed, "you're not so gullible, are you? If a local guy proposes to be your guide, or your friend, he's hitting on you. I'll guarantee it." Amy couldn't place where Yarron's blended accents were from, but she could hear his English had been learn in the United States. A young man joined them with two bottles of beer. He gave one to Yarron.

"This is Guy, my friend who travels with me." Yarron introduced his quiet friend who held up his hand in greeting. "Anyway, the waterfall - the freshwater is good to drink, people stand under the drop so bring your bathers," Yarron was instructing, "the public transport is not so reliable, so as we want to hike before midday heat, we need to set out early - six o'clock, okay?"

"Six in the morning," Amy said in Spanish to Gabriel who clearly didn't follow English conversation.

"Tomorrow morning?" Gabriel asked.

"Yes."

"Ok. Are you coming?" he asked quietly as Yarron's voice continued explaining the itinerary. Amy shrugged a little and asked:

"Are you?"

"If you do. I think he is like a boss," Gabriel said nodding towards Yarron, making them both laugh.

The next morning Yarron paced the veranda, his walking boots clumping heavily. Guy sat daydreaming at empty plates and coffee cups when Amy strolled out on the veranda. It was half past seven.

"Sorry I've kept you waiting," Amy said chirpily, to which Yarron just muttered. Disappointment dropped through Amy's stomach, firstly at Yarron's cool mood, and then the lack of anyone else there. She'd overslept without knowing, and half hoped the party had left already. She'd given Gabriel a fifty-fifty chance. He was rarely seen first thing. Amy swiftly ordered a bottle of water from the kitchen hatch and wrestled it into her miniature backpack, designed for fashion rather than hiking. A few minutes later Gabriel emerged, his buoyant manner veiled by the early hour, followed by the kitchen woman Yarron had summoned to wake him.

"Can we go now," Yarron said flatly and set off down the veranda steps, followed swiftly by Guy. On reaching Balgue they soon learned that they'd missed their bus.

"No problem. A truck will pass soon for sure. We can take a ride," Gabriel tried to reassure a furiously cursing Yarron, who snatched a map from his bag and peered at it.

"We will walk to Santa Cruz, here," Yarron informed them, pointing at his map on where the isthmus joins Maderas' island, "we can catch the Mologalpa bus that passes San Ramon." Yarron and Guy set off at a steady pace, just short of a military march, leaving Amy to lag behind conjuring images of her party leader in army boots and green camo clothes. Gabriel bumbled along like a laborador puppy, shaking early morning midges out of his dreadlocks.

Once at the roadside, Yarron instructed Guy to watch for the expected bus whilst he fumbled with his timetables and maps. Guy did so, munching on nuts from a small paper bag as if viewing a film in the cinema, whilst Amy vaguely pondered the relationship between Yarron and Guy. They didn't look like brothers to her, but their hairlines and beard growth had a similarity. She planned to strike up a conversation with them later, when Yarron had calmed down. A sharp squeaking noise caught Amy's attention, making her cast her eyes around the hedges and verge. Gabriel sucked his front teeth to get her attention, then raised his eyebrows, looking up towards a rustling sound. A few seconds later she saw a prowling Howler monkey saunter along a

141

branch above her. It moved like it was free of any worries, despite a potential fall of over twenty meters, peering around in apparent oblivion to the humans below. She cast a glance at Yarron and Guy, but they had their backs to her, so she carried on watching the beady-eyed little fellow with a huge grin on her face. It was the first time she'd actually seen one of the noisy monkeys she'd become so accustomed to hearing near the language school in Castillo. The minibus rumbled around the corner and the monkey strolled off out of sight. They squeezed in next to tittering school children and elderly women in quiet contemplation, their gazes fixed outside of the windows as if they'd find the answers to lifelong predicaments somewhere along the roadside.

San Ramon biological field station had neatly mown lawns, bordered with tall palms and bushes with variegated leaves, shining as if washed and polished. To Amy's surprise, the entrance fee wiped out almost all of the cash she had brought for the day. She deduced, from the length of time it took Gabriel to liaise his fee, that he too was down to his last córdoba. Gabriel and Amy shared the rather bruised bananas from her rucksack, giggling at a group of tourists in full safari clothing, including knee-high socks and wide-brimmed hats.

"We should top up our water bottles before starting the hike," Yarron advised his group - his first words since La finca.

"Can we get something to eat here?" Amy asked, hoping to engage the group on better terms. But Yarron just frowned at her.

"Tell her, she obviously wasn't listening," he said to Guy, as a commander would.

"Yarron explained that there are no facilities here, so bringing food is essential," Guy said with a slightly embarrassed expression. Amy wasn't sure if she pitied Guy or not.

"Come on, let's go. It takes two hours to reach the cascade," Yarron shouted coolly.

"What is his problem?" Amy blurted to Guy, who sheepishly blinked and followed Yarron. Amy noted how she'd never heard Guy speak before, that he was younger than Yarron, and he was under some obligation to him. *Maybe they are cousins. I wonder what happened to the cousins that dropped me off at Santo Domingo?*

The track to the waterfall was lined with stonewalls, beyond which, lay scrubland of long grasses, coarse bushes, sparsely-growing trees and grazing long-horned cattle. *Nature just living, reproducing and dying, seemingly to its own accord at the fertile feet of Maderas,* thought Amy. She took a photo of the fields that looked to her like a patchwork picture.

"I love Ometepe. It's so beautiful," Amy said to Gabriel but looked around to find she was alone. "Wait! Where's Gabriel?" Amy shouted ahead to Guy and Yarron, fearing Gabriel had bailed out of the grumpy, expensive touristy day. Guy turned and saw her, but they carried on. Amy looked all round her. *He'd been right by my side a minute ago.* "Yarron. Guy," Amy shouted as they disappeared around a corner, Yarron shaking his head in a disapproving way. Squinting under the climbing sun, Amy peered into the surrounding wilderness of tranquillity and beauty, hands shielding her eyes. Facing back along the track they'd just walked, she could see no sign of Gabriel. On the westward horizon the lake sprawled proud over the farmlands, framed by the looping overhead electricity cables on angled posts, and just visible beyond, was main land Nicaragua. Seconds pounded slowly. Suddenly, Gabriel emerged from a hedge giggling like a toddler. He had a load of bumpy objects bundled in his T-shirt, making his tummy appear large and lumpy. He gleefully presented four oranges and two huge avocados. Amy beamed at him with glee. A few seconds later, orange juice was running down their chins. Whether it was their thirst or hunger, or a pleasant relief from the aggrevation of the day so far, they agreed that the orange was the most deliciously sweet orange they'd both ever eaten. Then they shared a creamy avocado, by peeling off the skin and eating it like a banana.

"That is better now, no?" Gabriel said with glint in his eye.

"Delicious," Amy smiled back, with a warm sensation of success in trusting her own instincts again.

After following the direction Yarron and Guy had disappeared in, Gabriel and Amy came to a fork in the road. They followed the arrow of the wooden signpost engraved with a waterfall symbol. Before long the track entered dense jungle with wizened old trees covered in mosses, vines and bromeliads. The air tasted of sweet humidity and wafts of peppery scents. Amy's peripheral vision kept catching sight of the silent, erratic flutter of highlighter yellow butterflies. The further they proceeded into the jungle, the more heightened Amy's hearing sense became. It tuned in to the tropical milieu - sounds of vibrating

143

insects, distant growls of Howler monkeys and squawking parrots. She loved the feeling of being encased in nature, and she imagined it possible to spot a little fairy or wood nymph buzzing round as inconspicuous as a hummingbird. In less than an hour, they began to hear the sound of gushing water and soon after, the forest gave way to a clearing with a powerful, vertical flow of water plummeting down from over a cliff fifty meters above. Beside the waterfall clung vivid green mosses and miniature trees precariously rooted to the wet rockface. The water, falling faster than the eye could follow, slammed on to a piece of jutting rock just before ground level and spraying off at an angle, creating the illusion of a giant taking a shower.

"What do think?" Yarron shouted at Amy and Gabriel in English.

"Wow. It's very long," Amy replied in Spanish.

"It's very high," Gabriel unwittingly corrected Amy's adjective.

"Very high, yes," Amy repeated, noting the Spanish adjective correction with Alvero suddenly springing to mind.

"It's too cold!" Gabriel exclaimed as they waded in to join Yarron and Guy. The sound of tonnes of cascading water drumming on to rock loomed loudly.

"Amy. Please," Yarron said, positioning himself next to her so to face Guy holding a camera, and put his arm around her waist. And so the photo shoot commenced. Amy felt like the meat in a man sandwich. Firstly with Yarron and Guy posing either side of her, and then with Yarron and Gabriel. By the end of it, Amy's lower jaw was trembling uncontrollably, her toes were numb and white, and she knew her lips had turned blue. Glad to get out of the water, Amy put her feet on a rock in direct sunshine hoping to warm up her toes. Yarron joined her. His anxious glances at his wristwatch denoted to Amy that he didn't want to waste any time in setting off. He dried his feet with a little travel towel. "Ok, the plan to climb to the summit of Maderas is for the day after tomorrow," Yarron said to Amy in English, "will you manage to get up in time?"

"You're keen to be a leader, aren't you?" Amy replied, and looked at him. His eyes paused upon her, strikingly feline and bright.

"I like to explore, discover, experience. Not just sit around," he replied.

"Is that your plan? To see everything on Ometepe?" Amy asked, pleased that the ice was broken between them, but wanting an apology.

"Why not?" Yarron shrugged back at her. Amy thought of the bar brothel near Castillo called 'Why not?' and smiled to herself secretly.

"Yarron's a 'go getter'," Guy chipped in, "we've got an itinerary." Amy paused for an elaboration on this comment, but none came. She decided to leave the question of her joining them in the balance, and the group retraced their route back to the field station, this time together.

Back at the San Ramon field station they discovered, to Yarron's rage, they had missed the last bus back to Balgue. Dismay felt more apt, but Yarron's eyes blinked and flashed with an emotion that Amy could only fathom as pride or arrogance.

"This guide book has written there is a later bus," Yarron protested to the impassive ticket seller, whilst Guy and Gabriel sat on a nearby boulder discussing the time of sunset.

"The village of San Ramon has cabinas where you can stay the night," suggested the ticket seller.

"Ok. This way - let's go," Yarron instructed his group coarsely. Down a steep track, rain-washed wooden huts huddled along a small lakeside beach. Yarron went to lengths to negotiate an evening's accommodation with the pushy proprietor.

"I have no money," Gabriel whispered to Amy seriously.

"I have no money too," she replied.

"La finca," he said, gesturing hitchhiking with his thumb.

"Maybe we look somewhere else first, but this is an option," Yarron announced.

"Why don't we try to flag a ride down back to the farm?" Amy suggested.

"That's not a good idea, you could walk all night, with no food or water, and get lost," Yarron frowned and glared his eyes disapprovingly. *Such a waste of such beautiful eyes,* Amy thought.

"No, it is too risky," the proprietor joined in after catching on to the discussion.

"Me, I go," Gabriel announced in English, accentuating his motives with his hands, and walked off towards the main dirt track of the village.

"I'm going too," Amy jumped in quickly, "I don't have any money left either. I'm sure someone will pass by."

"Listen," Yarron addressed Amy, stepping into her path, "I will pay. You stay." For a moment his eyes seemed to command her.

"No. I'm going back to the farm," she responded.

"We can have a good time," Yarron said softening his voice, "drink rum, have a smoke, whatever you feel like." Amy retracted her neck and blinked blankly into Yarron's gaze that seemed to have gained some power over her, and then winced. *How did he know that?*

"I'm going back to the farm," she said into his eyes, imagining Luka and incense.

"I should have known you were one of those girls," Yarron said with disgust.

"Excuse me?" Amy said, now craning her neck forwards.

"You like to chase the local men," he stated, "the guide, now Gabriel."

"I climbed Maderas with a guide because I wanted to, ok? And I don't want to stay here, so I'm going," she said with an effort to keep her voice steady. "Gabriel is a young boy, well big, young boy, but I'm not up to anything like that."

"You sneaky, stupid, English girl," he said, as if she was a nuisance to him, to which she responded with upturned hands and a frown she would have once used at secondary school. Guy silently alternated his gaze between her and Yarron, before eventually letting it rest upon the ground where he privately considered his own thoughts. Amy sighed at Yarron, turned and walked away.

"I don't know what your deal is?" she turned back, "and you Guy. Why?"

"Have a good time on the roadside with your Latino boy," Yarron replied. Up on the roadside, Gabriel was crouching on his haunches waiting. He smiled when seeing Amy, who thought how he looked like an oversized child, and felt relief drain back into her face. They set off down the dusty road in the direction of Balgue, her hands still trembling. It reminded her of the argument she'd had with Giles.

"Where are you from?" Amy asked after they'd shared the last orange and mouthfuls of water.

"Honduras," he replied, swiping tall grasses at the verge with a whip of a stick. She knew that was north of where they were.

"How old are you?"

"Sixteen."

"You are travel alone?" she asked, to which he nodded vaguely. "Why you are travel alone?" He looked at Amy as if to assess whether his efforts to answer would be matched by her ability to understand.

"You know Honduras, no?" he asked. She shook her head. "Ok. Honduras has big problems. Because of drugs," he started, "gangs, you know? Groups of criminals. These gangs completely rule Honduras. Drugs, crime, poverty. The president says: 'it is the geography of our country that is the problem, and we can't change that'." Amy waited without empathic words and asked:

"Your family in Honduras?"

"I lived with my grandmother out in the farmland from the age I was three. My family, all of my family was killed by gangs in Tegucigalpa, the capital. I don't remember my brothers or father or mother really. Now I am sixteen -" he explained until Amy cut him.

"Wait," Amy had stopped walking. "You say your family, all, dead?"

"It is so sad, but I don't really remember them," he answered with a smile belying the tragedy that he spoke of, and continued matter-of-factly, "my grandma had always told me that I would leave when I was sixteen. She says that there is no future for me in Honduras now. It is too dangerous and I must go to seek a better life."

"Why geography is problem?" Amy asked as they commenced their walking.

"Honduras is part of the trade route of cocaine," he stated as if obvious.

"Route? The travel?"

"Yes. It is grown in Bolivia and Columbia, mainly, and travels up to the United States and out to Europe. Honduras is on the route." Amy fell silent as she acknowledged what he'd said. "But I am here. Life is not so bad for me. I trust in God to look after me," he smiled softly, shyly avading eye contact, "some people live a happy life in Honduras, too. Maybe my family had bad luck?"

They walked in silence for some time as they both digested the impact of Gabriel's story. Amy saw his peaceful attitude, his cute innocent smile, wondering how he could have been born from what he had described. She felt, all of a sudden, her Britishness made her, and millions of others, spoilt brats. Brats arrogantly unaware that so many British desires, tastes and vices are fed through deep, penetrating roots that have grown a tight grip around the globe, sucking the life blood out of so many people's lives. People like Gabriel. For party people to sniff cocaine in Britain, miles away from where it's grown.

After about an hour of walking into the pensive dusk, they heard an approaching truck. Standing in the verge waving their arms the truck rattled past without slowing, just as the previous ones had done. Then about a hundred meters on it stopped. Looking at one another, they simultaneously smiled. Gabriel grabbed Amy's hand and, like giggling school children, they ran after the truck. Without hesitation, Gabriel jumped up on the rear wheel and scrambled on the back, which was empty but for a few large plastic barrels that were securely fasten down. He pulled Amy up with a strong arm and slammed his hand on the cab of the truck. They bounced and jostled all the way to Santa Cruz, where they'd anticipated disembarking. But to their joyful surprise, the truck continued to Balgue. Somehow, the luck that Gabriel seemed to magnetise, child like in his acceptance of, made Amy resolve to this fact - that Gabriel trusted in God to provide for him, and his belief made this agreement a reality.

The journey was far from smooth, some of the bumps throwing them right off their backsides, making Amy regret her slimness. Other potholes jerked them from side to side. Amy tried squatting, lying flat and even standing, but the bumps pounded her flesh and bone.

"Here. Sit back to back," Gabriel said, leaning his back against her's, linking an elbow each and using their body weights to steady one another. Their ascent, on foot, up the steep farm track was starlit and spurred on by the paraffin lamp glow of La finca, the sweet scent of night jasmine, and fried plantain.

Alone in her little camp bed, Amy was kept awake by Gabriel's words in her mind. *All of my family was killed by gangs. Drugs, crime, poverty...it is the geography of our country that is the problem, and we can't change that.* She saw herself in a London supermarket carefully selecting fair-trade bananas and chocolate bars, to hypocritically later on sniff cocaine having travelled right through, in some proportion, Gabriel's ravaged country.

The next morning, Amy felt the need to reacquaintant herself with the glorious view from the balcony. She perceived a brewing uneasiness, perhaps the anticipation of Yarron and Guy's return after their overnight stay in San Ramon. *Grow up Yarron,* she rehearsed countering a verbal attack from him. But it was really Zan who was loitering in the background of her mind, and the situation she'd left behind in Castillo - the men who'd demanded money for cocaine, the way she was, in some unremembered way, embroiled in scuffles over drugs. Amy sighed at her past always seemingly close behind her, like a shadow, and just when life had started to become clearer.

"Hey Amy," said a soft, female voice in English. It was Luka, wearing a purple tie-dyed cotton two-piece, with a soft lilac and silver scarf in her hair. The sight of her instantly lifted Amy's mood. "The energy here is so pure." She inhaled deeply, squeezing invisible sponges in her palms "So - how do you say - opulent?" Amy raised her eyebrows.

"It certainly feels opulent," Amy replied, *opium, opulent,* she thought. They spent the following couple of hours nibbling salads and sipping juices, chatting and taking in the view, and it struck Amy that Luka was the only person who really chatted to her. It felt good to have a female friend again.

"How are the local men?" sneered a voice from behind Luka, who didn't turn but instead monitored Amy's face.

"Luka isn't a man, or local," Amy said flatly to his turbid eyes that seemed to smoulder in the dimness.

"How was the Honduras? As good or better than the guide boy?"

"Why do you want to provoke me?" Amy responded steadily, yet could feel her blood pumping faster and her scalp prickling.

"You like to taste the local cuisine. I know what girls like you want. British girls," Yarron informed, apparently indifferent to Luka's presence. Amy could feel Luka's eyes studying her face as if checking for tension, as Amy rapidly pondered British girls' reputation. Ibiza, Spain, her mind catalogued and concluded he had a point. *National reputation and self-identity can only truly be understood when abroad,* Amy recalled Rick saying over cocktails one evening.

"Go away Yarron, you're spoiling the peace," Amy said quietly.

"I came to ask Luka if she is still interested in climbing Maderas early tomorrow with the group I have arranged. Of course you only go with local boys for one-to-one tours," he baited Amy. Luka blinked and twitched first at Amy, and then turned to Yarron.

"I'm not sure, now," she said feebly.

"Well, everybody is still interested, except Amy of course," he said pointing but not looking at Amy.

"I would like to climb, but only in peace."

"Take the day to think it over and let me know," Yarron replied politely.

"I wouldn't recommend it, personally," Amy advised Luka.

"No, of course, you recommend using boys as prostitutes," Yarron directly stated to Amy, his eyes glinting with an unfathomable, cool emotion.

"I hope you get lost up there," Amy said to his glaring eyes.

"Bitch," Yarron breathed at her with a sultry sneer and strolled away.

"What was that incident about?" Luka asked a little stunned.

"I don't know what Yarron has against me, but it's his problem," Amy shrugged. Luka cleared her throat, frowned, and excused herself to bed. Amy, after sitting alone for a few minutes, ordered a Cuba libre from the kitchen and drank it whilst mulling Yarron's words. *I won't let him put me down, I've done nothing wrong. I'll be like Gabriel, who's suffered worse, much worse than I can imagine, who trusts in God to look after him. I'm over all of that getting frustrated vibe. If he doesn't like me, that's his problem. He's probably jealous that I haven't fallen for his eyes.* The cigarette, she'd cadged from a backpacker, burned her throat in a most unpleasant way, yet she dragged on it until it was finished, mentally noting how the rum and coke definitely tasted weaker than in the bars of Castillo.

A stolen dusk

Bright, thin light illuminating patches of faraway fields. Ominous, steely, blue-black clouds hung heavily all around. Amy felt as if she were magnetised to the hammock. Enveloped in the soft, woven threads, curved like a long banana, she hung, silently listening to nature. She was alone but for the quiet Scandinavian threesome who'd donated her a few cigarettes. She needed to eat but could still feel the simmering sugar heartburn from the previous night's Cuba libres. Her thoughts were trailing nowhere - her eyes were heavily blinking. Humidity hung heavily in the air - compressing, stifling - slumber-lulling.

Amy sighed into bouts of dreamless, sweaty sleeps punctuated by squawking and squabbling parrots, until a thunderous noise awoke her. She opened her eyes to darkness. Not a night-time darkness, nor the brief dusk darkness, but an untimely darkness - ominous and shadowy. The air tasted different - fresh, alive, thinner. The leaves on the surrounding trees started making a shaking sound as all of a sudden a loud drumming noise started. Water hit and rolled down the iron roof above, gushing from the veranda eaves in a sheet like a waterfall. Drips and plops and gathering insects invaded the quiet veranda, and the view was reduced to a blur of pouring water, mist and rising steam. It brought with it an unusual scene - farmhands outnumbering backpackers. They gathered near the kitchen wringing out clothing and patting hair dry with towels. They sat round drinking from mugs for hours, until premature night merged into real night. The daily dusk and sunset had been washed clear away.

"Ensalada verde con pollo a la parrilla por favour," Amy rehearsed. But she delayed her trip to the kitchen whilst the farmhands ate. An hour later, after her green salad with grilled chicken, Amy was still alone. She knew the Maderas climbing party, which included Luka and Yana, should have returned already, and imagined the party huddled beneath trees getting soaked in the dark. The rain started again and settled into a steady downpour. Little insects scuttled round the dusty, wooden floor in an agitated and disoriented manner. The farmhands were still grouped outside the kitchen, standing discussing the weather. Even the kitchen women, usually only glimpsed at in the dim depths of the cavernous kitchen, emerged to join the debate.

Suddenly a man ran up the veranda steps. He was drenched to the skin, his hair and clothes stuck down wet, and he was painfully out of breath. He was waving his arm in an uphill direction with every sentence he announced to the silent group. The kitchen women started shouting - one verging on hysterical. The men shifted and paced a little, glancing out at the night sky. Amy watched from across the empty veranda, only hearing pitches of their voices. Then the kitchen women all turned and looked across at Amy. A farmhand approached her, and Amy sat up in mild alarm, suddenly feeling suspected. *You had said a curse, no? "I hope you get lost up there", no? Did you not know that the spirit in the trees hear everything you say and whisper it to the gods locked in the volcanoes, no?* Amy's mind said, as he approached her.

"Senorita," he addressed her and went on to ask, "do you know how many guests have climbed Maderas today?" Amy blinked at him, only understanding the 'how many' and 'Maderas' part. His accent was heavy, and the rain hammered loudly on corrugated metal nearby.

"Maderas," he pointed uphill, "your friends, climb, today."

"Yes," Amy agreed.

"How many?" he asked.

"Yarron, Guy, Luka, Yana, the three American girls," Amy counted on fingers. "Seven, maybe?"

"Seven." The man turned and shouted across the veranda. The women started shouted again in high pitch objections. "What time did they leave? What time?" he pressed her urgently.

"Very early - six, I believe," Amy answered quickly. He jogged across the veranda and joined the farmhands donning waterproof jackets. The atmosphere had risen to panic. The kitchen women packed small rucksacks. The men flashed torches. A woman shouted down a telephone. Then, the men marched off down the veranda steps in silence, leaving the youngest kitchen woman sat at a table wailing in disapproval whilst a colleague patted her back. Two women hurried to the dormitories.

"What is the problem?" Amy asked a kitchen women, now cautiously approaching the women.

"The guests should inform us if they climb Maderas," the head kitchen woman preached to Amy, "we would have told them no. It is dangerous in this weather."

"We are missing ten people," a woman said, returning from the dormitories.

"Okay, two Germans - these two men went to Alta Gracia. The hotel telephoned to say," the head kitchen woman said.

"So, one we don't know where," the other woman replied.

"She is the other one, no?" the head kitchen woman snapped, gesturing to Amy. The woman shook her head and the head kitchen woman ordered her to recount.

"Which people you know climbed Maderas?" the head kitchen woman asked Amy, who now hovered at the frantic area around the kitchen door. Amy started to list them out by gender and nationality.

"Gabriel!" Amy suddenly remembered, "Gabriel - the boy from Honduras."

"Pass me the guest list," the head woman ordered and peered at the paper.

"Yes, it is him. Did he climb with the group?" she confidentially asked Amy.

"I don't know," Amy stammered just as a rolling boom of thunder drowned her out. The Scandinavian men came out and questioned the women in fluent Spanish.

"No, it is too dangerous," the head woman insisted, shaking her head. Amy leant over the balustrade watching the wild flickering of lamp flames assaulted by raindrops and breathed in the chaos of damp vegetation and earth, rubbing her dry lips in a repetitive, smoothing motion. An hour later, a man arrived and spoke with the head kitchen woman. Amy heard him say the word *ticos*. The woman looked over the balustrade into the yard below. Amy copied. There in the farmyard below gathered a dozen or so men in wellies, carrying lanterns and long sticks. Then the men set off towards Maderas. The rain had eased to a drizzle, but the water still poured off the roof.

For hours they waited. No one drank or ate anything. Two of the women went to the kitchen and started cooking.

"You should go to bed, we can come tell you any news," a woman insisted to Amy, but Amy refused. Instead she sweated and shivered in the hammock, smacking at mosquitos. At 3.30am shouts were heard, followed by a man running up the steps. Amy opened her eyes, anticipating. Women jumped to their feet and grabbed blankets. Two of them hurried into the kitchen and re-emerged with large, steel bowls of steaming water. Chairs were pushed back to open a large clear space. A feeble crying could be heard. Sweating, mud-caked men struggled up the steps, shuffling and straining under the weight of two makeshift stretchers. The stretchers were clumsily lowered by fatigued arms into the space made by the women. One of the men was unconscious, his head bandaged and bloody. The other was moaning aloud and writhing so not to move his right leg. The women looked at the men. Amy didn't recognise either of them.

"The pathways were like rivers of mud, they had tried to walk through the forest and fallen into a deep ravine," one of the farmhands explained, still panting. Blankets were fetched and wrapped around the injured, despite the humidity. The unconscious man looked pale and lifeless. No one touched him. A woman knelt at the side of the man writhing in agony and helped him to gulp down tablets with water. Another bathed the bloody scratches on the arms and legs of the farmhands.

Half an hour later, a pickup ground slowly into the farmyard, its tyres spinning in the mud, a cue for the stretchers to be raised. The conscious man let out a sharp cry. The unconscious man just wobbled as he was carried back down the steps and slid on the back of the pickup. The pickup lurched forward and slowly set off back down the steep descent, the two men rocking and shaking cruelly, as the wheels bounced over the rough terrain. Their escorts, a couple of young farmhands, crouched at their sides with torches peering at the route ahead.

"The other people?" Amy asked the head woman.

"They are still lost," she replied. The young kitchen woman wailed a prayer. Amy felt numb. She gazed dumbly at the bowls of dirty water. The women emerged from the kitchen with plates of rice and beans, passing them to the remaining soaked, silent farmhands. Amy suddenly felt sick, in a queasy afternoon hangover way. Without speaking she walked to her dormitory. The room was dark, lifeless. She closed the door but still clutched the handle, slid down on to her haunches, head resting against the wooden door and swallowed hard. Then she sobbed out loud - long breathy sobs, tears rolling down her cheeks.

"Please forgive me. I didn't want this to happen," she sobbed through grimaced teeth. "Please bring them back safely." A length of saliva hung from her bottom lip. She slid on to the floor and sobbed until tiredness stole her away to sleep.

Amy was running through the darkness near the top of Maderas. She knew the way to the lagoon. A high, bright moon lit the way. Scrambling up rocks she reached the highest point. Panting hard peering down at the misty lagoon, her eyes rapidly searched for any sign of life. Through the mist she saw a movement. Was it the ducks? Or the missing party? She jogged down into the mist, was engulfed by the thick fog, then emerged beneath the thick cloud. She was at the lagoon. The water was black. Something was pulling her to focus on the middle of the lagoon. The water was moving - swirling wide and slow. She looked round. She saw something at the shore. It was Luka's purple tie-dyed clothing. There was Yarron's baseball hat. There were lots of Gabriel's bracelets and belts, all strewn along the shore. She looked back at the water. The centre of the lagoon had become a deep, sucking vortex. It was silent but visibly building. Amy tried to look inside the whirlpool. Did it lead to the belly of the volcano? Is that where they were? She knew she must go to look, but without getting sucked in. She saw a small canoe on the shore. She found it had a rope on it. She ran to tie the other end to a tree, she pushed it on to the lake then climbed in the boat and took the oars and started to row. When approaching the vortex, she felt its pull. The canoe pulled against the rope and stopped. Amy stood to peer inside. It was glowing red deep beneath the water. The canoe wobbled from her weight and the pulling. She heard a loud cry of a man's voice. Then a reply. Then a girl's voice. Then her head was being banged on one side.

Amy woke to find the door being pushed against her head. The room was lighter. One of the kitchen women was shouting something along the corridor. Amy scrambled to her feet and went directly to the veranda where the scene was one of tired relief. Yarron, Yana, Luka, Guy and the others sat huddled with blankets around their shoulders. They had steaming hot drinks in mugs. The young kitchen woman, who'd been wailing prayers earlier, was sitting placid and contentedly next to her beloved farmhand, bathing his bloodied elbow with a wet cloth.

Magdalena

"My spirituality is through having an intimate relationship with nature. Have you heard of the Sacred Circle of Life?" Luka asked two German guys that she, Yana, and Amy were sat next to on a veranda bench. "Animals, the plants, the rocks, the people - this includes the concept of reciprocity, as I believe in the Sacred Circle, where we are all inter-related. When we give, we also receive - and as we receive, we also give. It is dynamic," Luka enthused, making a large circular motion with her arms, accentuating it with a rotation of her torso.

"So, if you take too much, there isn't enough to go around?" Amy asked, thinking it reminiscent of school science lessons and the feeling of *ah I get it*.

"Exactly! The native American tribes believe in 'Mending the Sacred Hoop' which means: to heal the broken places of the earth, like stopping the toxic waste, preserving nature, and for people to connect with their ancestral roots," Luka enthused.

"Are you, achieving, the Sacred Circle of Life here at Ometepe?" the German with glasses questioned without sarcasm.

"I feel it here," Luka smiled, "but I believe that it must come from within."

"How from within?" he continued probing, to her delight.

"Meditation - the practice of yoga - and to become connected to the earth energy. I was told that the energies are powerful here because of the two volcanoes. Apparently, Ometepe is the biggest volcanic island in freshwaters. I believe that bathing in the lake and eating the food growing here is healing," Luka said.

"Swimming in the lake is special, and the fish taste amazing here too," Amy said spontaneously, feeling her skin prickle with just the thought of its freshness.

"Ometepe is amazing," Yana chipped in, "but also this finca. There is something very special, no?"

"La finca Magdalena," Luka said as if of someone she adored, "has much history."

"This building was constructed in 1888," the German with glasses seized his chance to impart facts garnered from his Nicaraguan travel guide book, "and was given to a cooperative of 25 families after the Sandinista revolution in 1983 - the year my sister was born."

"Why the name Magdalena, do you know?" Amy questioned, half recognising it.

"Perhaps the Bible?" Luka suggested, straightening her back and glancing around the group, "Mary Magdalena was one of Jesus' devoted followers. She is on pictures weeping at the crucifixion of Jesus, with Mary his Mother. I guess the farm is named after this holy woman."

"Was she a prostitute, or a bad woman, I think? And then became transformed by Jesus?" the German with the glasses probed.

"No, that is a misinterpretation of the Bible," Yana interjected, jabbing a finger, causing Luka's eyebrows to peel up. "No, she was a woman afflicted with seven demons, making her insane. Jesus healed her completely and she became equal to the other men followers of Jesus."

"Wow, you know the Bible," Luka said cautiously, placing her fingertips of each hand together and slowly slipping them from side to side.

"So, here in Catholic-land they must revere her like one of the saints," Amy added.

"That is a part of the Bible I don't understand," the other German man frowned, "I am planning to study in medicine and it always fascinates me, the concept of the Bible referring to crazy people - clearly people with mental health problems or perhaps epilepsy - as demon-possessed, like the devil comes and resides in these people."

"God made the world perfect, and the fallen angel, Satan destroyed this. So, all things bad - illnesses, diseases, mental health problems, addictions, nasty thinking - it all comes from Satan," Yana explained.

"And Jesus healed people with illness, or bad-ness, by driving away the demons?" the plan-to-be medic stated.

"Or forgiving their sins, not everyone was demon possessed. Some people just suffering, and he said to them: *your sins are forgiven,* meaning *I am taking away this bad from you, because I am more powerful than the power of Satan."*

"Why didn't he just take away all of the badness of Satan in one go?" Amy asked, sneering a little, "I just can't believe a God can be in charge over this world."

"That is the final book in the Bible, when Jesus is predicted to come back, and completely destroy all evil in the world," Yana said, with an air of reminiscence.

"The end of the world," Luka said.

"It's the epic story of good versus evil," the German in glasses smiled.

"So, demons sort of work for the devil, and come to take hold of spiritually-weak people, encouraging them to do bad things?" Amy asked, half daydreaming.

"Demons were angels, but the ones that followed Satan - so bad angels," Yana said.

"That's scary, thinking there are evil demons around us," Amy almost whispered.

"Driving away evil spirits is a fundamental global belief across the world," one of the men added.

"That is why people pray for protection and strength," Yana said wistfully. Everyone looked at Yana, the gentle, small girl, who never usually really said a lot about anything.

"You are Christian?" Luka asked, "You never mentioned this before."

"Well, my family are. I was always taken to church, so I understand the stories of the Bible. It does make sense, no? This explanation of why the world is like it is," Yana replied, before adding "but there are so many religions, I respect other people's beliefs."

"There is something special about people who believe - the ones who truly believe. Whether they have a God listening to them, or not, it keeps them going. It keeps them on a purpose, helps to stop bad thinking," one of the German men added, before clearing his throat, "not that it has always been the case through all of history of course."

"But medicine is good too - especially for mental health," the plan-to-be medic said, "I think this is where I will specialise - mental-health."

"Good evening," Gabriel said cheerily as he joined the group, slowly eying all.

"Good evening," they chorused back, reverting to Spanish.

"We are having a debate tonight? What is the subject?" he asked innocently.

"God," Luka said in Spanish, "Amy does not believe." Amy shot Luka a glance at her hypocritical statement.

"You don't believe in God, Amy?" Gabriel said to her, with a disbelief that would have been mistaken for mockery, had it not come from him.

"I don't know. I don't have a religion," she replied conscious that the discussion was now about her non-belief. The Germans had broken off into their own quiet conversation with Yana and Luka. Gabriel grinned kindly at Amy.

"Whom do you pray to?" Gabriel asked with an innocent expectation, as if Amy may enlighten him to the name of a new God.

"I don't, usually, to pray," Amy admitted.

"You don't have to think of religion to pray to God," Gabriel said simply, "God is the one who keeps us strong - gives us everything. Like the people on Maderas last night. God kept them safe."

"Thank God," Amy said.

"The devil tries to snatch us away," Gabriel said miming a snatch, "but with the mercy of God we can stay strong. He can protect us." Amy blinked into the weirdly-wise, baby eyes of Gabriel and felt a sudden and heavy tiredness. Vague memories floated somewhere five-thousand miles away in London, where she'd felt snatched into doing bad things, bad things that had killed Gabriel's family and spun him off into a life of roaming aimlessly. Later, tucked up in the little camp bed, alone in the dormitory, Amy stared herself into somnolence at the soft candle glow. Her mind emptied of thoughts, yet the evening's spiritual debate had left her filled - overfilled, with the vast concept of belief.

As free and fragile as butterflies

Amy wandered back into morning sun's warmth in the rear farmyard, having taken a walk in the woodland behind La finca. She'd been having a go at finding that connection with nature Luka had spoken about, but had just gained scratches to her ankles from sharp reeds. Nothing as poignant as the children's lake baptism experience happened this time.   She pondered the vast rear elevation of the farmhouse. It was architecturally designed to be robust, hospitable and multi-functional. A farm worker appeared from across the yard, shouldering a large sack of grain, and made his way along a small pathway abutting the building. She watched him walk up a small set of external steps, set his load at his feet and reach up above the doorframe. His fingers tugged downwards at a vertical bolt and opened the door. Dragging his sack in behind him, he re-bolted the door from the inside. She stood for a moment, considering the little windows and deduced that the door was next to her dormitory. *That's what that little clanking sound is I hear early some mornings, not a monkey or clumsy bird.*

As Amy climbed the veranda steps at the kitchen end of the building, she was greeted by someone waving at her. It was Diego. He trotted down the steps to her, and in those few seconds Amy couldn't help wondering if he really was her age, if he had a body of a young man under his clothes. In that fleeting moment she imagined herself sweet and innocent, living a humble life with him, spending evenings weaving hammocks in their little backyard where chickens roamed around.

"Amy, how are you?" he asked.

"Good. Why you here?" she replied, concluding that he'd never be able to handle her.

"I have bicycles today, Amy. We can go explore," he answered twinkling. *Explore* echoed in Amy's mind for a couple of seconds as she reached her gaze into his warm-feel eyes, looking for his kiss, his passion, his taste. *If he attempts to kiss me, I'll let him* she thought in a schoolgirl enchantment.

"Ok," she said with a little lift of excitement, "first, we have breakfast."

After breakfast, the kitchen women insisted that Amy signed the guest book, including their planned route, and then they strolled down the track to the little shop in Balgue, where two mountain bikes were leant around the back. And off they set, bumping their way along the undulating dirt track past Santo Domingo beach. It felt weeks ago when she'd hidden herself away in that empty beach hotel, watching endless sunsets. She felt like a new version of herself now. *I've changed, improved, altered.* Amy frowned and smiled simultaneously, with a wisp of apprehension. Following Diego's zigzagging pathway between crater-like potholes, she breathed in the fine, chalky dust billowing up from his mountain bike wheels, and thought back to being ten years old on Worcestershire country lanes, before traffic had gotten fast - old minis and maxis with wind-down windows, and cab-less tractors that had chugged and jerked along. In her day-dreamy hue she contemplated the scores of butterflies that rose, in a consistently delayed reaction, from donkey dung, as they cycled past. A notion fluttered about her - that she was as free as they were. She remembered the rock group Mana and their mariposa song she'd thought so romantic, and granted herself, in memory of her ignorance, that she was as fragile as these butterflies too.

"Do you ride a bicycle in England?" Diego asked once they were parallel.

"Yes. In London. Very busy. No good for car. Bicycle is better," she replied.

Three hours later, they'd reached Alta Gracia. Coasting on the paved surface, Amy looked at the priest's house with a confused wistfulness, wondering what such a pious lifestyle would entail, and whether the cousins had been confined to a life of prayer and priest-assisting duties. They skirted the central park until reaching a cafe. Alta Gracia, compared to the few other places she'd visited on Ometepe, had an official air. Clean pavements and gaily-painted homes and shop fronts gave Amy the impression that it was a proud and well-organised community. Castillo, with its tourists and surfers, now seemed a hazy, distant, dangerous dream.

"Many tourists come to Ometepe because it is the most beautiful part of Nicaragua," Diego explained as they paused for more water, "both foreigners and nationals. Managua and other parts, well, are not as beautiful."

"Amy, Hello. You are still on the island!" a voice interrupted them. El Monstruo trotted up to Amy and sniffed her leg, causing Diego to jump back a couple of steps and pull Amy away from the dog.

"Allan! How are you?" Amy replied, instantly noticing his pockmarked face and the same black T-shirt and earrings from when they had first met. "Allan is the first people I know when to travel to Ometepe." Diego unenthusiastically greeted Allan with a single head nod. She elaborated on what she'd been doing since her arrival on the island and asked how Warner and the priest were. Sensing Diego was keen to move on, she bid Allan farewell with a twinge of guilt for not having visited him at the Priest's house.

"Oh Amy," Allan called as she spun the pedals ready to cycle, "do you want to come to the full moon party?"

"Good," Amy called back, only understanding the word party, assuming he'd referred to the local Crowning of the Queen party mentioned by the shop-keeper in Balgue village.

"We'll see you," Allan called behind her. Diego chose a café and ordered them lemonade. As she walked, Amy could feel, with satisfaction, the tightness in her thighs and calf muscles.

"Here, they have internet," Diego told Amy with a sense of pride.

"That's good! But first, do you want empanadas?" she asked him.

"You want empanadas? I'll order some," he said willingly and added timidly, "You have Hotmail? Yahoo?" Amy nodded, distracted by noisy Jay-like birds in a nearby mango tree.

"Maybe, you can do email?" he proceeded, "with me."

"Ok. You want email address of me," to which he broke into a beaming smile, rose to his feet and took their drinks into a back room. Amy followed, chuckling to herself. Once sat at a computer in a dimly lit room with four PCs, as directed by the waiter who turned one on for them, Diego gestured for Amy to take the seat at the keyboard and he pulled his chair in close to her.

"You me send a message," Amy confirmed to Diego, who had a blank expression. "Write me address of your email." Diego looked blankly at her and the pen she proffered him. The computer was still whirring into action and icons were appearing one by one on the dimly lit screen.

"You are Hotmail? Yahoo?" she continued, but Diego just gawped at her. She wrote her email address on an edge of a tourist map ajwoodywood@hotmail.com wondering if he might be familiar with her nickname - woody woodpecker derived from her surname, Wood. After some deliberating, Amy finally grasped that Diego didn't want to simply swap email addresses, but instead wanted Amy to set up his own email account. It took her a while to fathom the email account web link in Spanish, whilst Diego silently watched everything she did. The empanadas and more cold drinks helped to refresh them.

"Ok. You do," she announced and shifted her chair away from the keyboard. Diego cautiously placed his hand upon the mouse and watched the cursor travel around the screen from his hand movement. Amy pointed to where he needed to place the cursor and showed him the click action. She cheered when his new email opened. He smiled, biting his thumbnail. "Write. Email. For me," Amy encouraged.

"What do I write?" he smiling shyly.

"Write: Hola Amy, write to me." Diego took a deep breath, abruptly shed his embarrassed grinning and peered at the keyboard seriously. Then he pressed the H key and looked to see it on the new email page and continued to do this for every letter. It was Amy's turn to watch in silence as Diego typed out her suggested message. Amy saw how he had misspelt *escribe*, the Spanish word for *write*, and then realised he hadn't fully learnt to write. She pointed where to hit the send button and moved back to the keyboard to open her own account. Diego sighed a little as he regained his observing position. Opening her account, Amy noted over thirty unopened messages. She pointed to Diego's message.

"Ahh. That's mine?" Diego asked with surprise and they smiled at each other.

"This," Amy said, pointing to an unopened message on the screen from three weeks ago, "is from my Mum." Amy clicked it open and started to read:

'Amy – it's Mum here. I hope you are looking after yourself. Where are you now? Please drop me a line. Last time we spoke you were very upset about our wedding plans, we need to speak about it. I understand it isn't easy for you to accept that Giles and I want to marry. I just wish you could get to know him and the girls and see how lovely they are. I won't give up on hoping this will happen in the future. Rich and Anne want to speak to you too, neither will come to the wedding if you are not there. I just wish you could see things from my point of view. I want to be happy. I don't want to be a burden on Rich and you; I know you both worry about me being alone. I know you will be happy for me once you get your head around it. Love Mum.'

Amy saw a further four messages from Rosie:

'Amy – it's mum here. I wonder if you got my email from last week. Please call, I want to know how you are. I know you were upset before, but please drop me a line to let me know you are all right. I called the new eco-resort, near Castillo, the wife of the owner said they hadn't heard from you.

Amy silently read them one after the other, whilst Diego patiently waited, letting his eyes wander over the foreign writing.

'Amy – it's mum here. Please call I'm so worried. If it's the wedding plans that have upset you so much, then don't worry, we have postponed the wedding now. Everyone has sided with you. Maybe you need more time to come around to the idea. Even though you are planning to live over there. Is that your plan still? The lady at the eco-resort said that you hadn't shown up for the interview and the language school haven't heard anything either. I just hope you are ok.'

Amy sighed. The ceiling fan was losing the battle against the computer motor heat. *Everyone has sided with you. We have postponed the wedding.* A feeling crept upon her, something immediately undecipherable, but Amy's mind scrambled to remember her bubbling anger at her Mum, back in the days of Zan and Castillo. *Did I? Oh no. I didn't write emails to everyone,* Amy thought hitting the sent box with the cursor.

'Dear All

i am writing from Castillo, costa rica. sorry I can't download photos from my camera.

i am am very worried about Mum...as all you will understand. Giles has pushed mum to marrrying in shotgun wedding.

I know he is no good for mum from the way he has treat ed rich and me. he is a nasty piece of work. Mum is so lovely but doent see the danger she if in

He want s a steady home for his girls and stepmum form roses. Is this what she needs?????

Once married he is entiled to half the house and this is something I know he is intending to get.

I love my mum and want her to be happy of course...help me stop her making this MASSIVE MISTAKE IN HER LIVE

I NOT COMING BACK FOR WEDDING – NO WAY GOIN GTO SUPPORT THIS AND LIFE WITH THE GUILT FOR NOT STEPPPJNG UP ANDN SAYING THE TRUTH

Think carefully

Best regards

Amy'

She'd sent this message to Rosie's younger sister, Anne, her brother Rich, Stephie, and most of Rosie's friends that had given Amy their emails for exciting updates from her travels. Hastily, she opened the responses from the recipients, glancing over their joint concerns for herself and Rosie.

"It worked," Amy muttered to herself glumly, "I've derailed the wedding." But instead of triumph she felt empty.

"Your mother is well?" Diego asked with an empathic expression. She had almost forgotten him sat by her side. She nodded and shook her head, trying to remember the verb worry in Spanish. She hadn't needed to use it much during her travels. *He couldn't understand my life. How things are in the UK.* She opened another:

'Amy – its Mum here. Please respond or call, it's been over 3 weeks since I've heard anything from you. I am really worried. Please just get in touch, I can't sleep or eat not knowing if you are all right or not. I'm so sorry if Giles and I have made you feel that I don't care about you. Just get in touch.'

166

Amy drew a deep breath, hit the reply button and wrote, almost feeling the relief Rosie would experience when opening it:

'Hi Mum

I'm ok. Sorry for lack of contact, travelling in parts without much connection. I'm in Nicaragua now, travelling a little, staying at a beautiful lakeside backpacker hostel. I will call you soon, when I sort my plans out.

Don't worry – I'm fine

Love Amy x

Ps. I'm sorry I've been angry about the wedding plans. I just want you to be happy and do the right thing for yourself. You've looked after Rich and me for years, I just want you to think before committing to other young kids.'

Then she noticed the last unread message from Michael at the eco-resort:

'Dear Amy

I was disappointed not to meet you at the interviewing session earlier this week. Please do get in touch if you have run into any trouble at all. We are making good progress and hoping to open in the next couple of weeks, so I hope you understand the urgency of staffing.

I have found a suitable candidate for the assistant manager role, but before I offer this position, I am keen to offer you a final chance at the interview if you can make it in the next couple of days.

I hope to hear from you.

Best wishes

Michael.'

Amy checked the date Michael had sent it - over two weeks ago. Amy rubbed her eyes with the palms of her hands with a circular motion before letting out a protracted sigh. Diego blinked, silently contemplating her as if having second thoughts about his getting an email account idea.

"What's wrong Amy?" Diego gushed, taking one of her hands in his.

"Let's go," she uttered, suddenly restless with how the day was turning out. She wanted to ignore home, the UK. *So what if Mum gets married? Even if Giles does take half her house in divorce, why should I care so much? What I should be worried about is: what am I going to do now? Look for another hotel or eco-resort to try to work in?* It felt too much, too soon. Amy thought of the little hotel on the beach in Santo Domingo and the restoration of her soul, and the lake and the farm. *Why am I letting these echoes of stress and problems back in, all the way from the UK?*

The myth of Chico largo

"Cokghariiico" a cockerel boorishly announced into the dim dawn light. Amy's muddled dream of trying to catch running horses in woodland abruptly faded and she became aware of herself breathing, rhythmically in slumber. A tenebrous wooden-panelled room was just about visible. Amy sensed the heavy stillness, as if the world outside was momentarily empty of life, but for the cockerel. Then she remembered where she was - where they were - the awful, interminable, hacking cough throughout the night that had finally ceased in the early hours of the morning. Her attention turned to her position, more precisely, her bottom that was pressed against another body belonging to Diego. They were squeezed together on a tiny camp bed in Diego's uncle's living room. Together, they warmed the air in the tent-like space between them, beneath the blanket stretched from his to her shoulder, shielding skin from the night's clammy chill.

Amy lay motionless for minutes, listening for noises of activity, anticipating the cockerel's second call. Her mind sleepily recalled the previous day's stormy afternoon soon after leaving the internet cafe. The heat had gotten up to sweltering and Diego, ever the optimist, reassured Amy he knew a place that would cool her down. She knew he meant emotionally as well as physically. 'Ojo de Agua' he had said, as if offering her medicine. 'Eye of the water' Amy translated, reluctantly resuming her day trip with Diego. Diego had become to Amy all she suddenly needed - to lead her around, reassure her, keep her there and present. *Don't think of tomorrow, or the next. Just be, just breathe, just regain your strength.* Ojo de Agua, just off the road leading back to Balgue and La finca, was indeed the most cool, calm and tranquil place imaginable.

Diego had been surprised nobody else was there at the cool, volcanic rock pool. Lush vegetation surrounded the pool and a few simple wooden sun loungers faced on to the natural spring. So invigorating was the coolness of the tree-shaded pool, so refreshing, that Amy and Diego soon fell into many minutes without speaking. The sharp, keen bird calls penetrated the trees all around, dragonflies' wings hummed as they hovered and dipped and glided over the still water. A water that appeared dark, for it was coloured by the rocks deep below, through perfectly transparent water. No thought or worry could break the spell of arresting calmness of the pool, until their fingers were shrivelled, and their flesh cooled to cold. The light had pitched to a strange, bright darkness. Bright because the leaves and flowers all around shone, darkness because the woodland around was shadowy and dark. Diego had squinted up to the sky and said: "It will rain soon."

She felt Diego's warmth through her thin cotton knickers and imagined touching his smooth skin, embracing him, being embraced by loving, caring arms. Just breathing, eyes wandering around in the soupy dim and blinking, she imagined the one small patch of her buttock was pressed against his buttock and soon found the urge to shift her position. The moment's intimacy presided over her thoughts of where she was, or all the reasons she'd been sobbing like a toddler the day before. She shifted, as slowly as she could, on to her back and then rolled on to her other side. Diego stirred with a small jolt. She reached out her hand and touched his lanky, boyish waist.

"Amy," he whispered, rolling towards her. She held her breath for a second or two.

"Diego," she replied to his dark obscured face. Her whole being craved him, craved the sparks of physical interaction, to be desired, chased, explored. Wearing only her underwear she was sure he would at least want to touch her bare skin, like he did to her arm on top of Maderas. She prickled with anticipation.

"We must go," he said.

"Why?" she replied, aware that Spanish sounded like her natural language.

"I have work today, we must cycle to Balgue first," he whispered.

"But," Amy protested only to have her lips stilled by Diego's finger.

"Quiet, the people are sleeping," he whispered as he threw back the blanket and nimbly hopped over her to his feet. Any reaction she was about to feel, was suddenly cut by a nausea, a gnawing hunger pang somewhere deep inside her tummy. They'd not eaten since the empanadas yesterday lunchtime.

They slipped through the screen door into the yard and redressed in yesterday's damp clothes. The huge caldron, hung over a sodden pile of ash on its tripod in the centre of the yard, was just visible in the dim dawn. In the shadows beneath the yard's boundary trees Amy knew an outhouse was located, for Diego had accompanied her to it in the night with a small torch. She didn't recall from where they'd entered the yard last night for the rainfall was so heavy and stormy. Without seeing anyone, they left through a large wooden gate, took up their bicycles from the hedge and slopped their flip-flops around muddy puddles to the track.

"It should take an hour to reach Balgue," Diego said hastily, setting off without waiting for Amy's reply. She heard the spray of wet wheels and imagined his mud-splattered shirt. Scowling at his audacity to reject her, she hastily pursued him, so not to get left behind, which soon confirmed her imagination of soaking mud sprays to be accurate. The moon light, though obscured by the overhanging canopy, penetrated just enough for the puddles to glisten and outline the way of the track. Diego peddled slowly but steadily, bouncing in and out of large potholes they had previously avoided, now simply impossible to anticipate.

After a relentless cycle, void of all conversation, they approached Balgue. Amy, breathing heavily and sweating all over, was decidedly glad they hadn't kissed and was wondering how the sweet-natured, caring young Diego had mutated into this brash stranger. As they coasted into Balgue, the familiarity of the village was all at once upon Amy: the flatness of the road, the open space of the junction at the foot of the track leading to La finca, the little village shop, dark and shut-up.

"Good-bye. See you next time," Diego said wearily taking hold of Amy's bike.

"Thank you," Amy answered, wondering if she should offer him more money since they had to stay out the night, but dismissed it as she had no more cash on her. Diego slowly started to cycle off into the darkness, one hand rolling Amy's bike alongside his.

"Goodbye. And thank you," Amy called after his rapidly evaporating silhouette, feeling sorry for his day's farm work. The dark hike up the track to La finca was surprisingly invigorating. She panted hard and sweated, focusing solely on feeling her footing on the rocky ground beneath her steps. With eyesight sense shut down to barely anything, hearing, taste, smell and feeling became heightened. The sound of her own flip-flops crunching stones, the cicadas in the grass verge, the taste of the dust and damp grass, the faint wafts of flowering trees and shrubs, the feel of light puffs of breeze on her bare shoulders.

Back on La finca's veranda, Amy was relieved to see empty chairs. Only one hammock looked occupied, perhaps by Gabriel, but she couldn't tell. By then the dawn had emerged enough to reinstate most shades of green and she desperately hoped that none of the kitchen women would suddenly appear and rebuke her for not returning as planned. *They'd know that the storm stopped me getting back,* Amy told herself, knowing also that the storm would give them even more reason to worry for her safety. But it was still too early for the kitchen women to be bumbling around the front of the kitchen. At the communal sinks, under the soft, orange glow of a naked bulb left on at night, Amy gulped down handfuls of cold tap water. In the mirror she caught a glimpse of her mud streaked face and noticed her filthy vest and shorts. She stood in the little shower cubicle, fully dressed and turned on the tap, bracing for the cold water. Once she'd showered her clothes and skin clean, Amy peeled the soggy clothes off until naked, rung them out as best she could then hugged the bundle of wet cloths to her front and tiptoed towards her room. Once in a dry vest and pair of knickers, Amy wriggled under her bed sheet and pulled it right over her head, enclosing herself in a cocoon-like private space. There in her little camp bed, smelling the familiar, musty wooden scents, she closed her eyes and drifted into instant, muddled dreams of returning to the UK.

Confusion lingered and clung to fading dreams as she slowly awoke. The musty air scented with ash from Luka's incense sticks, footsteps on a vast, wooden floor vibrating beneath her camp bed beyond the sheet cocoon. She pulled down the sheet to the empty, dim room. Her head felt fuzzy, as she tried to know if she was happy to be there or not. She opened her eyes and looked squarely at the wall. Her legs and arms were weak and aching. *What the hell am I going to do?*

Amy had found that teeth brushing at the open communal sinks gave opportunity to discreetly observe the veranda, if particularly positioned at one of the trough-like sinks. Amy had taken to doing this whenever possible after the unpleasant incident with Yarron. It was already dusk, meaning she'd slept all day. Last night's sodden clothes were almost dry, having been hung on the end of her metal-framed cot bed. The veranda was busy. Backpackers she didn't recognise were being served dinner. Gabriel was setting up his wares. Luka and Yana were with the German guys, which made Amy fleetingly wonder if romance was spawning. Yarron and Guy were playing cards with two female backpackers Amy hadn't seen before. One of the girls wore a pretty scarf and smiled openly at Yarron as she turned her cards over to beat him. Amy frowned momentarily at an unexpected pang of jealously. Her mind scrambled for her own evenings' possible options: stay in the bedroom or sit on the veranda? But so vexatious were her thoughts they somehow weighed her heart down, as if a huge heavy brooch was upon her chest. *I need something,* she said to herself. She slipped back to her room.

Hastily, Amy fumbled with her bag - cash, lighter, cigarette papers, and thin tie-dyed hooded top. She paused. She couldn't face Luka and Yarron and the rest of the veranda. To her they were all floating along their allotted days at the farm, their aimless, relaxed, stress-free ways disguising their meticulously planned adventures. And Luka with her sidekick Yana, advocating the pure energy, basting in the simplicity of their current lives. It was all utterly unbearable.

Quietly closing the bedroom door behind her, she tiptoed down the dark corridor to the external door she'd watched the man enter by the previous day. It was pitch dark in there. With one hand she felt up the wooden door, cringing in case of any lurking spiders. On tiptoes, she ran her fingertips along the frame until feeling a bump. It was the bolt. She grasped the bottom of it and tugged. It slid easily down, instantly releasing the door. There were no lights at all in the back yard. She managed to fumble the bolt back in and feel her way down the steps. Once crunching her way down the farm track, she felt a strong sense of freedom, a restless freedom - a freedom verging on being lost. It was freshly dark. The cicadas were chirping with force. She sighed heavily, making her plans. If the shop didn't have liquor, she'd head for the bar on the beachside she'd seen when swimming with the kids. And if that didn't work, she'd head all the way to Santo Domingo hotel, a place that conjured a sense of safe reclusion.

Suddenly the sound of a crawling car engine became apparent, followed by crushing, spinning stones under grinding tyres. Then bright headlamp beams burst into the darkness. Amy stood in the verge, hood wrapped over mouth and nose against the dust and head turned away, averting her eyes from the bright full beam of the pickup. Five minutes later the pickup returned down the track, but this time it stopped next to her.

"Amy!" shouted a voice from the cab window. It was Warner in the driving seat.

"Let's go. La fiesta!" Allan shouted leaning into view.

"Allan, Warner, what?" Amy peered inside the cab.

"The full moon party, Amy, you remember?"

"Now?" Amy asked, glancing up to the dark sky.

"Bring shoes, sometimes the beach there gets muddy," Warner advised Amy as she climbed in the backseat, "do you need to return to the farm?" And so, Amy trotted back in the rear entrance door to avoid the veranda once again. Nothing had changed in the empty bedroom. She grabbed the plastic bag with her walking shoes in and a few more bank notes. Slipping back out, she had a feeling of relief for her evening's unexpected companionship. The bumpy ride in a pick-up reminded her of when Allan and Warner had first taken her to Santo Domingo.

"I need something for the party?" Amy tried to ask, "for example, rum?"

"Don't worry there is a restaurant near to the beach where we can buy liquor," Allan replied. The road got progressively bumpier. They lurched up and down huge washed-out sections of track winding through dark woodland. Two men became visible in the headlights. Warner and Allan muttered under their breath. Warner slowed down and hung his head out the window to speak to them. The back door opened and in climbed two local men wearing baseball caps. Allan explained where Amy was from and how they'd met. They all exchanged Buenas noches and happily chatted between bumps.

"Chico largo," the chattiest man emotively asked her "you know the story?"

"Chico largo," Amy repeated.

"You don't know about Chico largo?" the man replied with mock shock. "I tell you now. This is where we are going right now, the lagoon of Chico largo. Chico largo is said to live in the lagoon, and he appears sometimes on the roads. Not everyone can see him, but those who can see him make a pact with the devil, because Chico largo is like a demonic figure."

"Chico largo is dead?" Amy asked trying to understand.

"It is a local myth around here. Charco verde, this area, is famous for this myth," Warner offered to explain.

"It is more than a myth," the man next to Amy interjected, "my grandfather knows someone who saw Chico largo."

"Your grandfather drank so much liquor he wouldn't have seen Chico largo in his own home," jested the chatty man, to which everyone chuckled.

"Not just my grandfather - your father was the man who said he heard screaming in the woodland one day and refused to even drive near here," he retorted.

"He just wanted to scare his friends in the pub," the chatty guy grinned casually.

"Why Chico largo like devil?" Amy interrupted the two joking men.

"Don't worry Amy; it is a myth about the lake where the party is tonight. Chico largo is a story from a long time ago," Allan reassured from the passenger seat.

"Chico largo," the storyteller continued, accentuating the first vowels of each word, "is the governor of Charco verde area, and if a person steals from his area, for example fruit from the tree or hunt any animals, Chico largo transforms the person into a cow, or a crocodile, or a turtle, or maybe a pig. The butchers say that they sometimes find cows with gold teeth like humans."

"It is said that any person who gets rich has made a pact with Chico largo, and after he serves Chico largo he will turn into an animal and go to live in el Encanto, the city in the bottom of the lake," Warner added.

"It is always a mystical place. A long time before, the people made sacrifices to their gods here at the lagoon," the man smiled, "but now we take tourists on boats."

When Warner eventually turned off the engine and let the pickup roll to a halt in the sandy clearing, Amy caught her first glimpse of the magical lagoon. Clouds had finally dispersed enough for the low

175

milky-white moon to show. Its light cast a clear outline of the lake's expanse of water, the dense surrounding woodlands, and Concepcion, the larger of the two volcanoes, silhouetted beyond. If the lagoon's lush daytime beauty wasn't so easy to picture, the scene would have been perfectly eerie. Concepcion's virility conjured a magical, everlasting awesomeness whenever in view, which was enhanced, this night, by the moon's cool, white light from the clear sky. At the water's edge was a small beach where a few people had gathered, some with wooden drums. A couple were painting each other's faces with white streaks. At one edge was a rack stacked with canoes and paddles, and at the other, matting and blankets had been laid out. A newly built bonfire was starting to crackle. Amy wandered to the murky water, gazing out at the glimmering darkness and caught a familiar whiff of marijuana smoke drifting over from the blanket area. There she could just make out the shapes of two people sitting, one with blonde dreadlocks, and the other a shadow with the red orange glow of a joint tip. Amy thought of Arenal's lava flow glowing in the night seen from the luxurious hot-spring resort. But she quickly dismissed thinking of that evening at La Fortuna with Louisa and Rick. *Burnt bridges.*

"Can we buy beer, or rum, or something?" Amy asked her companions.

"Come with me, I will take you to the hotel," Allan replied, leading her into the dark woodland.

"Are you from Ometepe?" Amy asked after a few minutes.

"I am not an Ometepian. My Father was from Managua and my mother, the sister of the priest was Ometepian. My parents met in Managua and later, with my brother and me, they decided to come to live in Ometepe," he explained.

"How old?" she asked, a little out of breath in the evening warmth.

"I was ten years old when I came here."

"It is better or worse than Managua?" Amy asked, remembering the game in the language school of turning over cards to match opposite adjectives.

"It was - difficult for us to adapt to life here, especially my father. My mother loved it here, but then my mother died."

"And your father? Where is he?" she tentatively asked. Amy sensed him wincing.

"My father? He left Ometepe. Nobody liked him."

"Why people no like him?" Amy persisted.

"The family of my mother blamed him for her death, and he was - he had addiction to alcohol and drugs, and he went back to Managua," Allan said sombrely.

"Are you, to speak with your father, now?"

"I haven't seen my father for more than ten years. I think he is probably dead. And my brother is just the same as him, maybe in Nicaragua or probably dead now."

"So now - what? For you, and el Monstruo - you like life in Ometepe?"

"Managua holds bad memories for me, it is a place no good for me now. I want to return to Ometepe and live as my mother's family did. No troubles, tranquil, eat fresh fish from the lake. I will find work here. My uncle is a good man. He will help me find work. Maybe I can save money and travel to buy produce to sell on Ometepe," he aspired as they tramped on into the darkness together. A loud squawking from above startled them.

"You fear Chico largo?" Allan asked without a hint of humour, as the disturbed bird flapped away. Amy replied with an unsure sounding giggle. The woodland path gave way to a softly lit terrace humming with music. It was the hotel. As they approached, Amy saw a guitarist, serenading guests wearing loose linen shirts and trousers whilst waiters graced their tables with bottles of wine.

By the time they made it back to the beach with six bottles of beer, a scant number by Amy's reasoning, the number of partygoers had swelled to around thirty. The little beach was crowded. Amy's mood had lifted a little. Rhythmic drumming thumped and tapped. The painted faces were spinning and jumping a synchronised dance, sand flicking from their bare feet, and the moon was higher, shining brightly over the revellers. Joining Warner and the Chico largo storyteller from the car, who were shyly loitering at the periphery of the beach, Amy offered a bottle of Toña to each of her three companions, whilst Allan went to check on el Monstruo, who was chained to the back of the pickup.

"My name is Gustavo. And you?" the storytelling guy asked Amy, as he carefully prised the top off a bottle of beer with his molars and passed it to her. She looked him in the eyes, blinked, took it and introduced herself. Such machismo mannerisms never failed to arouse in her a forgotten femininity. "I am the canoe instructor here," he said gesturing at the rack of canoes on the beach, "If you want to explore the lake, Amy, we can take canoes all around. It is very beautiful; you can see many birds and monkeys from the water." *This is more like it,* Amy told herself privately, noting his muscular arms and strong-looking hands. He took a swig from his bottle, glancing at her for a reply. His small goatee beard and rounded cheeks reminded her of someone she couldn't place. His stature was larger than Diego or Allan or Warner.

"I like lake and canoe, but I don't know here, perhaps 'largo Chico'," Amy said. He flashed his set of white teeth. It was Bandu he reminded her of.

"I take many tourists on the lake," he smiled, "Chico largo is not a concern for me. I respect the lake and Charco verde. The city under the water is for bad people." Smiling, she took a swig at the beer and sighed at the bright fire light, wondering why she couldn't just be a happy tourist, dancing without inhibition, mingling with other travellers. Gustavo broke into her daydreaming, offering her a lit joint, which Amy took and dragged on with open-mindedness. *Not bad,* she thought to herself, nodding as she blew the smoke across the moon's lustrous face and passed the joint back to Gustavo, who was watching her with polite amusement. Allan stood by silently, as if caught in his own thoughts, meek without his canine companion. They all watched the beach revellers at a distance for some minutes. Amy remembered Castillo beach at night - a mingling of ticos and gringos getting high, uttering Pura vida through cheeky grins. The backpackers they now watched, stomping to conga and bongo drums, or clapping at the juggling fire poi, appeared so incomprehensibly joyous to Amy. With a sense of being removed, she was glad to be with her local companions, rather than the backpackers or the Castillo locals. She slapped her ankle.

"Sand flies," Gustavo said, "flip-flops are no good here at night."

"She has other shoes in the car," Allan said, quickly adding "I can get them."

"Do you want this beer?" Amy offered Allan as they walked towards the pickup. She was conscious that she'd ignored him since meeting Gustavo and he'd obviously gone out of his way to bring Amy along to the full moon party. She wondered if it was his first time at the party too but didn't ask.

"No, I have one here," he gestured at his own bottle, still full. She felt a pang of empathy for Allan. She too was always the outsider. Back at the car, Amy searched in her bag and pulled out her walking shoes, hoping to find socks stuffed inside from last time she'd worn them. Allan leant against the pickup patting el Monstruo's nose and ears. She was in luck - a pair of socks balled up in one shoe. Taking pleasure at getting an itchy foot inside a sock, despite the caked-on crud, she swiftly put on the second sock and slipped her foot into the opening of her shoe. But something prevented her from putting it on. There was something inside. She peeled at the plastic wrapping with her fingers, but the solid object was tightly rammed and stuck fast, as if moulded to the inside of her shoe.

"Allan. Help," she said after a few seconds, which made him start and look at her. After over ten minutes of tugging and manipulating with his fingers, he finally yanked out the gaffer-taped parcel.

"Amy!" he gasped, fumbling in his pocket for his lighter "is this?"

"What?" she asked as he squinted at the packet, perhaps a piece of scrunched up rubbish, in the flame light.

"What is this?" he asked her, looking her in the eyes. It was the most lively she'd seen him so far. She shrugged. He fondled it with his fingers and intensely questioned her with his eyes.

"I don't know," she said innocently, "look". Without hesitation, Allan began trying to tear the parcel with his teeth and then sparked his lighter, squeezed a corner of the parcel into a point and carefully held it over the flame. The singeing plastic slowly burned and curled giving off little puffs of toxic smelling smoke. Amy coughed and backed away, but Allan peered closely. He flicked off the lighter abruptly, evidently burning his fingertips and set about prising his finger into the heat-deformed corner. He muttered the name of a saint under his breath and held up his finger before his eyes. He smelt it and then put his finger to his lips. He swore in a serious way.

"Cocaine, Amy. A lot of cocaine," he said shiftily. She felt numb, blank, flat, then confused, followed by a slow dawning of something finally making sense.

"Where did you get this?" Allan demanded in a forced whisper. His urgent tone startled her. She said she didn't know. "Did you get this in Nicaragua?" he persisted.

"No."

"Where did you get this?" he probed, hardly able to contain his excitement, "How much did you pay for this?"

"I don't know. Còsta Rica. Nothing," Amy stammered, knowing that this was what the men in Castillo wanted from her. *But why do I have it? Surely Zan and I hadn't stolen it.*

"What will you do with this?" he asked leaping on the back seat next to her and slamming the door. He took a deep breath and looked at her.

"We must try some," he said, "I think it is good."

Buying some time

Allan dug a key into the parcel and carefully extracted a little clump of cocaine with its tip. With a shaky hand he held it up to Amy's face. For a few scrambled seconds events flashed into Amy's mind – the angry men in Castillo who'd tried to bundle her, the ranch, the cowboys, the horses galloping in the woodlands, Zan's accusations, the local bar she had vague, bitty recollections of. Sadness sank through her stomach. Blank-minded, she held a nostril closed and with a sharp head jerk she sniffed the sticky pile of powder up her nose. Allan reloaded the key and sniffed - in a practised manner - a portion himself. *Why now?* Amy thought, *Now I've burnt all my bridges in the UK and Costa Rica - would I suddenly try to stop and pretend to be someone else? I am a walking disaster.* They looked at each other, breathing and smiling and slowly started to chuckle, as if at a bad but vaguely clever joke.

"This is for someone in Costa Rica," Amy started to attempt her explanation. Her head lolled back with a sensation of wet heat wafting over her skin.

"Amy listen," Allan enthused, as if brought to life by the turn of events, "this is a lot of cocaine. You understand how much money this is worth?"

"Not my money," she uttered, blinking slowly at the blur of moments.

"If we sell this, Amy, we can have enough money to stay on Ometepe for a long time. We, you, can live in peace, life tranquil and calm, no problems," Allan sang almost poetically. Amy looked at him suddenly.

"Buy myself some time," she said in English.

"You could have *big* problems travelling with this Amy. I don't recommend prison in Nicaragua," he said seriously, his eyes wide. A knocking noise at the cab window stole their attention and the door opened.

"Hey. Do you have your clothes on?" Gustavo's voice entered the cab followed by his body.

"Ha, you are funny," Allan replied, shifting along the seat as Gustavo climbed in.

"What you doing?" Gustavo asked, closing the door on to the warm darkness. Allan, clutching the parcel in the palm of a hand, casually leant back on that hand to support a leaning pose.

"We're just chatting," Allan said way too happily and laidback to be convincing.

"Chatting?" Gustavo asked, and leant forward to peer around Allan at Amy.

"Amy? Chatting?" he asked chirpily.

"Chatting." Amy repeated the Spanish word *charlando*, giggling at its sound.

"You guys are not just *chatting*," Gustavo said, emphasising the word for Amy's amusement "come on, what you got?"

"Nothing," Allan protested unsuccessfully as Gustavo grabbed his rigid arm and yanked it easily before their eyes. Amy burst out laughing.

"What is this?" he asked with interest.

"This is Amy's," Allan said, as Gustavo peeled the packet from his hand.

"Is this what I think it is?" Gustavo asked, flicking on the interior light.

"Turn it off!" Allan jerked upright with alarm, "are you crazy?"

"Am *I* crazy? This is more than, perhaps, one kilo of cocaine," Gustavo exclaimed.

"Turn the light off. Someone may see us," Allan fretted.

"Relax my friend. We're surrounded by trees city boy," Gustavo smiled then turned the light off. "This is a lot of money," Gustavo said to Amy who slid herself back upright from an unnoticed slump.

"Not my money," she said, "me. I no have much money."

"Ok. You want to sell this? I think it's not good here," Gustavo warned, "it is better to go to Managua or San Juan del Sur than sell it there."

"You must know tourists who want to buy some," Allan replied, "come on."

"You know Ometepe, my friend, it's too small for this. Everybody knows everything here," Gustavo said and paused, "you know that."

"I know that. But just tonight - you know lots of the tourists here. They know you. Full moon party my friend. Come on," Allan replied. Gustavo looked at Allan and grinned a pleasant surprise.

"Have a taste," Allan urged him, pushing deep into his pockets for his key. "Tell me. Some tourist asked you for cocaine tonight?" Gustavo was quiet, glancing over to the distant firelight, key in hand. He dipped it in and sniffed a little up a nostril off the end of the key. Amy just listened with eyes closed. She felt contentment, escape, bliss, space, time, details of sounds. It fell silent for a few seconds.

"It's good, no?" Gustavo chuckled into the silence.

"That's what I'm telling you," Allan urged in a whisper.

"Listen," Gustavo said, leaning forward and looking out of the car window towards the beach, before touching Amy's knee momentarily, "Amy and you." She opened her eyes and peered around slowly.

"Ok. I sell for you just a little for the tourists who asked me for it, but the rest is your deal. If the hotel hears of this, I'm in trouble. If backpackers give this place a bad reputation, my job is gone, you understand me?" Gustavo said rapidly, seemingly to himself, "but those guys have money to burn…" He glanced back over at the beach and hesitated. "Give me some paper to wrap some in," he said decisively then snapped his head around to face Amy, "It's good for you?" Amy breathed a few times trying to fix a focus on Gustavo's silhouette, which looked to her exactly like Bandu. *Addicts always find the road to what they want,* Bandu's voice said in her mind.

"It's good stuff, Amy, Pura Vida Costa Rica," Allan grinned.

"Pura Vida, Costa Rica," Amy laughed back, happy with her nonsensical notion of contentment in buying herself some time.

Full moon beach party

Amy woke, still sitting in the back seat of the car, blinking, breathing. She looked around. She was alone. She didn't know how long she'd been there. She recognised the beaded cover on the car seats. The presence of Allan and Gustavo lingered in the humid air. Peering through the nearest window, she could see nothing but darkness. Through the other window there was light. It was the bright orange blaze of the beach bonfire, approximately fifty feet away. Suddenly, the light disappeared, and a face appeared at the other side of the glass. The door opened.

"Hey Amy. Where's Allan?" Gustavo asked her with a serious expression, looking around the interior of the car.

"I don't know," she replied after six seconds of her mind blankly questioning. *Adicta,* she heard Bandu's voice in her mind, *Adicta always find the road…*

"OK. We got to split. We got to go. Warner is suspicious now, he's coming back to the car now, look," Gustavo said, glancing over his shoulder towards the beach.

"Hi. Did you sell it?" Allan said appearing behind Gustavo.

"Yes, where is the rest of it?" Gustavo turned and asked Allan, who responded by pointing at his jeans pocket.

"Look, Warner is coming now. He will not be happy about this," Gustavo urged. Allan turned to just make out his cousin's silhouette against the backdrop of bonfire light. He cursed.

"Let's go join the party now. Come on, let's go Amy," Gustavo motivated her out of the car, "you have only one shoe on. Where's the other?" Amy tapped her foot around the foot well.

"Amy. There's a man, from the United States, who wants to buy more of the cocaine. He's already bought a lot. He paid a lot of money and -" Gustavo spoke hastily.

"Wait. Where is the money?" Allan said loudly. Gustavo lurched at him and seized both of Allan's arms firmly. Face to face, Gustavo was almost twice Allan's size.

"Stop shouting," Gustavo snapped, "be cool my friend. You know me. You can trust me. But things are heating up over there. These tourists are paying big bucks for this stuff. You understand? Warner will spit like a snake if he finds out what we're doing. His Uncle is the priest."

"My uncle is the priest also," Allan said coolly.

"Really? I didn't know that," Gustavo said looking Allan up and down, as if wondering whether that was true, "but we need to keep this under control. We can't make this party go crazy."

"Ok. We do the last deal and split before any trouble," Allan agreed.

"Amy, you must be happy?" Gustavo asked reverting back to his jovial tone. He took her foot into his hands, slipping it into her other trainer, then pulling her out of the truck and to her feet, he tucked her under one of his arms. "But don't speak about anything. We must not be seen," he added nervously. Gustavo, Allan, and Amy converged with Warner just as a loud shout came from the beach, followed by a cheering crowd. They all turned to see a fire poi whoosh high up into the sky, slowing to kiss the moon, before dropping.

"Ok. The United States only - after, we split," Amy heard herself say feeling fluent, as she and Gustavo strode ahead out of earshot, leaving Allan to deal with Warner. Glowing sparks of orange danced up into the star-spangled sky as more branches were thrown on the fire. Sharp, slapping drum beats assaulted Amy's hearing. A few meters away, backpackers were dancing so vigorously Amy wondered if they were in a trance.

"I'll be back soon. Wait here," Gustavo whispered in her ear, sending a wave of tingles over the skin down her neck, shoulder, and arm and to her fingertips. She stared into the fire flames, finding dark shapes beneath the licking flames. Allan and Warner stood either side of her, seemingly doing the same. When Gustavo returned, his eyes were wide with excitement.

"We should go," he shouted over the drumming.

"Yes. We should go," Allan repeated, "this party is too loud on the drums."

"What?" Warner frowned, "Every other place will be closed now." Gustavo shrugged a little at Allan.

"Let's get another beer," Warner suggested.

"I go for more beer," Amy said spontaneously, fearing the flames might be melting, else hypnotising her.

"I'll come with you," Gustavo said, swiftly following Amy, steadying her stumble.

"I knew he would," Warner warned, watching Amy and Gustavo disappear.

"Do you? I don't know," Allan responded.

"You can see it. Come on," Warner scowled to his cousin. Allan waited, his gaze snagged upon the firelight with wide, glaring eyes. "Gustavo is heated up for Amy. I don't want it to be any of my business. Gustavo's wife hears about anything, whom do you think she will come questioning? Eh? Me of course, the driver of the car," Warner explained.

"Ah. Don't worry my cousin. They will just get beer," Allan cheerily shouted.

"You know his wife has had a new a baby. That's when women get suspicious of their husbands you know," Warner went on.

"What do you know about women?" Allan laughed out loud.

"More than you, I believe. I have had some luck recently," Warner bantered back. Gustavo and Amy were half way back to the beach with hands full of beer bottles, when they suddenly heard shouting. They stopped walking and Gustavo held up the paraffin lamp the bar had lent them. They watched each other's illuminated faces and listened into the surrounding woodland. Then they heard it again. It sounded like laughing or crying.

"Let's go!" Gustavo cringed and broke into a light jog back to the beach. Amy followed as best she could on the sandy track. At the beach, they were greeted by the sight of a figure stood on top of the canoe rack, howling loudly up to the sky, his long dreadlocks shuddering from the vocal effort.

"That's the canoe rack," uttered Gustavo as he quickened his pace, leaving Amy behind.

"Hey! Hey man! What are you doing? Get down," Gustavo shouted loudly, but the werewolf impersonator continued full heartedly. "Look!" Gustavo bawled at Amy as she joined him, "the canoes!" Amy saw, glimmering beneath the moonlight, figures paddling canoes across the lagoon. "Come back!" Gustavo wailed in vain at the lagoon. Amy suddenly wondered if Gustavo would start to weep. "They are crazy. People are very drunk. This is bad," he hollered.

"A couple of backpackers from the United States had the idea, others followed," reported a distraught local man, "I tried to stop them, but they are crazy."

"We should go," Allan urged Gustavo, suddenly appearing beside him.

"This looks like trouble," Warner agreed, "the hotel owner will somersault."

"The hotel owner is my boss. I am the canoe guide. I have to get the canoes back," snapped Gustavo. After Gustavo had aggressively dragged the werewolf man off the canoe racks, he went to the lakeside and waded in. A backpacker girl was returning to shore. Ignoring her babble, Gustavo took her canoe and paddle, jumped into the canoe with practised ease, and launched himself off into the water.

"It was so beautiful, but scary," she reported to her friends. Gustavo was panting hard as he approached the first group of canoe-thieves drifting towards a bank he knew caimans favoured basking on in the morning sun. Four canoes jostled together, bumping and splashing. Cigarettes were being lit and passed. Laughter rippled over the lake into the darkness, where roosting birds squawked their disapprovals.

"Crazy boys. Time to go ashore now. Follow me. Before big trouble," Gustavo ordered seriously before saying in English, "Come. Go. Finish." The group followed him reluctantly. On approaching the shore Gustavo gave a high-pitched signal that was returned by the local man waiting on the beach, who obediently waded knee deep in the water to receive them. Amy, Allan, and Warner were in the shadows by the shoreline.

"Where are the others?" Gustavo demanded to the backpackers he'd just escorted, "the American man?"

"Two American guys went in first, but kind'a disappeared out into the lake," a girl babbled in English, "it was too spooky to carry on." Gustavo just blinked at her figure, and she pointed out into the lake.

"Two more American men?" Gustavo snapped in English, shaking his pointing arm lake-ward. Gustavo paddled out again, sweating and panting heavily. The drumming and voices faded until he could only hear his own breathing. He rummaged in his shorts pocket for his pen torch. He pressed in the button and cast its light around him. He made out the bank from the flashes of red reflecting eyes in his torch light - turtles, caimans, birds. He let his canoe drift over towards the bank as he scanned out into the darkness of the lake. He shivered and pushed away his dread at the situation. The moon was obscured by thin wispy clouds. Frogs loudly croaked; a fish plopped. He listened and flashed his torch light in all directions. Impatiently, he paddled further along the banks, peering into the mangrove roots and beneath the overhanging trees. Until, with another shiver, he turned back to the beach. In his mind he tried to see the lagoon as he knew it in daylight, for he'd never dared nor desired to paddle at night before.

"Are the others back?" he called to the beach in a hoarse voice. No was the answer his local friend called back. His sweaty T-shirt clung to his back and a gentle puff of wind penetrated it giving him a chill. "Get me a drink," he shouted as the tiny waves bobbed him closer to the beach. He swigged a few gulps of fizzy pop his friend had in his pocket as they both gazed out across the lake. Further up the beach the drumming continued, the bonfire had burned down to a large mound of embers, but still branches were being thrown on it, making orange sparks stream wildly up into the darkness. Gustavo paddled off across the dark lagoon again.

Warner, with threats of leaving his companions, had returned to his pickup, leaving Amy and Allan sat on a low, flat rock at the shore, obscured from sight by the drop in the beach level. They watched the lagoon in silence, scanning the moonlight-specked surface. Warner had threatened to leave them both there as he wanted no trouble. Allan twitchily looked over past the bonfire to see any signs of the pickup leaving, but was almost sure Warner was bluffing. He'd claimed that he wanted to help Gustavo sort the feral backpackers out, but of course was waiting for the rest of the cash from Gustavo's sales. Amy yearned for her camp bed in the depths of the quiet farmhouse, the fragrant scent of Luka's incense, surrendering to sleep in her safe stretch of privacy. Then they heard shouting. It came from the lake. Amy saw three canoes being paddled erratically in tandem, sloshing towards the beach.

"Get a doctor! Get a doctor," Gustavo was shouting urgently. The two flanking canoes were being rapidly paddled, oars jabbing into the water as if locked in a race, with the linked inner canoe being bounced and bumbled along with the motion. Three local men gathered on the beach, yet the partying backpackers were obviously oblivious to the commotion.

"He's not breathing," the man paddling the third canoe shouted in English, which immediately commanded Amy's attention. She recognised that voice. She froze still in the darkness, a spectator of the struggling silhouettes, her hands locked over her mouth. Allan was silent and still. Men dragged and beached the canoes. A body, clearly deadweight, was lifted from the middle canoe and shuffled up on to the sand, only a few meters from Allan and Amy. Gustavo knelt and breathed his own breathlessness into the motionless man's mouth. The man who'd shouted in English staggered off some meters away and sobbed into the sand alone. Amy stared hard at that sobbing figure. She'd stopped breathing. Blinking. Numbness. Rigidly poised. Unable to move.

"It's the man from United States," Gustavo said in a pained voice between breaths. The local's voices chatted urgently for what seemed hours rather than minutes.

"A doctor is here now. With your boss," one of the local men announced.

"My boss is going to explode," Gustavo whined through clenched teeth, as the doctor rushed to the body. Amy stood up, as if guided by remote control. She walked slowly over towards the body and the kneeling doctor. He was listening through a stethoscope, his eyes squeezed closed and a halted grimace on his face. Gustavo and his boss were talking sharply to one another. Amy knelt with a thud in the sand next to the body. Time had seemed to slow down, the crowd around the bonfire felt miles away, and she was in a space-suit protecting her from feeling or hearing anything around her. She leant over the face just as the doctor rolled open an eyelid on one of the eyes. Torchlight illuminated the bright, green eye staring up to the sky. The eye glared obsolete, just a hole into a dark place that once held a soul.

"Yarron," breathed Amy. The doctor turned to her frowning, but she didn't look at him. "I'm sorry," Amy whispered. The doctor stood up signalling and speaking to Gustavo's boss. Arms went around Amy's waist and she was walked between two people. Allan muttered under stilted breath. Then Amy found herself on the backseat again. The engine started and the pickup lurched forward, back into the woodland.

The journey was a jumble of bumping and bouncing, blurring headlights in dark shadows. It lasted for what felt like hours. Her eyes had closed, her head ragging, bashing, and tossing about, until her face hit against the door again, to open her eyes to the blurring headlights. She felt alone, in a tumbling washing machine nightmare. Not with people, but just figures, passengers, strangers, distant strangers. Nobody spoke. Then the engine stopped. Allan opened her door and she tumbled out into his arms. He struggled to support her. She slid out of the truck and on to her feet, attached to legs that somehow stayed vertical. He led her firmly by the arm around the back of the farm building. It was La finca, she could tell by the taste of the air. It was so dark she felt her eyes could have been closed. He pushed her in front of him. She felt her hands along the rear of the building, hand over hand, until finally she felt the steps. She breathed hard. She groped at the steps, crawling up them, hand then foot, hand then foot. At the top she palmed the door until standing upright. Dizzily she grabbed the door handle, clutching it in the darkness - wondering if Allan was with her or not. Gasping fast, forcing her dried out throat to swallow, she clutched the doorknob so firmly her shoulder cramped, she reached up with the other arm, released the bolt and entered interior dark. Hope filled her. Her camp bed - her sanctuary - her hiding place. Only meters away. She had to reach it. And she knew how.

"Amy," whispered Allan close behind her, "you must not speak of tonight." She turned to him in the dark, feeling his breath, holding his hand - it was dry and cold. "You understand?" he whispered, "this is big trouble tonight. Gustavo will be questioned. Gustavo sold the drugs. People must have seen him. Other people must know it was Gustavo who sold the drugs to the American man, who is now dead," Allan almost wept the last words. Amy blindly looked at his direction, listening. Her mouth hung open. "Gustavo - I don't know him. He doesn't know me, or you. When he is questioned, by police, I don't know what he will say," Allan paused. The cicadas were only just audible, somewhere in the bushes, and the silence seemed so loud in the darkness all around them, but Allan's whispers melted into it. "I don't want police hunting me down," Allan whimpered, "but you too, Amy."

"Police," Amy repeated, trying to swallow again.

"Ometepe doesn't have drug problem here. The hotels, the town, the people here, don't want drug problem reputation. But also, more importantly, Ometepians don't like this kind of bad luck. This - evil," Allan's words broke, "God have mercy on us." Amy knew Allan was crying but couldn't feel or think or care. "Don't speak of drugs, ok?" he whispered to her, "nothing."

"Nothing," she whispered back. She thought he was trying to kiss her, but he touched her cheek with his finger, pushed the package of remaining cocaine into her hand, clasped her other hand over it and crept away. In her bed she lay rigid, listening. She oscillated between being sure she was alone in the room and being convinced she could hear faint snoring. *Or can I hear myself slipping asleep?* Eventually, she slithered slowly on to the floor. There she froze still for some seconds. Then she rolled quietly on to knees and hands - her tummy contracting and stretching like a wild cat as she waited and listened. She crawled forwards across the dusty floor, stopping and starting, until reaching Luka's bed. She crawled her hand up the bed sheet and across the top until reaching the middle. It was made. It was empty. She did the same on Yana's bed. Now Amy knew she was alone. She sighed heavily. A little surprised. *Where could they be?* she wondered. Back under her sheet, safe, she shook, as if cold. She hugged herself with a sudden feeling that the thin sheet was not safe at all. She snatched it down to expose her face. The musty-smelling room pressed in on her, darkness, and heaviness. *I want Zan to rescue me,* she whimpered. *No not Zan. Alvero, and his prayers. But prayers could never save me now.* She opened her eyes after a pause, or sleep. *Where are Luka and Yana?* Some minutes later a thought arrested her. *They're at the beach party.* She clenched her teeth - cold tears ran from the corners of each eye and down her head and into each ear. Turning over, she buried her head in her small flat pillow. Cold but hot. Tired but over alert. Until, unknowingly, she stopped and fell, exhausted, asleep.

Eye of the water

Loud, stern voices tore into the silence. Amy's eyes opened wide. It was dim. Not quite morning, but no longer night. Yarron's eyes lingered in her dream, their iridescence shining through cold water. Unusually heavy footsteps thudded about the old farmhouse. The door opened and then closed. It was Luka.

"The police are coming," she warned. Amy just stared at her. *How does she know? Did she see me?* "Something awful happened last night Amy," Luka said leaning on the edge of Amy's bed. Amy continued staring at Luka. *Is she asking me or telling me?* Luka shook her head sadly. "You weren't there," Luka eventually said, to which Amy breathed out and raised herself up on to an elbow. "It's Yarron. He's dead." Luka hugged Amy. Amy couldn't hug her back.

Then came a knock at the door. A kitchen woman opened it and demanded everyone's passport, and then announced that everyone must go to the veranda. The woman held her hand out to Amy, who was already fumbling in her suitcase for her passport. In the seconds before the British passport exchanged hands, Amy felt her mind realise that the small, maroon booklet was her liberty. If it were to be confiscated, her freedom would go with it. As she handed it over, Amy's gaze met the kitchen woman's emotionless gaze for a second and then, as her eyes unfocused, it was as if her mind warped, muddling to think how she should act in the ensuing dramatic course of events. Luka left Amy alone, joining Yana and the others on the veranda. Amy rummaged through her suitcase for fresh clothing, hastily yanking a shirt and clean shorts on.

"Amy," a voice whispered, startling her forwards into her case. It was Diego stood in the shadow against the closed door. Amy peered at him seriously, deciding if he was an apparition, or perhaps a hallucination. He'd been crouched beneath her cot bed the whole time.

"Amy," he beckoned her towards him. "The police are looking for an English girl, like you - with drugs."

"The cocaine," Amy whispered, wide eyed at his shadowy, serious facial expression.

"You have cocaine?" Diego whispered back through a grimace that contorted his whole face, "quickly. They are coming now. I heard the police discussing this in Alta Gracia this morning. I was on the back of the banana truck, heading this way. They will be here soon". But Amy just sadly looked to the floorboards and swallowed hard against a surge of fatigue, nausea and sweat. *This is where I pay for my sins,* she thought. Diego's face turned to a horrified expression as he glanced nervously around the room. "You must throw it," he urged, "Can you get out the window?"

"No. I must tell the police. I am bad, so bad, so terrible."

"Where is it? The cocaine? Give me, quickly," Diego demanded in a haughty whisper that awoke Amy's senses. She fumbled through her case once more, unwrapped it from her hoodie and gave it to Diego, who cursed with stilted breath.

"This is a lot, Amy," he glared at her angrily. "This is prison."

"I'm sorry, it an accident," Amy stammered noticing it was well under half the original amount - almost a quarter.

"Get out, now, and throw it away. Quickly Amy," he urged, shaking her shoulders.

"I don't know. I want this to stop. Maybe, I am too bad."

"Amy get on my shoulders, you need to get out of the window, now," Diego demanded, almost raising his voice to speaking level. He climbed on the small dresser and pushed at the wooden window frame.

"Diego. This door," Amy pointed to the wall that separated the room from the corridor. Hand in hand they plunged out of the dormitory door and tiptoed into the dark corridor. Nobody passed them. Voices were only audible from the veranda. Diego fiddled with the door latches. "Wait. I know," Amy said unbolting the door with practised dexterity. The cool dawn air hit them.

"Go, quickly," he whispered. Down the steps, then pausing, she scanned around like a prowling fox. The lack of daylight gave a patchy image. Amy's eyes were wide to absorb every drop of available light. Through the languid humidity fell light, hypnotic rain. Then she broke into a shoeless jog, limping and splashing across the wide yard towards the trees and coffee bushes. Once under the blindingly dark tree cover, she eased onwards, dried leaves and twigs cracking beneath foot. Until, seconds later, bubbling was heard. Below a flurry of ferns, she found a flowing stream babbling and plopping down the volcanic slope. With a fleeting glance towards the still empty farmyard, she crouched at the stream's edge, fumbled out the stash of cocaine, un-wrapped it, briefly thinking about frogs, and held it in the water flow. The plastic bag filled and overflowed, then hung soggy and empty. Digging her fingers into the muddy bank she formed a hole, stuffed the empty plastic bag into it and smeared earth back over it. *I'm like a curse,* she whispered into the cold stream water that washed her hands. She felt suddenly queasy, cold and hot simultaneously. She thought of continuing up the mountain to the lagoon in the crater to hide. She peered into the eerily quiet woodlands that seemed to silently scream 'GO BACK'.

As she made her way to the yard, she saw no signs of police but constantly envisaged vehicles suddenly emerging up the driveway, bursting their headlights into the pale dusk, catching her, the killer, in the act of dumping the evidence. She was verging on wanting this to happen, almost regretting releasing it into the water. Yet, fear pushed her to skirt round the yard's perimeter close to the trees and shrubs. Only once back inside the corridor next to Diego - incriminated by her mud-plastered feet - did the pinpricks of sweat bead on her forehead.

"Amy," Diego said to her shadow after verifying where she'd dumped the stash. "Did your friends here see you at Charco verde last night? The police will ask."

"No."

"What did the kitchen women write in the book?" Diego whispered, with a concern that made Amy anxious.

"The book?" Amy brooded for dust-scented seconds, recalling her route sneaking in and out of the very threshold they were stood upon.

"The book every guest is to mark their departure and arrival time," Diego urged.

"Yes. I understand. The last one is for bicycle with you." Diego paused and asked:

"Are you sure?"

"Yes. The women of the kitchen, me not see, after the bicycle. After, I leave to Charco verde," Amy's voice warbled "at this door."

"This door?" Diego confirmed. "Nobody saw you?"

"I don't think." Amy let out a small wail "I no wanted to -"

"Ok. Stay calm. If you are sure nobody saw you yesterday here."

"I am sure," Amy interrupted.

"And nobody saw you at the beach party?"

"I with Gustavo, Allan and Warner. They see me."

"The police are questioning which man was selling, but now they look for the English girl who brought the cocaine to sell."

"I no bring for sell. It an accident," Amy sobbed, "I found -."

"Stop, Amy," Diego blindly gripped at her arms, "listen. The police are arriving very soon. You are the only English girl here. They will question you. You need to answer them. Prison in Nicaraguan is very bad."

"Maybe I need a prison?" Amy sobbed louder, leaning dizzily on to Diego. Diego held her before his face.

"No. The man who died, it was his fault. It will not help him for you to go to prison for this."

"Me fault," Amy wept.

"The cocaine is gone now. The police cannot find that. You have to say nothing about the party. You have to deny it."

"I say I no go to party?"

"Yes. No. You did not go to the party, ok? You say you were with me. One day we cycle and stay at my uncle because of rain; that is true. The next day you with me too, here in Balgue, after I work, we go to the Eye of the water. You remember Eye of the water?" he urged, Amy reluctantly nodding. "We spent the whole night together, in a little hut near there." Amy wished it were true, that they had spent the night together, wondered why he was going to such effort for her. Then, vehicles rumbled into the yard, headlights piercing the dawn. "Good luck," Diego whispered to her, "I have to go now."

"Thank you," she whispered back, squeezing his hand as he slunk down the steps.

"Remember, Eye of the water, with me, last night," he whispered, then ran away into the gardens towards the terrace for drying coffee berries. Amy locked the bolt and crept back up the corridor. At the end her eyes locked on the showers and toilets across the main corridor. She took a breath and boldly walked towards the sinks right into visibility of the veranda. Resisting the urge to glance, she instead faked a yawn and went straight into a shower cubicle, where cold water washed away the mud.

There were over twenty backpackers, quietly chatting amongst themselves. *Yarron is dead, do they know?* Amy's mind demanded, before answering herself, *I guess they didn't know Yarron.* With a wave of nausea, Amy joined Yana and Luka on the veranda. Simultaneously, policemen filed on to the veranda, one, two, three, four, five, six - each wearing an authoritative expression. Amy suddenly became angry with Yarron, like he'd somehow wanted this trouble upon her. *I didn't ask for that cocaine. I just found it. I didn't decide to sell it. The other guys did. Now because Yarron got himself drowned, police are hunting for me. He must have been the American wanting more. I knew there was something dodgy about him. And he knew there was something dodgy about me. That's what he didn't like about me.* Amy broke into a sweat and could feel the droplets of perspiration around her hairline. Luka chatted to Yana about tea, herbs and plants. Amy wanted to act casual and join in, but she couldn't take her eyes off the police. Then Amy saw the kitchen women pointing in her direction. Two policemen immediately approached, slowly and observantly, eyeing backpackers purposefully. Amy saw it all unfold before her, like a football match when your team is slowly and surely being terribly defeated. She was in the final minutes awaiting that final whistle blow - when the struggle will end. *There is nothing I will be able to do.*

"Come," demanded a policeman, having reached Luka, Yana and Amy. In a surreal, slow motion, Amy felt the policemen march her over to the kitchen hatch where the kitchen women now held all guest's passports. The police methodically looked at everyone's passports.

"You are a British?" a policeman said directly to Amy in Spanish who felt a sudden and strong dizziness, as if her head would drop off and hit the wooden decking.

"Amy Janice Wood," the poker-faced policeman read out in a hopelessly strong Nicaraguan accent. He looked directly at Amy and asked "Where were you last night?" Amy froze - her gaze unfocused so to take in view of both policemen. Through the corner of her eye she saw the other policemen filing towards the dormitories.

"Last night. I am with my friend," Amy replied in a voice a little louder than she'd expected.

"With friends, where?" the policeman probed. Amy froze again. Her head could only think of the beach, Yarron's eyes, the car, Chico largo, the lake, the doctor, Gustavo, Allan, Warner, the fire, the poi juggling.

"With Diego, a guide," she said, blinking but still unfocussed, "Eye of the water."

"Eye of the water?" squinted the policeman, "At night? Why?"

"We go bike," Amy stammered, imitating cycling a bike, "After swim. After sleep in trees, little hut near."

"Were you at the beach party at Charco verde lagoon?" his colleague snapped, with narrowed eyes.

"No," Amy answered, confident at her honesty in not actually being *at* the party.

"Diego, the guide, what is his full name?" the policeman continued now with a pen and paper poised.

"Only Diego. He work - at other farms. And, he live, I think, on the other island Concepcion, with his mother."

"Enough. Thank you," the policeman abruptly halted her, as a colleague came and spoke to him in a low voice, handing him an item of clothing. He held up the shawl.

"Is this yours?" he asked Amy with sharpness in his eyes.

"No."

"That is mine," Luka said. The policeman smelt the garment.

"You were at the beach party?" he turned his attention to Luka. Amy's sigh deflated her by a couple of inches as questioning turned to Luka.

"Did you see this woman at the beach party?" the policeman asked Luka pointing at Amy.

"No," Luka replied with a small frown at Amy.

"Look at me," snapped the policeman to Luka, who bristled at his tone. And so, the questions continued for nearly two hours, whilst policemen relayed messages from phone calls. All the while, Amy felt that she might collapse, but instead, her spine and legs, feeling like pipe cleaners, held her up. When the police eventually left, everyone found the dormitories ransacked, possessions turned out and Amy's cot bed sliced and decimated. Amy felt nothing. She just shook her head with Yana and Luka as they retrieved their belongings together.

197

Tears

The veranda felt surreal that evening. To Amy every mention of cocaine felt a direct accusation. She sat dumbly listening to everyone's opinions, one after the other, drawing breath to speak yet unable to find any words to commence.

"I was thinking, local people are just suspicious. But with more time here, I find myself in consideration to the mystical powers of Ometepe," said the German man with glasses, with an apparent need to chat.

"Suspicious or superstitious?" Luka asked.

"Super*stitious*, thank you. The belief in mystical energy," he replied. Amy tried in vain to contain her worried frown.

"It certainly has an awesome energy here. I can feel it," Luka replied, which made him swivel his whole body towards her.

"I feel it too," he said to her with a touch too much emotion.

"Me, also," his friend chipped in, "the night on Maderas was like a warning to respect the nature here. They were told by the staff here not to climb alone." *And I wished for them to get lost,* Amy added silently, *what is wrong with me?* She thought of Diego's words on ancient people sacrificing to the volcano god, when Luka dragged Amy back into the present.

"How did you feel when climbing Maderas?" she asked Amy, having watched her silence for some time, perhaps in avoidance of the German's eyes. Amy blinked at Luka for a few seconds before grasping the question.

"Maderas, I was told, is sacred - the spirits of the ancients still live up there. It seems strange for us foreigners to come roaming around, without knowing about the ancestors of a place," Amy said spontaneously. Then Guy entered the veranda after a long day with the police and other officials. He walked directly over to their table and plonked himself down next to Yana. Amy stared at how pale and tired he looked. He shook his head and wiped his eyes with his thumb and forefinger. Luka stood and took him in her arms. Yana copied. And he sobbed into their arms and breasts. Amy couldn't move, watching, yet hardly bearing to. One of the Germans went to the kitchen.

"I, I, I have spoken to Yarron's family," Guy uttered eventually, emerging from the hugs, "they are of course very sad. I cannot tell them the truth. They think he just -." There was silence all around. A bottle of beer was placed in Guy's hand; he nodded and placed it on the table.

"What truth?" Luka gently asked.

"Yarron is, was, my good friend," Guy said to the floorboards, "we are like brothers. We are from the same place. We go to study together in United States. But, he -" Everyone sat silently, waiting to hear the truth of his dead friend. Guy winced to himself at his private thoughts, lifted the beer bottle then placed it back down. "It was his idea to travel to Central America. He wanted to discover the Aztecs, the Mayans, all of that," he waved a hand and smiled sadly. "His family did not know he had a drug problem. *He* did not know he had a drug problem. He said he just wanted to party. But his uncle, in the States, knew how he was. His uncle always paid for me to be with him, to look out for him." He broke down into tears at the last words. Tears silently tumbled down Amy's face. Yana and Luka enveloped Guy back into their arms.

"It wasn't your fault man," the chatty German said, clamping a hand on to Guy's bouncing shoulder.

"How can I be forgiven?" Guy wailed out of the arms before sinking back in. *How can I be forgiven?* Amy's mind screamed.

"It wasn't your fault," the chatty German repeated. *It was my fault,* Amy wanted to scream. Luka and Yana pulled back from Guy again after his sobs had subsided.

"I knew it wasn't a good idea coming to Central America, I knew trouble would find him, I knew something would happen," Guy said, softly shaking his head, then stopped as if realising something, "but then, we reached Ometepe. And I thought it would be ok."

"The cocaine was super strong," the other German man said, breaking his silent staring.

"He never learned," Guy said bitterly through tears.

"How did he - drown?" Luka asked slowly.

"He just stood up," Guy retorted loudly, his sobs jolting his voice, "in the canoe, and the next moment I heard a dooosh in the water. Then I looked everywhere, and I could not see him," he blurted through a desperate frown, "then he was floating - his face in the water."

"Supernatural," the quiet German uttered to pained frowns all around.

Confession

Alta Gracia, Amy found, was as peacefully splendid as the first day she'd arrived. But her presence felt wrong, unwelcome, as if the town's colourful flowers and bright sunshine were not for her enjoyment. With a hand upon the priest's gate, she hesitated, with a feeling that she was an imposter infecting a sacred land. *I need to find him.* Amy bolstered herself as she pushed open the gate, unsure if she meant the priest or Allan. Immediately, she saw the priest crouching alongside an elegant flowering bush halfway along the footpath. He glanced up at her, wiped his forehead with the back of his dirty hand, and continued with the delicate procedure of splitting apart the roots of a large shrub.

"Can I speak with you?" Amy eventually asked, after watching him at work for several seconds. Without acknowledging her, he continued the task of transplanting the two halves of shrub along the border. After he'd finished trowelling the dry, crumbly soil around the base of the plant and watering in the roots, he slowly stood up, turned his back to Amy and walked towards his front door, casually beckoning her to follow.

"So?" he said once they were seated across his large, formal desk. He kept his eyes lowered towards his desk, slowly nodding, and twirling a hand in a gesture for her to proceed. He reminded her of a typical school headmaster. She peered at him, licking her bottom lip.

"I want, explain and sorry," she started, her mind scrabbling for Spanish words and phrases from the Castillo language school. He placed his elbows on the desk and clasped his hands, eyes remaining lowered. "I am stupid. I do accident. I bring drugs to Ometepe. It is an accident," she said, now lowering her eyes to the desk too. He didn't move. "A man. Dead," Amy continued, her voice wavering, "I am sorry. I do accident." The priest nodded very slightly and firmly blinked several times. "I know, now, it is bad. I no respect Ometepe, the island, the people. I think, it is bad," Amy pleaded to the desk, "last night I, to place drugs in the water."

"You have destroyed all of the drugs?" the priest finally asked, lifting his gaze and giving her his cool, eye contact.

"Yes. I have destroyed all of it," she copied his verb use, "I am sorry, for the trouble. For the people of Ometepe," she said, surprised by her own sincerity.

"Are you sorry to God?" the priest calmly asked, to which Amy sheepishly nodded. He blinked at her for a few moments, then closed his eyes and lifted his hands. "Great father, almighty God, this woman comes before you in confession," the priest prayed, "she confesses her sins and repents the evilness that the devil himself tempted her with. Great father almighty God, forgive her sins and rescue her from the grasp of the devil. From this day on, let her prayers and confessions be made to you, and her dealings with the devil rejected." Amy watched and listened, understanding the words, father, God, confession and devil. "Blessed be your kingdom Lord, forever the most powerful and glorious. Amen."

"Amen," Amy repeated.

"Do you have any other confessions to make today?" he asked, to which she shook her head, although unsure. Behind his thinly-rimmed glasses, the priest's eyes were watching Amy, intensely and solemnly. "You need the Lord God as your guide. You must confess, repent and pray," he advised. "If you reject to acknowledge the Lord, you will fail to lead a good life. The only way to reject the devil is to acknowledge and honour the Lord." His words trickled around her, yet she fully grasped the priest's sentiments. "Do you understand, Amy?"

"Yes. I understand," she replied, noting that he'd remembered her name.

"Tell me then," he demanded.

"The devil, to reject, I must, to know, God," she uttered. She'd expected condemnation, a confession booth or police intervention even.

"Have you ever read the scriptures of the Holy Bible?" he continued, tapping a finger on a Bible upon his desk. Amy shook her head. "The scriptures are here for you. You have been educated to read, I assume, yet you behave as if you have nothing for guidance," he said with steady words, then stood and went to the wall, shelved entirely with books. "Perhaps God led you to Ometepe, so you will know Him," the priest said, sliding a book from a shelf and returning to the desk.

"Allan and Warner? They are here?" Amy blurted.

"Allan has left Ometepe and returned back to the mainland," the priest replied with a fleeting look deep into her eyes and handed her a pocket-sized book. She took the faux-leather Gideon's Bible and saw it was in English. "This is the New Testament. I pray you will find answers in the text."

"Thank you."

"Amy, I will pray for you," the priest swiftly continued, "and I ask you to pray for the people you have harmed through your sinning."

"Me pray?" Amy confirmed.

"You *must* pray to the Lord" he said seriously, behind glasses masking his emotions.

"Yes, I pray," Amy replied. He stood and bowed slightly, which Amy copied, and without hesitation ushered her out of his building. Whilst exiting through the garden gate, Amy turned to thank him or repeat her apology, but refrained at seeing his hands crossed, head-lowered posture, as if guarding his threshold. Instead, she walked in the direction of Balgue with an unexpected sense of liberation. His words had been simple - turn to God, yet his certitude in this solution was absolute.

All the way back to la finca, Amy tried to figure out how she'd come to have the cocaine. Her mind went back to that day at the ranch. It had all started one afternoon.

"Come. Let's take a car again. We'll go exploring," Zan had suggested, stood bashfully on Hacienda Gloria's veranda. Amy had wanted to say how tired and ill she felt, but as he hung his head to one side, she'd looked into his eyes and knew being with him, being high, was the only thing that would make her feel better. A quick phone call to his old school mates at the out-of-town car hire, and they were on their way. As it had been a Friday afternoon, the office doors were locked behind them, cold beers and feet up on the desktop - pura vida, before settling any deposit. It wasn't long before piles of cocaine were being scraped into neat lines on the desk with a car-hire flyer. On their way back to Castillo in the hired car, they'd stopped at a petrol garage for cigarettes, when Zan bumped into a friend he'd not seen for a long time. Rasta, as most of the darker skinned, dreadlocked locals seemed to be named, was from Limon on the Caribbean side of Costa Rica.

With much handshaking and hugging between the friends, Rasta climbed aboard. As they cruised into Castillo at sunset, Amy having sussed driving an automatic, she felt she was in a real-life movie. Free, wild and carefree. On the beach that evening, they smoked with the surf junkies living in makeshift tepees strung beneath the branches of a little forest at the far end of the beach. Until, surprisingly soon, the dawn broke.

"We will show you a little *real* Costa Rica – Guanacaste," Zan promised Amy, hugging her shoulders as the threesome strolled up the beach at daybreak. It was nearing lunchtime when they'd reached their destination - a ranch somewhere inland. On the rear porch of the ranch's hacienda, cowboys offered them an obligatory shot of local liquor called *guaro*.

"Homemade from sugarcane," a cowboy grinned at Amy. On the first sip Amy felt her face flush, then her whole body warm. By her second shot her head somehow warped and her vision had a touch of sepia. And, as had happened at the rodeo, Amy became fascinated by the cowboys, their hats and spurred boots, and leather chaps with coiled ropes looped on their belts. A small tan-coloured horse was led out into the yard and paraded back and forth. It was a frisky gelding.

"He beautiful, very strong," Amy slurred in a hazy state of admiration. The coloured tassels hanging from the horse's halter around his eyes made him even more exotic to Amy, whose excitement was wafting higher with the effects of the potent liquor. Rasta showed a couple of the cowboys a handful of something they found interesting from his pocket. Everyone was in good spirits, laughing and chatting in a most friendly way.

"His name is Hijo del cacique, because he is the son of a strong stallion," one of the more mature cowboys explained to Amy. "His father was a chief of many mother horses. Horses of the wild fight for their group of women horses. He was the chief of a big group, and he fought many other father horses, so only he can keep his group of females," he continued. Zan and Rasta chatted to the other cowboys across the table. More shots of guaro were being poured out.

Amy approached the poor creature as if admiring a Porsche, followed closely by the proud cowboy, who took the horse by its halter and, to Amy's surprise, lifted her with one arm by her waist. Instinctively, she grabbed the saddle and clung to the back of the horse, pulling herself astride the saddle. The horse's fur rubbed coarsely against her naked legs as her knee-length skirt hitched up around her hips. She felt dizzy from the height and movement. The last time she'd mounted a horse was as a ten-year-old taking riding lessons. Dazed and giddy, she beamed, not daring to glance back at the porch. She pushed her flip-flopped feet into the stirrups anticipating a walk around the paddock, the horse led by the cowboy at the halter. But, to her surprise, there was a heavy thud behind her. The cowboy at the halter was astride the horse's rump. Glancing behind, she saw the cowboy who'd been parading the horse. He leant in tightly to her back, grasped the reins and kicked the horse into a trot that took them right on out of the paddock. He urged the horse on with kissing sounds and flicks of the reins. Swiftly, they entered woodland shade. The horse slowed to a walk and Amy attempted to address her kidnapper.

"Redondear," Amy shouted, thinking of the rodeo chants, hoping it meant *turn*.

"Si!" he exclaimed, "Redondear."

"No! Mi amigos, mi amigos!" she shouted back impatiently. She could hear him babbling encouragingly to the side of her head, pointing at the reins he'd let hang loosely on the horse's mane. *What's he doing dropping the reins? He wants me to take them. I've got to turn this horse round.* Bending at her waist, she leant forward and reached for the reins. The soles of her feet dug down firmly on the stirrups and her body weight rose up as she grasped. Then, when she sat back into the saddle something had poked her firmly on the backside. What happened next was a swirl of drunken panic. Turning abruptly, she jabbed the cowboy's torso with her elbow.

"What the hell?" she protested loudly in English, unintentionally jabbing a stirrup into Hijo's side making him flinch and jerk sideways. Then she saw the cowboy lay on his back on the ground shouting angrily at her. She shouted back at him. He scrambled to his feet, reaching for the halter, but Amy pulled the reins sharply away from him, bounced her heels against Hijo's belly, and sucked loud kissing sounds. Hijo clumsily broke into a canter. Worn leather reins clutched tightly in each hand, braced legs, feet pushed onto the stirrups bending her flimsy flip flops, heels bouncing uncontrollably at Hijo's belly, urging him on and on, further into the dim woodlands. Amy panted heavily, audibly. Her hair trailed behind her shoulders. Hijo's mane flapped between her hands with every lurch forward - his feet thudding the hard, dry ground - his ears flattened and his body tense.

"Hiiiiiiiiiiiiijo! Hiiiiiiijo!" the cowboy bellowed behind them. After a few seconds, Amy knew she'd not got tension enough on the reins to slow Hijo, and her feet were slipping in the stirrups too. Clinging to the saddle was just making her feet bounce and inadvertently kick him on. Amy could just about see something moving ahead in the dim woods. It looked like a white and brown horse prancing sideways along the track, with a rider all in white clothing. Hijo pricked up his ears and picked up speed. As they approached, Amy saw the rider of the horse was a woman, her long dark hair rippling as she turned her horse and struck out ahead, deeper into the woods. She was wrapped in what looked like padded cotton bandages and had a wooden bow and arrows strung across her shoulders. Amy hugged down closer to Hijo's neck, clutching the front of the saddle, and clinging with her knees. Hijo was almost galloping. Amy could just make out the horse ahead - jumping, landing, and forging on. Then a large, fallen tree was coming up fast. Hijo surged. Amy squeezed her eyes closed. The galloping suddenly stopped as they lunged upwards, shunting the whole saddle backwards, and then hard downwards, flinging the saddle loosely upwards. Amy gripped Hijo's whole neck, and they thudded down hard. Amy continued to cling to his neck, as Hijo's feet went on thumping the path. Hijo brayed loudly, wildly.

"Niiiiicoyyyyyaaa," the distant but clear voice called out. It was a woman's voice. Amy squeezed open her eyes again.

"Niiiiicoyyyyyaaa," the voice wailed again. Amy heard her heartbeat thumping fast and Hijo's grunting. Her legs and arms and groin were aching to breaking point. That voice again, sounding like from within the trees all around. Amy snatched glimpses about her - she saw other horses galloping alongside them. In amongst the trees, these horses were running fast as if they were on the footpath. *The cowboys?* Amy's mind thought fleetingly. Amy was panting hard as Hijo relentlessly galloped on - flashes of woodland and horses galloping and the sound of hooves crashing on undergrowth. *I've got to stop him,* Amy realised with a gripping fear. She focused on getting her left foot back into the stirrup that swung below. Once she'd managed it, she dared to bring a hand back on to the front of the saddle, and slowly raise her head. With the thundering of hooves crashing around them,

Hijo started braying loudly and tossing his head, showing Amy his wide-open, white, staring eyes. Up ahead, she could just about make out a blockage in the pathway. A great fallen tree all swaddled in green climbing plants. It looked at least twice the size of the one they'd jumped before. A horse soared up and over it. The wailing woman on her horse struck further ahead, increasing speed.

In a pang of raw fear, Amy leant forward, and deftly grabbed the reins and yanked them back hard. Hijo flung his head down and then up and dramatically skidded on all four hooves, lowering his whole body until Amy thought he might sprawl right to the ground. But then, with impressive strength, he rose back up and reared his front feet high into the air. Amy tried to shriek in horror - yet her throat had dried up - clinging to his mane, feeling the saddle slip beneath her, as if it would come clean off. Hijo dropped his feet to the ground, flailing his neck wildly. Amy slumped forwards once again hugging his neck, her mouth full of his mane. To her surprise, she was still upon Hijo, who was skitting sideways, catching their right side on the great tree trunk. He circled, braying loudly and panting hard through his splaying nostrils. Amy fumbled her left foot back into the stirrup quickly, vaguely aware she still had both flip-flops on. The forest was quiet but for Hijo's loud blowing - not a sound, nor sight of the other horses. A branch dug sharply into her arm and she squeezed Hijo's belly with her right leg and pulled firmly on the right rein, turning him around, urging him on with desperate kissing noises. He walked slowly back down the path they'd come, shaking his mane and pricking his ears. The woodland was eerily quiet, and Amy felt a sudden chill and tiredness. For minutes, less than an hour, Hijo walked on slowly, stopping to tear mouthfuls of grasses, until Amy saw the sun break the woodlands and the cowboy stood waiting. Hijo approached his fuming master with apparent indifference. The cowboy quietly took hold of his horse's head collar and started to walk alongside.

"What happened?" he asked seriously. *What happened indeed?* Amy thought and sneered at him for a second. Back at the ranch, the cowboy explained his version of events to the eager listeners on the porch, including the clearly perturbed Zan and Rasta, whilst Amy shakily dismounted. Without even glancing at Amy, the cowboy led Hijo away, who bid her goodbye with a tired braying. Amy could barely walk. The insides of her thighs were so wet she wondered if it was sweat only. Her right arm smarted from the graze. Zan gawped at her as Rasta helped her to a chair.

"He said that you took his horse, running very fast, into the woods?" All the other cowboys were watching her with stunned expressions and waiting to hear her speak.

"Yes. Accident," Amy said, accepting a glass of water with trembling hands. "But. I see many horses in the woods - running fast."

"What? I don't think so," the mature cowboy said.

"One horse - with woman - running very fast. After, many horses. I see. I hear woman - long black hair, singing "Nicoyyyyooo" like a song," she blurted wiping sweat from her face. The cowboys exchanged confused glances.

"There are no horses in the woods here," one cowboy strongly rejected.

"Lots of horses," Amy almost said to herself, "the woman she have -" Amy, struggling to think of words to describe the wrapped clothing, imitated wrapping herself with a huge bandage, patted her shoulder, and acted pulling an imaginary arrow in a bow. Three of the cowboys, with faces aghast, simultaneously jerked their heads, frowning at each other.

"Nandayure!" two cowboys breathed, simultaneously.

"Who is Nandayure?" Rasta blurted, impatience breaking his laid-back composure.

"It is said, that this is the land of the battle over the beautiful Chorotegan Princess – Nandayure," the mature cowboy said wistfully. "When the Princess fell in love with Nicoyan - the great Chorotegan chief, her father, forbad it. Nicoyan was his rival. So, he made alliance with invaders from faraway lands and offered his daughter - Nandayure as a wife to the Spanish conquerors. There was a great battle, with much blood lost. Nicoyan killed the Spanish conqueror with his spear, and then the Chorotegans in the region were brutally killed. They say, the dying Nicoyán, crawled to a well for water. There he found the body of his beloved Nandayure." Everyone had been silent as the cowboy told the story, and after he stopped, they were all looking at Amy as if she could verify it or not. Amy could do little more than blink, having caught the gist of this story harking back to the Spanish invasion days. But she'd started to pant hard and felt suddenly nauseous as the afternoon heat stifled her.

Zan and Rasta helped Amy to the car, after bidding a swift farewell. Amy tipped water from a bottle over her head, trying to cool down and sober up. Zan was impatient to leave, pushing Amy into the driver's seat. Once out of the ranch and driving slowly up the road, Zan could contain himself no longer.

"You had sex with that cowboy, didn't you? On his horse," Zan loudly shouted, slamming his fists on the dashboard. With perspiration popping from pores on her forehead, Amy could hardly focus on the road, but knew without even looking at Zan that his eyes were glaring wildly at her. Rasta tried, in vain, to calm Zan from the back seat. Zan grabbed her right arm and twisted it to see the scratches.

"No!" Amy protested. "He, the cowboy, he bad."

"You were a very long time, Amy!" Zan shouted, enraged. Amy swerved the car on to the highway, frowning at Zan. She would have stopped but she wanted to get away from the ranch.

"Amy, you are a prostitute. No – worse - you are just a dog, having sex with every man you see," he ranted. This carried on for a few minutes, as Amy shifted up the gears and squirmed in her seat, her sticky wet thighs pulling on the seat cover.

"Let's talk friends. Let's stop driving and talk," Rasta suggested diplomatically, whilst watching the road ahead between them. Amy tried to ignore Zan's insults, deducing from his unusually raised voice that he'd had a few too many shots of guaro. But, the repeated use of the word prostitute and his refusal to listen to anything she said, suddenly sparked something like rage in her.

"Me prostitute? Oh, thank you. You no boyfriend now - you bad boyfriend. You no love me - you no good. You and me together no more!" she shouted back at him. Her foot accelerated faster and faster. The car jolted and shuddered over the rain-washed gravel road.

"Slow down Amy. Slow down," Zan and Rasta both shouted. In her peripheral vision, she saw an appalled expression across Zan's face. The car rattled and shook aggressively over the ruts of the road. Her hands and wrists numb from clinging to the shaking steering wheel. She saw the road as a blur of grey boarded either side with green.

"You bad, you horrible!" she shouted. A loud, distinctive truck horn sounded from nowhere visible to her, until a fast approaching hunk of painted metal was before her vision. *Which side of the road?* Amy tried to think, frozen.

"Zaaaaannn!" screamed Rasta in a girlish voice. Zan lunged for the steering wheel and swerved the car right, as a painfully loud and long horn-blast passed them. Then the shuddering started. The car lurched dangerously on to its right side, tipping and almost banking into a roll. Amy braked hard and the car slid off the road into the verge. It jerked to a halt with its tail end up and nose sunk down.

"Shit!" Amy said.

"Mierda," Zan unknowingly translated. Amy couldn't remember much of the rest of their journey home. They'd smoked for a long while, sat on the bonnet of the car. Rasta had managed to judge the quarrelling pair. With the help of some passing farmers, they'd managed to pull off the creased wing to allow the car wheel to rotate and pushed the car back on to the road. They'd made the long, slow drive back towards Castillo without further delays, where they ended up in a local bar in a village a mile or so out of Castillo. Amy could find no memories of what had happened in that bar, but this must have been where she'd ended up with the cocaine. Why? She had no idea. She wouldn't have had enough money to buy it.

Concepcion

Coffee dripped through the *chorreador de café*. Paraffin lamp glow melted darkness. A distant dog's bark occasionally ruffled the quiet pre-dawn.

"Try this," Diego said and slid a cup towards Amy from under the sock-like filter hung in its little wooden frame. As she brought the cup of hot, dark coffee closer to her lips, a pungent aroma, reminiscent of marzipan and burnt chestnuts, made her gag.

"I want water, please," she frowned distastefully. Silently, Diego watched her return the cup to the table and squinted a thought.

"You look tired. Are you sure you want to do this?"

"Yes. I'm sure. Let's go," Amy insisted, despite the dragging heaviness in her eyeballs, and aching in her elbows and knees. Letting Diego down was not an option Amy would consider for a moment, not after what he'd had done for her. She might well have been in a Nicaraguan prison if it weren't for him. Besides, today was a special day.

Half an hour later, droplets of sweat trickled down the muscular valley of Amy's back, following her spine and soaking into the waist of her shorts. With blushed cheeks and mouth hung open, her chest rose rapidly with each inhalation. They'd not even left the cover of the foothill woodlands. In branches just above their heads, a magpie let out a loud rasping sound as if startled, and was answered from a short distance away with that distinctively piercing whistle. The birds had awoken Howler monkeys, as their slow, low-pitched growling and the sound of cracking branches soon followed. Diego turned to wait for Amy, watching for a few seconds before twisting his bag off his shoulder and plunging his arm into it.

"Here. Take one - you need more energy," he said, offering a small hand of bananas. They were the browny-red skinned, stumpy variety, no longer than six inches long. Amy snapped one off and instantly caught a whiff of its sweet, confectionary aroma. It brought a lump to her throat. She chewed a mouthful of its firm flesh over and over before forcing herself to swallow it, whilst Diego patiently watched her. The forest around them breathed out crisp oxygen in its sleep, and the air was lightly tinged with the perfume of wild jasmine. Mindful of Diego's urging to get as far as possible in the coolness of pre-dawn, Amy pressed on up the slope. By the breaking of first light, even the cicadas sounded subdued. The forest had started to thin out as the pale sunrise threatened to fade away the night's darkness.

"Normally, at this time we should be near the top," Diego stated. Amy just blinked at him, aware she appeared indifferent, an easy manner to adopt when not speaking your own tongue. He placed the back of his hand on her forehead and looked thoughtfully at Amy.

"Please, we continue," Amy insisted.

As the pathway steepened and the last trees gave way to naked rocks, the sheer size of the beast became overbearing and awesome. Amy felt miniature and irrelevant. She imagined beneath her feet, in a cross-section diagram from a geology textbook, a vent deep into a chamber of boiling rock stewing to its own accord - a mysterious energy forbidden to man. Taking a moment's pause, Amy looked out over the vast lake below. Perception seemed to warp for a moment. The great body of water seemed heavy and dense - the solid rock beneath her feet once flowed like liquid. But soon her feet were finding their footings upon loose rocks. Diego insisted on pausing for Amy to catch her breath, offering his water bottle and guide speech.

"Concepcion is the second highest volcano in Nicaragua, famous for its perfectly symmetrical cone. It last erupted in 1957, but now it only spits out rocks and gas and has small lava flows," he explained, politely ignoring Amy's panting.

"I hope today no eruption," Amy replied through a crinkled face, wiping sweat from her brow and retying her hair. Diego looked at her for a few seconds and put his hand on her brow again. *The tourists usually sweat a lot and turn red-faced,* he reassured himself.

"I don't think the volcano will erupt. But today is a special day. Do you know what day?" Diego asked cheerily.

"San Diego fiesta," replied Amy with a smile that doubled as a grimace. She'd broken their plans to climb the volcano twice before by simply over sleeping. Letting him down a third time, in her mind, would affirm all her failings in life. But from that lingering thought arose the question of why she felt so determined to climb Concepcion. It wasn't just for her indebtedness to him, or to keep a promise. And it was not for the personal challenge. She realised, forcing herself to ignore a wave of nausea, she had a strong, urgent *need* to climb it. What satisfying that need would achieve fully, she couldn't really be sure of.

"You no think it sad? The religion Aztec stop for the Catholic put by the Spanish?" she asked. Diego smiled and shrugged.

"Why? You prefer a human sacrifice today? Perhaps a girl thrown into the volcano?" he asked with a coy smile, "Perhaps you?" They both laughed. "That's what I like about you. You care about people." Amy raised her brow at the irony of his statement.

It was almost ten o'clock when they finally reached the summit. Three hours later than Diego had expected to. He always aimed to make it by seven to beat the clouds that form a crown around Concepcion's head. Yet by some act of fate the clouds dispersed for long enough to reveal the marvellous panoramic view. Mapped out below was the outline of the lakeshore and ahead was the adjoining sister island with the crouching, dormant volcano Maderas. And all around, like an expanse of sea, was the glorious, flat, blue-grey water of lake Concibolca. Diego, squatting with both hands to his eyes, beckoned Amy to join him.

"Look! Alta Gracia," he said grinning and pointing, "we can see the dancing." He passed the pair of binoculars to Amy. It was true. Looking back over the forested area that they had walked, Alta Gracia was a patch of tiled roofs contrasting against farmland, coast and woodland. Amy focused in on the green linear section that was the tree-lined streets of the central park where they'd sat upon the hotel veranda earlier, and sure enough she saw specks of movement.

"Like trees moving," Amy said squinting, a wave of exhilaration and nausea rising within.

"That is the dance of the Zompopo," Diego said, still grinning like a child at a circus and pointed his finger at his right ear for Amy to listen. The faint drum sound reached them through the silence.

"This is my first experience of San Diego day on the top of Concepcion," he whispered in a way that made Amy check his face for tears.

"Dance of the Zompopo," Amy said, remembering the woman

in the little shop.

"An ancient victory over a ferocious tribe of ants is remembered by a precession of dancers waving branches of trees. Now, always on the sacred day of Saint Diego - the patron saint of Alta Gracia. Before, it was the Aztec god of fire - in pre-Columbian times."

"San Diego lived in Alta Gracia?" she questioned, narrowing her eyes. Diego grinned.

"San Diego lived six hundred years ago in Spain," he answered.

"I understand today a very important day, but why so important saint Diego from long time before?" Amy asked struggling to speak Spanish in the past tense.

"San Diego," Diego said, as if speaking of a friend, "was a hermit. He lived in seclusion to be close to God, even when he was a child. Like Jesus, he healed the sick. He healed many people just with the power of his belief in Jesus' words."

"Healed the sick?" Amy copied his words.

"When you are sick, ill," Diego explained to which Amy nodded, "doctors give you medicine to be healed. But, like Jesus, San Diego healed with the words of Jesus."

"With words," Amy said.

"Not only words, but belief. Your belief in the power of God can heal you." Amy removed her sunglasses and wiped the sweat from her eyes and nose, turned and peered down into the vast wide crater behind them.

"If I am sick, I will remember San Diego," Amy said. Diego looked at Amy hesitantly.

"Sick is in the head as well. And in the heart too," he almost whispered. "Sickness like this makes you do bad things. Makes you have bad luck." Amy gazed into Diego's eyes, hooked on his sincerity, knowing he meant her. "San Diego believed and taught us all to believe in healing," Diego spoke softly and gently touched his finger on Amy's breastbone, "Belief can heal your heart too."

And then the reason why she was climbing the massive volcano Concepcion came to her. It was for that magical feeling she had when she was with Diego. Something of his words she knew she would cherish forever. An elated feeling of love, or freedom, or triumph, she wasn't sure what, but it was synonymous with the land of Ometepe.

This magic seemed to emanate from the ground, the air, the lake. Amy was now sure it was what made the lava flow and the bananas and coffee berries grow. It was what the Aztecs feared and revered and gave their blood to, and what the Catholics had celebrated in their patron saints for hundreds of years. She had reached out and grabbed it, despite the effort and guilt and doubt - she'd made it to the top of the volcano with Diego - to hear and accept and believe his words.

Half an hour later, whilst descending, Amy felt flushed with heat, followed by shivers. Her quadriceps in both thighs were cramping painfully. She trembled all over as one knee gave way with a sharp pain and her foot skidded downhill on the loose stone. When regaining consciousness, instead of blazing sunshine, Amy's eyes saw dimness. She instantly felt cold and damp from sweat. Her eyes tried to focus on the tree canopy way above her. She felt dizzy when trying to sit up and turned on to her side to relieve the pain beneath her ribs. After sipping water and getting to her feet with the help of Diego, she cast a glance back up the steep volcano's sides towards the sweltering summit and she knew Diego had carried or dragged her down into the woodland whilst she was unconscious. He spoke few words during the rest of their descent, Amy clung on to him around his shoulders and he supported her with his arm around her back. Her dizziness and weakness made the trek down an arduous task. They slipped on to their bottoms numerous times. They stopped to sip water every fifteen minutes. Diego strained to pull her back on to her feet to continue, not wasting his energy on speaking. As they eventually reached the road, she was staggering at his side, eyes closed, and her leaning weight causing Diego to lurch and stop every few steps. It was nightfall when they reached the La finca and instead of her own dormitory, Amy slept in a room next to the kitchen where the kitchen-women cooled her brow with damp towels regularly through the night and forced her to sip water.

Early the next morning, Amy was helped out of bed and carried by a wiry man across the veranda, down the steps, and placed on to sacks on the back of a waiting pickup, where her suitcase had already been placed. A man stayed next to her all the way. After a bone-bruising journey to the port, Amy was carried aboard a boat and placed upon a blanket draped across sacks of what felt like dried beans. She sensed people near her, but her perception of distance was muffled, and her eyes couldn't focus. The hot, fumy air and the shuddering engine made her doze uneasily without sleep for what seemed like hours. Next, she was pulled to her feet and carried by two men, one at her feet and the other under her arms, across the gangplank and onto the quayside. As the hot sunshine hit her face, she felt overwhelmed by confusion. *Why I am not at La finca having my brow mopped by the kitchen-women?* Amy tried to comprehend. She felt her shorts. They were soaking, with sweat or urine she didn't know. Her legs were shaking so much she couldn't stand, but could only slump against a large crate, where she drifted away into unconsciousness amongst the bustling quayside crowd. When Amy awoke, two nurses were swiftly wheeling her into a large building, which was unmistakably a hospital.

Thelma

Fresh chilli, picante pink peppercorns and zingy lemon - Amy could almost taste her new favourite dish – chicharrone, a local speciality that she had traipsed for almost an hour in search of. It was comida de calle - street food, and the ample-waisted woman dishing it out had perfected her service using a multitude of plastic containers of differing sizes and colours, carefully arranged on her tablecloth. The chicharrone stall was one of scores of street vendors in the Mercado el Oriental - a vast, hectic, colourful market place Amy had been attempting to absorb in short visits. Nowhere during her journey in Central America had she seen such a sprawling, bustling place with everything imaginable for sale. But this was Managua - Nicaragua's capital city, a place she'd not intended to visit but had been taken - without consent – to the city's largest hospital. Three days later, after nurses had treated her dehydration and exhaustion, explaining she had contracted dengue fever from mosquito bites, Amy had been taken by taxi to a simple backpacker hostel the driver knew to be popular, a couple of blocks from the market referred to locally as el Oriental.

In the palm of one hand, the street-vendor had laid two banana leaves in a cross shape, then scooped, from under a plastic lid of one of the buckets, hunks of yellow steaming yucca on to the leaves, and from another plastic container, smaller chunks of fried plantain. On top of this was placed a large scoop of cabbage salad in a citrus dressing, followed by the mouth-watering prize - succulent hot pork meat. The crispy fried belly-pork was kept warm over a steamer and came out as a chewy crackling. To finish with, the whole lip-smacking hand-sized bundle was offered with an optional picante sauce made from whole, fresh green and red peppercorns and mashed chillies. She then, as she'd done so the day before, expertly twisted and wrapped over the leaves into a neat parcel. With her hot banana leaf parcel in hand, Amy headed to the exit. After peaceful beaches and forests punctuated by howler monkeys, cicadas and frogs, the noise of heckling punters and hustling women with baskets on their heads was draining. Smells of fresh, raw fish and seafood mingling with smoky barbequing meats and wafts of open sewers was turning Amy's still delicate stomach. The labyrinthine covered market, built like a huge hanger with its sheet-iron roof, felt relentlessly busy, and Amy's vision had started to blur again.

The day before, she'd eaten the same hot lunch on a park bench that had taken nearly twenty minutes of wandering around to find. Just as Amy had tucked in, mindfully ignoring the day-dreamy gazes of fellow bench-seated folk, a painfully sorry-looking twisted old dog appeared near to her. It didn't take many seconds for Amy to see the dog was close to death from starvation, her long protruding teats showed her to be a mother. She had cowered beneath the shade of a thick, low palm-like tree, refraining from eye contact with Amy, too weak to shake the flies from her face. Each rib and vertebra showed plainly through her balding fur. Her eyes bulged and her mouth gaped open, as she took short panting breaths. At a turn of her head she swayed on her twisted feet and awkward-angled legs, threatening her to topple right over. She watched Amy without looking at her. Amy threw a piece of fat towards her and she hobbled forward in her twisted design and licked up the fat from the dirt, swallowing it whole. She didn't look grateful, or hopeful, nor did she approach Amy. She just stood. An old man turned towards Amy. The dog remained still for some while, regaining her balance on her twisted pose. Amy felt dire pity for the suffering dog and embarrassment at being a gringa throwing meat for a dying stray dog in a city where people lived in painful poverty. And it came to Amy then, that there are failures in humanity that are cut so deeply into a society, that suffering and despondency flourishes like fungus on dead wood. She gave the mother dog five morsels of soft, fatty meat, after sucking off the spicy sauce as best she could.

But today, back under the sky, Amy wandered off to one of the streets behind el Oriental to find a step to sit on and eat her delicious takeaway. She was acutely aware of her lack of strength and her quickness to tire. Heading to tree shade and finding a small stone wall, Amy perched and with relief unpeeled the shiny green leaves. There was nobody else around, a small stretch of wasteland scattered with litter fell into a ditch, but a dry ditch at least. Opposite, was a stretch of breeze block wall, graffitied in rough patches - perhaps the rear wall of some type of workshop-building.

Sweet steam burst up from the unwrapped meal, causing Amy's stomach to gurgle in anticipation. With every mouthful of chunky sweet plantain and fiery hot scratchings stabbed with the little plastic fork, she felt a deep satisfaction permeate through her whole being. Amy wiped away the delicious juices seeping down her chin with very bite. The sensation of taste and fulfilment was such a wonderful reprieve from the regret and shock of the full-moon party drama. Amy tore the soft fat from the meat with her plastic fork and left it aside as her stomach repulsed the greasy fat flavour despite the spiciness. She was still weak from the feverish sweating and loss of appetite over the last few days. With the almost empty leaf package clutched in her palm, just the spicy juices and shreds of fat left, Amy fell into a deep daydream of Castillo - the locals gathering at the estuary end of the beach, smiling students sipping cocktails at sundown, baby turtles swimming through the white sand towards moonlit waves, the low-lit banana plants around the brand new pool at the eco-resort. Her dream of staying forever, carving a future with dedication to the resort, falling in love with a scuba-dive instructor. An unsettling sense of lost, ungraspable dreams slipping into the past rose and with it emerged Alvero. Amy smiled in a shade of sweet sadness at the memory of the old friend she left behind.

"Me, I cannot live without praying. When I am alone – I pray. When I don't know which direction to go – I pray. When I am sad and lonely – I pray. The Creator always listens." Alvero's words echoed in Amy's mind. *"Pray for my forgiveness, do you promise?" "Ok I promise. I will pray."* Amy heard her own voice reply.

Staring intensely into the ditch, where a jay bird hopped and inspected the tufts of dry grass, Amy felt the culmination of encounters since meeting Alvero - Luka, Diego, Gabriel, whom had all, in their own ways, compounded a new truth - she needed to believe in the power of God. She sighed out heavily, dropping the banana leaves to the dusty ground between her feet. She cleared her throat and interlocked her fingers, clenching her hands together tightly. Squeezing her eyes tightly closed and leaning her forehead to her hands, Amy breathed in slowly and exhaled deeply three times. Her mind was swimming for the sentiments she wanted to grasp.

"Creator of the world, if you can hear me, forgive and protect

Alvero, your faithful follower. Help him, one day, to reunite with his family," Amy said into her clutched hands, "lead him on. And please, although I don't even know you, please lead... me .... on... to something, somewhere good." Amy came to halt, running out of thoughts, and just stayed poised for long seconds. Eventually she opened her eyes. For a second, the sense of calm serenity made her forget where she was. Then she saw her.

More than five seconds of blinking passed before Amy managed to engage her own thoughts to what she was seeing. The girl gazing back at Amy, with a casual but fixed, unblinking gaze that held Amy in a paused moment that tingled within her, like a supernatural destiny that hung, invisibly all around. She was a child, perhaps twelve or thirteen, sat on an upturned crate, leaning against the workshop wall the other side of the ditch. Her face and hair had the look of ground-in-dirt, unmistakable to Managua's street-children and her clothing was filthy and in tatters. Her bare feet had black soles. Her arms were scarred with cut marks. And in those arms, she held a wrapped bundle, in a woollen, colourful blanket, presumably a baby. Amy stared - hardly breathing - into the homeless girl's eyes that stared back, as if for those seconds their souls were speaking. The fading sunset light caught upon the girl's tired, distant face, seemed to reveal a lifetime of hardship. Then the girl glanced down to the baby, as if she'd almost forgotten it was in her arms and tugged down the front of her T-shirt to expose a tiny, but swollen breast. As the girl lifted the wrapped baby to her breast, Amy's breathing suddenly quickened, her eyes welled with tears and she covered her gaping mouth with her hands. Once the baby was latched on, the girl lifted her face to the sky, wriggling her toes in the dust. Tears were streaming down Amy's face in such force that her own T-shirt was becoming wet with tear drops. Amy's mind imagined herself sadly walking away to get her suitcase and catch the first plane back to the UK, away from the scene she was watching. But not a muscle could she move as she watched the girl-child sat breast-feeding the blanket-wrapped baby.

A boy emerged from behind the wall and approached the girl, who shifted a little on the crate and glanced at Amy with a flash of disdain. He looked to be a teenager, his hair matted, jeans torn, vest filthy and arms tattooed and scarred. When he spoke to the girl, his missing teeth were dark gaps. He staggered a little and pranced on his toes trying to steady himself. The girl asked him something and shook her head in disappointment. He held a hand up to his nose, wavering giddily and then extended the same hand to the girl's nose. She raised her face away from it after a second and lifted the soundless baby up to her shoulder, patting the blanket and staring at the dusty ground. The teenage boy grinned widely at the baby-blanket-bundle across the girl's shoulder, singing and swaying at the silent mother and baby.

Amy sat stunned, suddenly chilly from her damp T-shirt. *A child with a child*, her mind mouthed internally, *a child nursing a baby*. Amy steadied her thoughts and felt stillness within her. Something sure and clear emerged. It was an essence of that day she was sitting on the planks at the back of the barn at her family home when she knew she would leave the UK and travel far away. She saw something so clear before her, like the open empty sky after passing through a cloud seen from an aeroplane window - the miles below - and outwards. The girl was reluctantly releasing the baby from her arms into the crooning, swaying teenage boy's arms. She looked so tired, so forlorn. Amy knew this was linked to the prayer only moments ago - that it couldn't be a coincidence - that this moment was undoubtedly meant for her. She stood up and approached the little family, desperately wondering what circumstances would bring them to have care of the baby. Amy told herself the baby must be the girl's sister's or her mother's. As Amy skidded and slid across the ditch, the couple stood watching her, blank-faced. Amy picked her steps between dirty puddles and broken breeze blocks until reaching the children. The boy's face was heavily scarred and dirty; his eyes were rolling with each slow blink, clearly struggling to focus on Amy. The girl's pallid complexion and sunken eyes contrasted with her strikingly girlish beauty. Amy didn't have words ready; instead she softened her concerned glare into a sympathetic smile and said:

"My name is Amy. I'm from England." The two children looked at each other.

"Thelma," the girl said in a breathy voice.

"The baby?"

"Claribel," she breathed, without taking her suspicious, yet hopelessly intrigued gaze from Amy.

"Eduardo," the teenage boy slurred at Amy with a bolstered pride, "Claribel is an angel, a miracle, she is everything, I will do anything for Claribel." Thelma dropped her gaze to Amy's trainers and waited patiently. The baby remained a silent, motionless bundle of blankets.

"House? You live, where?" Amy asked carefully.

"On the street. No house," Thelma answered.

"The baby? Where is mother?" Amy asked, trying to be gentle with her prying. Thelma blinked slowly as if fathoming what life Amy had come from.

"Claribel is my baby," Thelma said with confidence, "I am the mother." Thelma watched Amy calmly, just blinking and breathing, her head tilted to one side. Eduardo had clumsily perched himself on the crate, singing to the baby-blanket-bundle. Amy noticed a blister or cold-sore on Thelma's bottom lip.

"How old are you?" Amy almost whispered.

"Thirteen years," Thelma replied without hesitation, still not expressing emotion. She tipped her head to Eduardo, "He is sixteen though. She has a kind father." Amy just watched Eduardo cradling the baby for a minute or so. He was so high on glue and so pigeon-chested from malnutrition he looked even more childlike than Thelma.

"Thelma. Are you hungry?" Amy asked spontaneously, to which Thelma barely nodded, "I've just eaten Chicherrone - the food of Nicaragua is very good." Thelma smiled shyly at Amy, revealing surprisingly white-looking teeth and replied:

"You like the food of Nicaragua?" Amy had a sudden feeling that Thelma knew more about life than she did. That this young mother's experiences on the streets made her wise and humble, attributes Amy seemed to have widely missed at every opportunity in her life so far.

"I buy you dinner tonight, please," Amy said, "You both." Thelma glanced at Claribel, who finally made a mere squeak of a cry, and nodded to Amy:

"Chicharrone."

"I go in el Oriental for Chicharrone. Together?" Amy asked slowly.

"No. We stay here," Thelma replied immediately. Amy nodded and left. As she returned to the bustling market to buy the meals, her mind was very still, contented almost. It felt as though she knew what she needed to do with her life with an overwhelming surety. It was simple - buy food and drinks for the homeless children with a baby. A surreal feeling emerged, a warming pang in her tummy, like coffee on an empty stomach, with mild giddiness. The market was as noisy and aromatic as ever, but the roped chickens and skulking, skinny dogs and short women in long skirts with baskets of strips of plastic sachets hustling with loud, husky voices all just blurred around Amy. She hoped that Thelma and Eduardo wouldn't just wander off, or gather other homeless youngsters expecting food too. *How many kids are living on the streets, so dirty and poor? Why does the government not do something? Why don't the locals do something? Why is the poverty so bad here?* In answer to herself, as if played on a cinema screen, came memory clips of those who had told the story of where she was - the restaurateur on San Juan del Sur beach, with his full historical account of the Nicaraguan war days and politics. Then there was Gabriel, sweet Gabriel, his dimples in his smooth, caramel cheeks. Sweet sixteen and all alone - wandering the dusty village tracks, making food money from tourists. Amy's heart sank at Gabriel's story - whole family murdered by violent criminals fuelled by drug money. Drug money - pouring in from Europe and North America.

"Two chicharrones with everything and three lemon drinks please," Amy ordered from the same the lady, who smiled politely back at Amy. "Large, please, extra."

Amy's mind wandered back to her student partying, clubbing nights - cash for a gram of cocaine from the local middle-aged drug-dealer visiting the house party, or the shady-looking man at the back of the dancehall whispering *weed, coke, pills*, or the dial-a-dude delivering bags of pungent smelling weed to your doorstep in his old, but trusty Ford Mondeo, that seemed to change colour each time, and then the hard working professionals of London, sniffing lines of cocaine with tenners any night of the week in the raucous, vibrant bars just to keep up the pace. Work hard, play hard. Had, at any point, Amy tried to fathom how, as the bundles of chicharrones were being bagged, she'd never stopped to think of the people being killed for the transit of the illegal drugs. *How could we be so blind to the suffering we cause to others?*

Back at the dried-up ditch, Amy sipped a sweet, citrus flavoured, fizzy drink whilst Thelma tucked into her dinner. She paused before taking a second mouthful, offering the other wrapped chicharrone to Eduardo, who slurred something in response. His eyes were keener though, at least facing the offered parcel.

"You want? The baby for me?" Amy instinctively asked, seeing that he had no free hands to eat. Eduardo refused, politely shaking his head.

"Eat," Thelma instructed, without looking up from gobbling her extra-large portion, "You can catch her if she wants to steal our baby. Chicharrones of the el Oriental are the best in Nicaragua." With a scratch of his head, Eduardo hastily passed the baby towards Amy who took the light bundle and sat back down on the dusty rocks. Eduardo sat close to Thelma and chatted enthusiastically over their meal together. Amy pulled the blanket back a little to peek at the baby's face, squinting at the miniature size of the baby. She was new-born sized, her tiny little face was angelic and perfect but for dirty smudges on her cheeks. Her arms and legs were wrapped in the blanket, and Amy felt no movement at all. Amy glanced at Claribel's child parents who were laughing and smiling with full-mouths together and realised the chance of the tiny baby's survival was slim.

Amy, gazing at the tiny, sleeping baby's face, knew at that moment that this was what she needed to do. Forget a future in hotel and tourism but find a way of staying there and helping children with no homes, seemingly no families, hungry, dirty, addicted, children. Children wasted to poverty at the worst level. It was a realisation as clear and fresh as sunshine after a rainy downpour. Amy almost didn't recognise this feeling of certainty. This was the reverse of her usual running-away-from-a-situation feeling - it was running towards something. It was purely a need, an urgent need. That if she didn't do it, she would not be able to live with herself - like herself. She smiled at herself - like herself even. She finally wanted to like herself.

Zan and Bandu

The afternoon storm had pounded Castillo beach, leaving the white sand pitted all over like the surface of a golf ball.

"Hey man, where have you been brother?" panted Bandu, jogging ruggedly along the beach. Zan turned to Bandu, beamed broadly and clapped him on his shoulders.

"Hey, I see you're getting athletic now, Bandu." Bandu panted heavily, his hands on his knees.

"How did the match go on Saturday? I only got back today," probed Zan.

"We won man, we won. You won't believe the top scorer," Bandu told Zan, after regaining his breath, glancing Zan up and down as he spoke. Zan smiled back, waiting.

"Jose? Snakey?" Zan guessed, but Bandu shook his head tutting.

"Manuel!"

"Manuel? He was upfront?" Zan beamed incredulously, setting the twinkle in his eyes alight.

"Hey, we were without our star scorer, we had to do what we could."

"Manuel scored?" Zan asked with a subtle squint.

"He scored one, two, three and four, against our nemesis," Bandu shouted becoming more animated, "didn't you hear man, where have you been?"

"I've been busy, I'll tell you. Four! Man, how did he do that?"

"Ha, I know - it's a revelation. He was like a different player. Weaving like a kinkajou through the trees. First goal - blam past the goalie, so rapid, then another within minutes. Second half, he just broke away - again blam, he blasted it in. And then, just before final bell, he chipped it over that massive striker, you know, the one whose Dad is from Liberia."

"Manuel," Zan chuckled shaking his head, "the star."

"Maybe he just saw the catastrophe we were heading for and rose up," Bandu concluded, frowning a little at Zan. "You appear very, very relaxed. Why you so happy? Where you been?"

"Ok, I disappeared, I had to sort out some business, and…"

"You went looking for her, didn't you? I told you she would break your heart," Bandu cut in. Zan stopped smiling and fixed his eyes upon his friend.

"You're right, my friend, she did go. I know why now."

"Just forget her - you and her together, big trouble man," Bandu pleaded.

"You're right, my friend, you were always right. But something else has happened - something good." Bandu listened. "Something like," Zan said, casting a glance over the sea towards the horizon squinting, "a new beginning." They started to stroll. The early evening breeze was refreshing and cool.

"What's going on man? What you talking about?"

"Bandu my friend. I have a new job. Out of town. Where the trees don't have eyes or ears," Zan smirked, "at the new eco-resort."

"The place the crazy English girl said she was going to work at?"

"I went there, looking for her," Zan nodded, grinning cockily sideways at Bandu, "and the owner wasn't there. Some tico was controlling the place - he was the builder for the whole complex. You should see it, swimming pools, Jacuzzis, spa, cabinas in little forests, the bar, oh man it's so sophisticated."

"I never heard you say that word in your life – sophisticated," Bandu hooted.

"So, I ask about her, and the guy tells me that they were expecting the English girl called Amy, but the boss had to go away on business. So, he calls the boss, an English man, who tells him that Amy had been in touch with him on the email. She had to split urgently, her mother's wedding back in England," Zan explained.

"I'm sorry man."

"No, don't be sorry - here's the good thing. This guy is from San Jose - he was struggling with the new pool filter system. I made a couple of phone calls, got it all sorted. You know how it is, *who* you know."

"I hear that one," Bandu agreed.

"So, we got talking about the little problems this guy was having getting things sorted in that flashy resort. I stayed on a couple of days. The boss returned. He seems sincere but has no idea what he's doing dealing with locals to make his business work, and now, I will, with God's blessing, earn four times what I earned before." Bandu stopped and faced Zan, his mouth opened wide.

"That is unbelievable. That is awesome," Bandu beamed.

"I got my own room there. I do twenty-four-hour maintenance in the grounds, the pools, the cabinas. It is so peaceful there. No parties. No craziness."

"No wait. You are sick. Are you ill?" Bandu glared.

"No. I *was* getting ill. This is it now. My chance. I'll meet clients from all over the world. Who knows what doors can open now? The boss is talking about me doing a qualification in plumbing. Over there, there's no trouble. No Castillo fiesta every night. I can pay mother and save some too. You know I will always be the king of Castillo in my heart. I will still return for some crazy parties - don't worry."

"Are you sure you're not getting too hopeful, man, this sounds too serious."

"It is," Zan agreed, shaking his head slowly grinning, "the boss loves me. Why? Zan sorted his biggest problem out - legal affairs."

"Legal?" Bandu puzzled, frowning and smiling simultaneously.

"Who you know, like I said."

"Your brother?"

"He knows his law," Zan smirked, "and so do his professor friends." They laughed heartily to each other.

"So, any scope at the eco-lodge for selling authentic Chorotegan pottery my friend?" Bandu said mock business-like.

"My friend, Zan will expand you into new business, a place where many new styles of empanadas are being fried," Zan joked, putting an arm around Bandu's shoulder and patting his friend's stomach. Bandu rolled to the ground, wrenching Zan on top of him and they play-wrestled like they had as children, spraying sand over a couple of tourists sat on a nearby rock, and sparking concerned whistles and shouts from fisherman on boats bobbing out beyond the wave break.

Casa Salvo

One year later.

The thin, pale dawn light re-coloured the lush garden. The creeping vines, exotically deep green and speckled with yellow, wound around the loops of barbed wire along the top of the high wall, softening the streets beyond. The neatly trimmed, thick carpet of a lawn was punctuated with blossoming frangipani trees, scattering their fragrant pink and white petals in the scarce breezes. Raised flower beds burst with meticulously watered herbs - mint, parsley and basil. Splendid chilli pepper plants - some with long, twisty, bean-like, red and green peppers, others boasting small, bright yellow, red or even purple-black peppers, nose-shaped and pointing upwards and outwards. Jacarandas and lilies sprouted from the flourishing flower beds, securing the garden as a sub-tropical piece of paradise. A piece of paradise usually preserved for the wealthy or tourists. It all filled Amy's heart with joy, and her breaths with peppery, sweet flower-perfumes, as she watched an early-starting bee go about its nectar collecting in the coolness of pre-sunshine. Amy, day-dreamily thought of the day ahead. The fifty-odd little white, silk-thin cotton dresses and tunic-trouser suits hung awaiting their excited little children. The girls each with fans decorated with gaily coloured feathers, for the boys wide-brimmed straw hats.

There was a niggling anxiety about the forthcoming events - something like failed expectations, disappointment, a bubble being burst. Amy turned on the tap to the hosepipe and started her daily circuit of the exuberant gardens. Her oasis from the madness of the city, the half-starved donkeys pulling carts, diesel fuming traffic jams with pushy hawkers, the sprawling rubbish dump. In a couple of hours, the heavy metal gates would have its chain unbolted and creak open to welcome in children as young as two or three years old that would have otherwise spent the day picking over that rubbish dump. Instead, they ate, learned, and played in the day-centre and its beautiful garden. For the weary, the hidden hammock yard behind the building was a refuge for peaceful sleep beneath shady trees. The older children, including Thelma, set about their daily lessons learning Spanish, English and mathematics, before sewing or cooking or craft making. Although it was late summer, Christmas was looming fast and handmade Christmas card orders and little dolls with hand sewn clothing needed shipping out to England in good time to sell in churches and schools and village-hall Christmas fairs. The older ones always helped feed the little children, delighting in giving out bowls of hot food they'd had a hand in preparing themselves. Even when Amy's face was struggling to smile, inside, her heart had a permanent smile.

"Good Mornin' to ya Amy," called the familiar voice of Brenda, the co-founder of Casa Salvo Centro de dia. Brenda was unfailingly buoyant, a determined problem-solver and a born 'Mama'. The kids loved her like a beloved Grandma, always imparting hugs and smiles and praise, never too busy to sit and help thread needles or untangle balls of wool. Amy had met Brenda the very day after meeting Thelma, in a backstreet internet shop. It had been empty but for the loud but jovial Brenda, clearly struggling to do some printing. The young man sat at the reception desk appeared nonchalant to his one customer's frustrations.

"Hey! I'm trying to shrink this poster to fit the paper page. You got an idea?" Brenda had asked Amy chirpily in her North American accent. Amy had immediately liked this buxom woman with grey hair curling to her shoulders and thick-rimmed glasses, instantly thinking how she looked and spoke like a teacher. "I'm Brenda, please to meet'cha . And also kinda Lucky I met ya," the lady chuckled as Amy started to make progress with the printer settings.

"I'm Amy. I think six is the maximum number of adverts we can fit on a single A4 sheet," Amy replied and gasped at reading the text of the handwritten advert she was helping to print. "Do you work with this day-centre?"

"Kind'a. I run my own charity called *Casa Salvo,*" Brenda answered. "I raise money back home to help provide basic facilities for street kids, but my house is small, and I only have five beds at the moment," Brenda added hinting regret.

"Do you teach in this day centre?" Amy asked.

"Sometimes. That's where I pick up the street kids. The day centre don't allow kids that are high on glue. They encourage the kids to look towards their future, through learning and getting the qualifications they should have got at school. These kids are the ones I can take into Casa Salvo. I have five kids right now. They have a safe place to sleep at night and they attend the day centre for classes. I also teach basic math and spelling and some English too. They love learning English." Brenda chuckled.

"I met a young girl with a baby yesterday, well a couple with a baby," Amy said with a sudden sense of relief to be sharing this experience with someone. "Thelma was the girl's name."

"I don't recognise a Thelma with a baby, honey. But there are so many kids out there. They don't allow abortion here, a child with a child isn't so uncommon. How was the baby looking?"

"Small, wrapped up, quiet." Brenda paused, waiting for more.

"Any deformity? Limbs?"

"I didn't see, the baby was wrapped up."

"I've seen babies born on the streets…" Brenda hesitated, "I've used up enough of your time young lady. Thanks a bunch for getting these advertisements fine and dandy."

"No, not at all. Well, actually, it's a coincidence I have met you like this," Amy garbled, a sudden sense of urgency swelling in her, "I don't know how to explain. Something quite…. profound has happened to me. I didn't plan to visit Managua - well not even Nicaragua - at all, but, it's a long story really. When I met Thelma and her baby yesterday, I believe that something happened to me. I think I'm meant to stay here and help these kids on the streets." Brenda had stopped rustling paper and was listening intently to Amy.

"What makes you think you are *meant* to work with the street kids, Hun?"

"Well this might sound crazy, but I've been travelling a bit recently and realised that I've been quite lost, quite distracted. Things have happened to me over the last couple of weeks that have changed me. Made me realise - well wonder - if what is missing from my life is having a faith - a belief in a higher force."

"You mean God?" Brenda asked, smiling warmly at Amy, patiently encouraging with small nods.

"Yeah, I do mean God. So yesterday, I prayed to God, for the second time in my life - well as an adult - for direction, to know what to do with my life. And when I opened my eyes, there she was - Thelma with her baby. And it all kind of made sense, right there. This is where I need to be." Brenda was smiling to herself and blinking as if remembering something else.

"Come here Hun," Brenda said simply, holding out her arms that Amy stepped into and received a big cuddly hug from this woman she'd never met before, but felt she'd known forever. Brenda took Amy off, right then, in her pickup to her modest apartment. It was split into a small living area for Brenda and her husband, and a five-bed dormitory with shared bathroom and basic kitchen facilities for homeless kids. Brenda had explained that the kids were taught and encouraged to wash themselves and their clothing as well as keep their kitchen tidy.

"The kids call me their house-mother, as I give them breakfast and provide a cooked evening meal," Brenda said with a motherly satisfaction. A man holding a large bag of groceries put his head around the corner for a moment and Brenda introduced him to Amy as her husband. "Part of what our charity does is attempt to re-home the kids with their families. If it's possible and appropriate," Brenda explained.

"This particular kid," her husband added, pointing at the photo pinned to the cupboard next to a neatly-made bed, "is very bright at day school, he's tidy and polite, he's clean. We've been engaged in discussions with his parents for some time now, and we're working with them to improve their living conditions. We hope he can go home one day."

"So, he's got parents? Why was he living on the street and not attending normal school?" Amy asked with a frown.

"Juan - this boy," Brenda's husband said affectionately, "is a typical example of the circumstances of how kids wind up on the streets. His parents have very little income and struggle to feed their family. He has three younger siblings. The father is in poor health and has an alcohol addiction. The mother would beat Juan, and he would go out to beg to get enough money to feed them. Eventually, he ran away and lived with the other kids that beg on the streets, and then got into glue. It's a sad reality for many folks here and around the world. It's a bad spiral of poverty when parents can't feed their children. That's why *Casa Salvo* works with the families; helping to educate them, helping with addictions, helping with securing income. That's the hardest part, really." Amy listened intently, trying to imagine an upbringing with hunger and beatings and begging in place of school.

"How long have you been running your charity?" Amy asked.

"What year was it, when we sold up at Eagle Creek?" Brenda asked her husband. He looked to be in his late sixties and had deep frown and smile lines across his face.

"Nineteen ninety...two or three I recall," he replied.

"It's been many years now since we sold up and moved," Brenda said.

"You sold your home?" Amy asked surprised.

"We sold up and bought the house we live in here in Managua. That's how we started the charity. When we can afford to go back *home,* we stay with friends and family, we've a son and two daughters. I sure miss my grandbabies," Brenda tailed off for a moment, "But this is what God has called us to do - help out the kids of Managua."

"God called you to do this?" Amy asked.

"It's a blessing to be here doing what we do," Brenda's husband picked up the conversation, "it can take years to help families scrape their way out of poverty, but the success stories, the children that do go back with their families and have a better life, is what makes it worthwhile. Of course, we can't be successful in all cases, and it can be heart breaking to try and fail to make inroads with some families, but we help those we can."

"And lucky for us," Brenda added, "we became great friends with the family who bought Eagle Creek, so we go visit from time to time."

"It's the most beautiful place you can imagine, along the Hood River, Oregon. Snow-capped Mount Hood, the gorge, the lakes... It's fruit-growing land, miles of orchards, vineyards and forests. Beautiful," her husband reminisced as if about a beautiful woman. *This pair of grandparents have given up everything to help these poor kids,* admired Amy.

"You guys have big hearts to do what you do," she said seriously.

"Yeah, well, we got God with us, and so do you too, Amy," Brenda said, glancing at her husband.

"I don't know much about that," Amy said quietly.

"Sure, you do. It shines within - when you care for your fellow humans. Besides, you must trust in God's protection as a lone female traveller," Brenda said seriously. Amy smiled at her and nodded a little.

"The Bible teaches us to love our neighbours. Matthew twenty-five says: 'For I was hungry, and you fed me. I was thirsty, and you gave me a drink. I was a stranger, and you invited me into your home. I was naked, and you gave me clothing. I was sick, and you cared for me. I was in prison, and you visited me,'" Brenda cited. Amy gazed at Brenda feeling humbled. "And what's more, life works better that way. You don't get hung up on all the little, insignificant details, you know," she added with a kind smile.

Amy smiled to herself, thinking of how she'd met Brenda, how it was like setting sail from a dock she'd been trapped in after failed voyages, finally at full tilt; she was starting a real trip, fully prepared to weather any storm. There had been no looking back from that day onwards, until now.

It had taken nine hard months of fundraising to get Casa Salvo Centro de Día functioning. Amy had pulled on all her contacts back in the UK. Brenda and Amy had chosen to set the day centre up in a part of Managua where street children had previously had no help at all. It hadn't taken long for the day centre to be visited by over fifty children a day. For some it was free, safe childcare whilst parents worked, for others - completely homeless - it was food, healthcare, support, hope, and love. Although Brenda was a co-founder and involved on a weekly basis, Amy managed and ran the day centre every day. And today, Amy reminded herself, untwisting the hammocks and trimming straying Jasmin branches from the wooden frame, was a special day for her. She hoped there wouldn't be troublesome, drunken family issues to resolve, children high on glue shouting through the gates, or a toddler with diarrhoea to nurse to absorb Amy's attention.

At midday, the children were all dressed, as planned, and Brenda and her husband had shown up to help, bringing with them, to Amy's delight two local musicians - one with a little snare drum and the other with a guitar. From out of the kitchen wafted delicious smells of empanadas and baking bread. The gate creaked open and the moment had arrived. In walked Stephie and her now husband Rupe, both looking super-cool in white linen and sunglasses. The children sat quietly watching the arrival of the visitors. Stephie slid her glasses on top of her head, grinning at the children, and gave Amy a little wave across the yard, then Rosie followed and stood next to Stephie. Her hair was tied up with a bright orange scarf and she beamed at the children sat in rows along the patio area. Amy held her breath and in sauntered Giles, looking as tall and cool as Amy remembered. Amy walked over to her visitors, hugging Stephie firstly, who didn't seem able to find any words and then shook hands with Rupe.

"Thanks for coming," Amy said, feeling self-conscious. Amy hugged Rosie, who whispered:

"I love you sweetie."

"Giles," Amy said shaking his hand.

"Amy," Giles replied.

"Welcome guys," Amy announced, pulling her dress straight, "come and make yourself comfortable and then the children have prepared a little show for you." Amy glanced at the children, sitting patiently, hoping they weren't getting too hot. Most were under the shade. After being offered freshly-made lemonade and shown to their seats, alongside the other guests, the dancing began. The musicians played traditional folk music and the guitarist sang with his warbling, warm voice. The children did well to step and swirl in time with the music, as directed by Flora, the local cook/volunteer. The costumes looked a lot better on the children than Amy had anticipated they would. The beaming faces of the children when the special guests clapped them touched Amy.

"We are gathered here today," Amy announced after the music and dancing had finished, Brenda translating afterwards in Spanish, "for this special occasion, to show our gratitude to some very kind, and special people." Amy paused and savoured the moment, wondering why she felt so emotional. "The special visitors here today have come from England, where I am from," Amy smiled at Thelma, "my mother and her new husband and my best friend and her new husband. We also have residents - the lovely owners from Hotel Mariposa, as well as Tropicana Lodge and Spa." Amy grew in confidence in the moment. "You children will remember helping to prepare some special wedding gifts for me to take to not one, but two special weddings in England earlier this year. My Mother and best friend, Rosie and Stephie, both made a lovely gesture by asking their wedding guests to, instead of buying traditional gifts, donate money to Casa Salvo. Between these two weddings, over three thousand pounds were donated." After translating into Spanish, the audience clapped. "On behalf of all Casa Salvo, Brenda and I, we want to thank you all. Especially Hotel Mariposa and Tropicana lodge and Spa, for their ongoing support, allowing us to host our fundraising events, reach into the community to raise awareness, and simply point their guests with interest to us." Amy paused for further clapping and nodded for the bouquets of flowers in hand-made vases the children had fired in the local pottery shop, to be carried up front to be presented to the hotel owners by two of the older children. Two other children stepped up with woven baskets and handmade dolls and presented them to Rosie and Stephie. Everyone's hands were aching from all the clapping except the children who sat with wide eyes watching the events around them. "Let us eat." Amy finished the formalities, and the musicians sprang back into jolly, salsa-sounding, folk music.

The lace coverings were taken off the bowls of salad, dressings, bread rolls, and the hot stacked empanadas. The children were given a bowl of food each, and then the guests milled around, eating and sipping mint tea, exploring the gardens, chatting with the children.

"We're so happy for you," Giles said to Amy, "it's just great what you are doing. The girls' school is happy to make you their charity."

"Thanks Giles," Amy said, reflecting on the fact that her Mum's new husband had morphed into a steady-headed, kind sounding man. She momentarily reflected on how she no longer felt the need to analyse and judge what kind of man he was any more, how completely she had relinquished her responsibility for Rosie's life-choices. Later that evening, at a hotel bar, Amy found Stephie sat on a bar stool.

"Look at you!" Stephie exclaimed as she saw Amy entering the bar, "running a charity to help street-kids. Who would have thought?"

"Thanks for coming to visit." Amy beamed at her best friend.

"I'm proud of you," Stephie said, "I never knew how these kids lived over here."

"Me neither," Amy said.

"How did you decide to do this?" Stephie gushed, gulping at her cocktail.

"I was lost, Steph." Amy said, "And I decided to pray for help - for guidance. I didn't know what to do. And when I sat and prayed for this - for the first time really - I opened my eyes, and there I saw a young girl, with her baby. And I knew that was the answer to my prayer. This was what I should do." Stephie wiped a tear from her eye, jumped to her feet, and grabbed Amy into a huge hug. The friends hugged for a long time. The barman watched, half smiling, half wondering.

THE END